MW01534934

Other Sammi Evans mysteries available:

Thinking Out Loud
Your Thoughts Can Trap You
Thoughts Can Be Murder
Sinister Thoughts Kill

Maxine,
Merry Christmas 2010

Enjoy the mystery,

Jeanne L. Drouillard

THOUGHTS CAN BE DEADLY

JEANNE L. DROUILLARD

INFINITY
PUBLISHING

All rights reserved. No part of this book shall be reproduced or transmitted in any form or by any means, electronic, mechanical, magnetic, photographic including photocopying, recording or by any information storage and retrieval system, without prior written permission of the publisher. No patent liability is assumed with respect to the use of the information contained herein. Although every precaution has been taken in the preparation of this book, the publisher and author assume no responsibility for errors or omissions. Neither is any liability assumed for damages resulting from the use of the information contained herein.

Copyright © 2010 by Jeanne L. Drouillard

ISBN 0-7414-6215-X

Printed in the United States of America

This is a work of fiction. Names, characters, places, and incidents either are the product of the author's imagination or are used fictitiously. Any resemblance to actual events or locales or persons, living or dead, is entirely coincidental.

Published November 2010

∞

INFINITY PUBLISHING
1094 New DeHaven Street, Suite 100
West Conshohocken, PA 19428-2713
Toll-free (877) BUY BOOK
Local Phone (610) 941-9999
Fax (610) 941-9959
Info@buybooksontheweb.com
www.buybooksontheweb.com

DEDICATED TO:

Those who believe in the Power of the Mind and continue on, despite occasional failures realizing that therein lies our greatest lessons.

SPECIAL THANKS:

Vicki Wettach and Maxine McCormack – whose belief in me has always helped. Thanks.

Ellen Linville – I hope we have more steak dinners soon. It's great spending time with a competent and resourceful woman.

Susan Marks – who helps me understand the Double Queen of Clubs.

And to the many other fans that I haven't met yet, but hope to someday.

CHAPTER ONE

There was a difference in the air that first day of April when Sammi Evans Patterson slowly opened her eyes. She didn't know what it was immediately, but a feeling of impending curiosity entered her entire being and teased her with hidden facts just outside her realm of knowing. Her husband Dave had left for work earlier and she was trying to decide if she should treat herself to an extra half hour of sleep or arise promptly and have a chance to read the morning paper at leisure with that extra cup of coffee. The extra half hour of sleep won.

To be honest, she didn't actually sleep, but enjoyed stretching out her comfortable, contented body as she lay there daydreaming about her life, how she ended up where she was at, and of course imagining thoughts about the universe that she felt had all the answers she'd ever need in her lifetime. As she stretched out on her more than ample-sized bed, she realized how far she had come from the early days when she had spent some time with Papa Logan on his farm. Her grandparents were her saviors in those days. They had the only home where she was welcomed that didn't have constant active arguments and disagreements of every kind bombarding her day and night. She treasured her time with them and occasionally longed to go back and relive those moments. However, that wasn't possible anymore; they had both passed on. Yet she felt they were always around her and that she could still enjoy them in a different way.

Satisfaction claimed her attention as she remembered the quick conversation she'd had with Dave before he left for work. He was a police officer and anxious to close up a few cases that were winding down because they were finally going on vacation. Every time they planned to take off for that week of fun and sun in Aruba, something came up. However, this time it seemed like a go.

"Don't forget to pick up the tickets or do you want me to do it?" he asked from the doorway of their bedroom. He was shifting from one foot to the other, needing to rush on to work but also feeling the excitement of their approaching trip.

"I'll pick them up; I'm a lot closer," she answered. "We're finally going to make it."

"Can you believe it? Nothing's going to stop us this time."

He waved as he walked out the door and she was happy to see contentment completely cover his face. The last time they planned this trip was around Christmastime, but then a good friend, arrested for the murder of his wife was heavy on his mind and he couldn't leave until it was solved. As their departure date came closer and the details of the murder scene loomed out in front of him, she could tell that Dave couldn't get his mind and heart away from Scranton and its problems. In truth, neither could she. She was instrumental in all of the cases Dave worked on and utilized many times by the FBI as well. She had a special talent known only to a few of her closest confidantes – she could hear what other people were thinking. This gave her a major edge with criminals or anyone trying to lie and cheat their way through life. She didn't know how she did it, but it had started when she was seven years old and it kept on throughout her life. It wasn't anything she'd ever practiced, but her Grandpa Logan was the only other person she'd ever met who matched her ability. Their special bond helped her to strengthen her gift and use it responsibly.

Because they could be of assistance and felt a strong link to be here in an emotional and heart-wrenching murder case, they had postponed their honeymoon trip until later and luckily, it had concluded a short while ago reeling in a bizarre murder scheme against women. Now it seemed that finally they would get their vacation. They had been married well over a year and still hadn't had a honeymoon. However, happiness hadn't escaped them and with their honeymoon trip less than a week away, they felt one of their goals would soon be met. Still, Sammi had a strange feeling since consciousness had flooded her mind this morning and she lay there trying to assess the nervousness that would not leave. She had a foreboding feeling and couldn't deny it. And she couldn't understand why. Usually when she entertained a premonition, along with it came an instant knowing. However, this time it was simply a feeling, an almost knowing, which was irritating. Possibly, it was the excitement of their upcoming trip. The mind had a funny way of playing tricks sometimes, usually when you least expected it.

* * *

Getting out of the shower brought her back to reality in her world and she felt awake and alert. Still, something in her mind wouldn't let go. She hated the uncertainty that rushed through her thoughts. She had many things to do before they left on Friday and she couldn't let her mind be sidetracked. However, at this moment she was distracted and didn't seem to have any power to stop it. As she dressed she thought back to the time she had met some of her 'clients', as she referred to them. These were people she'd helped in the past, but they were sworn to secrecy. She remembered Father John Meyer, a Roman Catholic priest in Tecumseh, Ontario who had needed her help. Then, there was her college friend, Professor Harley whom she had known from Scranton University. He had been instrumental in getting her involved in solving a child trafficking ring, as well as working with the FBI at different times. It seemed there were always a few more cases, either from the police or from the FBI that needed her attention.

* * *

Suddenly she shook her head. *Why am I thinking about all this now? There must be a reason, what could it be?* She knew there weren't any coincidences in life and so, she again wondered why her thinking was so targeted. Finally, another client that she hadn't thought about in many years crossed her mind. He was Billy G. Simpson. She took a moment and enjoyed the warm feeling that caressed her body whenever she thought of him. He was a very special person in her view.

Her dog Kali barked suddenly startling her out of the daydreams. She looked at the clock and realized she had barely enough time to let her dog outside, put down some food for her and get to her job at the Citizens Bank. Some other day when she had more time, she could continue her daydreaming.

* * *

Working alongside some of her colleagues at the bank always gave her a feeling of belonging, although there were always a few who still wondered why she had so many special privileges. She could take extra vacation time with pay and have many more leaves of absence than anyone else did and yet, she kept her status as an advantaged employee. No one questioned her about this. It was a private matter between her and the president of their branch, which many attested a special relationship.

After returning from her morning staff meeting, she noticed that she'd received a phone call from Cuyahoga Falls, Ohio. It gave her a moment of apprehension. She didn't know anyone from Cuyahoga Falls and there was no message as with usual business calls. Although her mind dismissed it

4

quickly, she came back to it several times in the next few minutes. She took a deep breath. She couldn't believe what was happening to her today. She was definitely off track.

Her phone rang. She quickly looked to see if the call was from Cuyahoga Falls; it wasn't. It was Dave.

"Hi, what's going on?"

He laughed, "Nothing, honey. I just needed to hear your voice."

"Right and I know you're trying to butter me up before our vacation."

"No, honestly, I always like to hear your voice. But," he said and paused. Since he got no reaction he continued, "I need to know if you might have some time tomorrow afternoon."

"Sure, what do you need?"

"We've got a new guy coming in from the 11th precinct who'll be starting in our group soon. He's been transferred around a lot and I have an uneasy feeling about him. He doesn't have anything worrisome on his record, but ..."

"Not a problem, I can be around if you want to see if I'll pick up something."

"You know, this time, it's not just me. Tom and Jim thought it'd be a good idea if you could be here."

"Of course, what time?"

"I'll let you know tonight. I'm hoping it's nothing."

"I understand. If the referees want me to listen in, I'm happy to do it."

Dave, along with his friends Tom Harrington and Jim Mucci called themselves the three referees, but kept the reason mysterious.

"Thanks honey. And I do like the sound of your voice."

"Okay," she laughed as she hung up.

She smiled for a moment relishing the thought that she loved her Dave Patterson. It had taken her a while to find someone, but at forty years old, she'd partnered with someone who had been a close friend for years. And after almost two years of marriage, she was happy in her choice.

After a few more afternoon meetings, she returned to her desk to find another phone call from Cuyahoga Falls, Ohio. Her phone gave her the city and phone number on her caller I.D., but not the name of the caller. Again, there was no message. She felt frustrated. Sometimes she could hear people's thoughts over the telephone, but there had to be someone on the other end of the line. She'd have to wait again for another call, possibly another day or two and the wait was getting harder.

* * *

Sammi picked up the airline tickets for Aruba after work and still managed to beat Dave home. She had dinner almost ready by the time he walked in the door. He gave her a hug and a kiss as usual and then looked at the mail.

"How was your day?" she yelled from the kitchen.

"Rather quiet for a change. I like it that way."

"Good, we need to keep it quiet this week. I don't want you worrying about anything in Aruba."

He laughed, "Well, I'm still going to worry about you."

She peeked around the corner. "Me, why? Why would you worry about me?"

"Because I love you and I always worry about people I love. Just get used to it."

Sammi made a slight grimace and returned to the kitchen.

Later that evening she told Dave about the two phone calls she'd received.

"Cuyahoga Falls, Ohio. Where's that?"

"Somewhere around Akron; that's all I know."

"Is there a bank branch there?"

"Don't think so. It could have been a wrong number, but the person called twice so ... oh well, maybe they'll call back or maybe not. We'll see."

After another moment, she asked. "So who's this new guy coming in?"

"Don't know very much about him. I understand he's late forties and has been a cop for maybe twenty years, but he was still a street cop until a few years ago. That gives me questions right there."

"Why?"

"Street cop and walking the beat is the bottom rung on the ladder. Within two to five years there's usually a promotion, so I wonder, that's all."

"What's his name?"

"Roy Dawson, and no, I'd never heard of him before Sergeant Brady told us about him. Even Amilio's never heard of him."

She wrinkled her nose. "And Amilio does get around and hears a lot of things. Anyone know why he's being transferred?"

"That's a good question and we asked Sergeant Brady. He said that his precinct wants him to get more experience, which usually means that they want him out of the way. That comment is what made us suspicious."

"And he comes when?"

"In a few weeks, I think."

They were both quiet after that, reading the paper and enjoying quiet time.

Sammi broke the silence. "Did Randy and Denver move back to Kingston yet?"

Randy Baker's acquittal on the charge of murdering his wife was one of the highlights of their efforts in the past several months. It took everyone's talent working together to get him acquitted and capture the actual killers. In addition, his ten-year-old gifted son needed help in getting through the ordeal.

"No, not yet. They don't have a place to stay and Randy wants to sell the house and buy another one. It would be too hard for them to move back there. Besides, this will give

Denver time to finish this semester at school and have all summer to readjust to moving again."

"Yeah, that sounds like a good plan. Jill said that he was doing well last time we talked. Sure is a bright little guy."

Dave laughed. "Sometimes I feel like I'm talking to an adult inside a little kid's body. Seems weird, but he's so likeable and down to earth. He's just a nice kid."

She smiled. No one could disagree with that.

Later on, she felt Dave's hand on her shoulder nudging her awake. "It's time to get to bed, honey. It's after ten o'clock."

"My word. How long have I been sleeping?"

"I don't know, about an hour I guess. You need more sleep than you get."

She struggled to find consciousness, but relented and welcomed sleep.

Through a few involuntary yawns she said, "I think you could use more sleep, too."

"Yep," he said in agreement, "and I'm heading there myself."

* * *

The next day Sammi arrived at the police station early for their three o'clock meeting. She'd given herself a little extra time to get the feel of the place, which made her more confident and strengthened her ability to focus. She wanted to pick up as much as she could in this short introductory meeting with Roy Dawson. She was also hoping for a moment with Julie Mucci, a friend of hers since high school who worked as an expert on the computer system. She was saddened at times when life's demands seldom left time for that occasional lunch with someone important; and Julie had been significant in her life for many years.

"Well, you're looking good," said Julie as she gave her a slight hug.

"And you always look great," she replied. Julie was quite gorgeous but had her memories of many dates who only wanted a lovely girl on their arm. She had finally met someone who appreciated her for other qualities as well. She made a good match with Jim Mucci.

"You're here to check up on Roy Dawson, right?"

"Yeah, and I hope he's straight. So many people are infiltrating the good guys these days."

"But they're lucky they have you to listen in. That goes a long way for them to be able to trust each other. Jim mentions that often."

"I'm glad I can do that. Our guys have tough enough jobs and craziness to deal with. How're the girls doing lately?" Julie's husband had two daughters from a previous marriage.

"They're great. We have a good relationship going. I really love them," she smiled. "We've even managed to get a decent rapport with his ex-wife Kathy. She's on the verge of divorce again and the girls stay with us a lot these days. She likes that, and it's fine with us."

"Jim used to say that she couldn't seem to find what she really needed in her life. I hope she does."

"Me, too. Life's hard enough anyway."

About this time, Dave wandered over to retrieve Sammi. Sergeant Brady was ready for his meeting with Roy Dawson and anxious to begin. He was insistent on her being there saying that he would explain her as a note taker of some kind, if necessary.

* * *

The three referees, Amilio and Sammi were already in Sergeant Brady's office when Roy Dawson walked in looking rather cautious and slightly edgy as he glanced around the room. Rather handsome in an interesting sort of way, his tall, husky build commanded attention. He definitely thought he could match anyone in the room. His body language conveyed self-confidence and a knowing that he displayed for the world to see. Even though he was transferred to this precinct against his wishes, he wanted people to know it had been noted that he'd been a valuable asset to the other station as well. He took pride in his work and felt he could stand face to face with anyone in the room. Sammi was hoping to find out if he felt as confident inside as his physical demeanor was desperately trying to show. His thoughts were rather crowded at the moment.

"I wanted you to meet with your team ahead of time," said the sarge as he introduced everyone in the room including Sammi, whom he said worked with the group quite often. "LeBron Harper and Tyrone Pittfield are out on assignment today."

A tiny history of everyone and a few previous assignments topped the discussion list to give Roy a feel for the work policies utilized at this station. In an effort to let them know he was a cooperative type of person he said, "Yeah I like to be up front about everything, too, and I'm big on sharing information to help any case along."

Amilio said, "That's good, amigo. We need cooperation and support within our group. We're all big on sharing around here."

Roy nodded. He hated having to start all over again with a new group, but he couldn't seem to satisfy many at the 11th precinct. He hoped to get the officers at this station to accept him. That would make his job a lot easier.

Then the sarge told him that he'd be working under the supervision of Dave Patterson. He almost wrinkled his nose, but stopped short of displaying a negative reaction.

Jim Mucci looked over and said, "Dave's our leader, so to speak. It's rather informal but he's sort of the lead detective."

Dave smiled as he said, "That just means that I get to do most of the paperwork. I consider us all on the same level."

Amilio added, "But you're sort of the big brother for all of us, right amigo?"

That made everyone smile and lessened the tension somewhat.

"I'm told I'll be starting in two weeks so until then I have some loose ends to finish up at the 11th precinct. I'm looking forward to working here and I'll do my best for all of you."

That ended the meeting for the group, but Roy stayed behind to talk to the sarge a little longer. He had more questions for him and the sarge needed to settle a few more things with a new officer that at times seemed to have his own way of doing business, regardless of what he had said in this meeting.

* * *

On the way home Sammi was quiet as usual. She always took time to assess her thoughts and make sense of her findings in what she termed quiet conversations. That's how she referred to her ability to hear what other people were thinking. She could feel Dave's tenseness as he waited for her report. He was anxious to know what impression she'd received from this Roy person. Nevertheless, he knew enough to give her the time she needed to collect her ideas. When she was ready, she would begin the conversation; they both knew that.

It took quite a while before she took that deep sigh that was so familiar to Dave. It signaled she was ready to speak.

"Okay Dave, I know you're anxious to hear what I've picked up."

She saw him nod and knew he was a lot more than simply anxious. This guy had been tossed at them without any options on their part. Still, he knew this type of situation could develop in several ways. Maybe Roy would turn out to be an asset for them, maybe not. But he needed to know what his mind was thinking and Sammi could tell him that.

"He's interesting, Dave. It's for sure that he's walked some shaky ground in the past. In fact, I get the impression that he believes his reassignment was because of cutting too many corners and working through too many leads by himself. He was certainly not a team player up until now, but he seems to have realized he caused himself many problems by acting as a loner. Bottom line right now is that he wants to change his luck and play by the rules, instead of keeping things to himself and trying to be a star along the way. His thoughts told me that he wants to change his ways, be a team player and hope he does better here. And he does love police work and wants a fresh start."

Dave nodded a few times during her assessment. "So you didn't pick up anything devious or underhanded that I should know about?"

"I didn't and that's what I always look for in people, especially at first. Now I do believe he did that in the past and although he wasn't caught, the many innuendos about him caused people to slowly shy away, and he became the lone ranger. He really wanted respect and to become a leader of some kind, but it all backfired. To what I can figure out, this happened more than once, but I didn't pick up anything criminal or illegal, etc., at least not yet. I'd like to get a chance to be around him again later on. This was a rather short meeting."

"But you usually pick up things real fast, especially if they're dangerous or illegal. Therefore, he might be on the edge and hoping to make a comeback. It's happened before. Some get too anxious to make a name for themselves and dig a hole with no escape, but from what you've said, I'm willing to give him a chance. Let's see what he does with it."

"And remember people usually think a lot more in thoughts than they say in words. I didn't pick up any thoughts of prior wrongdoings when he was thinking about his past career; that's what I would have expected. Mostly he's disappointed that he hasn't done better and is trying to figure out how he can improve."

"That isn't all that bad," said Dave, "as long as he becomes a team player. He does have a lot of experience in several areas, mostly from the streets, but that can be good. Time will tell, I guess."

Dave was quiet for a few moments and then asked. "You want to stop for dinner at Archie's or go home?"

"I'd like that. Then we can relax for a change. Our schedules have been so hectic lately. And I want to start packing tonight."

"Already? We still have three days before we leave. Everything will get wrinkled."

She laughed. "No, I meant I wanted to check clothes that I want to bring with me and make sure they're clean and all. I might wash some stuff so if you've got anything..."

"Can you believe it?" said Dave, in a quick show of excitement. "We're actually leaving for Aruba this Friday."

Sammi sighed in anticipation and her thoughts were already on a greatly anticipated vacation. "Yeah, it's about time we get away for a while. I'm not sure how I'll be able to handle all this relaxation and sun and just being a carefree tourist."

Dave laughed. "Well, it's about time you get a chance to find out."

* * *

Sammi welcomed having a hectic day at the bank on Wednesday. She was finally letting her enthusiasm for the upcoming vacation sink in and felt almost like a teenager escaping for an exciting spree. She couldn't remember the last time she'd been on a real trip. It certainly wasn't in the last few years since she'd been married. It must have been six or seven years ago. Oh, it was true that she'd planned many getaways, but something always happened and changed her plans. However, this time it was real.

"Sammi, we need you in a meeting at one o'clock. Mr. Marconey is requesting that you be there; it's in the main conference room."

That was one of the employees from the accounting department. Whenever Mr. Marconey invited her to a meeting out of her realm of activity, it meant that he had suspicions of his potential clients and needed her expertise. He knew she was a shrewd judge of character and could usually pick up trends and decipher the hidden meanings behind the words or speeches. She would be ready.

She planned to take a quick lunch at her desk to finish delayed paperwork, which she wanted completed before she left. She didn't want anything overdue when she returned or postponed details on her mind in Aruba. After lunch, realizing she still had more than a half hour before her meeting, she decided on another cup of coffee and started making a list for her trip. She hated when she forgot something essential at home. Then her phone rang and the call was from Cuyahoga Falls, Ohio. She felt a slight chill rise from the bottom of her spine and slowly inch its way upward. Here was that call she'd been subconsciously waiting for and it put her mind on alert immediately.

"Hi, Ms. Sammi, it's been a long time; do you remember me; it's Billy Simpson?"

She almost gasped into the telephone. She'd been thinking about him a few days before. He was part of those past memories that she couldn't get off her mind. Her very sweet friend Billy was calling her, but his voice didn't sound very steady.

"Of course I remember you Billy and sometimes I still think about you and the great class we took together at Scranton University."

" "You do? That's nice. I was hoping you'd remember me."

She heard him take a deep breath, which was shaky at best. He had a lot on his mind and felt that this was his one big chance with her and was nervous about asking his question.

She decided to help him along. "Is something wrong, Billy? You sound somewhat upset."

"You always know, Ms. Sammi. I knew you would."

He paused for a long moment and that gave Sammi time to hear some of his unbelievable thoughts. He wasn't simply upset; he was in great distress and needed her help. And she knew he was having a hard time asking for it.

"I'm kind of nervous, Ms. Sammi, just a moment, okay?"

"Sure Billy, but you don't have to be nervous with me; you know that."

"It's been a long time since I've talked to you. I always pray for you, Ms. Sammi. You've been such a special person in my life, but I'm not sure if you'd be willing to help me now."

Sammi felt the hesitance in his voice, but also heard the desperation of his thoughts. She had to get him to open up to her.

"Tell me what the problem is and then we can talk about it."

Sammi already knew his problem as his thoughts were coming through loud and clear, but she needed him to tell his story. Shortly he began.

"I've got a real bad problem, Ms. Sammi. Do you remember Ms. Lily Caulkin? She was the one who became my mother when I was fifteen years old. I thought she was my mother for a long time before then, but that's when she adopted me."

"Sure I remember her. She loved you, took you in, and adopted you. And she did a good job with you."

"Yes, she did. I consider her my real mother, because she is. She's a nice, kind person," he said and then he took another deep breath and blurted out what he had wanted to say from the beginning. "She's in a lot of trouble, Ms. Sammi, a lot of trouble. And she's in jail right now; that's where she's sitting. She's accused of murdering someone and I have to help her, but I don't know how. Could you come and help us? She didn't murder anyone and she told me so. I don't know why people are being so mean to her."

The request shocked her. She'd picked up Billy's alarming problem, but still wasn't prepared when he put his request into words. Billy's thoughts didn't always translate like other people. Sammi was quiet for a few minutes; she didn't know what to say. She would find it hard to refuse and, to be honest, she didn't know how to deny him; he was so desperate.

"Ms. Sammi, please come and see if you can help Ms. Lily. She doesn't have much money because she spent it all trying to take care of me. I need to help her now and I don't know how to do it."

Just then, someone stuck his head into Sammi's office. The meeting was about to start and she needed to be there.

"Billy, I need your phone number and where you live, okay? I'll have to call you back, because I have a meeting right now, but one way or another we'll get help for Ms. Lily."

She could tell he was half-crying and she knew his heart; a sweet, kind, humble little heart that didn't have the anger and prejudice of ordinary people. He was one of the few truly loving souls she'd ever met. She'd have to talk to Dave and felt together they could think of something.

"Thank you, Ms. Sammi. Thank you so much. I asked a few people around here but they don't want to help her. I asked them two or three times and, you know, they think I'm stupid, or at least not very smart, but I know she'd never hurt anyone."

"Look, I've got to go right now, but I'll call you later. This is the phone number where you live, right?"

"Yeah, I live right here where the phone is at. Please call me back and tell me what to do."

"I will, Billy, I promise."

And she put down the phone with lingering regrets, but she'd call back later.

* * *

Keeping her concentration on target for Mr. Marconey's meeting was probably the hardest thing that Sammi'd had to do in a while. But she knew how to do it. She could control her thoughts and she knew how to focus, yet personal feelings could get in the way at times and create havoc in her thought atmosphere. Yet she realized, right now, in this moment, her job was to help Mr. Marconey. She couldn't help Billy right now anyway, but she vowed to herself that she would.

As the meeting progressed, she got right into the thought atmosphere of a few people in the room. The new customers for the bank wanted to get operating rules determined so that no one would have any problems later. However, Sammi immediately picked up that one of these men wanted the bank to bend the rules in their favor and would continuously make an attempt in that direction. He had his own way of doing business and acted as if he was doing the bank a favor rather than the other way around. She eyed Mr. Marconey who caught her cautioned glance. In these circumstances, he usually avoided making a final decision until he'd talked to Sammi. Business seemed to move smoother that way.

"Well, I know they weren't happy that I wouldn't tell them yes or no today, but you had a curious look in your eye, Sammi. What bothers you about them?"

"Well, the young guy in the blue shirt, the one who was always the first to answer your concerns, I have reservations about him. Let me tell you how I see this group. The president is okay and he wants to play by the rules and his associate ah …."

"John Sharden?"

"Yeah, John Sharden, he seems to be a pretty straight player. Those two you can trust to be whom they say they are and what they seem. They will stand behind their words. But Kip Jordan was it …?"

Mr. Marconey nodded and smiled a bit. For all her smarts, remembering names was not her best talent.

"Right," she smiled as she caught his look. Yes, she was bad at names; she was so much better at remembering thoughts.

"Anyway, he'll try to play everyone against each other. Those other two will have problems with him, but I don't think they know it yet. He's out to make a reputation for himself and that's okay, but he'll eliminate anyone who gets in his way. And that includes everyone. Right now, he wants the bank to buckle under to all their requests and you'll see, Mr. Marconey, at your next meeting with them, he'll be more boisterous and mouthy and antagonistic in his behavior; that's the way he believes he needs to go to achieve his goals."

Mr. Marconey simply shook his head. "You know I picked up a few things, and the president is Rob Porter and I've known him for years. I talked to him before today and he had concerns about this Kip, whom they hired about three years ago. I may pass on some of this information to him. He's very honest and wants to keep his company that way. He says in these modern days, it can be hard to find honest and loyal employees. I think he'll be glad about your assessment."

He caught the look on Sammi's face.

"Don't you worry? I'll be very subtle and discreet. You must know that about me by now. I've never once asked you how you figure out all these things about people so fast. I know you've talents hidden to most of us, and that's okay with me. If I get the benefit of them, I'm happy."

Sammi was comfortable with the president of the bank. He'd realized many years ago when she first started working for his bank that she was a very shrewd judge of character, and as such was also able to pick up some hidden data easily. He didn't know how she did it, but the FBI and police appreciated her and requested her help on many occasions. So she was given time off whenever anyone needed her. Sammi liked the fact that he had never questioned her. He left her alone and allowed her the privacy she wanted and needed. Because of that, they had been able to form a trusting relationship.

* * *

On the way home, she realized that she had a major problem on her hands. This was the third time she and her husband had planned their honeymoon trip and something always happened to delay or cancel it. Yet they needed this trip now, especially after all of the hard felonious cases that they'd worked on in the last few years. They certainly deserved it. Yet how could she deny the help that her friend Billy needed? Not many people understood him the way she did. She realized his tender and faithful heart, even to those who didn't deserve it. Yet, she also had a loyalty to Dave. He was so excited about this vacation. How could she deny him? She took a deep sigh as she felt a tear run down her left cheek. She didn't know what to do. Where was her first loyalty? She needed time to think about this. She'd talk to Dave tonight. He could help her straighten out her allegiance, and he had a caring heart. She knew that she'd need his support on this one.

CHAPTER TWO

Sammi was surprised that Dave was already home. When she pulled into the garage and saw his car, she had to admit she felt some disappointment. She was hoping to have a few minutes to mull over her thoughts and work them out in her mind in the comfortable setting of her home. She didn't know how she was going to present this dilemma to him, but she had to tell him and it had to be tonight.

"Hi sweetie," he said as she walked through the door and then added, "tonight we're having steaks, salad and mushrooms. I hope that wets your appetite because mine is already in gear."

She walked over and planted a kiss on his cheek. He was such a loving personality and deserved the best. He treated her so well, and they were incredibly compatible, not only in their personalities and in views on life, but also in their dreams and goals. She felt unbelievably lucky to have found someone like him as her life's partner.

"I need to change and relax some, then I'll come back and help, okay?" She hoped her voice was steady, because usually he was incredibly sensitive to her and it was hard to fool him even for a little while.

"Sure, you go and relax and then we'll eat and later you can tell me what's so heavy on your mind."

She was almost out of the kitchen doorway, but had to turn around and look at him. He simply smiled at her, shrugged his shoulders as if it were a forgone conclusion that he knew she had something distressing her. He always knew. She smiled back and left, shaking her head a little realizing she was happy he knew her so well.

Later, they talked about their schedule for that day, about the circle of friends that they had and about their upcoming trip to Aruba. That's when Sammi's shoulders got somewhat tight and her face tried so hard to hide her feelings. But she couldn't and there was no use trying any longer.

She started to say, "Dave, I need to talk to you about something..."

"I know," he said, interrupting, as he took her hand. He knew she was having a hard time with this one. "And I'm glad you're finally going to tell me. I've been waiting patiently to find out what happened to you today, honey. You've been so different since you walked in that door. So tell me."

She didn't know how to start. She paused and looked at him trying to find the right words. Would he be upset if she wanted to help Billy? Would he understand and stand behind her all the way? Her mind was still wondering if she should go down to Cuyahoga Falls, Ohio in person or possibly get in touch with someone ...

"Hey, come back to earth and just tell me, Sammi. This is me, remember? You can tell me anything."

She nodded. She knew that was true so she finally began in earnest.

"Remember when I first told you that I could hear other people's thoughts."

"Of course," he said, "I'm not likely to forget that."

"Okay and then I told you about Father John Meyer, the priest in Canada and then there was Professor Harley of Scranton University. And of course you met him when we worked on those abduction cases in Philadelphia."

She paused for a moment trying to get her thoughts together. It gave him time to comment, "Yeah, I remember."

"Well, you knew that I said there was a third person I'd helped, a fellow named Billy, but I never told you his story."

"That's right, now that you mention it. I remember that you said there was another person who'd been sworn to secrecy like the other two, but you never got around to telling me his story."

"He's the one who called me from Cuyahoga Falls, Ohio and he finally called again today and I talked to him."

The concern showed all over her face. She took a few minutes before she continued. "I need to tell you his story first, okay? Then I can tell you what he wants."

"Fine with me."

She saw Dave shift in his position on the couch getting comfortable in his spot as he waited for her to begin.

"I met him at Scranton University; we took a political science class together. Dave, he's one of the nicest people you'd ever want to meet and also one of the most vulnerable. He has Down syndrome. That makes him an automatic target and some took advantage of him when we were in that science class. He's fairly mild in his syndrome and his motor skills and learning abilities are only slightly lower than a regular person, so he does quite well. Moreover, he works incredibly hard. His physical features show his syndrome slightly, but not to the point where everyone knows immediately and stares at him. However, it didn't take very long in our class for everyone to realize his obvious weakness. In that particular course you had two major tests, each of which counted for forty percent of your grade, so it was important to do well on both of them. The first one was a long and detailed paper that had to be turned in on time in great condition … you certainly must remember how tough some of those professors can be."

"I remember only too well. They were so particular that you'd get knocked down for anything at all."

THOUGHTS CAN BE DEADLY

Sammi smiled in remembrance. "Billy worked very hard and was always prepared; he felt proud of his work. But about three days before he was to turn in his paper, it disappeared. He had no chance to recoup and was utterly desperate and extremely agitated. I'd been a friend of his for a while, had lunch with him on several occasions and he trusted me. He was totally upset and through his tears told me that he couldn't imagine what happened. You see, he's so incredibly organized and exact about his routine ... he says he has to be otherwise his mind gets confused. It was because of his unbelievable attention to every detail that he couldn't figure out what went wrong. That day in class, I realized what happened. There were three boys who took his paper."

Dave looked disgusted. Unscrupulous people usually targeted the vulnerable; they were the first to be harmed or harassed and needed protection.

"Two reasons really. Billy was doing quite well in this tough class. These boys were goof offs and didn't want to be beaten by someone like him. And they hadn't done any work so they each took part of his paper and worked out extra details to make three papers out of one. They were jerks."

"And you figured it out, of course."

"Yes, well, their thought world was around the fact that they were so happy to have a paper to turn in and who would believe a somewhat stupid guy like Billy."

Dave could only shake his head. "So what did you do?"

"I knew this professor quite well so I talked to him first. Of course, he knew Billy's dedication to getting his work done on time and in impeccable condition so he had to lean in my direction. I wanted this professor to call a meeting with these three boys, myself, Billy, and the dean of the college as well. I thought that would be the best way solve this problem and ensure that it wouldn't happen again."

Dave puckered his lips and then laughed as he said. "These guys got a real surprise, didn't they?"

"They did. Of course, Billy was unaware of the reason for the meeting with the dean of the college and he was scared. However, I couldn't tell him in advance so I simply tried to comfort him. But these guys were so smug. They thought they were home free and could use Billy's mental capacity against him. But they didn't understand Down syndrome at all, which of course worked out in our favor."

"Don't keep me in suspense, what happened?"

"Well, talk about incredible stupidity, one of the guys still had Billy's original paper in his duffel bag; I already knew that from his thought world. So throughout all of the protests and denials, which I hoped they'd toss aside and admit their crime, this one guy sat there with all the ammunition we needed in his bag. Billy was confused because he thought they were his friends and so finally, I had to ask the professor and the dean to have them dump out their duffel bags. One of the guys broke into a sweat that was obvious to all. The paper was there and they all had to admit to their escapade."

"What happened to them?"

"Now that's the great part. The dean said it was up to Billy if he wanted to press charges and have them kicked out of college. But, have you ever known any Down syndrome people?"

"We had a neighbor once who had it, but I never got to know her very much. Said hi occasionally, but that's all. Why?"

"They're such loving and forgiving people. Billy had his paper back, the boys were begging him not to press charges, and he agreed. They promised never again to do anything like that and of course, they were put on probation until they graduated. Billy thought that was a good idea."

Dave smiled.

"The best part of the story here is that these guys couldn't believe that Billy didn't want any revenge and their attitude really changed toward him and life in general. It took a little time, but later you'd see them sitting with him for lunch and I joined them a few times. I could tell they'd learned a lot from him. I always wondered if they continued with their new attitude in the future, but these students had changed tremendously during their sophomore year. I know that for a fact because I checked their thoughts. And I understand at graduation that one of the guys dedicated his success to Billy."

"Wow, that's great. Maybe it all worked out for the best after all.

* * *

Dave knew there was more to come. He went into the kitchen, got some wine, and was on his way back when the phone rang. Jim and Julie wanted to know if they had time for a quick dinner on Thursday before they left for vacation. Dave agreed they did. That being settled, he was back to his spot on the couch waiting for Sammi to continue.

"Okay that's the background so what happened today?"

"I have a little more to tell you. Briefly, Billy's parents gave him up when he was four years old. They couldn't cope, or didn't want to; they were alcoholics and had social services after them several times because they were not doing right for this special needs child. After that, he lived at an orphanage for quite a while. He always wondered why no one was interested in adopting him, and that's when he truly realized he was different and began getting increasingly depressed. In his early teen years, Lily Caulkin was hired and she proved invaluable to him. She took extra time with him, explained him things about life and people in his terms and began to care for this little one who had no adult in his corner. After a time, she asked to be his legal guardian because she didn't think she could adopt him since she was single. But since she was a social worker and had experience with special needs children, they agreed she could adopt him. I believe she was in her middle thirties and Billy about fifteen when the papers were finalized."

"That's one of those stories that makes you feel good, isn't it?"

"Yes it is. Apparently, she brought him out to his full potential, which isn't all that much lower than some people. He went on to get some type of business degree."

Sammi stopped for a few moments. She was getting to the hard part and she was emotional. Her heart was torn in two directions.

"Okay, so what's the part you haven't told me yet?"

"Okay, Dave, this is it. Lily Caulkin would be about fifty-five years old now, give or take a few years. Billy still lives with her, but apparently, something dreadful has happened. She's been accused of first-degree murder and she's presently in jail. Billy has been everywhere trying to get her help, but no one will listen to him. She has no one on her side and Billy said that she told him she didn't do it."

Sammi blurted out the last part – kind of dumped it on Dave's lap. She couldn't even look him in the face right now. He must be so disappointed that this happened just before their vacation.

"So I take it what's so hard for you to tell me is that he's asked for your help, right?"

"He has," she said as tears began to roll down her cheeks. "But I didn't tell him yes; I simply said that I'd call him back. I know we can't break our plans again, yet I don't know how to say no to him and he's so desperate. What should I do?"

"You're asking me? What do you want to do?"

"I really want to help him, but we've postponed our honeymoon too many times already. We need this vacation."

"You didn't mind delaying it when Tom Harrington's friend was in trouble."

"He's a friend of mine, too. But you don't even know Billy."

Sammi sensed Dave's sympathetic glance. She felt a few tears still coming down her face, but truly tried to show some semblance of control. No, she still wasn't sure what to do.

"And?" said Dave, waiting.

"I thought maybe we could find someone out there that could help them. We could ask around for a good attorney."

"And would that satisfy you?"

"Well, at least I would have tried to get him some help."

Dave paused, waiting for Sammi to continue. She was confused and her thoughts weren't coming very clear right now.

"Since you don't want to, I guess I'll make the call."

Sammi looked over at Dave with a question mark on her face.

"I'll change our plane reservations from Aruba to Cuyahoga Falls, Ohio. It's the only thing that makes sense, Sammi. There'll always be an Aruba and some day I know we'll make it, but I feel we both need to go to Ohio and see what we can do."

Sammi resumed crying now. She couldn't hold it in any longer. "Really, you don't mind?"

"Sammi, I'd love for us to go to Aruba some day. But remember last time, you knew that my heart and mind would be here in Scranton with Tom and his friend. Well, I don't think your mind would be in Aruba anyway. Besides, I've never been to this Cuyahoga Falls, so let's make that our vacation this year."

Sammi grabbed onto Dave and gave him a big hug. "You're really terrific. Do you know that?"

"I think your caring so much about other people is what's terrific. And that's one of the reasons I like to be partnered up with you."

"Oh yeah. Are there any other reasons?"

Dave smiled, took her hand and they headed for the bedroom.

* * *

It was with great satisfaction that Sammi called Billy the next day. To say he was delighted and excited wouldn't cover the subject. He trusted her completely, and although he was a loving and forgiving person in general, he wasn't always totally trusting of people. He'd had too many experiences growing up that prevented him from doing so anymore.

"Oh, Ms. Sammi you're really gonna come to help me and Ms. Lily. I'll tell her. She'll be so happy and she remembers you. I told her I was going to call you and she was happy."

"I want you to know that I got married a few years ago and my husband will be coming with me. You'll like him, Billy and I've told him about you."

"You told him about me. Does he still want to meet me?"

"He's very excited about meeting you. We're going to leave on Friday night so I'll get in touch with you on Saturday morning. Where will you be?"

"I'll sit and wait by my phone all day. I'm so happy Ms. Sammi. I'm so happy."

"Okay, then let's wait until we get there and you can tell me all about Ms. Lily's trouble."

"Yes, I will and then we can go and see her. Oh, I'm so happy right now. I know you can help us."

"Billy, all I can say is that we'll try to help, okay? I can't promise anything, but we'll try our best."

"Oh, you can work miracles, Ms. Sammi. I know that. You found my term paper remember? No one else could've done that. I know you can find the real killer."

"Okay, I've got to go now, but I'll see you on Saturday morning."

"Thank you, Ms. Sammi and tell your husband thank you, too."

"I will. See you on Saturday."

Sammi felt complete contentment as she put down the telephone. She couldn't deny it. There was something about a person who totally believed you could do anything and everything that struck a note somewhere deep inside her heart. It was hard not to get overly excited about life when working with Billy. He believed. His wonderful mind had the capacity to believe a lot easier than the rest of us. And he loved life so much. She was happy that he had finally learned to trust people selectively; that was so necessary in order for him to protect himself, but other than that, she wished she had his capacity of total belief. He amazed her at times.

* * *

The next day found Jim Mucci coming up to Dave's desk asking what time they wanted to meet for dinner.

"Seven o'clock is good, but does it matter that we're not going to Aruba but to Cuyahoga Falls, Ohio instead?"

"No kidding." Jim showed surprise and inquisitiveness on his face as he sat down for a moment.

"An old friend of Sammi needs her and she can't refuse. Actually, I couldn't refuse either once I heard the story. So I guess Aruba will be some other time."

Just then, Amilio approached and he'd heard the last part of their conversation. "No Aruba again? Another friend needs you two. You're a good pair to know."

"I only hope a week will be enough, but we'll see."

Amilio added, "With Sammi around, you'll get it done."

Dave laughed. He knew that Amilio was still trying to figure out Sammi; actually, many people were. He marveled at the circumstances that had brought them together and put him in a world where nothing was ordinary or predictable. But he loved it; he had to admit that.

"Where are you staying?"

"Not sure. Sammi's going to find out where these people live and try to get a place around there."

"Good idea, amigo. If we can help in any way, you let us know."

"Thanks," said Dave. "I was counting on that."

Sergeant Brady called them in to make sure Dave had transferred his work to one of the others and found out about his change in plans.

"Well, that means you won't be too far away." He saw the look on everyone's face and added, "Now, look, I'm not planning on calling you for anything frivolous, but you never know, and since this is more business than pleasure, we may be able to help you as well."

Dave smiled. It was great to be working with people like these professionals. Solving crimes always came first and extra help was usually available.

"Roy Dawson won't be coming for one more month. It turns out that he had many loose ends that he left dangling in some of his cases and they're making sure that he completes everything before he moves here. So I guess we know one thing up front that we'll have to watch him on."

"Okay, we'll have to get him on the right path straight away," said Jim. "Those loose ends can be quite important."

"Right. Now Dave, I'm assuming you have all of your cases and priorities covered by the others. You guys make my job easier; you know all the rules and stick to them. I don't have to be watching over my shoulder all the time to make sure of it. That's a big relief to me."

They looked at each other and nodded. All of them were interested in one thing. Get the job done right and keep the details solid. You never knew when you might need them again. Police work was an exact science, even though it didn't always seem so.

* * *

Meeting Julie and Jim for dinner was a delight. The four of them never had enough time to get together anymore and relished any excuse for a happening.

"So you're not going to Aruba, I hear," said Julie, "you're going to Ohio, right?"

"That's right," said Dave. "There must be something about Aruba because every time we plan to go there something else more important comes up and prevents us. However, I do believe sometime in the future, we really are going to make it."

Jim said, "Julie and I've been talking about it, too. We've never had a real honeymoon either. Maybe we could make it a foursome someday."

Sammi was quite excited. "That would be great. However, you can imagine with the four of us if we could ever get our schedules in sync, but let's see if we can do it. When we're supposed to get there, the universe will find a way."

They all laughed. That was a typical Sammi answer. She didn't believe in coincidences and she believed they had made the right decision this time. She spent a few minutes telling them about Billy Simpson. They were both fascinated, and they could tell how much Sammi held him in admiration.

"He's very special. It's hard to explain it, even to myself, but this guy is so intuitive. I mean I can hear people's thoughts, that's true, but Billy knows many things because he is so in tune with the universe. I used to love being around him. Sometimes, I believe he puts me to shame."

Jim asked. "Does he know about you?"

"Well, ever since I found his term paper, he believes I perform miracles, but I don't think he knows exactly how I do it, although I might be surprised."

Jim laughed, "And I think you're a miracle worker, too. You sure can do some things that no one else around here can do."

"But that's a gift. I think everyone is intuitive but we have to learn to use it. And some special needs children, like those with Down syndrome and some with autism pick up information and are clued into things that I wish I could figure out. I think that they're not as concerned with the daily motion of the world, you know, so that keeps them free to be fine tuned in to other things."

"You mean, that they don't get involved in prejudices, anger, revenge, and any other of the unpleasant aspects of humans and so are opened up ... to the light, so to speak," said Julie.

"Exactly," said Sammi, "and very well put. Their own thought atmosphere around them is pure and untainted; therefore, it is open to pick up mainly the positive. And that way they are given a lot more information than those of us who get mired down with the petty stuff."

Jim said, "You know that I don't get involved in all of these technical bits and pieces, but what you said makes sense. They say you can't concentrate on a bunch of things at the same time, so if you stay on the positive side, that's what you'd be dealing with."

"I think you're getting the hang of this, too," said Dave jokingly. "But I have to admit that it does get rather complicated."

"Yes," said Sammi, "and no one knows it all."

"So when are you leaving for Ohio?" asked Jim.

"Tomorrow night as planned and Billy will be waiting Saturday morning for our phone call. Then we can get started with something but I don't know what it's all about, do you Sammi?"

"He did mention that he thought he had found an attorney, but not much had happened yet. And he said that he thought the attorney wasn't very sure of himself."

Jim and Julie looked at each other.

"I'm telling you that a lot of times Billy can be a very shrewd judge of people."

Dave asked, "How old is he?"

"Let me think ... he's got to be in his middle to late thirties by now."

"And his name is Billy Simpson?" asked Julie.

Sammi smiled. "His name is Billy G. Simpson. You see Billy has a great sense of humor. When he was about fourteen years old, Lily adopted him. At that time, he realized that he didn't have a middle name like many other people, so he asked Lily if he could add one. She knew that she could add it to the adoption papers so she agreed. But Billy didn't want an entire name; he said that he just wanted the initial G. Can anyone guess why?"

They were all silent. "I wouldn't have known either, but the extra generic material from chromosome 21 is what causes Down syndrome. It's also referred to as trisomy 21 or the G factor." They all smiled realizing what was coming. "Now Billy was told that he has this extra chromosome so he decided to add that letter to his name because that's who he is. But there's no name attached to it, only a letter. His name is Billy G. Simpson."

That warmed everyone's heart. Here was a person with Down syndrome who had a beautiful sense of humor.

Sammi turned to Jim and Julie to ask, "How are the girls doing?"

"Great," said Julie. "Sarah is seventeen and Donna is fourteen. But their mother is getting divorced again and they're sad about that."

"Yeah, it's kind of funny in a way," said Jim. "Neither one of my girls was that crazy about this particular step-father, but they're tired of seeing their mother unhappy and unable to find her niche. And they know that she'll find another guy and they'll go through this again and frankly, they're tired of it. But they love their mom so they're kind of torn."

"I can imagine," said Sammi. "It must help them being with the two of you."

"We have a good rapport now and of course neither one of us talks bad about their mother. Kathy used to badmouth me all the time and it upset them, but since we've developed a better relationship with her, mostly thanks to Julie, she doesn't criticize me that much anymore, so that helps a lot. I wish she'd find what she wants in life."

"Some people never do," said Dave. "They search all of their lives and come up empty."

"That's sad," said Sammi.
Everyone agreed.

* * *

After dinner, they all sat around with Jim already missing
Dave. When the three referees weren't together it was as if
part of the wheel was missing; their minds were so much in
sync with each other.

"Just like me," said Dave. "I'll be working without the
two of you."

Jim said, "We're only a phone call away."

"But you've got me covered if anything happens on that
burglary case, right?"

"Of course, I do, but I don't think anything will happen
while you're gone. We've got some leads, but it's gonna take
a while to follow up on all of them."

Sammi looked confused.

"We've got some burglars breaking into homes, scaring
the hell out of the occupants to steal jewelry, watches, money,
anything that will convert to quick cash. We think it's for
drugs."

Sammi nodded; she hadn't heard about this one.

"You've got LeBron helping, too."

"Yeah, I know, but ... we'll see. We'll be ready if something happens."

Then Jim had his own questions. "What do you know so
far about this case in Ohio?"

"Nothing. Honestly, we don't know anything at all. We
know they've arrested Billy's mother for first degree murder
and that's about it. We don't know the identity of the victim or
any of the circumstances yet. I checked with a few people at
one of the Ohio stations, but they seem to be quiet about this
one."

THOUGHTS CAN BE DEADLY

"Yeah, nothing on the news either," said Jim. "But then one murder in Ohio probably wouldn't make any news unless it was a sensational story of some kind."

Dave nodded. "But in a way that's probably good. We'll get all the details when we get there and sometimes the news can distort the details anyway."

"Boy, that's for sure. We know that to be true, don't we?"

They remembered in past years how some of their cases were blown away on the news and they hardly recognized them anymore.

"Maybe you'll hear from me. Do we know anyone there? I need to ask the sarge about that. It would really help a lot if I could get in with some of them. Sometimes they're open to it and many times, they're not."

"That's true; it really depends on the details of the murder, the scenario, who's involved and other ramifications. If you get into some delicate territory, you'll see a blank wall come up against you because you're an outsider."

"I'm sure that's true, but then she has an attorney working for her and maybe he can open some doors for us. Who knows? I'll have to wait and see."

"Just remember, if you need any secret or sneaky ways of doing business, you can always call Amilio."

They all laughed at that one. Amilio had experience as a double agent and was considered quite adept in many covert situations.

"Even from a distance I'm sure he'd have some good ideas," laughed Dave.

It was almost like a secret situation they would be walking into. Depending on the lawyer's expertise, and what Lily could tell them, they might have a huge fishing expedition on their hands.

* * *

35

Sammi was somewhat withdrawn on the way home. She seemed a little anxious and her concern was showing.

"Okay, what's up with you?" asked Dave.

"I'm thinking this could be tough for both of us because even though you're a police officer, they may not accept you anyway and then where would we be? I'm trying to figure out things before we even get there and I know that's not possible, but my mind wants to worry about everything right now, ahead of time."

Some habits were hard for her to break and a tendency of worrying had been part of her past and present. She'd always hoped to change that for the future.

"We have to wait until we get there and study the situation. It might be simpler than we thought or maybe more complicated. But when we know what we're facing, then we can devise a plan."

Sammi nodded. "I know that's the only thing that makes any sense at all, but I was thinking about Billy. He's such a simple person in a way, and so vulnerable. I'm hoping that the police and others haven't tried to take advantage of him. They could easily do that and get away with it."

"Lily usually looked out for him, right? Moms do that anyway. But it sounds that he does pretty good most of the time."

"If he's got someone around to watch out for him, he does fine. But he can't be out there in the world in scary and exposed situations. When you first see him, you're relatively sure he has the syndrome or something else similar and that puts him immediately at risk. That's all some people look for. Therefore, even though he can take care of himself and holds down a job, someone has to protect him from the shrewd and underhanded players we have out there in the world. In normal circumstances that's bad enough, but with Lily in jail and him fending for himself, that's just too scary for me."

Dave thought about it and said, "We'll be in a situation to ensure his safety; that should put your mind at ease."

"It will. I'll feel a lot better when I know he's in a safe environment with protection around him."

Sammi remembered back at different times when she'd known him in college. They were great friends from the moment she retrieved his term paper. Oh, they'd been friends before, but after that, he thought of her as a miracle person. He'd put her up on a huge pedestal and no matter what she said to make him realize that she was an ordinary person with a special gift, he didn't accept it. To Billy, Sammi was a wonder woman. And she hoped she could live up to his belief in her this time.

CHAPTER THREE

When the plane started making its decent for the Akron-Canton Regional Airport, Sammi felt the pulse of excitement rise in her. She had been able to keep it under control most of the time on the flight, but now that the moment had arrived, she couldn't contain herself any longer. Soon they would be in Cuyahoga Falls, Ohio and tomorrow she would see Billy G. Simpson again, after more than ten years. She wondered how much he had changed. Oh, she figured he'd probably look pretty much the same – fairly short stature of about five feet four inches, and his blonde hair and blue eyes made him look like an ad for an all American boy magazine, but she wondered what level of maturity he had been able to attain. It was obvious from his conversation that he'd gained knowledge of the world around him and able to protect himself from risky situations most of the time, yet he still needed to depend on an adult to strengthen his abilities and awareness. A lot of that had to do with his mother Lily who kept him abreast of danger and explained to him repeatedly with unbelievable patience about the information he needed to know to remain safe in the world.

She grabbed Dave's hand as she said, "It's like another adventure for us. We don't know what to expect; we don't know for sure if we can even help in this situation, but here we are hoping for the best."

"It's no coincidence that Billy found you and wanted you to come here and try to help. Remember you said how intuitive he is so maybe he knows that you're the one to rally around him right now."

"You sure know how to keep me on track; you're right. Well, for now, I'm really hungry and then we can get to the motel and grab a good night's sleep. I'm not sure when we'll get another carefree evening for a while."

Dave smiled. She knew he felt her tension and would try to keep her relaxed. They found a nice family style restaurant and had a good home cooked meal. Adding a glass of wine gave them the momentum that they needed for relaxation. They slowly drove to their motel, which was roughly twelve miles from the airport and would be close to Billy's home. Tomorrow would come very quickly and then they would find out all of the facts of this murder charge against Lily.

"What do you think of Lily?" asked Dave as they were relaxing and trying to fall asleep.

"She's a great person. I think she was an orphan herself and never adopted, so she really understood about Billy's situation. I believe it helps a lot when people have walked the walk. She became a social worker because she wanted to help in this particular field that consumed her passion. I spoke to her on several occasions while we were waiting for Billy at some function or other and she's so caring."

"She never married then."

"No, she didn't. I understand she was engaged one time, but her fiancé was killed in an accident. Yet instead of being bitter and miserable about it, she just went into another direction, namely helping others. And she's very good at what she does; I understand she's received recognition for her work more than a few times. I told her that I thought Billy was so lucky to have found her and, of course, she felt that she was the lucky one."

"You don't think she could have done this crime, whatever it is."

"I can't imagine, Dave. Her entire life was facing in the opposite direction, but we'll know for sure when we talk to her. I'm quite anxious to hear her thoughts. That'll go a long way to knowing what we can do to help."

Dave yawned some and then began breathing heavier. But Sammi continued, "I can't imagine her even harming anyone let alone murdering someone, and I know people can change but that would be a complete reversal of her personality. And with her caring and affection for Billy, it doesn't seem to me that she changed, does it?"

There was no answer from Dave's side of the bed.

"Do you think so, Dave?" she repeated again rather quietly.

Then she realized he had fallen asleep. That was okay; she was glad. He needed a lot of rest right now. He would be doing a lot of the hard work on this case. After all, she heard people's thoughts, but then she gave Dave the information and he was the one who had to follow up and do something with it. Usually he had Tom and Jim around and he consulted with them, which made things easier for all of them, and she had a feeling that he'd be calling them before this case was solved.

* * *

The next morning at ten o'clock, they were ready to leave, have breakfast and then meet Billy. She put in a call to him to settle his mind that they had finally arrived.

"You're here, Ms. Sammi; you really came. I'm so happy. I talked to Ms. Lily last night and she's scared, you know. She doesn't know what to do and her lawyer isn't too much help yet. She'll be glad to talk to you."

. "Okay, we're going to eat breakfast and then head over to your place. We'll see you in about an hour or so."

"I'll sit right here and wait for you. I can't wait to see you again. And I still believe you can make miracles happen."

"I told you I'd try, Billy, but I can promise that we'll do our best."

"Okay, then you do your best and I'll do the believing for all of us, okay?"

Sammi had to laugh. "Okay, that would be just fine. See you later."

* * *

As Dave started the car he said, "He gets to your heart, doesn't he?"

"Yes," she sighed, "and he'll get to yours, too. There's so much innocence about him and yet he's a functioning adult in most ways." She raised her hand, started to say something, and gave up. It was too hard to put into words.

As they started driving, they passed the sign that said, "Welcome to Cuyahoga Falls, Home of Blossom Music Center."

Sammi said, "This does seem like a nice little community, probably about 50,000 to 60,000 people, yet they're close to Akron to get some bigger city life when they want it."

They passed a beautiful golf course and came close to the Cuyahoga River. After eating, they drove around for a little bit before they headed for Billy's house. Both wanted to get a feel of the area and it did seem like a quiet district and one that would be conducive to living a simple and uncomplicated life.

When they approached the area where Billy lived they realized it was a nice neighborhood, definitely middle class and not showy or ostentatious in any way, but a comfortable area where you could know your neighbors and have block parties as you watched out for each other. When they approached a light grey brick ranch house with a little white picket fence in front, they knew they had arrived at Billy's house. They saw him peek out behind the living room drapes, and as soon as they pulled into the driveway, the front door flew open and he ran out to meet them. His steps were still a little unsteady, especially when he was excited, but he managed to convey his unbridled enthusiasm. Their world would never be the same again.

He ran around, opened Sammi's door, and gave her a long and tender hug. Billy had always been affectionate with her, but had learned to curb it with many other people. But Sammi was special to him and he was thrilled to see her.

"Hi, Billy; it's so good to see you again."

"I'm so excited to see you, too. You still look so pretty to me." Then he turned toward Dave. "You must be Dave, her husband. You've got to be one lucky person. Sammi is very special."

Dave smiled as he said, "I'd have to agree with that."

Sammi thought that he hadn't changed all that much. Certainly, he was older and more mature, but the innocence remained all over his face and his wholesome excitement was there for the entire world to see. He still had his determined walk as if he was contemplating where he was going and quite serious about getting there.

"Come on in and talk with me for a while. I'll tell you what I know, but it isn't very much."

They walked into a clean and beautifully decorated home. Billy offered them coffee and then they sat down to discuss the case.

"Lily didn't do anything bad; she never has. Someone has made her a goat or something."

Sammi said, "I think you mean that someone tried to make her a scapegoat; that means that the guilty party is trying to blame her so they can get away with their crime."

Billy looked slightly bewildered. He occasionally got confused on slang terms.

"Oh yeah, I said the word wrong. That's what I meant. She didn't do anything bad."

Dave looked at Billy and realized that he shared Sammi's assessment. This was a totally innocent child of thirty-some years. He could hold a job, relate to people, and take care of himself to a point, but his deductive capabilities were naïve. He knew Lily didn't commit this crime, but couldn't begin to speculate anything else.

"Okay," said Sammi. "Let's start at the beginning. First of all, who was killed?"

"This man who had been here a few times and took Ms. Lily to dinner was shot somewhere when he sat in his car. They said that Ms. Lily did it because she was with him that night and she had just found out he was married to someone else. Ms. Lily never would date a married man. She told me that wasn't the right thing to do. But he was already coming over and she said she would tell him that it was finished and that would be the end of it."

"Had she dated him very long?"

"No, just a few times I think. But I was home when they returned and she walked into our home alone and he took off in his car. He was still alive and Ms. Lily was home. She didn't do this."

"What was his name?"

"Matthew Belten."

Dave asked, "What do you know about this Matthew Belten?"

"I don't know anything important. He came over and took Ms. Lily out to dinner two or three times. I think she kind of liked him. The last time she saw him she told him that she found out he was married," he looked down before he continued, "I saw a few tears in her eyes when she came home. I don't know why she can't find a good husband; she's so nice."

"Where does Mr. Belten work?"

"He works for an engineering firm somewhere in Akron, but I don't know what he does. He was always nice to me when he came over; I mean he took the time to talk to me and people don't always do that, but I understand."

Sammi continued. "When was she arrested?"

"Let's see," said Billy. He was thinking hard for a moment. "She went out with Matthew on a Friday night and I think they found his body on Saturday afternoon in a car somewhere. He was shot in the head; I remember the police saying that and they said it on TV, too. We were both in shock because he had been here on Friday night. Lily cried. I knew she was mad at him, but she said that he didn't deserve to die like that. I think it was Sunday night that they came and arrested her. She cried at first, but then told me everything would be alright."

Dave turned to Sammi and said, "That's a pretty quick arrest. I wonder why."

"Do you know if they have any evidence against Lily?" Dave asked.

"I don't think so, but they said that she was the last one to see him alive and that she must be the one who killed him. Anyway," he said, suddenly excitedly waving both of his hands, "they didn't say she murdered him, but that she was being arrested on suspicion of murder."

Sammi smiled.

"What's the difference, Ms. Sammi?"

"It means that they think she *could* have done it, but aren't absolutely positive yet. That's why we have judges and courts to make those decisions."

"I'd like to get over to the jail and see her," said Dave.

"I'd like to come with you. Is that okay?"

"Certainly," said Dave. "I think you should come with us."

Billy smiled. He could never hide his emotions and never wanted to. He now felt like he was part of the process that would be helping to prove Ms. Lily's innocence. And that was important to him.

* * *

On the ride over to the jail, Billy pointed out some of the scenery around town. He indicated the direction of the Mary Campbell Cave, named after its most celebrated resident. And they passed a golf course, which Billy was happy to offer the name as Brookledge Golf Course. Then they approached the jail where Lily Caulkin was being held and Billy got very quiet.

"I'm nervous when I see her in there. Once they gave us a special room where we could talk, but another time I had to see her through the bars of her cell. I cried a lot. It's not right, Ms. Sammi, I tell you. It's not right."

"You hold some positive thoughts, okay? We're going to talk to Ms. Lily and find out what's going on. Then we can find a plan of action."

Billy's eyes got a little wider and he felt that was the way to do business.

Entering the jail, they gave Dave special consideration for being a police officer and extended him particular courtesies. The special room was available and they told him that they'd bring in Lily shortly. Dave nodded and expressed his appreciation.

And when Lily entered the room, Billy ran for her and just held her. They were both crying and gathering strength from each other. Then she extended her hand to Sammi who in turn introduced her husband.

After noting that it had been a long time since they'd seen each other and that a lot of things had happened since then, they both settled down to the critical business at hand.

"Well," said Sammi. "We've only gotten a little information from Billy. Maybe you could tell us what you know."

"I don't know much either. This is so crazy. First of all, I'm a social worker, for God's sake. I work for the Children's Aid Group and I help find parents for orphans or place them in good foster homes. I've never married, but I occasionally date, although, I must admit not too often."

"Where did you meet this Matthew?" asked Dave.

"I had been at a fund raiser for the Children's Aid Group and his company was making a donation. We met and talked for a while and had coffee later. We seemed to have hit it off, but I didn't know he was married. That's one line I don't cross."

"How did you find out?" asked Sammi.

"Some article in the paper about an event at his company where he'd taken his wife. And there was even a picture of them with another couple. They all had their arms around each other. I was furious."

"What's the name of the company where he works?"

"It's called Premier Tenner Engineering, but I have no idea what they make. They're an average size company I hear, but out of the realm of anything I know about."

Dave nodded. "What can you tell us about that Friday night – the last time you saw Matthew?"

"I had just found out he was married. I tried to call him from home and cancel the date, but I couldn't get in touch with him. I didn't want to have a scene in front of Billy, but I wanted to let him know what I thought of him. We went for a drive and of course, we never made it to that dinner that we had planned. I told him very quickly how angry I was for him being dishonest with me and let him know firmly that I don't date married men. At first, he laughed and tried to talk me out of it. But when he saw I was serious, he drove me back home and that was it. We didn't even talk; I opened my car door and walked myself up to the front door. I don't think I was gone more than half an hour. He wasn't even that mad, not really. He was acting more frustrated like a jerk that had been found out."

"So you didn't actually fight about it?"

"Not exactly, I mean I did yell at him; I was hurt and upset and he knew it. He tried to tell me that we were both adults, you know the drill, but I told him he should have told me and let me make up my own mind. Then he dropped me off and sped off before I even reached the front door."

"And no one saw you?" asked Dave.

Lily pursed her lips and slowly shook her head in remembrance. "No, I don't remember seeing anyone. I mean we never went to a restaurant. We barely got two or three blocks from home. And then considering my attitude, he said he might as well take me home right away."

"I see," said Dave.

"I don't know anything, that's the problem. I've been arrested and I have no idea who didn't like him or what type of enemies he had. I didn't know much about him at all. I keep wondering what type of proof they could have against me, because I didn't do this."

Just then, the door opened and a police officer brought in a folder for Dave.

"Here's the information you requested."

"Thanks," said Dave. "I appreciate this."

After he left Dave said, "These are the charges and evidence they have against you so far."

Dave read quietly for a while and then said, "Well, they found some hairs in his car on the passenger side and they're having these tested now." He looked at Lily and said, "They'll probably prove to be yours."

She nodded disgustedly.

"And someone did see a man and woman arguing in his car, but they don't name anyone specifically. They say the car had pulled over to the side of the road and it was in a residential area. Someone passing by heard loud voices, and looked over to see a man and a woman arguing. Then the car peeled away like the driver was in a fit of temper."

Lily agreed. Matthew did speed off after she told him she was finished.

"So that might mean that they do have a witness and any prosecutor could make that look bad." Dave read on more. "It also says that you were wearing a green blouse and had a scarf around your neck."

Lily nodded. "But that only proves I was there and I've already admitted that I did have a date with him. But he dropped me off at home and got out of there as fast as he could."

Billy said, "I told the police that, but they didn't believe me. It's probably because they think I'm stupid."

Dave said, "No, not at all. Most police officers seldom believe a relative, you know. They think a relative might lie thinking they were helping out."

Billy looked shocked. "I wouldn't lie. No, I wouldn't. Ms. Lily can tell you that."

"I'm sure that's true," said Sammi. "But we have to convince the police."

"Anyway," said Dave. "Could anyone else in your neighborhood have seen you return home and confirm that Matthew left?"

"I don't think so. At least, I didn't see anyone."

Dave paused for another moment and then asked. "So to what I understand, you didn't know him very well. You didn't know much about his life so if I asked you about any enemies or bad business dealings, or anything shady in his life, you wouldn't know?"

Lily put her head down in frustration and disgust. "No, I barely knew him – just a few dates, that's all."

"And he didn't talk much about himself?"

"No, I'll try and remember anything I can and write it down, but I can't think of anything right now."

At this point, she had tears coming down from her eyes; she didn't even bother to wipe them away.

"This is only the beginning, Lily, hang in there. We're going to talk to your lawyer on Monday and see if he's found out anything."

Now Lily looked up toward the ceiling. "Billy did the best he could, but I don't have much faith in that guy."

"Why not?"

She started to answer and then stopped abruptly. "I think I'll let you meet him first and decide for yourself."

Dave thought it was a strange comment, but let it go. As they were about to leave, Billy ran over to give Lily another hug. "Now you be sure to lock your doors tonight, okay? Don't forget."

She turned to look at Dave and Sammi as she said, "He's okay alone. He's been alone a few times before, but I remind him about locking his doors like any mother would do."

Her expression as a caring and loving mother was the last they saw of her, as she was led away, somewhat unsteady on her feet.

* * *

When they left the jail, Dave didn't ask Sammi any questions. Billy was so sensitive about things he might interpret the comments as a secret being kept from him so they decided to wait until later.

"Let's have some dinner before we go home," said Dave.

Billy looked a little hesitant which caused Dave to ask, "Is that a problem?"

"No, I'd very much like to have dinner with you, but I was supposed to take Marsha to dinner. We have dinner every Saturday night."

Sammi looked surprised. "Who's Marsha?"

"She's my girlfriend. I have a girlfriend, you know."

Dave smiled and asked. "And how long have you and Marsha been dating."

Billy thought about it and answered, "It's been two years now. She's really nice. Marsha Cordell, that's her name. I met her at a party. She has Down syndrome, too and she's just a little more serious than I am, but I understand how she thinks and we have fun together."

Dave said, "Why don't we pick up Marsha and then we can all have dinner together?"

Billy was happy; he couldn't hide it. "Would that be okay? Marsha will be so excited. I'll call her right now."

And he did. He couldn't contain his excitement about Sammi and Dave wanting to have dinner with the two of them. Billy didn't yet realize how special he was in his unpretentious heart.

* * *

Marsha lived in the same vicinity as Billy, only about three blocks away. Her parents invited them in for a few minutes.

"It's so sad about Lily. She wouldn't harm a fly but she doesn't have anyone on her side. Do you have any other suspects yet?"

"No, not yet," said Dave. "Did you know the victim?" he asked.

"Not personally," answered Mrs. Cordell, "but I heard many rumors that he was quite a ladies' man. And I think his wife had a bit of a reputation, too."

"Oh really?" That comment seemed to perk up Dave's interest.

Sammi remained quiet observing and concentrating. Dave found that waiting for her assessment was difficult.

"Yes," added Mr. Cordell. "I knew Matthew slightly, had only met him a few times, but he was definitely a ladies' man."

"Do you know anything about this Premier Tenner Engineering Company where he worked?"

"No, I don't. It's on the south side of town, which is considered strictly a business district and hardly anyone goes there unless there's a reason."

"What does this company do?"

"I think they deal in specific types of engines used for cars and trucks and he was a chemical engineer and had been working there for a while; that much I know. He was one guy that people talked about because of his reputation, but that's really all I know about him."

"What about his wife?"

"Don't know much about her either. But like my wife said, I understand she did her running around, too."

Dave nodded, but he was happy that they'd learned a little here, something he hadn't counted on. Since Marsha was ready, they left for dinner.

* * *

Marsha Cordell was twenty-nine years old, attractive and a little more into her world than was Billy. Still, she was a delight and enjoyed meeting Dave and Sammi and the fact that they wanted to have dinner with them.

"You're from Scranton, Pennsylvania," she said. It was obvious that she liked the word Pennsylvania, said it several times, and pronounced it slowly.

"I like that word," she said.

Billy answered, "Yes I do, too. It's a nice word."

Then she offered. "I have a job. I work at the Children's Aid Center and help clean up dishes and I do other stuff. I get paid a salary and they said they like me."

Sammi asked, "How many days a week do you work?

"Usually three or four days, and I like my job. I do good work."

"I'm sure you do," said Sammi. "I'll bet you're a hard worker."

Now Marsha sat back and smiled. She felt comfortable with Sammi and felt she appreciated her. Sammi knew this from her thoughts. She wasn't as comfortable having Down syndrome as Billy and she was hurt when people stared at her. She knew she was different and understood that her difference was more obvious. Her face was quite round and her neck was thick, which was a noticeable outward sign. In her heart she wished it didn't show as much.

"Marsha is smart and has written some poetry," said Billy. "Maybe someday she can get it published."

Marsha was shy about this. She looked down, obviously slightly embarrassed, but also happy that Billy had mentioned it.

"You have to keep trying and you never know when you'll get lucky." Dave was getting into the mood of these two people.

He wanted to build up a rapport with Marsha. "If you work at the center, you must know Ms. Lily quite well?" He was hoping to get an assessment from a very honest person who probably couldn't lie even if she tried.

"Oh yes, I see her every day. She's very nice to me, but then Ms. Lily is nice to everyone. I'm sad she's in this bad trouble."

"So everyone likes Ms. Lily and you don't know anyone that doesn't like her?"

Marsha took some time with this question. Before she answered, she puckered her brows, rubbed her hands together and thought seriously. Then she shook her head. "No, she doesn't have any enemies at work. She helps everyone all the time. That's what she does. If I have a question about anything, I go to Ms. Lily and she'll help me. She'll find a way. She does it all the time."

The dinner conversation confirmed that everyone seemed to appreciate Lily in the community. Dave felt they received important information out of Marsha, who luckily worked with Lily on most days. Yet it was pretty much as expected. She was a nice person with no known enemies. She cared about people, helped them out, and everyone seemed to appreciate her.

* * *

On Sunday after lunch they decided to go back and visit with Lily alone, hoping she would talk about other details when Billy wasn't around. Again, it would give Sammi more time to sort out Lily's thoughts. On Saturday, her thoughts confirmed everyone's suspicions; she was no killer. But her thoughts were mainly a mother's concern about Billy. Oh, she felt that he would be okay alone for a while, but the stress of this situation was a lot for him to handle. His pure mind had trouble with her being accused of anything bad. He knew her so well and she was a good person in his view. That was what she was worried about the most.

"I'm glad you came back alone," she said and they all understood why. "I don't have much else to add, except that Matthew pursued me quite vigorously after we met at that charity party. I didn't know he was married and I have to tell you that I was flattered by his constant attention. After all, look at me. I'm not very pretty." She put her hand up when she saw their expressions, "No, no, I'm being honest. I'm rather plain, not ugly or anything, but no men were fighting to get to my door, ever. But I've had a good life and a few suitors along the way. Once a long time ago, I met someone and we almost married. I think it would have been a good match, but he died rather unexpectedly and shattered my dreams. I was twenty-seven at the time."

"That must have been quite difficult for you to handle. I understand you have no family," said Sammi.

"Yes, that's true. I was one of those orphans who wasn't adopted, but for me it made me strong. I learned not to depend on others and I worked harder in school because I knew I had to depend on me alone. And it's worked out fine. I did well in school and got my degree in Social Work, which was the perfect niche for me."

Lily paused for a moment as if looking back in time. Then she shook her head sending her short light brown hair in several directions. A few tears escaped her eyelids, although she tried to prevent them from doing so.

"I can't believe I'm in this predicament; me of all people. I'm accused of killing my married lover. Before Matthew, I probably hadn't dated in over ten years. There was this one guy at work; we went to dinner a few times, but only as friends, not a date or anything like that. Like I said, the offers didn't come in that often. So I guess this situation is rather ironic at best."

"So you think it's unusual that they accused you at all."

"Well, yes I do. I mean what motive did I have? He was married and didn't tell me? Come on, how many times does that happen? And that's usually after people have dated a long time and they're involved deeply with one another, but we dated casually three times, that was all. This would have been our fourth date and we weren't intimate or even that close yet. I thought we were just beginning to establish a friendship. We found we could discuss things easily with each other."

Dave asked. "What type of things did you discuss?"

"He liked to talk about his work, much of which I didn't understand. But I know that he liked his job and it came up quite often. He was some kind of manager and sales rep and got to move around a lot. He didn't have to sit at a desk all day long and felt he had finally arrived."

"So he never discussed family," asked Sammi.

"No, I don't think he ever did," she said slowly. "He did discuss a couple of buddies he was quite close to. One was Rodney Belford, in fact I met him briefly at the Charity meeting, and another was Don something; I don't remember his last name. But they both seemed to be a big part of his life."

Dave had been taking notes throughout this session. It seemed that Lily was coming up with some important details; some that needed to be pursued.

"Have you told any of this to your lawyer?"

Lily looked distressed at the mention of her attorney. She simply shook her head. It was obvious she didn't have much confidence in him, but she still wouldn't give a reason. She apparently wanted them to make their own assessment. Dave was quite intrigued and looked forward to meeting him.

"Have you tried to make bail yet?"

"So far no luck. They think I'd be a flight risk, even with Billy around. They said I could take him with me. So guess I stay here, at least for now. It's okay, but I worry about Billy. I think my lawyer has a bail hearing set for sometime next week, so we'll see."

"Billy seems to be doing quite well and we met Marsha on Saturday night."

Lily smiled. "They really care about each other and are very compatible. She's a little more serious in the syndrome, but well within any bounds of living a fruitful life with a little bit of help and guidance. And she's a good worker at the center."

"He seems to watch out for her," said Sammi.

"Oh yes, he's very protective of Marsha. It's nice to see."

The rest of the time, they talked about any and all the details Lily could think of, which weren't that plentiful. She was in a quandary after being arrested for murder and hadn't been able to resolve the issue in her mind. Sammi felt she was quite stable and could hang on, but couldn't be counted on for any rational help. She was at a loss for what had happened to her.

* * *

Sammi had been able to confirm that Lily was genuine in her thought world. She was no killer and just as confused about the circumstances of her being held in jail as she had told them in words. Her thought world contained purity not unlike Billy in the fact that her life had been sheltered and simple as she tried to survive alone in a complicated world. Billy had made a huge difference in her life as it took the main attention off of her concerns and targeted her primary focus on someone else who needed her help. They both won in the situation.

"She's rather uncomplicated, isn't she?" asked Dave.

"Yeah, she's very straightforward in her approach to life and her thoughts confirm that she is exactly what she seems to be."

"We need a smoking gun here, but I have no idea what direction we should go. I'm going to call the sarge and see if he knows anyone in the Akron area police force. I meant to talk to him before I left but never got to it. That could help in finding out why she seems to be the only suspect. The evidence is rather flimsy and there must be something pointing in another direction. Look, Sammi, we know she didn't do it, so there has to be something else. I wonder what else this guy was involved in and I want to know if his wife was even checked out. She'd have a better motive."

"Maybe we could find a way to talk to her; I'd love to pick up what's on her mind."

"Yeah," said Dave. "That could be very enlightening."

"So tomorrow we meet her lawyer – what's his name?"

"Joey Larson. And Lily seems to have strong opinions of weakness about him."

"Yeah, she doesn't feel he's up to this task at all. Kind of makes you wonder why. Her mind didn't give up too many hints, just that he was too inexperienced for her murder case. She's quite worried about him."

"Not a good spot for her to be in. I mean, a good lawyer should give her confidence and that could help her to relax. Yet, that doesn't seem to be happening."

"No, it doesn't and you have to wonder why they chose him. Billy said he couldn't find anyone else. I guess we'll find out for ourselves tomorrow."

CHAPTER FOUR

Entering the office of Joey Larson was like walking into the world of a mainly disorganized and scattered mind. He met Sammi and Dave at the door with his arms full of files, a pencil behind his ear, something resembling a toothpick in his mouth and wearing horned rimmed glasses. He wasn't more than five feet nine inches and slight of build. His light blond hair and deep blues eyes didn't help him to be taken seriously, as he looked like someone who should be designated for a magazine cover. He ushered them to the two chairs in front of his desk, but they looked at each other and back to him as they saw two seats fully occupied with more files.

"Oh, I'm sorry; I'm so disorganized right now. Let me get those files out of your way."

In an attempt to clear a pathway for his visitors, he accidentally dropped all of the files in his arms and watched passively as they went in several directions. He stood there for a moment wondering what to do or what to say. He looked at them sadly and said, "I'm not always like this, but I haven't been on my own for more than six months and can't seem to find any workable system yet."

"Where were you before this?"

"I was in a corporation and worked with several other lawyers constantly in some type of litigation. But it wasn't what I wanted to do so I went out on my own."

"Have you had any cases yet?" asked Dave.

"Yes, I've had five cases so far. Two were plea bargained satisfactorily for my clients. One was a hung jury and the decision hasn't been made as to its future fate. The last two cases were dismissed, so my record really isn't too bad."

His concerned look connoted he must be wondering what they were thinking about him, no doubt a disheveled, bumbling idiot. Sammi almost felt sorry for him. His outward appearance came across as a total incompetent, but she knew from his thoughts that his mind was organized and shrewd. He needed to get himself together in order to convince others of his capabilities. Although she knew why Lily didn't have much confidence in him based on his outward appearance and style, she thought he would prove to be valuable if given a chance.

After they were finally seated, he poured everyone coffee, spilling his own on yet another file. But, when he began to speak about his new client he showed serious interest in Lily's case.

"So you two are friends of Lily and want to help her?"

"No," said Sammi, "Actually I'm a friend of Billy and he asked for my help."

He smiled. "Oh yeah, Billy; he's a great guy and smarter than he seems."

Sammi couldn't resist. "I think you are, too."

He smiled. "Thanks, but it doesn't seem like it today, and I think Lily thinks I'm a total nitwit. I can't blame her, but I have been looking into her files. I know there's not much there at this time, but we need to follow up on several leads that haven't been investigated yet. I only got this case last Wednesday so I haven't had a lot of time to get anything done."

"What's your take on it?" asked Sammi.

"I don't believe she had any real motive; his wife seems like a stronger suspect to me, but for some reason no one is targeting her and you have to wonder why. I tend to believe

Lily's story. Guilty people usually make up extravagant reasons and alibis for their innocence. Lily pretty much tells it like it is. If she were guilty, it would surprise me that she didn't even take the time to think up a good reason for her innocence. No, no, I'm convinced that she didn't do it. But the police seem to think ..."

"So what road do you plan to take?"

"Right now I have to get out and talk to people. I'd like to get over to talk to those two buddies of his at that Premier Tenner place where he worked. What was this Matthew person all about? We know that he was a well-known womanizer, which means his wife had the biggest motive. However, maybe he was involved in other shady things, too. I heard he had a rather big ego."

Sammi sat back in her chair. She looked over at Dave who seemed surprised that this bungling, cluttered human frame sitting before them seemed to have a sharp mind after all. Sammi gave him a look that he understood; she felt this lawyer would be good. Lily had a positive surprise coming her way.

Dave said, "We'd like to work with you if we could and see what we could turn up together."

"I'd like that. What do you think you could do?"

Dave then told him that he was a police officer, which could open doors to a certain point. Joey was thrilled.

"Yeah, maybe you could find out what evidence they have against her."

Dave produced a folder that he knew would be of interest to Joey.

"I've been waiting for this. I've requested it twice and haven't received anything yet."

"I know; there are many reasons for delays."

"This is great and at least we'll know what to prepare against."

They told Joey where they were staying and he gave them his card. Sammi thought that although his outward appearance would deceive some it might prove to work to his advantage. She knew his mind was sharp and his wit was clever while his capability was above average. She hadn't figured out his clumsiness or his awkwardness, but he could be first rate if he put his mind to it.

"I plan to make it out to his place of employment tomorrow. And I want to talk to that Rodney Belford you mentioned and see if I can find out anything about a Don somebody or other. They could tell us about his other activities. He may have had some sheltered interests going on that few knew about. Your closest friends always know."

"That's true," said Dave who was now becoming increasingly impressed by Joey the longer they talked to him. "We want to get out and talk to his wife, if we can. She may have some information as well."

"Great, maybe we could meet later in the week and compare notes. I do have a bail hearing for Lily later this week so I'll have to work around that. I need to get her out of jail."

As they left his office, Dave had to comment. "I sure do have a better impression of him now than when we first arrived."

"Yeah, but did you notice how clumsy he was just before he shook your hand. His thinking process is getting in the way of him being smooth and more reserved in his physical world. I wonder why."

Dave thought about it. "It really is strange, because his mind is sharp. He can talk and discuss like any of the pros, but there's a total difference between his mental world and his physical world."

Sammi said, "And you know that there's got to be a reason for that. Anyway, as long as he's a good lawyer and does well by Lily, I don't care. He may catch others off guard with his double demeanor."

"That's right. I'd like to be in court on ... what did he say? ... Wednesday ... and see how he does in action."

"I would, too. I'd like to see how he performs in court surroundings."

* * *

Dave's cell phone rang as they were driving back to the motel. It was Jim Mucci.

"Hey buddy, you missed me so much that you had to call, right?"

Jim laughed. "That's right and we do miss you and Sammi around here. But I have a news flash for you. They've decided to let us have Roy by next Monday. Makes us wonder what they're doing over there. They keep changing his exit date, but they said it's solid this time. Even the sarge is scratching his head on this one."

"That's strange. I wonder why. Oh well, time will tell."

"Yes, it will. So how's your case going on down there?"

"Not really sure. We haven't found out much yet, but they don't have much evidence against her and apparently they're not even looking in another direction."

Dave took a few minutes to tell Jim what he knew. It wasn't much and it didn't take very long.

Jim said, "I would think the wife had the better motive, even if she was running around, too. Doesn't seem that cut and dried so it makes me wonder why they aren't looking at her as well."

"My thoughts exactly. But it was fun meeting with Billy G. Simpson. He's a great guy and a good thinker as well. I think he's got a crush on Sammi."

Sammi looked over and gave Dave her disparaging look. Jim answered, "I think everyone's got a crush on Sammi for one reason or another."

Dave told Sammi what Jim had said. She simply shook her head knowing these guys could really lay it on thick at times.

"Anything else new? What about our burglary case?"

"Nothing new on that, but no new burglaries either. So that's good for now. LeBron and Tyrone have a few leads that they're following up on."

Jim said, "Got to run. Keep in touch."

Sammi said, "Give my regards to Julie."

"Will do," Jim said as he hung up.

* * *

"Do you think we can set up a meeting with the wife tomorrow? I mean it'll be Tuesday and we only have a week, right?"

Dave thought for a moment and said, "I'm not sure how all this will work out, but I think you'll have trouble leaving here without some kind of resolution. I'm not sure that can happen in one week. You'd want to stay around, right?"

Sammi's face said it all. "I would have trouble leaving, but if we could get it going in the right direction and get confident about this Joey Larson, then we could keep in touch and if they needed either one of us, we're not that far away."

Dave looked over and smiled at her. She realized he knew how she thought and he knew what she was thinking. If he wasn't on any hot topics right now back in Scranton, maybe Sergeant Brady would let him take a short leave. After all, they were all police officers wanting to solve crimes. She thought he would understand. But before she had a chance to say anything, Dave had something more to say.

"I might be able to get another week or so. I don't think Sergeant Brady would fight that. And he has that buddy of his in Akron, Detective Fred Anchor. He might even be able to get me here officially until we can do some good."

Sammi leaned over and gave him a kiss.

He said, "Well, we're a team here. We fight crime to-gether. That's what I've wanted to do all my life and you've helped me a lot. This is another strange crime and I think the sarge might be very interested in this one as well."

Sammi let out a deep sigh that was louder than she meant it to be. "You knew what was on my mind all along, didn't you?"

"Sure, and I would have been thinking the same way. This case is not going to be cut and dried, but I'm anxious to know where it will take us. I think it's going to be one of those cliffhangers until the end. Something real unsuspected will show up; we know that Lily didn't do it and for some reason I don't think his wife did it either."

Sammi shifted quickly. "I've had the same feeling. I think this guy had some underhanded dealings going on ... but I don't know ... that doesn't really feel right either. Something will start to fit in soon. As we talk to more people we'll be getting more ideas."

They were both quiet as they drove along.

Then Sammi turned to Dave and said, "I love you Dave Patterson."

He smiled and grabbed her hand. Nothing else was said, it wasn't necessary.

* * *

Dave contacted Sergeant Brady, who in turn contacted Detective Fred Anchor of the 13th precinct in Akron and they got permission to put Dave on the case in a semi-official capacity. This would open some doors for him and it did get him permission to interview Mrs. Matthew Belten. They made an appointment on Wednesday morning with her which would ensure that they would have plenty of time to get to court for Lily's 3:00 PM bail hearing.

The Belten's home was in an upper class area on the outskirts of Cuyahoga Falls, which sported manicured lawns, wider streets and fancy lampposts with most homes having impressive doors that caught your attention with their ostentatious trimming. Although not considered totally upscale, it was one area that had no problem enjoying life in the fast lane, if desired.

After using the fancy gold doorknocker, which intrigued them both, Jessica Belten answered the door. They introduced themselves and she let them in.

Jessica was a tough person to read. She was somewhat reserved, yet sociable enough to extend niceties and led them into the living room where a coffee tray was already set up. She was possibly in her early thirties, which meant that she was considerably younger than her husband Matthew who was in his middle fifties. A woman of average height and slight of build, her stylish blond hair was obviously her favorite asset. She was congenial as they sat down and began.

"We're sorry for your loss," said Dave as he tried to convey a tone of caring.

"Thanks, I'm still quite upset right now. We'd been married for three years and somewhat settled into each other."

"I have some questions I need to ask that are mostly formalities, but we need to get some information filled in."

She nodded and her hands twisted in her lap. She seemed rather timid and shy at this point.

Dave looked over at Sammi, but she was holding her attention straight ahead and didn't give him any hint of what she was picking up in Jessica's thoughts.

"Did your husband have any enemies that you know of?"

"No, I don't think so. He seemed congenial with most of his workers and associates."

"So you don't know of anyone that would want to have him killed?" asked Dave.

She simply shook her head.

Sammi took over for a moment and was as delicate as possible, but Dave knew she was fishing for something else she'd picked up in Jessica's thought world.

"You said that you'd been married to Matthew for about three years?"

She nodded, but it was obvious that she was more congenial with Dave. She didn't flirt with him outright, but her attention was always in his direction and she never lost eye contact with him.

"Was he married before?"

She stuttered a little and it was obvious that she didn't like the question. "Yes, he'd been married twice before me."

She had raised her head in pride answering a question she thought was none of their business. She immediately turned her complete attention back to Dave.

However, Sammi continued. "And this was your first and only marriage?"

She hesitated but ultimately said that it was.

"Did Matthew have any children in any of his marriages?"

That did it; she was irritated and her entire personality changed. "Are these questions necessary? I don't see what this would have to do with finding my husband's killer, which was not me, by the way. I figured that was your next question," she said throwing an unkind glance toward Sammi.

Sammi persisted since they were both seeing another side of this woman who had been so demure a few minutes before.

Sammi didn't forget her question. "Did Matthew have any children?"

"Yes, he had one daughter whom he seldom saw or cared to see."

"And where were you at the time of the murder?"

This infuriated her and her cover was completely blown. She turned to Dave and asked, "Do I have to answer this impertinent question?"

"Yes you do. I was going to ask it myself."

Now she knew where the cards lay. These two stuck together and she hadn't been able to lure him onto her side.

"Well, okay," she said knowing she had no other course. "I had gone out to dinner with friends and didn't get home until well past midnight."

"And you do have the names of these friends, right?" Sammi paused as she added, "Just for the record."

"Do I have to divulge who I was with?"

Dave took over. "Yes you do. This isn't a social party; this is the murder investigation of your husband and many people will have to account for their whereabouts and that does include you."

Dave looked slightly disgusted. Why wouldn't this wife want to be more helpful in solving her husband's murder?

It was obvious she knew she was beaten. Actually, she knew she'd be forced to answer many personal questions from the beginning, but was hoping to avoid some of them. Her answers would not only be embarrassing, but also could spell trouble for her. And that was no surprise to either Dave or Sammi.

"I was out with a friend of ours, Jason King."

That's all she said, but neither Sammi nor Dave said anything and waited her out. She decided to continue.

"No, my husband didn't know I saw him occasionally, but he did have a score of women of his own anyway. I guess you could say we had an unconventional marriage."

Now she was finished and her look connoted that she had every right to live her life in the way she saw fit. This wasn't any of their business.

"So he was the only one you were with? You said earlier that you went out to dinner with some friends," asked Dave.

"I was covering for myself. I didn't think it would look too good for me to have been on a date the night my husband was killed. But then, I've heard he was on a date as well. Why are you asking all these questions? I thought you had the murderer arrested. That's what all the news is saying?"

"The investigation is only beginning and it won't be finished until we have a trial and a conviction. Some evidence points in other directions."

That unnerved Jessica. "What other evidence do you have?"

Dave simply said, "It's confidential."

"Oh," she replied with a slight pout on her face.

After a few more routine questions that weren't going anywhere, they adjourned for the day mentioning that they might have to interview her again at some other time. She nodded realizing by this time the futility of refusing.

* * *

"This was one time that I could almost read this gal's thoughts," said Dave. "But I'd still like to know what you heard."

"Yeah she was quite obvious, wasn't she? She kept making a play for you hoping that she could score some points."

Dave laughed. "That didn't work, but I can't figure out what she hoped to gain; she still had to account for her whereabouts and it finally came out after a lot of probing."

Sammi began to tell Dave what was on Jessica's mind. "Apparently this Jason King doesn't have the best reputation. And he isn't a friend of her husband. Matthew had a fit a while back when he realized what was going on and forbid Jason to come around his house again. I understand it was quite a battle they had."

Dave looked interested. "This could be a lead to follow."

Sammi wrinkled her nose. It prompted Dave to ask, "What? You don't think it's a good idea."

"Not really. Neither one of them had anything to do with Matthew's murder. Jason is probably not too sorry he's dead, but for Jessica he was sort of a cushion from the outside world. Nevertheless, their marriage had become ... unusual almost from the beginning. He wanted a pretty, young girl on his arm and she wanted someone who could give her security. I guess they both got what they wanted, yet they both wanted more."

"You mean they were both surprised at how their marriage turned out?"

"No, I don't mean that. I believe that they both knew what they were getting into and that's what they wanted at the time. Later they settled into their old patterns of behavior and although Matthew wasn't crazy about Jessica going out on him, he was doing the same thing so he didn't have much to criticize."

"Interesting. So you don't think they had anything to do with his murder?"

"I really don't think so. They were at a motel at the time of the murder and stayed there for quite a while. I didn't get the name of it, but I'm sure she'd provide it if we needed it, because the truth is out anyway."

Dave let out a bit of a chuckle.

"What?" she asked.

"I was thinking how much her personality changed from the time we walked in until we left. She kept changing to see what would work with us."

Sammi smiled. "Yes, she's quite an actress and Jason isn't the only one she meets either. I believe she has at least two more and no one knows about the others. Kind of a dangerous game she plays."

Dave whistled slightly under his breath. "Such complicated lives these people live. What are they searching for?"

"Hard to say isn't it? Some don't even know what they want?"

Dave was thoughtful for a moment and then said, "Let's have lunch now because I want to make sure we get to the court on time. I'm anxious to see how our Joey behaves in court."

Sammi had to smile, but she was confident he'd be quite effective and surprise a few people, including the prosecution.

* * *

The courtroom was slightly smaller than others Sammi had seen, but then Cuyahoga Falls was definitely a small town. When they got there, early as Dave had wanted, they sat in one of the back rows to get a better overall perspective of the procedures. The prosecution entered first and he looked like a tough, harsh character who could as easily been on the other side of the proceedings. Several minutes later in came Billy and he spotted them immediately.

"Hi," he said with a happy smile on his face. "I'm glad you came."

"We wouldn't miss it and we're hoping for good news today," said Sammi.

Billy puckered his lips and looked down at the floor. "I think Mr. Joey has a good heart, but I don't think he's very good."

Sammi grabbed his arm as she said, "you never know Billy. Keep some good thoughts, okay?"

"Yes, I will, Ms. Sammi," he said as his expression definitely brightened. "I remember when you used to tell me that. You said good thoughts can make good things happen."

"And they can."

"I want to go sit closer so I can be near my mom. Do you want to come with me?"

"I think we'd like to sit back here," said Dave. "But we'll talk to you after the hearing."

"Okay," he said and he turned quite purposely and walked down to the second row behind where he knew his mother would be. He turned and smiled at them and then waited patiently in his seat for the proceedings to begin.

It was only a few moments later when Joey Larson came in stumbling and fumbling as usual. Sammi couldn't understand the disconnect occurring between his mental capability and his physical ability. Obviously, something bothered him with his perception of the world around him and he was overly concerned how he was perceived. Yet when he concentrated on business at hand, he was quite effective.

Lily Caulkin looked tired and nervous when she walked in with her protectors. She smiled at Billy and tried to hold a strong look, but the strain of the last few days were there and obvious for all to see.

When the judge came in and pounded his gavel to begin the proceedings, Lily's shoulders humped and then drooped. Sammi hoped she could keep her composure because although she was a strong person, she was under unimaginable stress.

The judge read the charges against Lily and then announced that this was a bail hearing and the prosecution immediately jumped up and began.

"There is absolutely nothing to keep this defendant from running and we'd never find her. She could take her son with her and have no reason to return. Her ties to the community are minimal at best and it seems that she'd have good reason to flee from the scene of the crime. The fact that we have solid evidence that she was in the car the same night that the murder was committed is a strong case in itself and along with other substantial proof in our possession, it would seem that any defendant would want to run and hide. I must insist, Your Honor, that no bail be set."

The prosecution's voice had been strong, sarcastic and unnecessarily loud. It caused the judge to mention, "I'm not deaf and I'm only a few feet in front of you. Keep it down."

The prosecution apologized to the court. In his exuberance and his belief that he would win the bail hearing easily, he let himself get out of control.

Joey had sat there listening and watching and hadn't interrupted once, but kept a close watch on the judge's reactions. Sammi knew that he was clever in a way that no one would usually suspect, and she could detect his knowledgeable and skillful thought process. She knew that Joey realized that the prosecution had hit a few sour notes with the judge by telling him he insisted there be no bail and his sarcastic and derogatory tone didn't help him make extra points for his side. Sammi was happy with Joey's plan to use his methods against him.

The judge turned to the defense attorney and said, "Mr. Larson, it's your turn."

The person who stood up and straightened his tie and fastened the middle button on his dark blue suit jacket, was not the one who'd walked into the courtroom disheveled and seemingly unprepared. This defense lawyer was obviously confident and well primed.

"Your Honor, I must disagree with the prosecution. Ms. Caulkin has extremely strong ties to this community. She's worked here for the Children's Aid Group most of her adult life as a social worker and has showed compassion for the orphans in our area, as you well know." Joey did his homework and knew that Lily was instrumental in the adoption process of the Judge's granddaughter. "Even though there is evidence against Ms. Caulkin, meager as it is, Ms. Caulkin is not a flight risk and will stay and fight these charges to clear her name and stand proud before her son. The Children's Aid Group does stand behind her and will help with her bail. I respectfully request that bail be set within limits that Ms. Caulkin can afford. Thank you."

The prosecution jumped up at this point, loud and boisterous again, setting off the judge once more. "Keep your voice down and your temper under control. Mr. Larson was well within the bounds of appropriate dialogue in his presentation."

"But Your Honor, it's not fair mentioning that this Children's Aid Group will help with her bail. That puts all of the sympathy in her corner and how do we know that they believe enough in her to do this? It's simply Mr. Larson's word."

The judge turned to Joey and said, "Any comment?"

"Yes, sir," and he was quite happy that the prosecution had taken the bait and kept up the conversation strictly on the subject of the Children's Aid Group. "I have a letter from the director of the group and it states they are willing to put up collateral for one of their most trusted employees."

He gave the letter to the bailiff who in turn gave it to the Judge.

"It would seem that Mr. Larson's statement is well documented and I must hold this in high esteem. This group wouldn't back just anyone."

All through his recommendation, Joey spoke with respect to the Judge and to the prosecution. He was clear, distinct and extremely precise in his wording as well as respectful in his physical demeanor, keeping his tone and attitude civil and considerate. There stood a well-versed and effective lawyer.

Dave leaned over to Sammi and said, "It's hard to believe that's the same guy."

Sammi smiled. "I know. This guy will be dynamite in this trial, if it comes to that and before I leave I've got to find a way to decipher his thoughts and find out why there's a discrepancy between his mental and physical world."

The judge took a few minutes, readjusted his glasses a few times and came back with the following. "Although there is a possibility of a flight risk with every defendant in a murder trial, I sincerely believe that Ms. Caulkin's flight risk is rather minimal and I'm willing to take the chance. Her bail is set at $500,000.00." And down came the gavel hard and definite.

The prosecution slammed his folder on the desk and glared over at Joey, who simply gathered up his files slowly and orderly. He seemed to be in complete control. Billy on the other hand jumped up and gave his mother a big hug.

"It will probably take a few days to get all of the details cleared for the bail, but you should be going home by Friday or Saturday at the latest." Joey wanted to make sure they both understood that the bail amount needed clearance and the Children's Aid Group's portion had to be notarized in writing.

Billy was so excited that he cried and ignored any tears that left his eyes. His mom was coming home and there was no doubt that new life had found its way into Lily's person. There was hope in her face. She spotted Sammi and Dave at the back of the courtroom and smiled. Then she shook Mr. Larson's hand and Sammi caught amazement in her thoughts.

Yes, it was true that Joey Larson would amaze many people in his lifetime.

After a few very moments, Lily again left the courtroom and Billy came over and hugged both Sammi and Dave. He had to share his happiness with everyone.

"I kept my thoughts good, Ms. Sammi and it worked. You were right again." He turned to Dave and said, "I just love Ms. Sammi. She teaches me so many things."

When they left the courtroom, everyone was stepping lighter than usual. There was hope in the air and belief for the immediate future.

* * *

Dave was more quiet than usual as they left the courtroom. Sammi knew he was emotional about what he had witnessed today. It is true that anyone would be happy to have won a bail hearing, but experiencing this entire proceeding through the eyes of Billy brought in a new set of feelings that were hard to deny. Billy lived in a simple world that found it much easier to believe in goodness than the general population. Being around him made it impossible not to be drawn into his magnetic faith and simple convictions. Even Dave felt that Billy lived in a magical world that would give any of us special coaching were we wise enough to try it.

"I can't put today into words, Sammi. I simply can't," he said in a poignant tone affected by deep feelings that he was unable to convey.

"I understand, honey because I can't either. There's certain things in this world that can't be talked about; they can only be felt."

Dave nodded his head. They both realized that they were living on the edge of an encompassing universe, which welcomed them wholeheartedly at this moment in time.

CHAPTER FIVE

In Scranton, work was piling up and Jim and Tom more than the others missed the expertise that Dave brought to the table every day. The only other person who felt this impact directly would be Amilio Hernandez with LeBron Harper and Tyrone Pittfield slowly understanding this loss. Yet they were still an effective group and by next Monday, they would be adding a new detective by the name of Roy Dawson. Jim and Tom especially would have liked Dave to be here during this time. To be honest, they would have liked to have the critical assessment of Sammi as well, although it seemed that they would both be gone for a few more weeks and that's just the way it was.

"Amigos, it seems kind of empty around here, despite the noise," said Amilio.

"Yeah," said Tom. "Sure does seem that something is missing, or somebody."

"Personally, I don't like it when Dave's gone," said Jim. "But at least he'll be back in a couple of weeks; they both will."

Sergeant Brady called Tom and Jim into his office for a briefing.

"Look, I know that we're getting Roy a little sooner than we had planned and with Dave gone for a few more weeks, I'm going to assign him to the two of you. From what we've heard, we're gonna have to keep close track of him from the beginning. I'm hoping he'll play it cool at first; I would think he'd be trying to make a good impression for himself here. I hope he realizes that this may be one of his last chances and act according to the rules."

"You mean he's sort of on probation?" said Jim.

"Well, no one has put it that way to me, but he has been moved around a lot and so I would think it's crossed his mind. It sure has crossed mine. Look, you two, if we have a lot of problems with him in the first few months and I complained about him, where do you think they'd send him next?"

"Good point," said Tom. "So how do you want us to play it with him?"

"Just do your work and watch him; just like Dave would do. But you report to me immediately about anything out of line. I'm not kidding about him. We can't afford to take any chances."

After a significant pause during which time the sarge was moving papers around his desk, he seemed to find his next question.

"There's nothing new on our burglaries I take it. I'm glad there haven't been any new ones, but I'd still like us to get a lead on the old ones. These break-ins are mainly on senior citizens and have all of our elderly residents in fear. And I don't need the mayor on my back for anything."

"He's been rather quiet lately," said Jim. "What's up with him?"

"We've got a good working relationship again and I believe he's trying to give us a chance to do our job. He's not said anything bad in the papers, but we need to find out something and fast. Let me know what's happening."

"Okay," they echoed and left. The look they gave each other said it all.

* * *

Back at his desk, Jim seemed a little out of sorts. He had so much going on that he was frustrated. First, he had his demanding workaday world and that alone required so much of his time, but his two daughters from a previous marriage were upset because their mother was getting a divorce again; this would make the third time. Those girls were always on his mind.

"You're in deep thought; what's going on?"

That was his wife, Julie. She had come up from the computer department for a few minutes. She was a computer expert who worked for the police department in another section of the building. Yet, she seemed to know when he needed her.

"Oh, I'm having a tough day and I'm not even sure why. It's really not any worse than usual; must be me today."

"You do have a lot on your mind and we both know it. Why don't we take the girls out for dinner Friday night? It would give Kathy a break and they always have a good time with us."

Jim looked over and smiled. He had really made a good choice in Julie. She understood so much. She was beautiful, that was true, but she was also smart and quite intuitive. And she had come up with a good idea.

"Thanks, I'd like that. And I'm sure they would, too."

"Well, so would I. We could do something fun. They could use it, but you know what? We could use it, too. And they are fun to be around."

He smiled, looked down at his desk for a moment and then said, "You're great, Julie."

She laughed. "I'm glad to hear that. And I love you, too, Jim."

She walked away satisfied. She couldn't halt thoughts of her first husband crossing her mind occasionally. He had been conniving, controlling, and wanted to extend her out for favors to further his career. She had lived a nightmare and after her divorce, she was shy of men for a long time. Yet when she met

Jim, who'd had his own problems with his first wife, she knew she had found someone stable who had real feelings about life and what was important. He treated her with love and respect and she loved doing things to make him happy.

* * *

Just then, all hell broke loose. Jim got a call from LeBron saying that they had picked up two men in their early twenties who fit the description of the burglars. They'd be brought in for questioning within the hour. Jim let Sergeant Brady know immediately. This seemed strange for him; usually Dave did that. But with Dave away, it was him or Tom. It wasn't anything difficult, but it did feel strange and out of the norm.

He called Tom and together they'd be ready for the questioning.

"I sure wish Sammi was here," said Tom.

"That's for sure. We'll see what we can find out. I sure hope we have some connection here. These guys had to leave some clues and I think I heard that one of them was spotted in the last burglary. We may have an eye witness."

"Let's hope so. These crime sprees have gone on long enough. But I wonder if they were working alone."

Tom added, "That's a thought. How many burglaries were there?"

"About five that we knew about in this basic area; I haven't heard about any others in surrounding areas."

Tom nodded. "Okay, then, let's hope this leads somewhere."

* * *

When they brought in the suspects Tom, Jim and Amilio were there to greet them. Brad Niemen and Carter Olsen were both twenty-three years old, angry and screaming for an attorney. Although caught unaware when brought in for questioning, they both had a crime sheet that was nearly one page for each year of their lives and an attitude that didn't do them any favors. When LeBron and Tyrone returned, they decided to interview them separately and compare their stories to see if they matched.

Jim decided to use the last burglary as a starting point and see if Brad could account for his whereabouts at that crucial time, but he had one answer only for any of their questions.

"I'm not answering any questions until my attorney is present."

Jim tried again, "Don't you want to give us your alibi; we could eliminate you that way."

"I'm not answering any questions until my attorney is present."

"So you don't have an alibi and no one could verify where you were, right?"

Brad almost started to say something and then remembered, "I'm not answering any questions until my attorney is present."

Jim looked at Tom and Amilio and realized that it was futile to continue. They'd have to wait until his attorney had arrived.

Going over and checking with LeBron and Tyrone, it was determined that they weren't doing much better. Carter Olsen had slipped up on a few answers at the beginning, but nothing significant enough to make a difference. It seemed of the two, he had the father with more money and influence and he was eagerly awaiting contact with the family's counsel.

"Damn, it's hard when even these young kids are covered by attorneys and connections that protect them from the start."

"No wonder they think nothing of committing these crimes. If they get caught they cry for daddy to come and get them out of this mess."

Well," said Jim. "There's nothing we can do right now but wait. I'm going back to the office; I really need a cup of coffee."

* * *

"Anyone heard from Dave lately?" asked Tom.

"I haven't," said Jim. "I wonder how they're doing down there in … what's it called?"

Tom offered, "Cuyahoga Falls, Ohio."

"Oh yeah, well I hope they're getting somewhere and fast. We need Dave and Sammi back here."

"Yeah, but it's a waiting game right now. The lawyers will come and tell them not to answer half of the questions anyway, so we'll be back to square one. We don't have enough to hold them without some kind of proof."

Jim said, "What did they have to bring them in?"

"One of them had a few pieces of the stolen jewelry from one of the homes in his pocket. But they said they found it somewhere or other so we still need proof."

"We need Sammi; she could sift through all of this stuff."

"They'll be back in a few more weeks," said Tom. "I'm sure these kids aren't going to leave town. In fact, by then they might think they're home free."

"That's true and then their guard will be down."

Word came down the lawyers arrived, but they told their clients not to say one word at this time since there was no real proof against them. In a week or so, if they presented some substantial evidence they could have another interview and then they might be more likely to cooperate.

And that was it. Everyone would have to wait and see what else turned up.

It seemed that bringing these suspects in for questioning didn't accomplish anything. Their lawyers were close to claiming harassment as they felt there was no solid evidence against them. After all, you didn't drag kids into a police station for questioning and ruin their reputation when you had minimal proof against them. It looked like you were on a fishing expedition, and that was considered borderline aggravation and character attack. They received a warning to back off.

When they approached Sergeant Brady about it, he was livid. He felt the police had a right to bring in these kids for questioning. They weren't arrested or even accused of anything, but simply interviewed. Yet these high priced lawyers could make it difficult, so he decided to wait until they found more evidence thereby surpassing the complaints of the legal minds. It's not as if this was a new angle; it was used before and would probably be used again. Everyone walked a narrow line on their particular side of the law. So for now it was back to the drawing board, get out there and question people and search around to see what else they could find.

* * *

By the time, Lily Caulkin walked out of jail it was Saturday morning; Dave and Sammi went with Billy to pick her up, and together they headed back to her home. She was happy to be out on bond and thankful that the Children's Aid Group stood behind her. She was still shaking her head about everything. This had been one of the most surreal times of her life. And, where it would end, no one knew.

When they arrived home, Billy needed to get to work for half a day. He liked his job as a supply manager and it paid quite well. He had missed some time during the week because of the trial, but would make it up today. This gave the three of them time to talk.

"Are they even looking for someone else? The police seemed so focused on me that I didn't feel that they even looked to anyone else."

"And the evidence against you isn't even solid, so you have to wonder why they made you their only suspect," said Dave.

"What do you mean the evidence against me isn't even solid?"

Dave looked at Sammi and said, "Do you want to take it or shall I?"

Sammi began. "Okay, well first of all you said that you only went several blocks away from your house and then parked in a residential area, right?"

Lily confirmed.

"Then Matthew drove you back home, dropped you off and took off again."

"That's what happened, but they don't believe me."

"Okay, but even if they don't believe you, they've got a lot of problems on their hands. They found Matthew about eight miles from your house in a vacant parking lot about 6:00 AM Saturday morning. The coroner's office puts the time of death about five hours before he was found. That means Matthew died sometime between twelve o'clock and two o'clock in the morning. The exact time of death usually can't be pinpointed closer than that."

Dave took it from here. "That would mean that the two of you drove around from 7:30 PM, which was the time he picked you up and one of your neighbors did see you leave with him, until twelve o'clock midnight or two o'clock in the morning. Since you said you didn't go anywhere, then no one could have seen you two together. That puts the burden of proof on the prosecution to prove you were with him all that time.

"And since I wasn't there, he may have gone somewhere else and other people noticed him."

"Exactly and here's another part to be considered. He was found in a vacant parking lot, which means you would have had to leave the car, no doubt they'll say after an argument and then double back already possessing some type of gun and shoot him from the left side of the vehicle through the window on the driver's side. That's where he was shot from the left side in the back of his head and the bullet came out the right side of his forehead."

"You know I think he was a total jerk and a coward, but no one deserves to die that way."

Dave nodded and then continued. "So you left the car after an argument and he just sat there and waited; that doesn't make a lot of sense. Then you had to get home and that would take time if you walked. If they said you had a ride, they'd have to prove it. But if they believed you walked, it would be unusual for no one to have seen a woman walking alone at night. Anywhere you look; their case has a lot of problems."

"But I didn't have a gun? I don't own one; never have."

"They'll say you could have gotten one, but this part alone doesn't make sense either. You leave the car after an argument and double back to shoot him. No guy who's just had a big argument with a gal would let her leave without watching where she was going. That's not logical. He would have watched you either in the rear view mirror or the side mirror or just turned around to see where you were going; that's common sense."

Lily thought about this for a moment. "I see what you mean."

Sammi said, "Also, they'd have to prove you had a weapon of some kind and the murder weapon hasn't been found."

"Don't a lot of killers just throw the gun away?"

"They do and you're right," said Dave. "But their important legal obligation would be to prove you had a gun in the first place. They'd just be building a huge case of insufficient or circumstantial evidence, which would help prove reasonable doubt and that would help your side."

"Oh," said Lily, "I see where you're going."

Dave said, "This case is full of holes, and our Joey Larson knows it. He's quite good when he gets going, isn't he?"

"Yes," she said, "I certainly got a pleasant surprise in court."

Sammi couldn't help but add. "I think he'll prove to be an excellent lawyer.

Lily nodded her approval and let out a sigh of relief.

"At first I was quite worried about him, but we couldn't find anyone else who'd take the case. Now, I think maybe we lucked out after all."

* * *

Leaving Lily's home Dave and Sammi decided to nose around a few places that Matthew frequented to see if any stories of enemies or recent encounters would surface. But people were actually cold to both of them and didn't say much past polite greetings. They were outsiders and that still counted high on many people's list of necessary precautions. Outsiders weren't to be trusted and although Sammi still picked up some interesting thoughts, they were hitting dead ends anyway. Matthew wasn't liked and was considered a troublesome person by anyone's assessment, but he seemed to stay out of the big trouble. He notched up significant dislike and considerable aversion by many of the town's people, but they hesitated to deride him to strangers. He had one of those 'I don't care attitudes,' as well as a troublesome personality that drove many away. Making a good name for himself was not high on his list, but having fun and doing what his needs required did. You treaded light when in his presence and even now that he was dead, that pattern seemed to be holding true.

"People's thoughts said they didn't like him and didn't trust him," said Sammi, "but mostly they ignored him and didn't want to get on his bad side."

Dave agreed. "People in this little town tend to mind their own business and they're certainly not going to open up for strangers like us. Guess we'll have to find another way."

"Who had it in for Matthew enough to kill him?" asked Sammi.

"That's the million dollar question. Is Joey working to-day? I'd like to connect with him and find out what he knows. He was supposed to talk with Matthew's boss and to that Rodney Belford and Don something or other. I wonder if they'd opened up about him."

"I've got his card; let me call him. Hopefully he's having better luck."

* * *

Joey was working Saturday and it was discovered that many times he worked Sundays when on a tough case. And this one he considered quite difficult. He knew the evidence against Lily was circumstantial and very weak, but he needed another suspect, somewhere else to throw suspicion. That would be the best way to get her freed. They decided to meet for lunch.

"Well, I must admit that you're a hard worker," said Sammi.

"Yes well, when a case bugs me I simply can't get it off my mind. I still don't understand why they arrested her. Their evidence is so flimsy; I haven't before seen a rush to judgment like this. Usually they've got at least one solid piece of evidence that's compelling."

"Maybe they needed to arrest someone real fast."

"Possibly, but I also think she was the most vulnerable and her son Billy irritates a few people around town."

Dave was surprised. "Why? He seems like a nice enough kid and does well for himself."

"I've heard rumors around that some people are leery of him. Many people just don't understand and don't want anyone strange around, as they say. That's the consensus of opinion. Now he has a lot of support around the orphanage and with others who know him and admire how far he's come, but you know how some people can be."

"So you think part of the case against Lily might have to do with the fact that they don't like Billy."

"A lot of people would like to see them move away, but they've made a very good niche for themselves in this town. Now they've both worked hard for it, but some type of prejudice is simply hard to erase."

"That's so sad," said Sammi.

"I'm not saying that this case had a lot to do with that, but it was just a thought I wanted to throw out there. Many ordinary folks like them both and think it's okay for them to be around, but the higher strata of this area, so to speak, have an aversion to anything that isn't perfect, if you know what I mean."

Dave nodded disgustedly. Some people didn't have any patience for anyone different from themselves. And it was hard to realize that Billy faced that type of criticism just for being who he was.

"Did you get over to talk to Rodney Belford and were you able to find out who Don was?"

"Simmons. Yes, I did and they are a strange twosome. I mean even after Matthew's death, they don't want to talk about him very much. They were quite tight lipped about his activities."

"Did they admit he dated a lot? I mean he was a married man."

"They did, but they seemed to believe that was perfectly alright. The strange part about them was they were almost apologetic for not saying a lot more about him, but said if they were subpoenaed, they would cooperate. Yet if they didn't have anything to force them to speak out, it was to their advantage to keep quiet."

"That seemed like a dead end," said Dave.

"Yes and no. If we come up with stuff and need them in court, they all but said they would be cooperative. I think it has to do with not seeming like a snitch."

"Okay," said Sammi. "So where do you go from here?"

"This week I plan to talk to a lot of people who knew Matthew and a few more who knew his wife and their unusual open marriage; I still think there could be pay dirt there somewhere. I mean, I have no idea where at this time, but something has to turn up. I'll just keep digging."

The only answer seemed to be to keep searching and hoping.

"What are the two of you up to?"

"About the same right now," said Dave. "His wife seems to have an airtight alibi, but I want to check it out more carefully."

"But again," said Sammi, "you didn't get any idea from Rodney or Don that Matthew could have been involved in any illegal activities?"

"I don't think so. It seems he pushed the envelope right to the limit, but stopped there. His idea of taking chances was mostly in his personal life."

Sammi relaxed on this one. Joey could be sharp in his assessments and his thought world related the same ideas as he was saying in words. These three buddies were mostly carefree and fun loving and played some dangerous games, but while staying close to the line, they never crossed it. The answer had to be somewhere else.

Sammi couldn't resist complimenting him on his court expertise. "You certainly did a good job in court during the bail hearing."

"And I think I surprised a few people, you two and Lily included."

Then Sammi heard the reason for his inconsistent personality and understood. In many aspects of his life, he had conquered his weakness, but not in all.

Sammi was happy that Joey was comfortable enough with them to explain. "I used to stutter a lot when I was a kid. My parents tried everything to help me along, but nothing worked. People sneered when I stuttered and kids laughed at me. Sometimes when I deal with the public, it's still there. But, as soon as I get working and concentrating on what I have to do, I straighten out; just one of those lingering memories from childhood."

"And we all have them," said Sammi knowing with certainty from the thoughts of many people she'd heard over the years.

Joey smiled realizing she was right, but he was happy he had come this far.

* * *

Waking up slowly that Sunday morning, Sammi decided to be lazy. Dave wasn't awake yet and sometimes she liked to lay there and simply watch him sleep. Usually when he awoke and found her staring at him, it drove him nuts. And today he threw the covers over her face and ruined her view.

"That's not fair," she said as she disentangled herself and prepared for a fight.

He was laughing and began sitting up and again threw the covers over her head. She jumped out of bed on her side, ran to the foot of the bed, tore the covers from his feet, and tickled them, which caused his knees to jerk. Now he was fully awake and prepared as he began a rather brutal pillow fight, which left many questions as to who actually won.

Later, they sat there at the height of their laziness trying to decide what they wanted to do today. Sunday was a free day and since the weather had cleared a little, he was thinking of heading to the driving range. Sammi felt she'd go watch him and then they could do some shopping and end up for a nice dinner somewhere. They got up, took their showers, got dressed and were close to leaving the motel when the telephone rang.

"Hi Mr. Dave, it's Billy."

He always seemed to have a song in his voice and especially today, he was a happy person.

"Good morning Billy. What's up?" he said. Sammi immediately took notice.

"I was wondering if you and Ms. Sammi had any plans for today."

"What did you have in mind?" he answered in a noncommittal way.

"Well ..." he said and paused for a moment. You could tell he was quite excited and trying to choose his words carefully. "Mom and Marsha and I wanted to go see some of the sights, like the Blossom Music Center and a few others and we were hoping you'd like to come, too. It would be more fun for us that way."

Dave laughed and gave Sammi an emotional glance. "I can't think of anything we'd rather do than that."

"So you don't have any plans then?" he asked again with a question mark in his tone of voice."

"Your plans sound like a lot more fun."

Billy giggled on the phone and Dave thought he was pure delight. Then Lily took the phone.

"I hope we haven't ruined any plans you had, but these two are so anxious to spend some time with the both of you."

"Lily, spending time with the three of you is the best way to spend today."

She laughed, "I suppose you can hear them both giggling in the background. This will make their day so special."

"And ours too. Where do you want us to meet you?"

"Why don't we pick you up, if that's okay with you?"

"Sure that'll be just fine."

"Okay then, it's after eleven now; we'll give you time to have breakfast and pick you up about one o'clock."

"That's perfect. See you then."

Dave put the phone down and said softly, "It's impossible to turn Billy down, isn't it?"

Sammi came over and gave him a big hug. "It is and who would want to? I think this will be a fun day. I mean you can always go to a driving range and I can always go shopping, but ..."

"I do agree, then let's go and have breakfast right now since I'm starving."

Sammi smiled, grabbed her purse and they both headed out immediately to the motel restaurant realizing that it did seem that they were on vacation, with some sightseeing on today's agenda.

* * *

At exactly one o'clock, there was a knock on their motel door. They opened it to find Billy and Marsha well ahead of Lily who was letting them have the pleasure they deserved.

"We're here," he said with a big smile. Marsha was standing next to him giggling a little.

Marsha said, "I'm so excited to be spending time with people from Pennsylvania." She still liked to say that word and repeated it in a long drawn out way. It caused them all to laugh.

"And we're ready to go. Hi Lily," said Sammi. "You're looking good today."

"It's so great to be out of jail and have some hope back in my life."

Billy immediately turned to his mom and said, "Remember, we said today would be a happy day; no sad talk about those problems, because they'll be gone soon enough anyway." When he saw a slight concern cross her face he added, "Don't forget Ms. Sammi can work miracles and I think she's got one waiting for you."

They smiled as they left and headed for the Blossom Music Center, the first place on their list. Sammi leaned over and said to Marsha, "You look very pretty today; you're wearing a nice outfit. I think blue looks nice on you with your pretty blue eyes."

There was no doubt that Marsha was tickled but also confused. She said, "I don't look very pretty, but it's nice of you to say that."

Billy immediately jumped on that statement and said, "I think you're very pretty, Marsha, in fact, I think you're beautiful."

Marsha got shy as she looked down at her hands that were folded carefully in her lap. She said, "Billy likes me."

"I like you a lot," he answered, "and you are pretty."

"But I show the syndrome more than you do. I have a thick neck and a fat face and my eyes have little slits in them."

"But that's what I like about you and I think that's what makes you pretty."

Marsha smiled and seemed pleased.

Sammi couldn't stay out of this game and said, "You know, Marsha, everybody has things about themselves that they don't like."

"Really? You're pretty. I'll bet you like everything about you."

"No, I don't. There are a lot of things about myself that I don't like, and other people feel the same way."

"What don't you like?" asked Marsha. She stared directly into Sammi's eyes, which made her realize that it would be hard to lie to a child like this. But she had no intention of doing that.

Dave added teasingly, "I'd like to hear this myself."

Sammi ignored his comment and kept her attention totally on Marsha, "Well, I don't like my nose and I wish I was a few inches taller."

Marsha looked at Sammi with a surprised look on her face. "I like your nose. It's a nice nose. How come you don't like it?"

"I don't know, but I never liked it."

"And you're taller than me. I always wanted to be taller, too." Marsha was quite thoughtful for a moment.

"I guess nobody gets everything they want," said Sammi and she knew that this gave Marsha something new to think about. She wondered why this perfectly normal person wouldn't like her nose and want to be taller. Marsha thought Sammi was perfect.

* * *

The first place they arrived at was the Blossom Music Center. The Cleveland Orchestra had long considered this amphitheatre to be its summer home, but it was also home to a full summer schedule of popular music arts as well as symphonic performances.

They got out and walked around the pavilion with Billy telling them what stars he had come to see here. He had seen the Moody Blues and James Taylor, but he especially liked the symphonies because they usually sat on the lawn and could sometimes look at the stars while they were listening to the music. There was well over 500 acres of undeveloped acreage surrounding this entire area.

They all sat down for a while and enjoyed the beautiful scenery as well as the warm sun that had showed up today just for them. Billy had said that it was a special favor he'd asked for. After a while of sitting and walking around, they decided to head for the second place that Billy wanted to take them – the Mary Campbell Cave.

American Indians used the Mary Campbell Cave for shelter and to house white captives. The cave was located in Summit County and legend had it that the Cuyahoga river carved out the cave approximately twelve thousand years ago. It was named after the cave's most celebrated resident. It seemed that during the French and Indian War, the Delaware Indians captured Mary Campbell when she lived in western Pennsylvania. For seven years, they kept her captive, but eventually released her and allowed her to return home. Billy knew the entire story by heart and didn't pause even once in reciting it. He was also proud that it had a Pennsylvania connection.

When the day was over they stopped for dinner at a pizzeria and everyone had at least one slice more than was necessary. It was a fun day for Billy and Marsha, a happy one for Lily and a totally memorable one for Dave and Sammi.

When they were dropped off at their motel, everyone had to hug everyone. Billy and Marsha's world liked to express emotions and feelings and all were happy to oblige.

Marsha kept shifting from her toes to her heels in an effort to express her happiness.

"It was such a fun day. Thank you for coming with us," she said.

"Thanks for inviting us," said Dave which made Marsha giggle again.

Lily said, "You can never get used to these two or take them for granted. They keep everything in a special mode all the time."

Sammi said, "I can understand that and it's quite catchy, isn't it?"

Lily nodded, said goodbye, realizing that she'd see both of them soon. Billy and Marsha had to go to work on Monday and Lily had decided to return as well. She said that she'd go to work while she could. After all, she felt that was what she wanted to do.

* * *

Dave and Sammi were both quiet after they closed the door to the motel. They went over to sit in the little area with the table and sofa and just stared off in space for a time.

"Their world is different, isn't it?" said Dave. "For the life of me I wouldn't know how to explain it."

Sammi nodded "I know. When I was in college and in close contact with Billy, I tried to figure out what made him so different. After all, his intelligence factor is only slightly below the low part of the scale for normal. Yet being with him was a whole world apart from what I was used to."

"Yeah, there's something so pure about him – both of them actually."

"And Marsha isn't that far below Billy. It seems so because she's a little embarrassed by her looks. She doesn't like the fact that her syndrome shows a lot more on her than on Billy. But he's made a big difference in her life. He keeps laying on all that confidence on her and she eats it up. He's just what she needs. And he likes her so much. Isn't that nice to see?"

"It is. I'm somewhat numb when I try to talk about their world and put it into words. It's so special, I mean ...." He couldn't continue.

Sammi went over and sat next to him on the couch. He put his arm around her and they sat quietly and thought over what they'd experienced today. Finally Sammi said, "Remember some feelings can't be put into words. I'm so happy sharing this with you. That's one of the reasons that I never told you about Billy; it would have been too hard to give it justice. But I knew you'd love him. Who could help it?"

Dave let out a yawn and it became contagious quickly. "It's been a fun day," he said "and one I won't ever forget. But we have to get out there and figure out who really killed Matthew. Lily needs to get some peace and security back into her life."

Sammi looked over and said, "Do you want the first shower or what?"

"You can go first. I don't mind sitting here for a little while longer."

Sammi got up and headed for the bathroom. She grabbed her robe and toiletries and was about to close the door when Dave said, "By the way, I love your nose."

"I'm glad," she said smiling.

"I love everything about you and wouldn't change a thing."

Sammi stood there for a moment looking at him with pride and said, "That's what love's all about."

CHAPTER SIX

Roy Dawson sat in his car for a few moments before he had the nerve to exit and head for the police station. His 6'2" frame and muscular build usually didn't have any problem making the strong and confident statement when he wanted, but today none of that mattered. The fact that his wavy dark brown hair and striking blue eyes could usually charm the women wasn't important either. He had thought all night about how to make a good impression, but his mind was blank on what behavior pattern would work out best.

This was his first day on the job at the new precinct and he had to admit he was as nervous as hell. He didn't like being transferred again, but he was always the first to go when there was an opening somewhere. No one seemed to want him around for very long. He couldn't understand it. He thought he was likeable and worked hard at making friends wherever he was. Friendships were always attainable for him although in an honest assessment he'd have to admit that they weren't close or intimate friendships, but he hadn't made any outright enemies either. He worked his tail off on every single assignment he'd ever had. He worked those extra hours that no one else had done, yet he found it hard to get into those secret little groups that every place had. He was always an associate, not disliked exactly yet more of an outsider than an insider; he always had been. How to make close friends and become part of the group always escaped him, no matter how hard he tried, and he had tried most of his life.

Remembering his childhood, he had one older brother who always seemed to fit in everywhere. He tried to study him, but was never very adept in matching his success. He couldn't believe as the years started piling up that he still had only a handful of friends most of which were the same ones that he'd had in grade school. He felt he was a loser and all losers stuck together. He shook his head. He had to get himself together. Today would be like a new beginning for him and he hoped that life would change for the better this time. Maybe he had to try harder, but for the life of him, he couldn't figure out how to do more than he already had.

Okay, he said to himself as he opened his car door, *think positive. Maybe this is the niche you've been looking for; it could be. Behind these doors might be a congenial set of circumstances just made for you.* And although he didn't really believe it, he tried to hold onto that thought.

He walked into the station, looked around rather sheepishly and walked directly to the office of Sergeant Brady. He waited for the signal to enter.

"Okay, Roy," said Sergeant Brady, "glad to have you aboard. We're rather informal around here and most refer to me as 'the sarge'." He laughed. "That's fine with me, but we all have mutual respect for each other and that's important here. I need to let you know that Dave Patterson is away on special assignment for a couple of weeks and you'll be reporting to both Jim Mucci and Tom Harrington. Don't worry about it. At this time, they report to each other, too. Just the way it is right now."

Throughout this information session, Roy actually felt comfortable. He felt the sarge was trying, in an awkward sort of way to put him at ease. And he was glad that they weren't sticklers on protocol. He'd been in stations like that before and hated it. Anyway, whatever the rules were around here, he'd follow them. He wanted to do well; he had to make it here. It could be his last chance and he knew it.

Then Sergeant Brady opened the door and called in Jim and Tom. "Okay, you two, our new recruit is here and you can get him up to speed with what we're working on. Anything new on those burglaries yet?" he asked.

As he waited both Tom and Jim shook their heads, so he continued. "I need to be kept up to speed. I got a call from the mayor. He wasn't nasty, just curious to see if we'd lucked out yet. He's trying to be long on patience right now."

"Nothing major," said Tom. "There aren't many leads, but we found two eye witnesses, one being the victim in that last home who was able to stay rational and aware and thinks he could make a positive I.D, and another one that just came forward. Don't know much about that one yet."

"Okay, well, that's good. Keep me up-to-date. Are you planning on a line-up yet?"

"Hopefully by the end of the week. We have a few more details to work out. We've got to keep everything clean or those lawyers will be all over us."

The sarge nodded about the same time that his phone rang. They all left his office.

* * *

They gathered at Jim Mucci's desk since Roy's desk was on the other side of him. They explained to him the procedures around the office, outside in the field, and what was expected of everyone.

"The next two weeks will be a little out of the ordinary; we don't have Dave Patterson around, but when he returns he takes over a lot of the details."

Roy got some kind of a questioning look on his face, which prompted Jim to add, "Dave's a great guy and knows what he's doing, and he and the sarge have a strong rapport."

Roy acknowledged the statement. Just then, Julie came up with some information that they needed. She stayed but a moment and then left.

Roy had a favorable look on his face.

"What?" asked Jim.

"Nothing, but she's quite a looker," said Roy.

"And she's my wife," said Jim.

"Oh, sorry, I didn't mean ..."

"It's okay; just so you know," added Jim. "Now we can get down to work. We've had several new leads in the burglaries around here and we need to at least make phone contact to see how valid they are." Jim took a few moments to explain this crime spree to Roy.

"How long have they been going on?" he asked.

"I think it's been over six months now, at least those we know about," said Tom.

"They've been quite frustrating, but then an eye witness came forward and a few other potentials that might help us along." Jim felt they were on the right track.

"If things go right, maybe we can have a line up later on this week or next week at the latest. We had these guys in for questioning last week, but their lawyers wouldn't let them talk at all because we had such meager evidence. We're hoping that will change and then we can bring them in again and have better luck."

Tom grabbed the phone messages and gave half to Roy. "You and I can start on this, okay Jim? I thought you had to finish that other report."

"Yeah, that'd be great. Then we can compare notes later."

* * *

With a copy of the file and a few phone messages to follow up, Roy started his first day at his new office. He was angry with himself for being obvious about Julie, but he didn't know she was Jim's wife. Still, he probably would have been better off not saying anything at all. Just his luck to start on the wrong foot. Then he thought that once Jim mentioned she was his wife, he sort of shrugged it off. Probably others had made a comment; she was quite stunning.

Roy snuck a few secret looks over at Jim; he couldn't help it. He seemed busy enough and not overly concerned about him. Taking a deep breath, he picked up the phone and started. He'd done a lot of this type of work before and knew it was boring and fruitless at times, but when you got lucky and that one lead panned out, it made everything else worthwhile.

A few hours later Tom came over and talked to him about whether he'd had any success. He hadn't, but he was waiting for some callbacks that might work. Tom brought over a few pictures of the suspects and it was all that Roy could do to sit quietly in his seat and try to look normal. He knew these guys. He'd run into them a few times when he walked the beat in another precinct. He almost broke into a sweat because interviewing them might be a problem for him.

Here's the way the story went. Several years ago, he was walking the beat and had pulled them in for attempted burglary on a liquor store. They were kids from rich and influential families in the area and were released on bail almost immediately. Then about two weeks later, he had another similar run in with them. Same ending, but their lawyers were threatening harassment charges and the kids had threatened retaliation someday. If they spotted him, he was sure they would try to involve him in some way. What a mess. He knew it; his luck was never good. Everything in this world was against him and he didn't think he'd make a very good beginning in this precinct.

For some reason Tom caught a look of apprehension on his face and asked, "Is there a problem here?"

He had to answer and said, "I think I might know these kids from a few years back when I was walking the beat. I was instrumental in getting them arrested for the attempted robbery of a liquor store." He didn't have anything to lose because Tom had caught a drift of something anyway.

"So if they remember you, they might want to finger you in some way to get the heat off their backs. That's what usually happens. We'll have to wait and see what develops on that."

Roy was shocked at how little stock Tom put into his concern. He certainly had given him the benefit of the doubt.

They were both silent for a few minutes. "It's almost lunch time and we go to the cafeteria or there are a few places around we like. Come on with me, if you want."

Roy tagged along happily knowing that Tom wasn't shocked at what he'd told him. And he was truthful because he figured he didn't have a chance anyway. Why did this type of thing always happen to him? My God, he was trying to do his best working a respected profession, but he always felt if there was one black ball in a pile of white ones, he'd be the one to find it.

* * *

After lunch, it was back to the office and Jim, Tom and Roy found time to compare notes on the leads they had followed. Jim had one lead he wanted to complete in person and planned the interview later that afternoon. He asked Roy to go with him.

"One of these gentlemen was in the house that was robbed and luckily wasn't blindfolded, but they broke his glasses and thought they were home free. But his glasses are strictly for reading and even at eighty-four years old, his long distance vision seems to be quite good. He's quite sure he'd recognize these guys. Anyway it's worth a chance and I've brought several other pictures with me, so we'll see what happens."

Roy nodded his head. At first, he wondered if he should tell Jim about knowing these kids, but decided against it. He had already given the information to Tom whom he felt would relate it at the proper time.

James Malloy, one of the robbery victims, led them into his living room where he lived with his wife, Mitzi and his friend William Schaefer. He told them he was glad that his wife had been out shopping when the attempted robbery occurred.

"Where were you when these guys broke in?" asked Jim.

"William and I were in the back room; we use it as a TV room and they probably thought the house was empty."

"How did they get in?"

"We heard a window break on the front right side of the house, that's our living room, and by the time we got in there to see what was going on, they were already inside."

William added, "It was obvious that they were as surprised as we were and one guy grabbed his face, realizing they didn't have any face masks on."

"Yeah, but they moved fast," said William. "They shoved me down quickly and took my glasses and did the same with James here. Now James needs his glasses for both near and far vision, but I can see far away just fine and I got a good look at both of them."

"So neither one of you was hurt?"

"No, mainly my pride," said James with a sly smile. "Back a few years we would have fought back and maybe won."

"Did you see any weapons?" asked Roy.

"One of them had a knife; I saw it before they broke my glasses, but I didn't see a gun."

"Okay, then," said Jim. "I've got a few pictures here that I'd like you to take a look at. Tell me if you recognize any of them."

Jim had brought along at least ten pictures of different suspects they'd had over the years. He wanted to make sure William could pick them out of a line up. He took his time with each picture and never hesitated until he got to the pictures of Brad Nieman and Carter Olsen. He didn't backtrack once to the other pictures; he knew these guys and pointed them out immediately.

"That's the two guys that broke into the house. I'm positive. I got a good look at them."

"Do you think you could pick them out of a line up?"

"Yes, I do and I'd like to hear them talk, especially this one," he said pointing to a picture of Carter Olsen. "He didn't talk real clear, like he had a lisp or trouble pronouncing certain letters. There was something different about his speech."

Jim said they'd be contacting them later in the week after the line up was set up. The old gentlemen were happy, hoping to be part of getting some young hoodlums off the street as they put it. James' new wristwatch had been taken. It was a present from his wife for their 50th anniversary and was the most important item he was hoping to get back. Jim didn't mention any recovered items.

Back in the car Jim said, "I think you heard that we interviewed these guys a few weeks ago, but they wouldn't talk because they were screaming for their lawyers. Well, this one Carter Olsen does have a speech impediment, so that's something I have to write in my report. God, this is a lucky break for us."

"It's good when things go right, isn't it?"

Jim nodded. He was happy; he was having a good day.

"This was a lucky break for your first day here. Not every day is like this. Usually we plod along for quite a while before anything turns up, I'm sure you know how it is. I don't know anything about these kids, but I'd like to look into their backgrounds and see if they had a troubled past or not. Their parents are rich and well connected so we have to make sure our details are correct and we haven't forgotten anything. Their lawyers will be up front anyway."

Roy felt he couldn't hold back so he let Jim know that he knew these kids had been in trouble before in a precinct he was in a few years ago.

"You seem concerned; why?"

"They always said that they would retaliate someday and I wonder what they'll say about me."

Jim nodded. "Yeah, a lot of them try to bring us down, too, but remember they have to have evidence or else it's all talk. And mostly we tend to ignore their attempts at linking one of us into their dirty activities."

"Still," said Roy, "I'm new here and it could look bad for me."

"Sit tight; we've got an eye witness, possibly two. Don't know about the second one yet. And we have them with some of the merchandise on their person. Things don't look that good for them right now."

Jim could tell that Roy was worried. And he tried to think of it from his point of view. He was new here, nobody knew him, and he'd moved around a lot mainly with the reputation of not being a team player nor having the best record. Yet he didn't have anything improper on his record and no infringements for anyone to question. His character and history of accomplishments were untarnished. Still, in his shoes, Jim thought, he'd probably have some uneasy concerns as well.

* * *

The lineup would take place on Thursday. The second witness was a neighbor who'd heard noise next door and looked out in time to see the guys leaving. He didn't think he could give a positive identity, but could describe the clothing they were wearing. At this point, every little bit helped on the details and on a list of clues that was adding up against them.

Friday came and the line up was set for 2:00 PM. A few minutes prior to that time, in walked the Olsen and the Nieman families with their lawyers well positioned on each side of them. The young suspects were noticeably quiet and when Brad at one moment went to make a comment, he was scared speechless by the look from his father. This line up and interview, obviously choreographed by the fathers and lawyers, did not give the children any consideration in the matter.

The line up time came. Nine suspects awaited their fate nervously. The victims, James Malloy and William Schaefer sat in a room with one-way glass waiting for their moment. Just as the proceedings were about to begin, there was a loud commotion outside. Jim went to see what was going on.

"I insist on being in that room," said Carter Olsen, Sr. "I have a right to see who's going to lie about my son and try to ruin our reputation."

Three officers were immediately on hand to calm everyone down. But it was Jim who answered, "You don't have any rights at this moment," he said. "The victims have a right to see if they can pick out their intruders without any worries about being intimidated or harassed." Then Jim turned to their lawyers, "You'd better explain the law to them."

There was a large huddle between the Olsen and Niemen families and their lawyers. It was explained that their time would come later as no one had been accused of any crime yet. Moreover, the rights, at this moment were on the side of the victims. Amidst loud cussing and angry tones, they had to turn around, leave the hallway and wait in another room outside the immediate area. This happened at the same time that Roy Dawson stepped foot into their range of view and both Brad and Carter spotted him.

"Hey, good seeing you here buddy," said Carter. One of his lawyers jumped on this action immediately.

"You know this police officer?" he asked.

"Oh yeah," he laughed. "We're old friends and did a lot of business together in the past, right Roy?"

Jim almost felt for Roy. This was the suspects' perfect opportunity to get the heat off themselves and onto a police officer, a much better target in their estimation. Then Brad joined in as well, "What's it been, maybe four years now? You wanting to do business with us again, or are you trying to play straight cop nowadays?"

With that, the lawyers shut them up and led them to the line up room, but not before they threw out a few more pointed and accusatory remarks. They acted as if Roy was their long lost friend who'd help them out of this mess or they would tell everyone what they knew about him. It was a tough and tense situation. Roy took it all in stride despite the critical looks of many onlookers.

Jim said, "This has happened before, so hang in there. Crooks always try to drag in the police and since they knew you from before, you're the perfect set up. I think it shows they're desperate."

Roy simply nodded. He couldn't speak. His mind was on fire as to what to do or say at this moment. *Damn, damn*, he thought. *I know this is probably my last chance and look what happened. I've never done anything illegal. Oh, I pushed the line a few times trying to catch a suspect, but I always stayed on the right side of the law. Maybe I'm in the wrong profession. Maybe this isn't what I should be doing with my life. Yet, it's what I always wanted to do. Just my luck; damn, damn. What's going to happen to me now? What else could happen?*

* * *

The line up was in itself quite dramatic. James Malloy and William Schaefer felt out of their element in any police station, but being eyewitnesses in an attempt to identify burglars made everything surreal for them. Their nervousness showed and the commotion in the outer hallway hadn't helped the situation. Marty Kennick, the neighbor who could only identify the clothes and give a general description of the suspects joined them at this time.

"Now remember," said Jim, "they can't see you through this glass, but you'll be able to see them. Take all the time you need and if you have any questions, ask me. Okay? Are we ready?"

They all nodded. The suspects paraded across the stage in accidental order. There were nine in all. Jim wanted enough so that if they identified them, no one could say it was a guess. But he didn't have to worry. As soon as Carter Olsen and Brad Niemen stepped onto that platform as Numbers 5 and 8, William Schaefer let out a gasp. Jim and Roy both turned to look at him.

"I don't need any time at all. No. 5 and 8 – they're the two who tried to rob us," said William Schaefer.

"Okay," said Jim. "But you can take a few more minutes to be sure if you like."

"Don't need any more time; I'll never forget those faces."

Jim had purposely separated the suspects during the lineup so that they wouldn't be next to each other. And the victims still knew them immediately.

William Schaefer asked if they could hear them speak. "I'd like to hear all of them say something so I could tell the difference."

Jim asked all of them to say, "Stay on the floor old man, or you'll get hurt."

Again, when they came to Carter there was no doubt at all. His voice and different way of speaking came through loud and clear.

William said, "That's the guy. I'd know that voice any-where and he talks differently. I'm sure you know what I mean. I don't know what to call it, but he has problems getting his words out." And James Malloy could verify the voice.

Jim nodded as did Roy.

"Okay, then," and Jim picked up the microphone and said, "Let them all go except No. 5 and No. 8."

They checked them out again in side view and front view and heard their voices again. There was no doubt at all in their minds. They were as sure as they could be. It was a positive identification.

* * *

Jim was ready for the wild grandstanding and uproarious exhibition expected by the families and their lawyers, but he was ready to detain the suspects. In preparation, he immediately called Sergeant Brady for advice and assistance.

"I'll send a unit down immediately and I'll be there, too. We can't chance that these guys will run now that they've been fingered. Wait for me; I'll be there in five minutes."

And it was probably less than five minutes when the sarge and his men walked through the door. Jim explained the problem they'd had before the lineup and needed to take precautions.

"I'll handle it from here. Let's get these victims out the side door first. We need to make sure they get out of here and home safely."

Jim nodded.

"You go and take care of the paperwork," said the sarge, "that should distract them, but you'll still get the brunt of the nastiness, I'm sure."

Jim smiled. "All in a day's work and I have a few more details for you later."

"Then meet me in my office as soon as this is over."

As soon as the victims were on their way and out of sight, the sarge joined Jim out front. By this time, the lawyers and the families were out in the hallway as loud and as boisterous as before, but upon learning their children had been identified, they launched unbelievable threats and insults at the police.

"You'll all be very sorry for how we've been treated," said Carter Olsen, Sr. "Where's my boy now? I insist on seeing him this instant. "

Jim stood his ground strongly as he answered civilly and without annoyance. "He's being processed as we are following procedure at this time. You'll have your moment to talk to him later. I'm sure you'll do all you can, but for now, he's being held."

There was a moment when Jim thought that Mr. Nieman wanted to hit him, even though he was only explaining the facts and procedures to them in a courteous and professional manner. Noticing his bullying tactics and attempt at physical assault, Jim said, "I'm sure you don't want to do that, Mr. Nieman. There's no reason for you to be in the cell next to your son."

That drew more anger from Jonathon Nieman and lessened his ability to control himself, but he made a strong effort knowing that hitting a police officer in a police station would be stupidity to the utmost degree. And he was able to settle down, although it wasn't easy. He had the attitude of the entitled people of our society and couldn't understand why these police officers were not cooperating. Jim could almost hear him saying under his breath, *do you know who I am?* And Jim was ready with his answer, *Yes, I do and I'm still following procedure.* However, it didn't get to that and the families and lawyers went into another huddle and sat on a corner bench quietly after that, much to the pleasure of the officers.

When the family realized that it would be quite a while before they could see their kids, they decided to leave and come back later, but not before they hurled accusations at Roy Dawson in an effort to keep up the pressure on the police. They yelled and shouted as they left saying that they would be looking into his past and taking appropriate action.

Sergeant Brady did not understand the comments, but Jim told him that he'd explain it later in their meeting.

"Fine; I want the both of you in my office as soon as you can so I get to know what's going on here."

Jim nodded and they went on to finish the endless paperwork.

"I sure miss Dave; he's the one who would have taken care of most of this paperwork. "

Looking over at Roy, he noticed the worried look on his face and said, "The sarge needs to know what's going on.

He'll want all the details about how you knew these guys in the past and anything else you know about them that might help us here and now. Any fine point that we need to know about these guys is what he'll be looking for."

"Of course," he answered. "This has been quite a first week for me."

"I can tell you're worried, but we all get targeted by crooks now and then; it's part of the game. Just tell the truth … tell it like it really is and then we can work with you."

Roy agreed. "Yes of course; it's just a worry for me."

"I'm sure because you're new here, but it's one way for us to find out about each other."

Roy threw a sly grin at him as they finished their paperwork and headed toward Sergeant Brady's office. This would be a telling moment.

* * *

As they sat down in the sarge's office, he offered coffee, a nicety he didn't always extend. However, the situation was tense and they all needed to relax a little, take a step back and reassess the situation.

The sarge said, "This was a tough day for the both of you. These parents and lawyers were almost out of control. What the hell's wrong with them? If they were on the other side of this event, they'd be screaming another state of affairs. Why these people don't work with us and even help us do our job is beyond me."

Jim said, "It sounds too logical. But then it was all in the heat of the moment and none of them were very calm out there."

Roy said, "That's for sure. I thought that one father was ready to take a shot at you."

"Yeah," said Jim. "I did, too. In fact, I'm surprised he didn't. But I guess he saw the futility of the situation in the nick of time."

After a few more moments of evaluating the situation, Sergeant Brady wanted to know about the other part of the comments hurled at them.

"So what about these kids, Roy? What do they have to do with you?"

Roy took a deep nervous breath, let it out slowly and told the sarge his run in with these kids before. He didn't leave out any details most especially that they said they would retaliate some day.

"Most of the crooks around would like to see us dead or at least hurt and humiliated in some cruel way. That's part of our way of life."

"Yeah, but, for the record, I know from the file you've got on me that they told you that sometimes I've come close to the line a few times. And I have. To be honest, I have pushed the envelope right to the edge more than once and was reprimanded for it. But I've never crossed over the line. I've never done anything illegal. Hell, I'm on this side of the law and that's the only place I've ever wanted to be."

Roy paused, slightly emotional, realizing that maybe he'd said too much. But it just flowed out of him as if someone had opened a faucet that couldn't be immediately closed. Maybe he had given more information than was necessary, but he felt like he had cleared the air.

"Well," said the sarge, "since you brought it up; your record does say that you like to be a loner out there and don't always embrace being a team player. We like team players around here so that's what I need you to be."

Roy admitted it. "It's true; but that's in the past. It didn't work out that well for me and I can see now that working with each other is a much better way to go."

"I hope you mean it," said Jim. "That's what we need around here and that's what I can really work with."

"Like part of my group here, Jim, Dave and Tom have been together almost since the beginning. They work together well because they share. They call themselves the three referees."

Jim smiled.

The sarge added with a smirk, "Are you guys ever going to tell anybody what the title means?"

Jim laughed, as he stated, "Not in the foreseeable future."

The sarge shook his head, "You guys probably never will. But they're a team within a team. Tyrone and LeBron have sometimes worked with them and then they're all a team. That's the way it works around here and that's what I must have. Any problem with that?"

"No, not at all."

"Good, then we should be able to master this latest challenge. And about what these kids said out there … it happens all the time. It must have happened to you before."

"Not where they were this serious about it."

"Well, we can worry about that later. In the meantime, I need you two back out there getting more against these kids. We got good evidence now, but we need more. And now we can really interview them."

Jim said, "We have all the evidence I think we can get on them."

"On this one robbery, but I was hoping to link them to some of the others with the same style."

"Oh right, well, I've already requested subpoenas; I wanted to search their home, and I should have that before the end of today."

"Good, if we can find more evidence from those other robberies, the better off we are. It's going to take a lot to put them away."

* * *

When they left the sarge's office, Roy seemed a little more relaxed.

"The sarge is a real straight shooter, isn't he?"

"Oh yeah, he's a great guy to have at the top of our entire group," said Jim. "He knows what he's doing and he's willing to work with us. I know some at the top almost work against their own people, but not here. Honestly, this is a great group so when we get this first one under your belt, I think you'll like what you see."

"You guys are pretty tight, aren't you?"

"Yes, we are. We know each other well; we know how we work and how we react to different situations. It takes time to get there, but well worth it."

They went back to their desks and talked a little more.

"So are you married Roy, now or ever?"

"Not now; I was once, but it didn't work out. No kids either, but that's probably for the best."

"I know. This is my second marriage and I finally feel like I've connected with the right one. My first marriage didn't work out so well, but I have two girls so we try to get along for their sake. Anyway, that was a long time ago, so it's a little easier now."

Jim's phone rang. The subpoenas were ready.

"I'd like to go today and get this done. I'm asking Tom and Tyrone, too, if they're available to come. I take it you'd like to be there?"

"Oh yes, I'd like to be in on this one."

"Good. We're going to need back up because this one won't be very pleasant. I'd like LeBron, too, but he's not around right now, so it's at least the four of us and one extra unit; that should do it. I'll let the sarge know. We need to get there now, before their lawyers get them out of jail and they have time to hide or dispose of the evidence."

As they walked out of the office to their car, Roy was feeling a part of something, a feeling he hadn't experienced in a long time. He would be working with a group; it was almost a foregone conclusion. They didn't seem to want to keep him on the outside as he'd experienced so many times before. It seemed he had tried often enough to earn his way into some of the other cliques, but they were quite tight and didn't take in any newcomers. That's one of the reasons that he became a loner in the first place. He knew it wasn't the best course of action, but he'd never had a choice. It seemed like this transfer might turn out to be good after all. And he realized as he walked out of the station with Jim, that he felt different. He glanced over toward his car parked on the left side of the parking lot and remembered how he felt that first day, leery about getting out and walking into the station. He had no idea what awaited him at that time and he was somewhat uneasy. But it seemed to be going well, and he was pleased. He didn't have to fight hard to get into a group; he was into a group because that's how they worked. He always knew that was the best course of action, but hadn't been able to find. Now he had, and it felt good.

CHAPTER SEVEN

Sammi didn't feel satisfied with this week's work. They had only learned a few more facts about Matthew Belten, namely, his strange activities that were close to the edge and which of his enemies to question. And there was another witness, other than Billy who had seen Lily dropped off at her house around 8:00 PM the Friday night of the murder. The case was inching along whereas she would have liked it to be charging toward the finish line. She hadn't heard anything significant from other people's thoughts, which confused her at first. Then she realized that they must be aiming at the wrong people, but for the life of her, she didn't know who the right people were.

Dave had planned to meet with Detective Fred Anchor of the Akron Police Department. He wanted to see some of the private files that were not available to anyone outside the professional world. With that in mind, Sammi decided to take advantage of a free day and stop to visit Billy at work at his supply job for a merchandizing company. He was so proud and repeatedly asked Sammi to stop by. She made it in time for lunch and after they headed to his office.

"My office's not very big, but it's mine. I have my name on the door."

When they arrived, Billy proudly showed her the upper part of his door, which was fancy glass and had the name,

Billy G. Simpson, Supply Administrator on it. He was so proud that his heels kept lifting off the floor. He invited her in, offered her some coffee, and was thrilled that she was sitting down talking to him.

"I'm happy that Dave is with you and that we had a nice day Sunday with everyone around, but I'm really glad that we have a few minutes to talk, just you and me."

"Me, too," said Sammi. "It's been a long time since we used to have those lunches at Scranton University."

"Yeah, and I was so proud to sit with you. I like to talk to you."

"And I like to talk to you, too. Your girlfriend Marsha is nice and she's pretty. I'm glad you keep reminding her."

"She's smart, too. She worries too much about her looks. She looks fine to me. It's who she is. And like you said, nobody's perfect."

"That's right, nobody's perfect," Sammi said with a smile.

"I think Dave is very handsome. You think so, too, right?"

"I do because he's my husband and I love him. But like you said, it's what's inside that really counts."

Billy thought for a moment and said, "That's true, but a lot of people don't act like its true."

"Maybe they haven't discovered it yet."

Billy thought about that and then he puckered his lips and nodded his head in agreement. "Yeah, I think you're right; some people don't understand, that's all."

They sipped their coffee and then Billy got to a few questions that had obviously been on his mind for a while.

"We don't know when my mom's trial is scheduled, do we? Do you think she has a chance to be free?"

"Today Dave is with some police officers in Akron trying to find more evidence and we'll keep working until we find the real killer."

"Mom is acting so brave, but I know she's very afraid. I can't imagine. People say she killed somebody and we all know that she didn't."

"I know."

"But I heard that this Matthew did a lot of bad things. He dated other girls and didn't tell them he was married. That's not right. Maybe one of them got mad and killed him."

"That's an idea. I'll have to mention it to Dave. They have files on a lot of people and Dave said that he hopes to find new leads today."

"I hope so. I'm worried, too. I want it to be like it was before. We used to have fun and didn't worry. We both had jobs and worked hard. That's what people are supposed to do, go to work and earn a living and then have some fun. So why did this happen?"

"That's hard to say. Sometimes bad things happen to good people."

"Oh, I know that, Ms. Sammi. I didn't want you to think we don't appreciate everything that you do. I just wonder why it had to happen in the first place, that's all."

"I don't know the answer to that Billy."

"That's right, like you said, nobody knows it all."

Then Billy opened his desk drawer and got excited and upset at the same time.

"Oh my gosh, I forgot. Oh gees, I forgot. Marsha will be so upset. I don't know what to do."

"What's the matter, Billy?"

"See this envelope. I was supposed to give it to Marsha last night and I forgot. She needs it this afternoon and it's my fault ... oh my gosh."

"I can take it over to her, Billy. I've got time."

Billy's eyes got very wide with wonderment. "You'd do that?"

"Of course I'd do that for you."

He smiled and relaxed for a moment. "But it's already 1:30 PM and I think she needs it for a 2:00 PM meeting."

"Then I'd better leave right away. How far away is it? You have to tell me how to get there."

"It only takes me ten minutes to get there."

"Then I'd better leave now and that'll give me plenty of time."

As Sammi got up to leave, Billy rushed around to give her a big hug. "You're still one of my favorite people ever."

"And you're one of mine. I'm sure we'll see you later – I'd better hurry."

"Yeah, hurry up, but drive carefully."

"I will. Bye."

* * *

Sammi drove carefully as she headed toward the Children Aid Group center. It would be nice to see Marsha working at her job. She'd also be proud to have Sammi see her at work. And of course, she'd get to see Lily in her natural habitat. These were close-knit people and Lily had the confidence of this group behind her; that must have given her warm feelings of belonging.

She pulled into the parking lot of a modern two-story building that seemed to house a lot of action. Most of the orphan and foster home activities filtered through this group and their business was usually high in any given year. When she reached the front desk, she asked for Lily who was out to greet her in a moment. When she explained the reason for her visit, Lily decided that she should see Marsha at work and give her the envelope herself.

They headed toward Marsha's area and as she handed the manila package to her with the explanation, both of her hands went up to her face in blank anxiety. "Oh my gosh. I forgot, too. And I do need this for my meeting. It's my notes to talk about things to improve the cleaning process. Thank you, Ms. Sammi. You've saved me today."

"My pleasure," she said as she watched Marsha scurry off to her meeting.

Lily invited her into her office and this time she refused the coffee offer, but welcomed the time to sit and talk with her.

"How're you holding up?"

"I'm doing okay. Sometimes a few hours go by, I'm busy, and I forget what's going on in my life. But it's never gone from my mind for very long."

"Of course not, but you seem to be holding it together."

"I just wish someone would find out something soon, you know? Just waiting and waiting for anything … that's the hard part. I haven't heard a trial date yet and I hope it doesn't get to that. Maybe they'll find out who did it before then."

"We're hoping. Dave's working with some detectives in Akron today. I hope we get some new leads."

"I wish I could think of something," Lily said, "but I know so little about the entire situation. I'd dated him three times, but it was casual, dinner and a movie once, and another time we went dancing. I knew very little about his life, personal or otherwise. It's so frustrating. To think the police would target me for killing him."

"That's only because you went out with him that last night he was alive."

"I know, I know. Bad luck for me."

Just then, there was a knock on her door and she waved in a guy from the outer office.

"Lily, I need to get this approved by you. It's for more than $200.00."

"Okay, give me a moment." Lily read over the paperwork briefly, signed it, and gave it back to him. However, she did take a moment to introduce Len Worley. He was an office manager and their positions were on par, and many times, they co-signed for each other as a security measure. He was possibly early to middle fifties, not overly confident, but appealing in a casual way and ready to be friendly. He seemed polite and pleasant until Lily mentioned that Sammi and her husband were here to help her in the murder case. Then agitation and anxiety immediately covered his demeanor. It was quite a switch as before that comment, his body language suggested that he would stick around for a few minutes and talk. However, after that one line, he seemed to shift his purpose and found reason to leave quickly.

"Sorry, I'd like to stay and chat, but I'm wanted somewhere else."

Sammi recognized his blatant lie immediately and realized that the colors around him were dark and dismal implying this person was hiding a lot. But it didn't make sense to her. Sammi's mind had been wandering as she heard Lily tell her that he was the guy at work that she had dated a few times years ago, but only casually as a friend. And she felt that he had remained a good friend of hers over the years. Sometimes Lily felt that he could be over protective, but since she'd never had a big brother, she relished the attention. Sammi was hearing these words over her own thoughts that were working overtime and had her almost spaced out as she tried to remember Len's few fleeting thoughts that were not what they should have been.

The moment she had a chance she asked Lily. "Do you know if the police ever checked out the people here where you work? That should never be overlooked."

Lily had a strange look on her face, as she said, "No, I don't think so, at least no one ever said anything to me. You think ..."

"I just wondered; you really can pick up clues everywhere. I'm one to cover all the bases."

Lily mentioned that she had a meeting she couldn't miss. "That's fine. Do you mind if I just look around here and get the feel of the place. I won't disturb anything."

"Of course not; look around all you want. And thanks again for everything."

* * *

As she carefully began her determined walk around the outer offices on the pretext of looking around the area, her purpose was to find Len again and see if she could get close enough to pick up something in his thought world. The flashing thoughts that crossed his mind earlier were shocking and worrisome to her. Lily had mentioned Len's multiple degrees and expertise that certainly helped them out tremendously, but almost made others wonder if he'd be enticed away sometime with a better offer. She was sure that Lily had no idea what his mind focused on during any given day. He had more than one purpose for remaining in this position and she wanted to know more about his extra curricular activities, because the one she heard of was vaguely bizarre. That was the immediate assessment, which came to her from beyond and she needed to follow up in her own way.

She took her time strolling around the area trying to look as inconspicuous as possible as she tried to pick up some hints of a controlling figure in their midst. Then, luckily, her intuitive feelings were at their height as she felt someone coming up slowly behind her. It wasn't that she'd heard anything, but thoughts were catching up to her ahead of the person. She turned around suddenly and surprised Len who had snuck up behind her, and without realizing it, had managed to stop and interrupt her private space. She took a step back before she began speaking to him.

"You surprised me," she said. "I didn't hear you at all."

Len smiled subtly as he said, "I guess it's these shoes I wear. I end up shocking a few people everyday."

Sammi waited. He had a purpose for approaching her and she knew what it was, but didn't want to arouse any suspicions in his mind.

"So you and your husband are trying to find Matthew's killer. We all know that it wasn't Lily, but the police don't seem to have another suspect."

His thoughts were saying, *and you'll probably never find out. I covered my tracks very well. I needed to get that creep*

*away from her. He wasn't acting nice toward her and would
have hurt her before long. Besides, if I can't have her, no one
can. Well, maybe if she dated someone nice I wouldn't mind,
but not a creep like that. I have to watch out for her. That's
why I'm around here; I have to protect Lily.*

Sammi was considerably shocked and yet she didn't dare
show it. She was standing face to face with Matthew Belten's
killer and he was so incredibly smug. He thought he had
committed the perfect crime, and he felt that he had the perfect
explicable reason. Matthew Belten was married and he had
lied to Lily. Therefore, he was dispensable.

Sammi had to recover quickly and answer him logically
with a steady voice. She couldn't let on that she knew his
secret and would soon lead him out of the shadows into the
revealing sunlight. She focused with effort and then replied,
"Yes, we're trying to see if we can find any evidence that
might point in another direction."

"Any luck so far?" he asked.

This she could answer honestly, "No, not yet, but we hope
to keep looking."

"I see," he said and he had a strange look in his eye.

Sammi was trying to decipher in her mind if this person
was sane or not. His reasoning seemed on target for him, but
his deed was not logical. There were other ways to help Lily
without killing this person. Then she heard the biggest reason
cross Len's thoughts.

*I've loved Lily for all these years. Before long, I'm going
to try for her again. When she sees how well we're working
together on this latest project, I think she'll start to see me in a
new light. She's the world to me and I won't let anyone hurt
her. She's mine and always has been.*

Sammi began to feel hot and flushed. She couldn't let on
anything was happening in her physical person, and that was
one of the good things about her gift. At times people thought
maybe she was onto something, but no one ever guessed that
she was completely aware of what they were thinking. She had

to distract him and leave quickly. This situation made her more than a little uneasy. Lily wasn't around; Marsha was gone to a meeting and a quick glance around the room caught Sammi slightly worried as she realized they were the only two people in the entire area.

"What time do you have?" she asked.

"It's about 2:30; why?"

"I'm running late. I have to meet my husband by 3:00 this afternoon across town. Can you tell me the fastest way to get to the Akron police station?"

That caught Len's thoughts off balance. He took a step back and his thoughts promptly decided he'd better move away from this woman quickly. Therefore, after giving Sammi some casual directions, he found an early exit the best strategy for himself.

* * *

Sammi couldn't deny that she was somewhat nervous as she walked out alone to her car in the half-deserted parking lot. Her physical person felt threatened although not necessarily in an outward fashion. Len's thoughts from the dark and dismal side of life attacked her and she had no idea yet how to rebound. Her guard was down at that moment; she hadn't been prepared, but she'd know better than to open herself up again in the future. She didn't care if it was the middle of the day, her mind was loaded and she had been particularly cautious not to let one word spill out that would give Len any clue that he had committed anything but the perfect crime. This one would be hard enough to figure out as it was, his crime was near perfect, except for one little thing; his thinking was giving out a lot of ammunition.

When Dave spotted Sammi walking into the police station, he immediately went up to her and led her into Detective Anchor's office. He introduced her and they talked for a few minutes. Sammi was trying to remain poised and laid-back, but one glance from Dave made her realize that he knew she had found out something serious. Since she didn't volunteer any information, Dave realized quickly that she had found out something meant only for his ears. He cut this meeting short and they went out for an early dinner.

"Okay, I know you. What have you got?"

"I know who killed Matthew Belten, but for the life of me I don't know how we're going to be able to prove it."

Dave was speechless, which was not a common occurrence.

"What? Where were you today? What happened?"

She recounted about going to Billy's place of employment and then bringing over a package to Marsha, which he had forgotten to give her. Because of that, she had met Len Worley and his spiraling feelings gave him away immediately when his worrisome thoughts realized the purpose of Sammi's visit.

"Holy shit, that guy she dated a few times years ago; he killed this Matthew Belten to protect her."

"That's what his thoughts were saying. Apparently, he's been in love with her all his life. He has a high I.Q. and holds two Masters Degrees in something or other and he's way over qualified for this job. You have to wonder why he's stayed around for so long, when he's had offers from other places. Once I picked that up, I started paying more attention to his thoughts and made a few comments that triggered his thought patterns. He thought that he was protecting her from a predator of some type who didn't tell her he was married, and he knew her life's values wouldn't allow her to go out with a married man. He thinks some day soon she'll realize how compatible they are and he'll win her over."

"And if not for you, I don't think anyone would have ever bothered with him."

"That's true and I don't have all of the details about the murder, but everyone was gone to a meeting and to tell you the truth, he gave me the creeps. I mean all of a sudden I knew that I was standing next to the killer of Matthew Belten, and whatever his reasons, he was a cold-blooded killer and I wanted to get out of there. But if I can get around him casually and we could get him in a telling conversation, I have no doubt that I could pick up enough details to check him out."

Dave grabbed Sammi's hand. "I think that's the first time you ever admitted you were scared."

She sheepishly said, "I wasn't exactly scared, but there wasn't anyone around and ..."

"No excuses; you were right to get right out of there and come to me. That's what you're supposed to do. Find out things and tell me. Now we have to work out a plan. I can't think of a way to tell Detective Anchor that all of a sudden I know who the killer is. I mean I love your gift, but sometimes it's hard to deal with."

Sammi gave him one of those looks that agreed that her gift sometimes put them out in left field somewhere with no one around them understanding what she could do.

"Do you think we should clue in Lily?" she asked. "I think she might be leery of him if she knew."

"Yes, I guess she would, but he certainly isn't going to harm her. I mean, he killed for her. Still, I don't think that would be the best way. She said that they were friends and got together at times for conversation or lunch. Maybe we could find a way to be with the two of them. We could invite them to have dinner with us and talk about her upcoming trial. We could bring up everything associated with it that's common knowledge. That would trigger his thoughts enough, don't you think?"

"That would probably work. Still, I think we should do it without Lily being aware. She has too much on her mind now. And when she finally does find out, I think she'll have even more guilt."

"It's not her fault," Dave said.

"But I think she'll have a little guilt over it anyway."

"Probably, I guess most of us would feel that way."

"Why don't we try for a dinner this weekend? I need to figure out what this guy's all about and I can only do that if

I'm around him. It might be tricky. I really don't want Billy and Marsha around this time. That would be very distracting for me."

"Didn't Billy say that he was taking Marsha somewhere on Saturday night? I think it was a get together with a few people from where he worked. That might be the perfect time."

"That's right; I forgot about that. Let me call Lily; that would be perfect."

* * *

"Detective Anchor has been a little stumped on this case. Everyone's been concentrating on Lily like it was a foregone conclusion, so when I talked to him today about the possibility of someone else, he was cooperative but realized they didn't have anything pointing in any other direction."

"I'm surprised," said Sammi. "Matthew was a character of loose morals, so he had several affairs in the last few years that we know about. And his wife knew about them, too. To me, no matter how casual she talks, I would think there would be something to look into there. No one is interested in anyone but Lily; makes me wonder about other cases, too. You, Tom and Jim never seemed to be so close-minded."

"That's true. We've always kept open to new possibilities. So many times in the past the answer came from a totally different direction."

"Exactly, and I think there will be a few surprised officials on this case. First, we have to find more proof that leads away from Lily. I'll call her as soon as we get home."

They drove on in silence each with their own take on this murder. Sammi had many thoughts to sort out. Len's mental activity was very fast; she'd grab onto one thought, and he'd immediately move to another random thought with electrifying speed. Other people did that occasionally, but mostly she found out that happened with nervous and agitated people. They could be harder to read as their thought patterns moved up and down quickly. When these patterns reached deep down into their minds bordering on the subconscious, she could lose them quickly. She felt if they had Lily and Len together in a casual setting, like a warm pleasant dinner gathering, it would be less likely to happen and she could find out more information.

When they got back to the motel room and closed the door, Dave grabbed her and gave her a long and welcomed hug. She knew he felt the tension in her and he had a good share of his own. This was one emotional case and they were the only two who knew what was going on, except for Len Worley, of course.

"Even though we try not to, we always seem to be carrying a heavy load," said Dave, "I guess that's just the way it is."

"We're lucky we've got each other. I was thinking on the way home that I used to have all this information and try to figure out things by myself. I couldn't tell anyone and that was hard. But now with you and our other friends, it helps so much to have others to discuss what I hear especially ...."

Dave smiled, "Especially what?"

"Especially because you don't think I'm a nut."

"Sometimes I do, but a loveable nut."

Sammi laughed, but that created an atmosphere for a fight.

"You picked me so you must be a nut, too," she quipped.

"I hope so, because it helps a lot. I mean we're always talking about the universe and how it crosses people's lives everyday. Honestly, you're the only one I discuss the universe with."

"Yeah," she said, settling down, "I know. Yet if people realized more they'd know how much help there is around them. They could get guidance and direction and maybe people like Len, would find a way to live a happy life."

Sammi stopped. She sighed. She felt worn out. She didn't like how this case had turned out. At first, she thought that maybe one of Matthew's ex-lovers had killed him or one of his wife's suitors; that would have made more sense. However, life didn't make sense many times, at least not when we looked at it from a human and earthy standpoint. However, when she stood back and got the universe involved, ideas and information came from unexpected places and then the direction was clear.

She decided to take a nap. She felt tired and a little glum. She lay back on the bed and tried to relax, but then she felt a gentle hand on her shoulder. It seems that Dave had other ideas on his mind and she was not opposed to them either.

* * *

A few hours later, Sammi called Lily. She caught her at home in a relaxed mood, which was a surprise for her lately.

"You sound good," said Sammi. "I'm glad you're finally taking it down a notch or two."

"And it's not by any effort on my part. I guess after a while my body and mind couldn't take all the high tension anymore and started to relax. I finally realized that there wasn't anything I could do and it was as if I took a deep breath inside and started to let go. Now I feel better and more positive for some reason. I'm sure this will work out in time."

"It will and I understand that you've been under so much stress lately that it's good to hear."

Sammi mentioned about them getting together for dinner on Saturday night.

"You know Len mentioned that he wanted to stop by. He wants to see how I'm doing; he's such a worrier and always very concerned about me. Why don't I make dinner here and we could have a nice, casual evening? I'm sure Len would enjoy getting to know the both of you better."

Sammi was surprised to hear the innocent and naïve thoughts that Lily had on her mind. Not even one single thought of anything but confidence and support crossed her mind when she thought about Len. Sammi had come up with some questions of her own. If Len loved her so much and wanted the best for her, then why was he letting her take the fall for this murder that he had committed? There was a lot more to Len's motives than was obvious at this moment, and for the life of her she couldn't figure it out, at least, not yet.

"That would be great, if it's not too much trouble," Sammi said.

"Are you kidding? I love to cook. This would be great."

"Okay then, what time?"

"How about 7:00 PM. Billy and Marsha are going to their own party, so we'll have some time to ourselves. I'm looking forward to it."

"Okay, then, we'll see you around 7:00 PM."

"Great."

* * *

Dave had heard the conversation, but caught the look in Sammi's eyes as she put down the phone.

"Okay, what's up?"

"Well, like you heard, we're on for 7:00 PM for dinner at her place. It seems that Len had planned to stop by anyway. However, I can't help but wonder why does he leave her in this vulnerable spot if he cares about her so much? He has to have another motive but I haven't figured it out." Sammi threw her hands up in the air in frustration.

"You think there's more to it, don't you?"

"There has to be, Dave. If you really love someone ..." her voice trailed off again for a moment, but then she continued quickly. "I'm sure he was shocked that she was accused of the murder; that's the first thing. He's probably just trying to figure out what to do and probably hoping they'll arrest someone else and that would let both him and Lily off the hook."

Dave thought for a few minutes. "You made a good point; I'm sure he had no idea that Lily would be accused. Everyone, except the police were surprised because she doesn't have any background or personality traits that would lead anyone to suspect her. But, I wonder how he plans to handle this. If he really does love her, he wouldn't let her be convicted and go to jail, unless ..."

Sammi's shocked look was obvious as she looked over at Dave. "Unless what?"

"Well, you picked up that he was protecting her, but what if it was more of an obsession?"

"I'm not sure where you're going with this," she said.

"I'm thinking of the usual ... if I can't have her no one else will either and, of course, if she was in jail, no one else could have her and he could play the really good guy and visit her and get her into his debt so that by the time she gets out she'd feel that she owed him. Either way he would have accomplished his purpose."

"Wow. I never thought of that. I'm going to be paying a lot of attention to him tomorrow night. That's kind of a bizarre and crazy way of thinking. I wonder what his story is; you know his childhood, relationships, stuff like that."

"I don't know, but we've both heard of possessive and controlling personalities. I've seen it before many times; you've heard of it, right?"

"Yes, I have," said Sammi. "That's human behavior at its worst. It believes that you have a right to another person regardless of what they want. It's not realizing that you can make your own happiness with being happy with what you've got, possibly in another direction."

Sammi got quiet after that, obviously lost in her own world of thought. Dave left her alone. His own mind wandered back to Linda Saunders for a moment. She was in jail for attempted murder, but still was able to convey her obsession with him. He wondered if she'd ever give up; would she ever stop.

* * *

It had to be more than an hour later when their phone rang. It was 10:00 on Friday night and both were rather sheepish in answering it. A call at this hour of night had a 50/50 chance of spelling bad luck.

"Hi Jim. Good to hear from you. What's going on back in Scranton?"

"It's fairly quiet. We did arrest Carter Olsen and Brad Niemen. The victims picked them out of a line up. So their families and lawyers are screaming at anyone who'll listen. They'll probably make bail by tomorrow and then we'll have a hell of a go at them in trial. But they were caught with some of the merchandise on their person and we have an eye witness against them."

Dave said, "But you know what high priced lawyers can do with that stuff."

"I know, and we have another twist to this story."

Jim told Dave about Roy's connection to the suspects. They tried to name him as an accomplice and acted out threats as well. He told Dave how nervous Roy was about the entire situation.

"That happens all the time. Why is he so nervous about this?"

"I think it's because he's new here and was just transferred over, like he's not had a chance to prove himself yet. He feels the other precinct wanted to get rid of him and he knows he doesn't have any strong ties here. Still, I have to tell you that when I worked with him this week, he seemed to enjoy being a team player. I know his reputation, but maybe in other precincts it was harder to make connections."

"We know how that happens; you, Tom and I have always been kind of lucky about that. Nowadays we've got Amilio as well as LeBron and Tyrone who've worked out well. Maybe Roy never found this before."

"That's exactly what I was thinking because we seemed to merge well, but we'll see what happens. We told the sarge and he told Roy not to worry about it and that seemed to settle him down a bit."

"Anything else going on?"

"We got subpoenas today and Roy, Tom and I along with a unit went over the suspects' homes and found more evidence from the crime scene. They had an entire stash of loot out in open sight. I guess they didn't think anyone would ever get over there."

"The suspects are still in jail, right?"

"Yeah, but the fathers and lawyers gave us a rough time when we arrived. We had to wait for a judge's order because they didn't think subpoenas were enough. The sarge didn't think we needed to break that barrier and let the legal system do it for us. Anyway, we confiscated a lot more jewelry and even some other stuff from some of the previous robberies, so we have them connected to a few more that took place a while back."

"That's great. You guys are doing a great job; probably don't even miss me."

"Are you kidding? We've been splitting up all of that paperwork that you usually do," he laughed. "God, I don't think either one of us realized how much reporting you have to do."

"Took me a while to get used to it," Dave said.

"I was wondering how your case is going there in Cuyahoga Falls and if you had any idea when you might be back?"

"You know it's finally starting to move a little. Sammi picked up some interesting stuff today so I think next week will be very interesting."

"Leave it to Sammi," said Jim in good cheer.

"Yeah, leave it to Sammi," Dave said as he turned to her and winked.

"Any new burglaries happening around Scranton?"

"No, they seem to have stopped, at least around here. We've linked into other nearby precincts on this one, and in the next few days, we're going to compare evidence. That should tell us a lot."

"That's good. Either they're taking a break or maybe these two are the entire group."

"That doesn't seem likely to me," said Jim. "They were too spread out in the last few months. I find it hard to believe that these two could cover all that territory. And besides, these young kids don't have that much smarts alone, I don't think."

"That's a thought. I hope maybe by the end of next week I'll have some idea of when we're coming back. If we can nail down just a few things, this case should move fast."

"It'll be good to have you back. I hate this damn paperwork you have to do all the time. No wonder you get behind."

Dave laughed. "Sergeant Brady is a stickler for that."

"Between us we get it done, begrudgingly. It certainly isn't my favorite part of the job."

"Mine neither. But hang on a minute, I need a favor."

Dave turned to Sammi and mentioned something to which she agreed enthusiastically. Then he came back on the line.

"Look, Jim, I need you to do a background check on a guy. I don't want it done from here because I don't want to raise any suspicions right now. Do you think you'll have some time to help out?"

"Of course, anything to get you back here fast," he laughed. "Between Tom and Amilio and I, we'll get you what you want."

Dave offered only a few details about Len Worley and asked him to find out everything he could as discreetly as he could.

"No problem. I'll get back to you as soon as we have anything."

"Thanks, Jim."

"Okay, and if you need anything else, let us know."

"I will, thanks."

CHAPTER EIGHT

"You really miss working with Dave, don't you?" asked Julie.

"Yeah, after all these years it seems like one piece is missing. Same thing when Tom is gone. We've gotten so used to each other, but maybe a break occasionally does us all good. We can work alone, but it's just better when we're all here."

Julie smiled. "I know the three referees are a very solid group."

He laughed, "Yes we are and working with people you can trust to back you up when needed really helps when you're in a tough spot."

Julie nodded.

"Dave wants me to check out this guy – Len Worley. It's confidential and he said to keep it quiet. Now you know how Dave is; he'll tell you a little about a person that he wants checked out, but this time he didn't say anything at all. He just gave me a name, approximate age and asked us to check him out because he didn't want to do it himself out there in Ohio."

"Isn't that unusual? Doesn't he usually tell you what it's about?" asked Julie.

"He does and the only reason he wouldn't is because he doesn't want to prejudice me in any way. He just gives me this name and says to find out what you can."

"They must be on to something, don't you think?"

"I do. He also said that next week should be quite interesting."

"It sounds like they're in the middle of a puzzling case with no straightforward clues or answers. A type of quagmire, isn't it?" asked Julie.

"Yeah, some murders are so unpredictable and this seems to be one of those."

"From what I've heard, I've got to wonder why this Lily is the only one being targeted. She doesn't seem like a logical suspect to me. How about some of those other women he was involved with? How about his wife?"

"But Lily was with this guy on that Friday night just before his death. That makes her a major player," Jim said.

"I guess you're right."

"It'll be interesting to find out about this guy Dave is concerned about."

Julie said, "And even more interesting when we find out why Dave and Sammi are concerned about him in the first place."

Jim frowned as he looked over at her. Intrigued as he was by the lack of information Dave had given him, he knew the reason. Still, he was anxious finding out about this person and knew that tomorrow it would be the first thing on his mind at the station.

* * *

Friday morning found Jim Mucci at the station checking all of the files he could find on one Leonard Worley. And he did find some information immediately. Dave had told him that he was in his early to middle fifties but that was about it. Not wanting to prejudice him yet needing to make sure he found the right person, he only gave him what was necessary. And what he found out was rather intriguing. He searched the database again which only added to his own confusion. *What was going on here? Was Dave suspecting something unusual would be turning up? Had Dave already guessed some uncertainty would surface or was it simply a request to keep the investigation as clean as possible? Okay,* he thought, *I have to start from the beginning again.* Therefore, for a second time he entered the raw data into his computer. And he got the same results. Len Worley had received a Bachelor's Degree in Education from Arizona State University and a Master's Degree in Business from Colorado State.

However, that seemed to be where the trail ended. There wasn't any other information on this guy; nothing. He seemed to have materialized at these two colleges, received his degrees and disappeared again for almost five years. He'd have to contact these colleges to find out any more information about him. There was no information about him prior to his college years. There was no high school data, no place of birth, no family data, no personal information, nothing. Five years after graduation from college, he ended up in Cuyahoga Falls, Ohio. He didn't seem to have any other positions prior to that, which in itself was strange. There was a five-year gap between his graduation from Colorado State and his employment at the Children's Aid Group, but no information about those missing five years.

Jim went over to talk to Amilio and called in Julie.

"Look at this data I'm getting; this is really strange."

And he shared with them the information he had found. Actually what he talked about mostly was the missing data. That didn't make any sense at all. Where was this guy born, where did he grow up and where had he been for those five missing years?

Amilio said, "Amigo, this is somewhat peculiar. There has to be a trail of him somewhere unless he changed his identity and then you have to ask why. I think our friend Dave has a real puzzle on his hands."

Julie broke in with, "Let me check my computer data base. I've got several areas that just might bring in something else."

"Like what?"

"Did you check registered offenders, or criminal records? What did you ask for?"

Jim said, "Good idea. I went in looking for basic information, you know, the type that would tell us the basics about any person, but I came up with some definite holes here. So then I went into those special files we have and I still found nothing."

"Give me a few hours. I have several places to look that will bring up information hidden from other areas, if there's anything available at all, that is. Let me give it a try."

"Great. I think Dave was hoping for something by tomorrow morning, if possible. They've got something planned for Saturday night and he'd like to be prepared."

"I'll get right on it."

* * *

Julie spent the better part of Friday afternoon going into one program after another. She had trouble finding out anything about Len Worley's place of birth or early years. Then she found another person who had been born and raised in Westerville, Ohio, which was near Columbus. It caught her eye immediately because the notation at the bottom of the page stated that this person later changed his name to Leonard Worley. Part of the file was wiped clean and there were a few strange notations written in bold print, but the important fact was that there was a person named Leonard Worley whose previous name was Jamie Buckley. These names were linked together and that's the only reason she found him. This could develop into an interesting story. Julie called in Jim and Amilio immediately.

"Now, I'm not positive this is the same person, but if it is, this guy might not be totally stable. It seems when he was around seven years old, he lived in Westerville on a small farm about three miles on the outskirts of town. One night some burglars broke into their home and killed his mother, father, little sister and older brother. Apparently, the only reason he survived and remained undetected was because he had fallen out of his bed and wedged himself between the mattress and the wall. The police figured he didn't move at all because of debilitating fear and horror, and the murderers didn't know he was there. Now the file I found is in a 'not to be opened' file, but police and high-level medical personal can get access. And I was able to do that."

"Damn, maybe he's the one that killed that Matthew and Dave didn't want to prejudice us but just see what we could find out."

"Well, we don't have positive proof that it's the same guy," said Julie.

"That's true," Jim said. "But I can make Dave aware of this anyway."

"Let me finish. There's more."

Amilio and Jim were both waiting anxiously.

"Okay, this little boy was totally traumatized. The file says that it took a few days before the crimes were discovered and this boy was still hiding in his secret spot too petrified to move. Neighbors and friends who hadn't seen any members of the family in days summoned the police. That means this little boy was alone in this horrifying situation for days. The notes say that the crime scene was quite gruesome, which is probably why this little one didn't speak or cry or anything for a long time. Placing him in a psychological facility seemed to be the best answer but it still took time before he began to respond. He stayed at this facility for years and that's where he graduated from high school."

"Well," said Amilio, "that would make sense why there's no high school record for him."

"And," continued Jim, "because this was such a high profile case, his name was changed probably because the authorities felt he could start a better life that way."

"Were the killers ever found?"

"Yes, and they were locals – three of them about the age of twenty-five with impressive records at the time. They were arrested with the guns in their possession, but a lot of evidence was thrown away before these criminals were caught. Their homes still held some of the clothes; it says they tried to burn them unsuccessfully and they had most of the stolen merchandise in their possession at the time of their capture. It was a solid case."

Amilio shook his head. "That little boy had about ten or eleven years of psychological therapy, but you've got to wonder if he ever healed inside."

Jim said, "Good point and this could be who Dave and Sammi are dealing with."

"I think there's a college graduation picture on file. I'm going to dig for that one. We could have it enhanced and that might help them. I haven't found out anything about those missing five years though."

"God," said Amilio. "Not sure I like what they're in the middle of out there. Maybe one of us should request to go and help."

"That would have to be Dave's call. He's been given a subordinate role with the Akron police, so he's not working alone."

"I'll have that picture for you in about an hour."

"Okay, thanks."

* * *

When Jim called Dave back late Friday night, he made sure that Sammi could hear his conversation, too.

"You guys are in the middle of a hell of a situation out there. Let me tell you what we found, actually Julie found this out."

Jim began to relate the entire details of the story, as they knew it. Neither Dave nor Sammi said one word, but they looked at each other in disbelief.

"I'm going to be faxing you a picture of this guy at graduation and also Julie had the picture enhanced and it could give you a better idea of what this guy might look like today. That could help determine if this is the same person."

"That's great Jim. Good work all of you. The picture will be priceless. That's the only way that we'll know for sure."

"But we don't know about those last five years before he ended up in his present job."

"Don't worry," said Dave. "I think Sammi will be able to find that out."

"Where do you want me to send this picture?"

"Let me call you. If I can get some privacy at the Akron station, I think that'll be the best place to have it sent. I want to keep this information private for now, until I know where it leads."

* * *

When they put down the phone, Dave could only stare at Sammi. Neither one said a word at first, lost in thoughts of confusion.

"At least it's beginning to make sense," said Dave. "They gave this kid an alias because he would never have been able to live a normal life in light of all the publicity surrounding those murders. But apparently he was still more unstable than they thought."

Sammi said, "Tomorrow night I want to get him thinking about those missing five years. I can't imagine where he was during that time. Why was that wiped clean?"

"You sort of wonder if Lily's in danger, but then he killed for her. Yet his mind isn't logical. This kid probably needed a lot more help than he got. He saw his entire family killed at seven years old; how does one recover from that?"

"Only with very definite and exact therapy, I would think. It would have to be therapy that taught you how to choose your thoughts and keep them off these dire happenings of the past. They would have had to help him transform himself into a very strong thinking person, if that was possible." She shrugged her shoulders. "Who knows what he was capable of doing?"

"You've got to feel sorry for him, in a way," said Dave. "I'm not sure how these murder charges will play out, but it doesn't seem that he's quite right, does it? He probably never has been."

"The one good thing is that we're aware. Tomorrow night even though some of our talk will definitely be about the trial, I'm going to make sure that we get casual and all talk a little about our personal lives."

"Even talking about the trial should trigger a lot of thoughts from him, don't you think?"

"I agree. And I'm going to be really curious how and why he's letting Lily hold the bag on this one."

"I've got an opinion," said Dave.

"Let's hear it."

"It's like what we've talked about before; he now has her where he wants her. Look, when he came here to work, they were friendly and even though nothing came of it, at least not from Lily's viewpoint, he may have had the semblance of some type of warm feelings from her and that would have been something that had been lacking from his life for years. Maybe he had partly his mother's image or his sister's image hooked up to her and it gave him relief from the anguish I'm sure he still carries around inside."

"That's interesting, and probably true. Yes, maybe he's put a tag onto Lily, but it worries me that it might be something she could never live up to."

"True, but I think that's why he stuck around even though nothing romantic ever developed. I'm not sure he even wanted that. He probably wanted her acceptance and could love her in any capacity."

Sammi reacted to that statement. "Wow, I see where you're going with this. That has to be a part of it, but still it makes me wonder. If either his mother or sister was in this type of trouble, wouldn't he help if he could?"

"I don't have the answer to that one. Still, he'd have Lily in a position where she'd need him if she spent years in jail. And in his mind, maybe that would feed him something that he needed."

Sammi thought for a moment and then tossed out some worrisome thoughts. "Maybe he's held on all these years because Lily hasn't had any boyfriends. By her own admission, she didn't date much at all. Look, Dave, as soon as she has a few dates with someone and something isn't right; he steps in and does something about it. What worries me is this? This time his anger went toward Matthew, because Len thought he was doing a wrong thing. But what if he wasn't married and they began a serious relationship, how do you think Len would have handled that?"

"Good point; it's hard to say. If he's still thinking of her as sister or mother, she'd probably be okay. But if his feelings changed, and they could, sooner or later she could have been in real trouble."

"I'd have to agree with that. Sooner or later something would have happened and she could have been the victim." Sammi added, "Do you think she's safe enough working with him everyday?"

"I do right now, but depending what happens in her trial, who knows? We'll have to make sure she's protected."

Sammi took a deep sigh. "I sure didn't see this one coming."

"Neither did I," said Dave. "At first I thought it was his jealous or angry wife. Then I thought maybe an angry husband of one of his girlfriends or possibly even one of the girlfriends themselves. But I never could have guessed this one."

After a pause, Dave couldn't help but add, "The good part is working with Jim and Julie and Amilio again. Even though they're miles away, it's like there is no distance between us; I like that."

"Me, too, but now I'm so tired that I don't want to think anymore."

"Right," said Dave, "and tomorrow will come soon enough."

* * *

Back in Scranton, a few phone calls placed to Sergeant Brady by the lawyers of the Niemen and Olsen families, consisted of threats and bullying centered on Roy Dawson. His name came up every other day as they called and tried to harass the sarge into dropping the charges or changing the accusations with strong hints that one of their own would be dragged into this quagmire as well. It didn't seem to matter that the suspects were caught with the merchandise from the robberies on their person and in their homes. This alone didn't make them guilty in the eyes of their families or lawyers. Finally, the sarge had to pull rank and told them to contact him through his department's lawyers only and failure to do so would prompt actions from their legal team. He told them clearly and directly that he had a department to run and other crimes to investigate and this was beyond his realm at this time.

"Go after someone that could do you some good. That's not me anymore; we're beyond that."

"But we could make your officer look real bad or we could help you. It's up to you."

"No, it's up to the law and courts and if you try to threaten or bribe me again, you'll have more charges to face than your clients. Do I make myself clear?"

With that rather brassy comment, the lawyer hung up. He was sure he'd probably hear from him again, but hopefully this time they would take a few moments to understand that they were crossing the line in their attempt to get a break for their clients.

The sarge called in Jim, Tom and Roy.

"I want to make very sure, Roy, that you've told all of us the extent of your dealings with those two kids. I get calls everyday from their lawyers threatening to make you a scapegoat, too."

Roy looked upset. "I've told you everything. I've never had dealings with them, but the first time I arrested them on a burglary charge their families got them off quickly. The second time it happened they almost started a vendetta against me. My superiors got some phone calls, too, back then. Yet everything stopped when they got away with it. I've had a few more calls stating that someday they'd get me and they'd never forget. I've heard nothing for the past four plus years and I figured it was behind me. But now, they'll connect me again and I'm sure they'll try to do a lot of damage."

"Well, okay," said the sarge. "This is not a new tactic, but I needed to make sure that you were upfront. They've got nothing but empty threats right now."

"But they could manufacture something," said Jim. "That's not beyond these types."

"I know, I know," said the sarge waiving his arms around. "I just want to know that I've got all the facts right now."

"That's all I know," said Roy, but you could tell he was visibly upset.

"Just settle down, Roy," said the sarge. "I'd be interrogating any of my other officers at this point just like you. If you think of anything else, let me know; I need to be prepared."

Tom said, "Where do you think this is going?"

"Don't know. The evidence against these kids is bad this time, but these high priced lawyers always try to make the department look bad to change the focus. You know that they'll get everything about us that's shady in their minds into the newspapers and on TV. I just don't want any surprise, that's all."

"That's a gimme," said Jim.

"Damn, I wish Dave and Sammi were back. We could use them, but I'm not ready yet to call him back here. It hasn't gotten to that point yet. I hope that they'll be back before all hell breaks loose here. Anybody heard from them?"

Jim updated the sarge to what he felt he could to say. Things were moving and possibly, in the next week he'd have some answers.

"That's good. That's very good. That crime down there needs a quick solution. Damn, everything seems to hit the fan at the same time. Okay, I guess that's all for now, but keep me updated."

* * *

Roy was clearly upset as they gathered at Jim's desk. He didn't say anything but it was obvious that he had a lot on his mind. He was fidgety and uneasy as they tried to hold a small meeting to discuss the facts. He looked down at the floor and then his eyes moved shiftily around the room making it obvious that his concentration was awkward.

"You've got to get control of yourself," said Jim. "This is likely to go on for a while. What's got you so uptight?"

Tom said, "You'd probably feel more secure if you'd been with us for a while, right?"

"Well, yeah, that's right. You people don't really know me; in fact, I thought I had a pretty good first week here, but now it's gone downhill; I really like your operation. Some other places I've been I always felt like the outsider, but here you've made it real plain that you work as a team and that's what I always wanted to do ... to fit in, you know. But now, who knows where this will lead."

"Wait a minute," said Jim. "We're still on a learning curve with each other. And to tell the truth, now we'll be able to see how we all work under pressure. These will be typical days, Roy. Come on now, suspects trying to incriminate us isn't new by any means, but I think I'd be nervous if I was new at a precinct, too. Just be who you are and we'll work this out together."

Roy put out a nervous smile. He was hoping against hope that this would work out. He liked it here and they had the type of loyalty he'd been looking for. But he was worried about what these kids might say. Oh, he'd been honest and told the sarge exactly what had happened. However, they could implicate in ways he wasn't thinking about right now, and that's what really troubled him. Their future allegations worried him most of all.

* * *

One of the officers came running up to Jim's desk. "Get to Sergeant Brady's office; they're gonna be talking about us on TV."

"What the hell ..." he began as they all headed toward the sarge's office. He waived them in immediately.

Jasper Conrad, the lead attorney for the suspects was holding a press conference already. His clients had made bail earlier in the day and he was already rushing to get public opinion on their side and against the police. He was an ostentatious and flamboyant type of personality whose show biz behavior could keep the public transfixed and in awe whether they were interested in the proceedings or not. He would be someone to guard against.

"I'm not taking any questions today, but I need to let the public know what's going on with their own police department. They are railroading my clients, accusing them in a string of burglaries that have taken place in this fair city. These young ones are innocent young kids and quite shaken up at the rough and unfair treatment they've received. We need to be especially careful of the type of behavior that our police department is exhibiting at this time. I definitely see room for improvement. And one of their own fine men in blue could have more involvement in these burglaries than my own young clients. This case will have far-reaching effects on this town. I beg you to keep these young innocent ones in your hearts as we move forward against the big police department. Moreover, don't believe all they tell you; they have ulterior motives in their hidden agenda that I'll speak about to you later. That's all for now. Thank You."

The crowd of reporters surrounded him as he waived them away in a fashion that was more beckoning than not. He seemed to be gesturing to them to follow him and didn't discourage them in any way. He was quite a performer. At this point, the news conference was cut off rather abruptly.

"Well," said the sarge, "he certainly is laying the groundwork heavily right now. He wants to broadcast his position by putting suspicion on us from the beginning."

"His line of fire is quite clear," said Jim. "I've heard of him before, haven't you?" Jim looked around but no one answered. "Yeah, he puts on a lot of theatrics and that's one of his methods for getting the attention where he wants it to go."

Roy looked like he was in shock. What the hell was happening? He couldn't get any straight thoughts in his mind. He hadn't done anything wrong and he was already targeted in these burglaries. What kind of luck was he having anyway? The usual and it was always bad. He kept shaking his head in disgust.

Just then, the phone rang.

"I've been expecting this," said the sarge. "It must be my friend the mayor."

"Hi Ron, how's it going?" he said as he shook his head in the affirmative. "Yeah I saw the news conference."

"What the hell's he talking about having one of our men in blue on suspicion?"

"I've got no idea at this time, Ron. You know that's a tactic that a lot of lawyer's use. You can't have called me about that?"

"No, no, I didn't, but I did wonder if you knew what he was hinting at."

"It could be a lot of things, Ron, but trying to throw suspicion on the police is not a new idea. God, you know that."

"Oh yeah. Do you know this guy Jasper?"

"Not really, do you?"

"Yeah, I do. I've seen his work and I've heard about it, too. He's one of the most underhanded and devious lawyers around. He's been up on ethic charges at least a few times that I know about. You might want to look into his background, which might be one way to get him to back off."

"Really? Well, that's good to know. Thanks, Ron. I think this one will play out for a wide audience, don't you?"

"Oh definitely. He'll use public opinion as often and as nasty as he can. He'll be a problem. Do we have good proof? I know we've got a lot of seniors who are scared and I want to make sure we've got solid evidence."

"We do, Ron. And these kids made bail this morning. You know their parents are rich and influential so I know that we'll have a fight on our hands."

"Okay, but we can't let the guilty go free, no matter what. I trust your judgment Sam, but keep me informed."

"Will do, Ron."

The sarge turned to his group. "Well, you heard most of it. The mayor wants us to catch these burglars that are terrifying our seniors, but he wants to make sure we've got solid evidence. He's familiar with this lawyer and didn't seem to be overly concerned about his speech. That's the type of method he uses all the time."

"It's good to know that we've got a good relationship with the mayor," said Jim. "It's good to have him on our side again."

"Right now, but when things begin to heat up, he'll start getting his dander up. Even though he's basically fair minded, he can still get ruffled by public opinion."

Tom said, "I guess we all can."

About this moment, Amilio came strolling in followed by LeBron and Tyrone.

Amilio said, "Looks like we're heading into the spotlight again. I hope everyone here knows how to take the heat."

They all smiled and Tom said, "We'd better by now. We're in the heat half of our existence here, but I handle it better when we're all together. I can't wait for Dave and Sammi to get back."

They all agreed on that and then broke up to get back to their regular routines, which would be there no matter how many speeches Jasper Conrad decided to make. He was one blurb on TV, but their other cases were with them all the time.

* * *

On Saturday morning, while waiting for Sammi to return from the beauty shop, Dave went down to the Akron precinct to get those pictures that Julie was ready to send. He almost wished they were wrong about Len for two reasons. One reason would be that Lily could be in danger if he snapped again. And two, it could mean that this cold blooded murderer was still a child inside and one who had witnessed a horrendous personal crime on his family. How did you punish someone like that? Oh, it was true that he couldn't be allowed the chance to hurt anyone else so he must be taken into custody for his own protection as well as others, because he needed help. He'd needed help all of his life and somehow no one had been successful in giving it to him.

When Dave saw the pictures come across the fax machine his heart dropped. He had only met Len briefly one time, but he knew that Len Worley, alias Jamie Buckley was the person working at the Children's Aid Group. He stared at the pictures a few minutes longer; he wasn't sure why. There was no doubt. He felt a cold chill slowly inch its way up his spine. *Well*, he thought, *we have a hell of a problem on our hands. Good thing we'll see him tonight and Sammi should be able to pick up a lot. But I have to monitor her, too. Sometimes these sessions are very hard on her, yet we need her to pick up everything she can tonight. Good thing I'll be with her.*

He thanked Detective Anchor on his way out.

"Okay, Dave. Check in with me next week. I'm going to need a second pair of eyes on some of this evidence; I want to go over it again. I figured you'd be the perfect person. I know some of it points to Lily, but that can't be helped. We need to be objective here."

"Thanks, I'd like that," he said as he thought by then he might be going in a totally different direction. And yet, he'd only read about the evidence and hadn't really had a chance to see it. Maybe with what they had learned he'd see the evidence in a new light. Yes, it would be a good idea for him to go over all the proof they had. It was hard to be objective when you were quite sure that one person had done it. To step back and be impartial seemed almost impossible at times like that. Yet he had a real good reason to be detached and neutral; he knew Lily was innocent.

He waived as he walked out and headed back to the motel to wait for Sammi.

* * *

She knew immediately as she walked in the door and saw the look on Dave's face that he was trying to hold steady. He didn't quite succeed.

"It's him, isn't it?"

"There's no doubt in my mind, but you've seen him more times than I have. Look at these pictures."

Sammi seemed to have a pained expression as she stared at the pictures.

"I know this will sound funny, but I'm not sure who to feel sorry for. Does that make sense?"

"Perfect sense," said Dave taking a deep breath. This case was so incredibly emotional at times that he couldn't even concentrate on it. There was too much pain all around.

Sammi went over and sat by him on the couch. "It's too early for a glass of wine, but I sure could use one right now. My insides feel all tied up. I feel so sorry for Jamie Buckley. That poor little kid," she said and paused for a moment, "but he's not a kid anymore. And he seemed to have behaved fine for what – twenty years?"

"We still need to find out about those five years."

"Yeah, I know. That could tell us something."

The phone rang. It was Billy.

"Hi, Ms. Sammi. How are you?"

"I'm fine Billy. How are you?"

"I'm fine, too. Thanks for asking. I called because I'm taking Marsha to a party tonight and I won't be home when you get here. I'm sorry that we won't see you tonight. Marsha says she is, too."

"Dave and I are sorry we won't see you either. But you have a good time at your party, okay?"

"We will. It should be a lot of fun. But I wanted you to know that I'll miss seeing you."

"It was nice of you to call and tell me, but I'm sure we'll see you soon."

"Okay, bye."

And he hung up rather abruptly. He was so refreshing. He was just what she needed at that moment. When she turned to look at Dave, her expression and demeanor were completely different than they had been a minute ago. Gone was the tension that she felt all over her body and gone was the worrisome expression that had covered her face. Billy had that type of effect on people.

Dave laughed. "You look better already."

"He's magic, isn't he? He has many worries on his mind, but he still called to say that he was sorry he'd be gone by the time we got there tonight. That's so simple that it's beautiful."

She decided to go back and sit with Dave. They had time right now and decided to enjoy their closeness and relax in each other's company. Her body leaned against his and they seemed to be able to communicate their feelings to each other silently, without words.

"Just when things look as scary and depressing as can be, Billy calls and he can brighten up your day even before he says anything out loud."

"I know what you mean. And that's why Lily has maintained a good life with him around."

"Yeah," she said from her own thought world. And nothing more was said for a while. They simply sat there relishing the beauty of some people.

CHAPTER NINE

Carter Olsen and Brad Niemen snickered as they got together for a leisurely Saturday afternoon. They felt exonerated after being bailed out by their parents and already vindicated in the arena of public opinion. A lot of publicity had accompanied their release; their fathers made sure of that and now it was over to Carter's house to do as they wished since their fathers had already put this unpleasantness behind them and gone on to more exciting business.

They felt that they had fooled many people and even confused their parents once again about their latest escapades. It gave their fathers another reason to try to crack down on the police department and keep the political machinery from settling down into a comfortable position. The boys had no doubt that their parents would be creating havoc for the community again and they were in their glory for all the excitement that they were causing. It was one obvious way to get their fathers' attention, a feat that wasn't always easy taking into account their busy schedules. They could sit back and watch everything unfold because their parents would be indignant about anyone trying to send their boys to prison. After all, they were prominent citizens and spent a lot of money in their communities, and they felt entitled to special treatment in return.

"Did you see the look on Roy's face?" said Carter laughing in a manner not too unlike some hyenas in their most confused state. His knees kept leaping up toward his chest as his entire body took in all of the hysterics it could handle.

"I thought he'd crap on the spot," said Brad as his body took on similar contortions, as it tried to handle what was deemed a hilarious situation.

"Boy, that's one cop we've got sweating and he knows we mean business," said Carter. "We almost got him in trouble last time. He's such a loner that none of the other police officers were ever ready to back him up. I wonder what he's doing here anyway."

"That's a good one. Probably trying to get as far away from us as he possibly could. I think we really scared him last time."

That sent them both again into crazy and peculiar laughter, which lasted for a few more moments. Then it seemed that the laughter was over and they got more serious.

"They've got some stuff on us this time," said Brad. "I didn't have time to stash the last stuff away and it was in my room when they searched it. I'm kind of worried about that."

"Don't sweat it. No one is going to cross our dads. They'll get us off. But I think we'd better lay low for a while after this one."

Brad said, "You really think we'll get off?"

"Yeah, sure. The worst we could get would be community time – no jail time, that's for sure. My dad would have a fit and wouldn't allow that to happen. But how did they know it was us. Those two old men couldn't see passed their noses. Maybe we should have roughed them up a little more."

Brad was the more thoughtful of the two. "You know, I'm getting tired of all this stuff. Maybe we could try some other stuff for a while."

"Like what?" asked Carter, not realizing that Brad had other interests on his mind and that he had gotten tired of their stimulating side adventures.

"Okay, look, we barely made it through college, but we did get a degree. I think I'd like to get some kind of real career started that was fun, you know, not too many working hours, but stimulating in some way or other. Then I want to try to see if I could get somewhere playing the guitar. We were both quite good at one time."

"Really? You want to go back to that safe stuff?"

"I think I would, at least for a while. This last job just wasn't as much fun anymore and we don't need the money."

Carter said, "I never did it for the money; I did it for the excitement."

"Think about this. Playing music in some hot band on the side can get us a lot of attention from girls and a lot of prestige. What do you say? Let's give that a try."

"It's a thought, at least for a while. Don't mind the girl thing, that's for sure. And we could even buy our way into some decent band. With my dad's connections, I know we could do it. Hell, wouldn't our parents love that? My dad's always on my back to start doing something responsible as he calls it."

"It's what I want to do," said Brad. "These last few jobs just weren't as exciting as the rest. I think this type of stuff has just used itself up with me. But think about playing at some of those hot spots in a real cool band; I could definitely handle that for a while."

"Yeah, I can see that. Let's contact Phil Eden on Monday. He might have something for us. Hey, we can go over to the Earthman Café tonight and see what's going on. It'll give us an idea what they're doing lately."

Brad laughed. "Okay, but let's wait on contacting Phil. I think I'd need a couple of weeks to practice up on some of this stuff. It's been a while since I played my guitar seriously."

"Okay, tell you what. Let's take a few weeks and get back up to speed. Shouldn't take us very long and then we'll contact Phil. He owes us a couple of favors anyway."

"That's right, and besides he was after us a while back to join them anyway, remember? Should be a shoe in."

They both sat back and got lost in themselves for a while. Brad was a little more timid than Carter; he'd always been the follower.

* * *

They were both avoiding one subject, at least aloud. Their home life wasn't as good as they tried to pretend. Carter's real father was never in the picture and this present one was always on the edge of politics but had never been able to win an election. He had money but even that couldn't buy him one of the offices that he'd wanted. And Brad's stepfather loved the power connected to his wealth. He flaunted it most of the time and was in competition with Carter's dad adding up enemies. These two boys were in the middle. This was Brad's second stepfather and he was surprised this marriage had lasted almost ten years. Carter was on his third stepfather although this one had been around since he was eight. Both had felt tension and frustration in their homes for quite a while, which left them wondering when the word divorce would come up again and where they would end up next time. Coming of age hadn't lessened the heartaches that were constantly around regarding the position they held in their lives. These two ignored and disregarded boys did everything they could for attention and succeeded best when they were in some kind of trouble. Then their stepfathers used them for publicity as well as to make their own point about the troubles in society. The boys didn't mind being used in that way, at least it was one type of attention.

"Was your dad very mad this time?" asked Brad, who at twenty-three was still very concerned about parental attitude.

"He was more pleased about getting attention and being able to use it. Honestly, sometimes I don't get it. I really thought this time he'd be furious at least inside our home where true feelings come out. Instead he was indignant and already practicing his role. How about yours?"

"He did yell quite a bit for about an hour or so, but then he shut up. I thought it was over until my mom came in. She was having a hissy fit about unwelcomed attention and then she went on a tirade about everything she's done for me; you know the drill."

"Mine ignore each other a lot; I think I like it better that way," Carter said.

"Yeah," said Brad but his thoughts raced around his head thinking he wished he'd had a more normal life. His mom and this stepfather argued and fought ever since he could remember, but he never thought they'd get a divorce; his mother was quite happy about having an upscale role in society. Yet she was running around as was his stepfather; it had been going on for years so he figured they were used to their lifestyles. Families never meant that much to him, only his grandparents understood him, but they had both died a while back and he'd felt alone since then.

"Hey, Brad, what are you thinking about?"

"Just getting my guitar skills back in order," he lied. He'd never want Carter to know how he felt. He'd never want anyone to know. He always hoped things would get better, but they never did.

"Okay, let's get started tomorrow – where? Your place or mine?" asked Carter

"I think there's more peace and quiet here. I think I need that, especially at the beginning. Do you have a problem with that?"

"No, not at all. My dad's going to be out as usual and it doesn't matter if my mom's home; she won't bother with us anyway."

Brad left shortly after that. He was in a crappy mood tonight. He wondered about life and where he was heading, something he'd never discuss with his friend. Carter never thought past tomorrow, but Brad did. He also thought a lot about yesterday. But answers never came to him, only more questions. He kept at it, hoping in time, some great idea would come to him about what to do with his life.

* * *

"I'm telling you again that I think we should find a place for that kid of yours to live; he's too disruptive around here. When's he going to straighten up?"

James Niemen hated it because Catherine always protected her son Brad. Finally, he had found a wife he was happy with, at least most of the time, but she always had a bug up about her son, even when he wasn't in trouble. Hell, he didn't know what to do with him; he never had. He'd always been a problem even as a small child, but now he kept getting into one mess after another. And he knew if he kept this up, he would end up in jail or prison. He didn't want to ship him off to an apartment or anywhere else where he didn't know what was going on. He could cause unwelcomed publicity.

"I don't know what's wrong with him; he's probably going through another stage, you know. He always was a thoughtful child and you never knew what was on his mind, but in the last several years I think he's trying to figure out what to do with his life."

"Well you'd better help him figure it out. This is more bad publicity and something we don't need. I hear all kind of rumblings around the club and it's embarrassing. We worked so hard to maintain a good status there and this one kid of yours is ruining it, I tell you. I'm glad you've only got one."

That irritated Catherine. James had two daughters from a previous marriage, grown and married now, but they had caused their share of annoyances being raised in the middle of privilege.

"Look, I've been in that club for years and there are always a lot of rumors going on. This isn't the worse I've heard by far and your girls caused some, remember?" she said.

"Well, we don't need to make any more enemies or give anyone more ammunition against us."

"Gees, James, how come this bothers you all of a sudden? You usually enjoy the attention, good or bad."

She knew that would shut him up and irritate him as well. She recognized the signs that it was time to drop the subject. Catherine knew she had stepped over the line this time and retreated. James wanted Brad to move out with restrictions and couldn't hide the fact, yet he didn't want to threaten her territory. Her son had been a sore subject for a while and she knew she'd better leave it alone. And with this added trouble, it was more annoyance to be overcome.

Catherine was James's third wife and it had taken her a while to get that status. She'd dated him for the last two years of his second marriage and was about to give up and then he finally divorced and married her. This was her third marriage as well; she'd finally climbed the social ladder a few rungs, had money, and status as she'd never dreamed possible and she really did love James, in her own way. But money and status were more important to her, a fact she usually kept well hidden.

Finally James said, "This'll all work out and be over before long, so settle down."

"Yeah, I'm sure it will," said Catherine trying to put out the fire that she had started. And with that comment, James seemed to relax some. Yet she knew her son was never far from his mind. He'd been looking for a solution, but not that forcibly, a mistake he was beginning to recognize. Just then, the telephone rang.

Catherine said, "Hi there Carter. Yes, we plan to make it tonight."

James nodded in the background.

"Okay, I'll tell him. See you then."

"George wants us to get to his house about a half hour earlier tonight. He needs to talk to you about something."

That ended the conversation. There was no doubt what Carter wanted to talk to him about; it was always about the boys.

* * *

By Saturday afternoon, both Sammi and Dave found it hard to settle down and keep themselves on even keel. Tonight's dinner was so vital in their eyes that they tried repeatedly to think what would be the best conversation to bring about the most fruitful results.

"If we get him talking about the past in any capacity, it'll have to trigger thoughts from him about his young life. Remember what I've told you, people say a few things in words, but their thoughts take in everything they know about the subject. And unless his thoughts get too deep, I should be able to pick up a lot."

"Do you think that might be a dangerous way to go?"

"I don't. It's perfectly natural to be talking about the past, about fun things you've done, or accomplishments you've made in your life. Maybe we can get Lily talking about how she and Billy first got together and you and I can talk about our background and that will have to get him thinking about the past, whether he says any words out loud or not."

Dave was thoughtful. "And to be sure, I imagine his mind constantly goes back to what happened to him as a child."

"I'm sure that it seldom leaves him and that should bring his thoughts to the present and have him thinking about the crime. However, I was also thinking of the loneliness caused by all those years he lived without a family that seemed to be close and loving before. That's probably part of the reason for his present anger. In some ways I think that Lily took him back to what he had lost and what he needed in the present and so he developed a great need to protect her because of the importance he placed on her."

"Yeah," said Dave, "this is going to be a tough case. I mean I know he committed murder, but he's also a victim. God, I hate this type of case."

"I know, but our job is to help prove Lily's innocence and then let the authorities deal with Len. I'll be curious to know how this plays out."

"The police hardly talked to anyone else; they were so sure that Lily committed this crime. Now you have to wonder what kind of alibi he has for the time of the crime. He may have planned something to say a while back, but he wasn't even a suspect, so now he may be caught off guard."

"Right."

Dave knew that Sammi wanted to relax for a while and take a nap. She needed all of her mental resources to be rested and prepared for tonight. Her concentration had to be in top shape to perform at her best. As she stretched on the bed, Dave noticed that it didn't take but a few moments before she was beginning to breathe deeper and slower. She had exhausted herself by trying to decide how best to take advantage of the evening. He knew she felt that this was their last chance, but it wasn't. It was an important opportunity yet there were other ways to get to Len. But knowing Sammi he knew she wanted it settled tonight if possible, and there was a good chance that could happen.

He looked at her sleeping so peacefully. He was happy with their marriage and felt their compatibility was one of the main reasons. Her talent certainly made their lives together more interesting and he never expected to hook up with someone like her. He wondered how they would have done had he married her right after college rather than her best friend Kelly. He couldn't imagine. After all, he had changed as much since college as she had. Although it took a while for them to get together, life could be unpredictable at times.

He looked out the window for a while. It was a nice day and the clouds were light in the sky against a medium blue backdrop. He always felt small looking at the upper part of the universe, yet he relished the feeling it gave him as he attempted to be a part of it. He wished he was a little sleepy, but he wasn't. There was no way that he could convince his mind and body to rest; it didn't work for him that way. Maybe he could read a little. Maybe he could … His cell phone rang.

* * *

"Jim, good to hear from you. What's up?"

"Wanted you to be aware of what's going on here. The boys made bail early this morning and they're on their way, but probably not for long. We've got good evidence on them this time."

Jim told Dave about the evidence found both on their person and in their homes, which was obtained with a subpoena and made everything legal and above board. He also mentioned how Roy was still nervous about the fact that these two guys had fingered him and why.

"You say he seems nervous about it. Why? That happens all the time. Do you think he's trying to hide something?"

"I don't think so. I worked with him all week and he seems to be trying hard to fit in. He said at other precincts that he found it hard to get into the groups; you know how some of them are, but he was happy how we worked around here. He was beginning to relax and I thought he was cooperative. Still, with this thing now, it has him worried. I wish Sammi was here; she could tell us for sure what was bugging him."

"That would help."

"Look, I know you're doing what you have to do right now and you'll be back before too much more goes on. Their lawyers are only starting to work on their behalf so it'll take a little while yet. We've got time."

"I appreciate the update. I feel like I'm torn between two places and both are important."

"Don't worry about us; we'll handle things until you get back. How's your case going?"

Dave told him part of what they had discovered. For some reason he didn't feel inclined to tell Jim everything and didn't make the dinner tonight sound as critical as it was. He didn't want to jinx anything so he held his information close.

"I think our robberies will take a while to work out. I've seen these cases before with high-priced lawyers and nothing's ever simple or quick with them."

"Yes, but everyone is entitled to the best defense they can find," said Dave. "And with these wealthy and influential people it always takes a lot longer than usual. But that's good. I'd like to be back in time for this."

"I hope so, Dave. I'm getting damn tired of doing all that paperwork."

Dave laughed. "Not too much fun is it?"

"No, it's not and Tom and I are splitting the task right now. He was saying just yesterday that this is one more reason that he wants you back here quickly. Besides, I'd like your opinion on this Roy guy. You always have sharp instincts on people."

"You and Tom do just fine. If you feel he's really trying right now, then he probably is. He may realize it could be one of his last chances so he's going to straighten up. I hope so. His file shows that he's had good experience."

"And most of his familiarity is in this part of Pennsylvania anyway. We could cash in on that since some of those robberies were a little ways away from Scranton. It's too bad he hadn't been here just a little bit longer and we'd gotten to know him better. It's hard for us to try to figure out everything at once and it's making him anxious, too. It's just a tough situation."

"It'll work itself out in time."

"Yeah, I know. I'd better go. Julie sends her regards and wants to have lunch with Sammi as soon as you get back."

"Okay, she's napping right now. She's so tired, and it's mostly mental."

"Right. Good luck to you both."

"Same to you."

* * *

Billy paced the floor of the kitchen area as Lily began preparing the preliminaries for the dinner she was giving tonight. He was frustrated and his mouth couldn't help a slight pout, which he found difficult to conceal. He felt his bottom lip move and pucker slightly, a habit that he'd tried to conquer, but failed. His purposeful walk and unsteady manner didn't seem to concern his mom, as she continued with her busy duties. However, he knew his mind was indecisive and wandering and he was quite sure his mom realized what was bothering him. She always knew.

He grumbled mostly to himself as he walked back and forth, although some of his complaining did spill outward as he paced slowly and usually at the same meter. Lily paid him no attention; she was busy cooking. That was good. Sometimes it took him a few minutes to straighten out his mind. Now he was ready, but began slowly.

Finally, he said. "What are you having for dinner?"

"I thought tonight deserved steaks and I'm going to have baked potatoes, my special Caesar salad and since I've got time, I plan to bake some sourdough bread. What do you think?"

"I think that's wonderful and I want to stay home tonight."

There he finally said what was on his mind. Lily knew that he'd already called Sammi and Dave sharing his disappointment that he wouldn't be here.

"You have another commitment tonight, Billy. I'm sure your party will be fun as well."

"I know, I know," he said as he waived her off with his arms trying to throw off something in the air that wasn't there. "And I always have fun when I'm with Marsha, but I want to be both places."

She laughed. Everyone felt that way at times, yet you knew that Billy would always express what was on his mind.

"I wouldn't cancel my party because I want to go there, too. I work with so many nice people that I know we'll have fun. But I want to be here, too."

"Life is that way sometimes," she said. "Everything happens at once. But Sammi and Dave will be here for a while yet and I'm sure we can have another dinner with them."

That made Billy smile. He liked Sammi a lot and thought Dave was nice as well.

"They make a nice couple, don't you think? Sammi made a good choice."

"I'd have to agree with that. They seem happy together."

"How come you never married, mom?"

There was that question again. Billy came up with it quite often and never seemed to be satisfied with the answer she gave him.

"It simply didn't happen, Billy. I don't know why. I've already told you I almost got married once when I was much younger but he died in a car accident and after that, I'm not sure why no one else came around. But I've always liked my job and worked hard and then I met you and life has been good to me."

It was obvious that Billy liked that part of the answer.

"But I think you'd be happier with someone to take care of you, kind of like I try to take care of Marsha."

"That might be true, but I am happy with you and my other friends. I'm okay, really I am."

Billy was thoughtful for a moment. "Maybe Mr. Len would marry you."

That was another comment that arose with frequency as Billy always thought they would be a good match.

"Len is very nice and we're good friends, but that's all. Sorry about that."

Billy smiled. He liked the way she always kept things light and uncomplicated yet still said what she meant so he wasn't confused.

"You don't think you'd ever want to marry Mr. Len?" He had to ask again; he was never sure if there was a possibility or not.

"No, I don't. He's a friend, Billy, a good friend and that's important, too. How do you feel about your friend, Maryanne?"

Billy nodded emphatically. "She's nice and I like her a lot."

"Do you like her the same way that you like Marsha?"

"Oh no, I love Marsha; she's my girlfriend."

"But you can see the difference, right?"

"Yes," he said with some hesitancy.

"I like Len the same way you like Maryanne. I always hope he'll be a good friend."

"Yeah, I understand now. Friends are important, too."

That seemed to satisfy him; at least he understood the answer. But he still felt that his mom would be happier if she was married.

"I guess I'd better start to get ready for my party. I have to pick up Marsha at 6:00 PM."

Lily nodded and watched him covertly as he left the room. He had the same feelings and attitudes as anyone else, but he always said what was on his mind. That seemed to be the only difference.

Then he peeked again into the kitchen from the doorway. "What are you having for dessert?"

"I'm having apple pie, your favorite."

He looked at her thoughtfully. "But there'll be some left for me to have later, right?"

"Absolutely, I'm making a big pie."

"Alright," he said gleefully as he left.

Lily heard his footsteps going into his room. He was such a delight and she treasured him. He had made her life worthwhile.

* * *

Her mind drifted back a little to her earlier life. She remembered living in an orphanage from the age of four. Her parents died and there was no one else to care for her. She barely remembered them anymore. Sometimes she still struggled to get a picture of her mom in her mind, but usually she failed. She only had one picture of her parents that had been pinned to her blouse when she arrived, but the photo was blurry and she couldn't make out their faces. Still she treasured it and took it out on occasion to view.

Her orphanage years hadn't been too bad, truly; she had fared well. Her meals were good; she'd received clothes as needed and got help with her homework on occasion. The only drawback was that she witnessed others being adopted and her turn never came. She hated being lined up with all the others when people came to view the available children. She wasn't an attractive child; there was no other way to say it. As an adult, she had improved somewhat, but she'd never be a sought after beauty and she accepted that. Yet as she saw the others one after another finding a loving home, it was difficult for her to accept. At first, she cried a lot, but later on she accepted her fate and believed it made her stronger and more self-reliant. And there was something positive in that.

Later she met Sonny Jones, a soldier who came home on leave. He loved her immediately and thought she was beautiful. Actually, he was rather common looking himself, but they found in each other what they needed. They were only weeks away from their wedding when he died. Her life shut down for the second time after that and it took a while before she put any faith in the future. As she grew past this second tragedy, she realized that good memories could help a lot in keeping a good attitude for the future. She chose a caring profession, which created a passion in her that satisfied her from the beginning.

Suddenly, there was a loud whistle sound. The kettle on her stove caught her off guard. She had drifted so far back into her early years that she had forgotten for a few moments what a dilemma her current life presented. She made her pot of tea, checked her pie in the oven and sat back at the table thinking. She had definitely gotten herself in a reminiscent-type mood and had to admit she was rather enjoying it. She remembered the first time that she had seen Billy. He wasn't happy and self-confident in those days. He'd been living at the orphanage since he was about four or five years old. His parents were alcoholics, couldn't cope with him, and honestly, didn't want him around. He'd never received any individual training for a special needs child and had mostly been his own teacher. He was about twelve years old when she spotted a very with-drawn and noticeably depressed child trying desperately to stay away from the crowd. When she heard his story, she made him her first mission. She knew she could help him and devoted her extra time during the day exclusively to him.

"Mom, which shirt should I wear? Can I wear a light blue shirt with my black pants? Is that alright?"

"Absolutely; that would look great."

"I thought so but I always like your opinion. Thanks, mom."

Then he was gone as quickly as he had appeared. Sometimes her heart would almost break with happiness when she realized Billy's meaningful position in the world. She had made a big difference in the life of this child. And looking back on her life many years from now, she knew that no one would care whether she had married or not; no one would care that she herself didn't get adopted and no one would remember that she was not considered a striking beauty. But it would matter that she'd been important in the life of this one child, a Down syndrome boy whom many had ignored. They didn't know what he was capable of and she had brought him up to his full capability. No matter what happened in the rest of her life, Billy was considered by far her greatest accom-plishment.

"Mom, which tie should I wear? I brought down two ties because I like them both but I'm not sure which one I should wear with this blue shirt."

Okay, Billy. This is a reality check," she said. "Which one do you think would look the best?"

She liked to throw decisions back at him. He could handle them, but sometimes he liked to lean on her.

"I personally think they would both look good."

Then he looked at her questioningly.

"Me, too. So which one would you like to wear with that blue shirt?"

"I like this one," he said. She could tell he was hoping that his mom would pick one out and make the decision for him. But she refused to do that.

"I think you made a great choice."

He came over and hugged her. He hugged her a lot. He always told her he was so glad to have a mom. She thought sometimes that her heart would shatter with delight; he had that affect on her..

* * *

She couldn't help but remember the first few times that she helped a twelve-year old Billy with his homework. He warned her that he was stupid and didn't think anyone could help him.

"Let me try anyway, okay?" she said and got an excited look in return.

His little heart was waiting for someone to look beyond his doubts, beyond his syndrome and prove him wrong.

"You want to spend time with me?" he said rather surprised.

"I'd like that. Is that okay with you?"

"Sure, I'd like that a lot. Most people don't want to spend time with me; I know they think I'm kind of boring and stupid."

Lily laughed and he looked at her strangely. He didn't know what to make of this person who had an important job at the Children's Aid Group, had an office of her own with her name on the door, yet she still wanted to spend time with him.

So they started first with math, which seemed to be most difficult for him. Surprisingly, after only a few sessions he began to catch on and improved considerably that first semester. Then his reading needed help, which had suffered greatly, and it improved as well. Yet most important was the fact that Billy began to take pride in himself and he began to feel smart. Within a short time came the possibility that he could help around the facility during the day in his spare time, and he performed tasks that no one would have believed possible several months before. He had a good mind, and thought deep and powerful thoughts. Other adults around were beginning to realize his potential and no longer shunned him, but included him in activities that previously were off limits. In addition, another important fact was that he and Lily became a team, a fact that she realized as well as he did. Then she tried to become his legal guardian, an idea that totally thrilled him. But because fate sometimes steps in, it happened that she was cleared for adopting him, even though she was single. It seemed that with her background in social work and humanities, she had an edge and at thirty-two years old Lily became the mother of a fifteen year old in a match that could only have happened with the angels involved.

"Okay, mom I'm leaving. Do I look okay?"

"You look mighty handsome. You have a great time and enjoy your party."

"Thanks and you enjoy your dinner party, mom. Tell Sammi and Dave hello for me and tell them I'll see them soon."

"I'll do that."

"Okay, my ride's here and I've got to go. Love you mom."

Although occasionally Billy was allowed to drive with supervision during the day for short distances, he wasn't allowed to drive at night alone and so a friend of his from work was picking him up and then they'd pick up Marsha. Billy was completely accepted and never had a problem getting someone to take him from one place to another. He was very sociable and considered good company.

Lily watched him get into the car and waved them off. Billy, a well-adjusted, congenial and satisfied person was a benefit to society. It had been a long walk from the disheartened and dejected child she'd met so many years ago, but his strong and happy heart made the journey worthwhile. Besides, Lily was happy to be part of that process; she felt privileged.

CHAPTER TEN

Jim Mucci and Tom Harrington felt that they had ample evidence when these burglary suspects came back in front of the judge in a few weeks. They had two eyewitnesses and another neighbor who could testify as to the height and approximate weight of these suspects. Plus this new witness could zero in on the clothes they were wearing the night of the robbery. They also recovered several items from the burglary, three of which were on their person during their arrest and four other significant pieces that were found on the dresser of Brad Niemen's home, which they had obtained with a proper search warrant. One of these items was the crucial watch of James Malloy that he was hoping against hope would be found and returned. His wife had a special inscription added for their 50th wedding anniversary that was priceless to him.

"You keep going over that evidence," said Tom as he watched Jim late on Saturday afternoon repeatedly checking what they had.

Jim laughed. "I know and I also know it won't change, but I keep wondering if maybe this has a bigger story than we're seeing here. Something doesn't feel exactly right to me."

"Like what?" Tom asked.

"These kids don't need money; they're loaded. Why would they be committing these petty robberies? And don't tell me that they wanted their parents' attention. There were plenty of other ways to get it like they've done in the past."

"You've given this a lot of thought apparently; what do you think?"

"I wonder if these kids were involved in something else. Nothing's clear to me right now, but this scenario just isn't doing it for me. It's starting to drive me crazy. Julie tells me to leave it alone until more facts come to the surface. I know she's right, but I can't seem to let it go."

"Somehow you're hooked on this one," said Tom. "It happens. Maybe you'll dream the answer. That's what Sammi talks about sometimes."

He laughed. "Don't I wish she was here right now?"

"Yeah, me too. Those two are powerful together. I hear they've got some hot leads to follow up right now in Ohio."

Jim said, "That's what Dave hinted at when I talked to him earlier today. He didn't say much; I think he's somewhat suspicious about a few things. I'm sure he'll let us know when he can."

"He's on a tough case this time. Wish we could help."

"Yeah, so do I, but I'm not even going to offer. If he needs us, he'll let us know. In the meantime, I'm ready to stop for the day. And I'm going to put this one in the back part of my mind until Monday. That'll make Julie really happy."

* * *

Sammi was nervous on the ride over to Lily's house; she couldn't hide it. She had to get herself in gear and be ready for whatever Len would be thinking. Plus, she couldn't take notes, which made it more difficult for her. She had to remember his main thoughts and let the others slide. Yet she realized if his thoughts were shocking enough, it wasn't likely she'd forget them.

"Trying to get yourself ready mentally, right?" asked Dave. He'd noticed her quiet yet fidgety behavior, which was unlike her.

"I am and sometimes when I can get myself worked up a little, I do my best work. And I want to get it right tonight. It's tough knowing that Lily is so unaware of anything that I feel like I've let her down. But I think it would be dangerous for her at this point."

"Absolutely. It would be too much to ask her to be that good of an actress. She's known him for years; they've been close friends and then for her to find out about his background and the fact that he was the one that murdered Matthew; I know few that could pull that off. It'll be hard enough later on when she has to be told."

"If I can get enough evidence tonight, then what?"

"Depending on what it is, I thought I might get Sergeant Brady involved. He knows you can learn things and let him get in touch with Detective Anchor and see what he can convey to him. If he's with us, we can check out your info and proceed from there."

"I'm hoping if we get enough tonight, this case may end soon."

"That might very well be true. Let's see what happens. Now I know under the circumstances it seems silly to tell you to relax, but you have to be calm and let me help. I know when you're in need of help and I can take over for a while, okay?"

"That's why it's good working with you."

"Well, here we are, right on time."

"Doesn't look like Len's here yet; I don't see his car. Let's get started."

* * *

As they walked in the door, it was clear that Lily was excited for this evening. She had no clue as to what she would face in the future and was looking forward to a fun evening with friends. Sammi felt a pain in her heart when she realized that Lily would soon discover one of her so-called friends was dangerous and unstable.

"Len should be here any minute. He's seldom late, but I didn't get a chance to tell him the two of you would be here. For some reason, I couldn't get in touch with him today and he'd been off work for a few days. Oh, wait, he's pulling up now."

It was obvious through the window that Len was concerned about the other car that was in Lily's driveway. He walked around it slowly and looked back and forth from the house to the car a few times, and he hesitated. Lily opened the door.

"Hi Len, come on in."

As he entered and saw Sammi and Dave, he definitely blanched. His thoughts were scrambled and he almost panicked. But he had inner strength and took control of himself rather quickly.

"Hello, Sammi, and you must be Dave Patterson. Good to meet you." And they went into the living room where Lily had hors d'oeuvres and other goodies ready for them.

What the hell are they doing here? he thought. *Can't believe this is just a social thing. These two are on a fishing expedition. I wonder if Lily knows. I have a strong feeling that I should get the hell out of here, but I can't. It wouldn't look good. Okay, okay, I must take control of myself. I can make it through this evening. Why in the hell didn't Lily tell me? I didn't have to come tonight.*

"I tried to call you yesterday and again this morning, but I couldn't seem to get in touch with you."

"I had some business to take care of and I wasn't around. What did you want?"

"Just to tell you that Sammi and Dave would join us for dinner tonight. That's all."

At least she tried to let me know. I feel better now. But I have to be on guard all night. I have to watch what I say and not get caught in anything. This guy's a police officer.

Without any special talent, it was still obvious to realize that Len was in a nervous state. Even Lily took special notice as she had previously mentioned that even though he was a quiet person, he usually acted quite reserved. But he wasn't reserved tonight. He was edgy and it showed.

"I hear you're both from Pennsylvania?" he asked in an attempt at civility. He felt his best defense was to be a congenial guest and remain friendly though totally alert.

"Yes, we live in Scranton," said Sammi. She knew his thoughts were scrambling, which showed he had some problems with them. Okay, they had to start talking, first casual and then get into some background.

Sammi added. "But I was born in Tecumseh, Ontario. I didn't move to the states until I went to college. Dave, you were born in the states, weren't you?"

"Yes, in a little town outside of Philadelphia. I never moved that far away from home," he laughed trying to sound casual yet realizing where Sammi was heading already.

"What about you Lily? Where were you born?" asked Dave.

That started Len sweating. He knew they'd be asking him next. *What should he say? Well, they didn't know anything so he could make something up.*

Lily answered. "I'm not sure. My parents were from Arkansas originally, but I'm not sure where I was born; maybe Arkansas or maybe here in Ohio. After they died I was put in an orphanage here, but that's all I know."

Len's thoughts had moved to the past as soon as Sammi had answered. They immediately went to a small bungalow house and a bloody bedroom, which Len could never quite get out of his mind no matter how hard he tried. It seemed over the years that he had put a lot of effort into forgetting and burying memories without success.

When the topic got around to Len, he lied as Sammi had expected. He said that he was from somewhere in Arizona originally and cut his answer short. He then immediately tried to change the subject by asking Dave and Sammi how they liked Cuyahoga Falls and what sights they had seen. In this way, he thought he was home free.

Sammi however kept bringing in little hints of the past. "I loved seeing that Mary Campbell cave and this gal did have ties to Pennsylvania. Funny how the past is always around in one way or another."

Everyone laughed but Len's expression was guarded and his thoughts said it all. He was struggling to make it through this evening, but vowed never to be caught in this situation again. *Damn,* he thought, *how could this happen? And they keep talking about the past. Well, they won't find out about mine. They changed my name a long time ago and for a good reason; I'm safe.*

After a pleasant and delicious dinner, they all sat around and talked again for a while. Although Len seemed to relax some, Sammi was convinced that he'd find a way to exit early. She paid attention to all his conflicting thoughts and kept digging for more hints. This time she brought up Matthew's murder.

"It's so strange that they didn't even investigate anyone else except you. The police must have other suspects." Then she turned to Len and asked, "Did you know Matthew?"

His expression was erratic. It seemed that even Lily noticed. "No, I didn't know him at all."

"Yes you did," said Lily. "You were at the same charity luncheon that I was at when he gave that donation for our group, remember?"

It was obvious that Len didn't like being corrected, and Sammi found his thoughts unreliable.

"Gees, Lily, I forgot about that. But that was the only time; I mean you dated him so you'd remember him more than

I." His comment was angry and confrontational and showed a different side of his character than Lily had ever seen.

She was stunned at his comment but pursued the subject. "But you were there when he came to the office a few times. You had coffee with him. Don't you remember?"

"I guess not," he answered aloud and his thoughts said that he had better keep his comments short and to the point. His irritation had already showed and he knew that Lily was surprised. He couldn't slip up again.

"Anyway," said Sammi, trying to rescue the situation, "he did seem to know a lot of people and had an impressive number of enemies, some rivals from work both inside and outside of his company."

Len simply nodded but wouldn't offer anymore. Yet his thoughts were telling Sammi a lot and she'd received some unbelievable clues already.

Lily asked, "They've never found the gun, did they? And I've never owned a gun, my God, where will this end?"

His thoughts now were in turmoil. He would always protect her but he had to protect himself first. No one else had ever protected him. Yet after he felt safe, he'd make sure that both Lily and Billy were okay. He wasn't sure yet how he could do that, however, if she had to go to jail, he would be there for her. After all, she shouldn't have dated Matthew anyway.

Sammi was having somewhat of a tough time and Dave knew it. Twice he eased them out of an intense conversation and kept everyone on lighter subjects. Yet it was Sammi who kept coming back to gather needed information. When she'd gotten all she wanted, her demeanor changed and then Dave knew.

It was still quite early when Len took his leave. He said he had early plans for Sunday and only meant to stop by anyway. He bid everyone a cordial goodnight and tried to rectify some of his earlier damage by suggesting they should do it again sometime. Yet his thoughts said that he would never again put himself into this type of situation; it was too dangerous for him.

* * *

After he left, Lily was the first to comment. "He didn't seem like himself tonight for some reason, but he does get rather aloof and abrupt at times. I guess he must be one of those people who keep everything inside."

Dave nodded and Sammi agreed completely. Len definitely was keeping a lot inside and unfortunately for him, it would all be coming out very soon.

Lily looked rather puzzled. "He certainly was different tonight. I really don't understand it."

Sammi decided it would be a perfect time to place a hint in her mind. "How much do you really know about him?"

"I've worked with him for more than fifteen years, on and off. I think I know him rather well."

"But how much do you really know about him personally? I'd guess not much if he's as private as you say."

That comment made Lily reflect. "I guess I don't. I've spent a decent amount of time with him, at least a while back, I did, but he never talked much about himself. I always thought he was more of a private person."

"So he never talked about his childhood or his parents, anything like that?"

"No, I don't think so." She looked at them suspiciously and asked "Why?"

Sammi had asked that question purposely. She wanted to put hints and doubts into Lily's mind, but she didn't want her to panic so she tempered it.

"We're looking at a lot of people right now, Lily. We know you didn't kill Matthew, but someone did and since the gun is still missing, we don't have that type of trail to follow. So expect all kind of questions from us in the future."

Dave jumped on that one. "Sometimes it's the one you least expect and we need a new direction to go in. If you can think of anyone who was acting suspicious about that time, let us know. That could help."

She understood. "I wish I could. I want this nightmare behind me, but I can't for the life of me imagine anyone I know who would commit murder."

"Of course not. Murderers usually hide their tracks pretty well. In case you think of something, let us know; any kind of suspicious behavior should be looked into."

All of a sudden, Lily thought of something. "I'm sure this is nothing … I mean I never thought anything about it at the time, but Len did come to visit me in jail within the first few days that I was there. He was nervous and edgy and I felt he shared my fear, but he did say something peculiar."

"What's that?" asked Dave.

"Well, he said and I'm quoting … 'this wasn't supposed to happen' and he said it a few times. I thought it was strange at the time, but then we were all in a panic. But looking back …" she stopped and didn't say anymore. She looked at Sammi with a few questions on her mind but didn't say anymore.

Sammi felt she had accomplished her purpose. She'd gotten plenty of information from Len and had fed Lily some preparation for what she was about to face.

"This has been an interesting evening. You've both given me plenty to think about and I will. If I think of anything at all that might help, I'll let you know. I guess sometimes we don't know people the way we think we do."

"That's very true," said Sammi. "And anything connected with crime can bring out the best and worst in people."

They gave Lily much to think about and as they left, Dave grabbed Sammi's hand knowing she needed some relaxation time.

"Let's stop for a glass of wine somewhere; I think you need it."

She laughed as she said, "I think you're beginning to read my thoughts."

* * *

There was a small beckoning café almost adjacent to their motel that Dave had noticed a few times. It was comfortable and quaint and had small tables perfect for private conversation. Dave picked one near the back wall where they'd have no one behind them.

"I know you're aware that I heard a lot, but let's just sit here for a few minutes and relax. I know I won't forget anything, but as I tell you I'm going to write down my notes – just in case."

"Forget everything until your second glass of wine. The first glass is for good memories and happy thoughts and for settling you down. On the second glass you can tell me what you've heard."

"Two glasses and I'll be whipped," she said, laughing, as he knew she always got giddy by the second round.

"And then you can get right to sleep when we get back. I know you need a good night's sleep after a session like this one and you won't get it without something to calm you down."

"I know. Honestly, I must say that I'm really beginning to be homesick for Scranton and all of our friends. I like it when we can share ideas with them. However, as long as I have you with me I'm okay, but I could never handle all this stuff alone anymore."

"And you won't have to because I'll always be around. I miss Scranton, too, and I wonder what they've discovered on those robbery cases. You know many robberies are usually petty stuff, but when they target seniors, and they've got half of the senior population in and around Scranton scared, well, that puts a high priority on it. Jim seems to think there's more to it than what appears."

"What do you mean?"

"He thinks that the robberies might be a cover for something else. I know, I can't imagine what either, but to him it doesn't make sense. These kids are from wealthy parents and they don't need the money. They hadn't even hocked anything and most crooks do that right away. So I guess he has a point."

"Still, what else does he think it could be related to?"

"He doesn't have a clue, only a gut feeling that theft is not the real reason."

"So he's not really satisfied yet?"

"No, I don't think so. I think Jim's mind is working overtime."

* * *

Sammi waited a few more minutes to get on the important topic and then she couldn't wait anymore. "I need to tell you some of this stuff, Dave. It's really bizarre. I was ready for some unbalanced thoughts but, well, let me tell you."

"Okay, but take it slow; we've got a lot of time."

She smiled, took a deep breath and began. "I do have some new clues to what he's been doing. He's actually tailed Lily every time she went out with this Matthew. In fact, he's tailed her most other times she's gone out, every time he could manage it. His thoughts said that he wanted to make sure she was okay and maybe with his background it was true. But he was doing a type of stalking as far as I'm concerned."

"So you mean he followed her a lot of times when she went out and not necessarily on dates."

"Exactly. If she met some friends, girls or guys many times he was around somewhere, but hidden. So he knew all her habits outside of work."

Dave's expression got worried. Even with good intentions, Matthew was a loose canon that would explode eventually.

"So he followed her the night Matthew was killed?"

"Definitely and he knew they'd had a fight. He saw her get dropped off at her house and then he proceeded to follow Matthew. His thoughts suggested that enough was enough and he was going to put a stop to this. It's sad, because if he had only waited, he would have found out that Lily had ended it already."

"But it sounds like there would have been another victim some other time, don't you think?"

"Yeah, I do. He was somewhat infatuated with her but not in the usual sense. I think he loved her in his own way, and would have married her if she had been interested. She represented family to him and as long as they were friends, his mind accepted the situation. Some days she represented his mother and other days his sister. Does that make sense to you?"

"Sort of."

"It's not 100% clear to me either but that's how he was thinking. Anyway that Friday night Len followed Matthew to a bar – the name of the place I didn't get – but he actually went into the bar as well and had a few drinks. When Matthew left, he was quite drunk and when he got to his car, he sat there and fell asleep for a while. That's when Len came up beside the car and shot him. In his mind, he thought he was protecting his family; I'm sure he had reverted to those years. When he realized what he had done, he walked to the other side of the car and leaned against it probably in total shock. Later, when he thought back on the crime he panicked. One of his fears is that he knows his handprint might still be on that car."

"We could have it tested. I'm not sure they would have been that thorough considering the fact they were positive Lily had committed the murder."

"I thought he was found in his car in an empty parking lot," Sammi said, somewhat confused.

"Actually by the time they found him in the parking lot of that bar, it was quite a few hours after closing time and it would have been empty."

Now Dave was taking notes. He explained he would use these points when he talked to Sergeant Brady and asked him to present the case to Detective Anchor. Dave sat back relaxed as if Sammi was finished. She allowed him a few moments to relax and then said, "Don't you think a few people in that bar, maybe the bartender would remember him and that could put him near the murder scene?"

"Sure and we should be able to find out the bar; it's probably one that Matthew frequented."

"Len has something else bugging him, but I didn't pick that up. That thought was too deep."

Sammi was miffed. There was something brewing in his thoughts but she'd have to wait for it to surface and that was always hard for her.

Dave sat up. "Okay, we've got a lot of clues here. We need to find that bar and also get an imprint off that car and I think we've got enough to get Lily off the hot seat."

"You think so?"

"We'll see, but I don't think they'll put her back in jail with another suspect and better evidence against this second one."

"That should be a relief to her and Billy."

"I'd like to call the sarge but I think I'll wait until Monday. The first thing Monday morning I'll be on the phone with him."

"That's fine. Nothing should happen before then anyway."

* * *

First thing Monday morning Dave was on the phone with Sergeant Brady, a very shocked Sergeant Brady at that. His sarge wanted them to move as quickly as possible and he had an ulterior motive. He wanted Dave and Sammi back in Scranton, before all hell broke loose on the robberies.

"Okay Dave and you'd like me to contact Detective Anchor."

"Well, yeah. I think he might have questions as to how·we obtained this information, you know the usual questions and he might not accept the answers from me, a relatively unknown as far as he's concerned."

"Okay, that's right. We're used to you and Sammi around here, but you could have trouble with him. What do you have in mind?"

"A couple of things. First, I'd like to know where Matthew's car ended up and have it dusted on the rear right door and fender to see if we can find either fingerprints or a palm print or something. We need to find that bar and could use some leeway as far as questioning his friends. Now if I tell him, he's going to try to pin me down to find out how I know all this stuff. He'd want to make sure it's reasonable info or he won't cooperate with me. You know that. But if you can convince him ..."

"Oh, I'll convince him; I've known him for years and he'll just take my word for it."

"Good, that's what I was hoping for. We need to get Len Worley in for questioning as soon as possible, and find out where he stashed the murder weapon. That would be the final nail in his coffin and then we could get Lily out of being the main suspect. We need to get this guy off the streets. I'm still wondering about those five unaccounted years. I still need to dig more for that."

"Do you want Julie to follow up on that?"

"Sure wouldn't hurt and maybe we can pick up something at this end."

"Okay, Dave, why don't you call me back in a few days or I'll have someone call you back before then if I hear anything."

"Thanks sarge. I really feel that's the only way to work this one."

"Oh, I agree. They don't know you well enough to go out on a limb like this, but he'll do it for me. I'll talk to you later."

* * *

By Monday evening, Dave got a call back from Sergeant Brady.

"It's all set and we've got one very excited Detective Anchor on our hands. He can't believe what you've come up with because they hit nothing but dead ends and that's why they won't let go of Lily."

"Sure that's what usually happens."

"He knows enough not to push you about where you got the information. Hell, he'll be like me now. As long as the information is good, he doesn't care how you got it. He'll probably end up looking real good on this one and that makes him happy. He wants you down there first thing tomorrow morning. I didn't push too much about Sammi; that's your call."

"Okay, we may play this one differently, I'll see. Thanks sarge."

"I have an ulterior motive you know; we want you two back here."

Dave was laughing as he hung up.

Sammi had heard most of the conversation. She knew that Dave was a little sheepish on this one so she offered. "It would be fine with me if you went down there alone. I don't have to be there until we question him. I thought I'd go to lunch with Lily and let her in on some stuff."

Dave smiled. "It's getting close. He'll probably push for an interview with Len by tomorrow afternoon I would think."

"That's what I thought. But, I'm glad this one will be over, except I have a few more things to pick up from him."

Dave was quiet and she knew what was on his mind. "Look I don't mind. I think it's the best way to handle this one."

"But you picked up all the clues and you don't get credit."

"Yes, I do. I always get credit from you and we're a team, remember? I don't want him getting suspicious; I get enough of that back home."

Dave laughed. He had to agree with that.

"Actually I'm more comfortable this time. After our interview with Len is over, this detective will probably start to wonder about me, and by then we'll be gone. That's my best scenario."

* * *

Dave walked into Detective Anchor's office before 8:30 AM. He was eagerly awaiting him after the phone call he'd received from Sergeant Brady.

"I don't know how or where you got this information, but Sam said I shouldn't be concerned about that. He said that your information is reliable and that's all I need to know. Sam only hinted at a few things but I'd like to hear it from you."

"Okay," said Dave and he began explaining about the palm and fingerprint that was left on the car. He continued with talk about the bar where Matthew stopped with Len in pursuit, as he waited for the right moment.

Fred kept shaking is head. "We've questioned a lot of people, but honestly we were all so positive that Lily did it. That ought to teach all of us a good lesson. And honestly, we don't usually rush to judgment, but it seemed so cut and dried."

"It can happen to all of us unless we guard against it."

"Yes," said Fred, "that's so true. The car has been impounded and I'm sending out my guys right now to totally dust it for fingerprints."

"Well, that's good, but we're mainly concerned about the right rear door and fender."

"Okay, but I've learned my lesson and I want to be thorough this time."

Dave nodded.

"I'm also sending out officers to talk to the bartender at the Gilligan's Armor. That's where he was found shot in his car. Maybe, if we're lucky he'll remember this Len and we can always find out who frequents the bar on Friday nights and have more people coming forward who saw him there. Hell, I'd like to bring him in for questioning by tomorrow."

"Once he gets suspicious we should move fast. This guy isn't the most stable person around."

Detective Anchor looked over at Dave curiously. "You know even more than you're telling me, don't you?"

"I do, Fred," he answered, "and I'll tell you the rest before we question him."

"Good enough. Let me get this done today and I'll call you later tonight."

Dave left knowing this was moving fast now and he needed to make sure that Lily and Billy were protected today, tonight and until Len was arrested. He couldn't take any chances.

* * *

Sammi preferred an early dinner with Lily, as she would have plenty of time to help her understand and digest Len's background before she had to see him again.

"You had a particular reason for wanting to meet me, didn't you? You sounded so urgent."

"Yes, I did. I need to help you face something that will be hard and I wanted you to have time to accept it."

Lily looked at her suspiciously. It was obvious she was nervous when they ordered dinner.

"Look, I'm only trying to prepare you because this information will be coming out very shortly, and you need time to prepare Billy as well. I mean, you might want to wait as far as he's concerned, but that should be your call."

"Maybe you better just tell me; I'm getting very nervous right now."

"Okay," said Sammi as she shifted in her chair realizing she was slightly uptight herself. "We have reason to believe that Len is the one who killed Matthew."

"What?" she said. "You've got to be kidding me. I know he's withdrawn and a little strange at times, but he's no killer. It's not in his personality."

Lily went quiet for a moment or two and then added, "No, No. I can't believe he did it."

"Then let me tell you a few things about Len Worley that I'm sure you don't know."

This was the moment that Sammi chose to tell her about Len's early childhood and continued all the way to his infatuation with her under several different scenarios. Lily had tears coming down her face that fell off onto the table that she failed to notice. She was in such shock and distress that her eyes couldn't leave Sammi's face. It was as if she believed if she kept staring at her that Sammi would change her story and tell a different one. Therefore, she sat and stared, but the story didn't change.

Sammi grabbed her hand and said, "I know this is a shock to you. It would be for anyone, but I needed to tell you and it had to be today. I think by tomorrow they'll bring him in for questioning and everything should happen fast after that."

"This is horrible for him; what a sad life he's had. He's been totally a victim. I wonder what will happen to him and me. I guess it means that I'll be off the hook, right?"

"Yes, it should."

"My God, I can't help but feel sorry for him, you know?"

"Dave and I can't either. Apparently, the state tried, but he didn't get the help he needed. You need to understand that he does love you, but since you never got into a romantic relationship, you're his substitute mother and sister at different times. I know it sounds weird ..."

"No I think I understand, sort of. It's just that I never would have guessed him. I don't think anybody would have. How did you know?"

"Different facts we discovered just started pointing in his direction. But look, Dave is concerned about you and Billy."

"Why, he'd never hurt me. God, it looks like he actually killed for me," and she started crying. "I just told Matthew I didn't want to see him again, if only Len had known."

"Even so," Sammi said, "there are other ways to handle those situations. You can see how unstable he is and we can't take a chance. His circumstances will be changing and he could blame you. Dave will have protection for you starting tonight and until he's arrested."

Lily sobbed. She was almost out of control but slowly she sat up straight in her chair and took command of herself. She simply kept shaking her head. "Who could have ever known?"

She planned to go and meet Billy at work and take him home with her. At this time, it was the only way she would feel safe. Len was truly unbalanced; there was no question about that. All this information had been thrown at her quickly and she'd had no time to prepare, but her first loyalty was always to Billy. He needed protection.

CHAPTER ELEVEN

The phone rang at the motel around 8:30 P.M. Dave was in the middle of a shower so Sammi answered.

"Hi Fred, let me get him."

It only took a moment; Dave was anxious for the news.

"Okay, what have you got?"

"Almost everything we need. The bartender remembered Len and can place him in the bar at the same time that Matthew was there. In fact, he thought he was one of those quiet ones, you know the kind you have to watch. He sat alone, drank alone, and didn't talk to anyone all night. Anyway, he remembered specifically that he left moments after Matthew. The main reason that he remembers is that Len was right behind Matthew when he paid his tab and our drunken friend Matthew fell into his arms as he turned to leave. The bartender thought there might be a fight, but it seems Len just let him go and didn't say one word. But that's why he remembers it all so well."

"Lucky break."

"And here's another one. We have a total handprint and four fingerprints on that right rear door just like you said. How could you have known that?"

"Lucky guess."

"Right, well I don't care, but we're bringing him in to-morrow and he won't be leaving. We've got plenty to hold him."

"What happens to Lily?"

"That'll take a little time. She's not completely off the hook yet. We'll keep searching for more and if we take Len to trial, which it looks like to me, then she'll be free."

"And hopefully we'll get more tomorrow during his questioning."

"That would be great, but like the others, he'll probably deny everything."

"Maybe not. This one might surprise you. Look, I have two things on my mind. First I'd like to bring in Sammi during the questioning; she may be able to figure out something. Also, I need to get to talk to you before anything goes down, so I'd like to come in earlier. I've got a few more facts that you need to know."

"Really? Well, okay. Anything that might help would be great."

"What time are you bringing him in?"

"We're going to let him get to work and pick him up there about 9:00 AM. I think that would work out best, and I plan to question him at least by 10:00. If you get here by 9:00, we'll have a chance to have that talk."

"Okay," said Dave. "See you then."

As Dave put down the phone, he turned to Sammi and said, "Tomorrow's a go; we'd better get some sleep. We need you rested."

* * *

By 9:30 the next morning Dave had already told Detective Fred Anchor the story of Len's childhood and the reason for the identity change. Fred hadn't said one word during the entire briefing and was slow to comment.

"My word, I've heard about that crime. I know it was a long time ago but anyone who's law enforcement in Ohio knows about one of the craziest crimes that ever happened. And Len is that little boy? My God." He couldn't say anymore.

Dave took over and told him what he thought his relationship with Lily was and how in Len's twisted mind, he needed to keep her safe. Fred only nodded a few times trying to make sense out of this bizarre repeat of history. Sammi kept quiet and never said a word. They both felt this was their best plan.

"We'll take over the questioning if you agree. I want to see if we can take him back into those years and maybe blow everything wide open."

"Okay, but I've got a sergeant that's rather a hot head and he'll probably butt in on anything you say. His ego will be quite bruised that the murderer is not Lily; he spearheaded everything about her."

Finally Sammi spoke. "But he's wrong."

"And he'll find it hard to take. However, I'll be there too and try to keep him in line. He's a good cop despite his arrogant ways."

As they went into the interrogation room, Sergeant Bill Warner came in and couldn't understand why Dave and Sammi had to be there.

"Because I insist," said Fred, "and Dave will do most of the questioning. You can sit back and relax or you don't even have to be here; it's your choice."

You could tell Bill Warner was already quite miffed. "I want to get some questions in, too."

"Fine, but I've told you how this'll go down. You cooperate or I'll remove you."

That settled it, no room for discussion and his attitude changed immediately.

* * *

The meeting was delayed until eleven o'clock since Len wanted his attorney present. Then a very agitated and confused Len Worley walked into the interrogation room, with reliable representation. He was advised to answer the questions truthfully and honestly in as few words as possible. He didn't even look surprised to see Dave and Sammi sitting at the conference table, but he did throw them an angry look.

Again Sammi sat on Dave's left side, as she usually did and Detective Fred Anchor as well as his sergeant Bill Warner sat in second row seats.

"Okay," said Dave wanting to be exact about everything. "You've been read your rights and are ready to proceed."

Both Len and his lawyer nodded.

"We need to know your whereabouts on Friday, April 22 the night that Matthew Belten was murdered. Where were you at the time of the murder?"

His lawyer intervened and asked, "What time did the murder occur?"

Dave answered, "Sometime between midnight and two in the morning."

Len conferred with his lawyer and answered. "At the time of the murder I was home."

Dave said, "Okay and where were you earlier in the evening?"

"I stayed home, but went out for a drink about 9:30 and was home before eleven."

"Can anyone verify your statements?"

"No, I live alone and didn't see anyone."

"Where did you go for a drink?"

"Just a corner bar near my home."

"Surely the bartender would remember you and could corroborate your alibi?"

"Don't know; probably not. I don't go there very often and he doesn't know me."

Sammi suggested he hint at the fact that he was at the Gilligan's Armor because that was constantly on his mind.

"We have reason to believe, Mr. Worley, that you went and had your drink at Gilligan's Armor and followed Mr. Belten out and killed him before you went home that night."

Len didn't even answer. He looked down. His attorney told him to answer, but he took a moment and conferred with him.

"That's the bar that I stopped at to have a drink, but I didn't kill anyone."

"But that bar is at least ten miles from your home and hardly what anyone could call around the corner. What were you doing there?"

"Just decided to go there that night."

"Well, Mr. Worley, the bartender at the Gilligan's Armor does remember you and he remembers you walking out right after Mr. Belten. In fact Mr. Belten was quite drunk and almost fell on top of you as he paid his bill."

Now Len was starting to sweat. He wouldn't look up at anybody and simply clasped his hands in front of himself on the table. He was shaking and obvious tears began to escape from his eyes.

Sergeant Warner took this opportunity to lunge at him to scare him and asked in a loud and sarcastic tone, "What did you do with the gun? Where did you throw it?"

Detective Anchor told him to back off, sit in the corner or he'd have to leave.

"This was my case and I have a right to question this crappy suspect."

Detective Anchor said, "Sit down and stop or leave ... your choice."

He chose to stay but with an anger that could only be second to Len's, who couldn't believe that the evidence was piling up against him. Len looked over at Dave and Sammi and scowled. *They must have had something to do with this,* he thought. *They must have picked up something during that dinner on Saturday. But I didn't say anything. How could they know?*

Suddenly Len began to whimper. His voice was almost like that of a little child again and he started crying. This made Sergeant Warner very disgusted and he had trouble controlling himself until Detective Anchor looked over and told him that this was his last chance. There were many distractions in the room, which made it hard for Dave to keep up his line of questioning.

Then Len's lawyer stopped the meeting. "Look, I've had very little time to confer with my client. I have to stop this questioning right now until I have time to give my client proper instructions. Also, to be fair, I need to completely familiarize myself with this case; he deserves that."

"Understood," said Detective Anchor in a disappointed tone. "We must comply with that."

"I'll call you in a day or two and we'll get together again. Then I can prepare my client properly and we'll be ready for a more in depth interview."

"That's fine, but we're arresting your client now. However, you'll be given all the time you need with him for preparation."

"Okay, that's all I can ask for right now."

They left a tearful Len Worley shocked and bewildered as well as horrified of an arraignment. It would take time for his lawyer to soothe his anxiety as he conferred with him and to strategize his defense. The angriest person in the room was Sergeant Warner as he felt that if he had gotten in a few more questions he could have gotten a confession.

"And one we probably couldn't have used under the circumstances. Even though he'd been read his rights, his lawyer didn't have time to properly advise him of his best approach. And once he stated that fact, we had to back off."

He saw the angry look in Bill's eyes and repeated. "His lawyer didn't have his time with him. Look Bill, we've got plenty on him right now and he's a much better suspect than Lily any day of the week."

"But there's no gun."

"There isn't one for Lily either. But his fingerprints were found on the outside of the car and we have people who can place him in that bar the night of the murder. Now settle down. We'll take this in the proper fashion so we don't lose him on a technicality. We'll have time to question him legally later."

"I don't think this stuff is good enough. We've got more of a motive on Lily."

"You're riled up right now and I'm telling you to go walk it off. I need to talk to Dave and Sammi."

"Right, a lot of good they've done for us."

Dave had used these few minutes to confer with Sammi, who seemed anxious to talk to him privately. He turned to Fred and said, "I need to confer with Sammi for a few minutes. How about we meet you in your office in about fifteen minutes?"

"Okay, sorry about Bill; he thought he owned this case from the beginning."

Dave shrugged it off. "See you in a few minutes. I'll come to your office."

* * *

Sammi had gotten what everyone needed. She decided she would like Dave to walk back into Detective Anchor's office alone and tell him and Sergeant Warner what they needed to know.

"What about you?"

"I'm going to wait in the car. That Bill is such a hot head, he'll want to know how you knew this and it'll start everything all over again. This is our best way. Just tell Fred and then leave. He'll know enough to believe you."

Dave had to laugh. Again, she had the best plan and one he'd enjoy carrying out, even though Bill Warner would be out in left field alone.

Bill was still arguing when he returned, but shut up apparently on orders from his boss.

"Okay, what have you got?"

"Len Worley has a key on his key chain to a safety deposit box. You'll have to figure out where it's at and get a warrant because that's where he's hidden the gun. It's been there for years; he only took it out the day of the murder. "

Bill sat up straight and looked quite indignant. Dave ignored him.

"Holy Shit," said Fred as he sat up stiff at attention. "You've got to be kidding."

"No, and here's the twist you're going to love. When the murder of his family happened all those years ago, one of the killers accidentally lost his gun. Apparently, he even spent a few minutes looking for it, but couldn't find it immediately. It had been stuck in the blankets on one of the kids' beds and his buddies were screaming for him to leave it and run. So finally he did. Len, as a tiny little kid, waited almost a day before he had the nerve to get out of his hiding place and he spotted the gun. He's kept it all these years. Apparently, at the time, he put it in his little duffel bag and no one ever searched it because the police thought the killers left with their guns. He's never used it but felt killing Matthew was the perfect revenge."

"My God, Dave. How could you know that?" asked Fred.

Even Bill looked at him with newfound respect, but Dave simply held his ground.

When Fred recovered he said, "You're telling me that this little kid had the gun all these years. I'll bet no one ever really checked his duffel bag because there was no apparent reason. What a travesty."

"Right and he's kept it all these years," added Dave.

"Unbelievable."

"Yes, it's a Smith and Wesson .38 special," said Dave. "And I think if you can check back on his brother and sister's murders you'll find that this gun and the bullets match."

Bill was stupefied. He started to say, "You can't know that ..." but stopped midway in his sentence.

"It will also be the same match to the bullets that killed Matthew Belten and to what we've been able to figure out about the second shot ..."

"What second shot?" asked Bill.

Fred looked at him in disgust. "You didn't know there were two bullets fired at Matthew? Why the hell didn't you check that out?"

"He shot him twice," said Dave, "one was for his mother and the other was for his sister. I think his irrational behavior will come forward now and he'll be in and out of reality for quite a while. Be prepared for it."

"Kind of a sad case in a way. But it will be good to have found the last gun from his family's murders and have total closure there."

Dave agreed. "Okay I'll be going, but I'll still be around for a few more days so if we can help further, let me know."

Sergeant Bill said, "I really screwed up on this one, but I was so sure it was Lily. And I owe you and your wife an apology; I can be real hardheaded at times. How in the hell did you figure this one out?"

"Just a bunch of little clues that started to lead in one direction."

"Oh, I think there's more to it than that," said Bill. "I won't push it, but you both have my respect."

Dave waived him off.

"But I've got to learn to step back and look at everything from now on. I was just so sure."

"We all need to step back once in a while. Good meeting you both and we'll talk again."

"Thanks," said Detective Anchor as Dave left smiling at both of them.

* * *

Dave left the station and met a waiting Sammi in the car. She smiled when she saw the satisfied look on his face.

"This was fun today. When we get it right it makes everything worthwhile."

She was pleased.

"I'd like to stick around a few more days, until they find the gun and match the bullets and we know for sure Lily's off the hook and they're both okay."

"I can't disagree with that," she said.

"I'm glad this is over but it'll be fun to get back to Scranton. At least things are a little more logical and calm there right now."

"And this way we'll have time to have another one of those home cooked meals with Lily and Billy, which I know they'll insist on anyway."

* * *

A few days later on a Tuesday night, Dave and Sammi again walked into the home of Lily Caulkin for dinner and certainly memorable goodbyes. The police found the gun in the P. O. Box that Sammi had determined. And the bullets from this gun did match the bullets that had killed Matthew Belten and also Len's younger sister and older brother. Len himself had reverted to his younger self mentally as well as physically in his voice tone and mannerisms staying mainly in an imaginary world of his choosing. Presently he was held in a psychiatric facility. Whenever the gun or his family's murder was mentioned, it seemed that his mind went into a shocked remembrance of the crime scene that had never totally left him. To this day, he couldn't handle any mention of his tragic past.

"It seems strange to me that he was able to appear relatively normal most of the years that I'd known him," said Lily. "You can't help feel sorry for him on the one hand, but on the other hand ..."

She couldn't finish. Everyone in the room felt the same way.

Sammi said, "But no one in his present day world brought up reminders of his past; they didn't even know about it. So he was able to hang on to what he wanted to be true, namely you at times playing two different roles for him."

Lily shook her head and took a deep breath. "I can't even think of any logical comment to make about this. It's so bizarre. I mean, it's crazy that he even made it through that murder scene being such a little kid. Then all those years of therapy, but no one realized that it had never ended for him in his mind. You can't help but feel sorry for him, yet …

"You know mom, I think part of Len died that day. I don't think what was left was really Len or Jamie or whoever. He wasn't a total person anymore and needed professional help. He did a bad thing in killing Mr. Belten, but his mind wasn't right; I don't think. Most likely the doctors will have to figure him out."

They all looked over at Billy. He cut right through all the confusion and made some telling statements.

Lily agreed. "I think you're right, Billy. No one really knows what's going on in his mind, probably not even Len himself."

"I'll bet you know, Ms. Sammi," said Billy. "You always know."

Dave had a broad smile on his face with that comment. There was no way to answer it. Billy laughed, too; he was happy.

"I knew you'd have a miracle for us," he said. He looked at his mom and added, "I told you she's the one person who could save you."

"That's what he said to me that first day. He has such faith in you Sammi."

"That's good, but I think you had a good lawyer, too."

"And," Billy said, "I think he likes my mom."

Dave and Sammi smiled. "I'll bet he does," she said.

"I'm serious, Ms. Sammi. He's called her a lot and didn't he ask you out for dinner, mom?"

"I think it's only a friendly business dinner because the case turned out so well. And he did do a good job. He does have a brilliant legal mind; it just doesn't always show."

"I think he likes you," said Billy. He wasn't going to give up on the subject.

"Well, I like him and we've had some good discussions. Maybe he'll only be a friend and that's okay, too."

Bill smiled mischievously as he said, "I think he likes you mom."

And you couldn't get Billy off that idea.

"What do you think of him?" Dave asked Billy.

"I like him. I knew he was nervous when he had trouble speaking, but after he knew us better he talked fine. He's very nice to me and I know he likes my mom."

They all laughed after that, but later as the evening grew to a close, sadness descended on all of them. No one wanted the evening to end.

"I hate nice things to end," said Billy.

"Just this evening," said Sammi. "But you and I will always be the best of friends no matter where we live, right?"

He nodded, "But I like it better when you're close by to us."

"Then maybe you'll have to come and visit us in Scranton. I'd love to have a visit from you and your mom."

Billy's eyes lit up. "Can we mom? Can we go and visit sometime?"

"I'd love it," said Lily. "It's not that far. I'm sure we can manage that sometime," she said.

"Okay, then," said Billy. "That'll make it a lot easier when you're gone. Because I'm going to watch until your car turns the corner just like I waited for you to get here."

The hugs and kisses were multiple and the evening did finally end, although everyone would have liked it to go on longer.

* * *

"This was a great time, especially since everything turned out so well. I'll miss them but I'm anxious to get back to Scranton," said Dave.

"Me, too. You can get so caught up in a new world, but I miss our friends, my job, my dog and the familiarity of all we know."

Dave grabbed her hand. They both understood.

Dave said, "I think Lily will be just fine now. When she visited Len she said that he didn't even recognized her. It seems that his mind has recessed so much."

"It'll take a lot of time for him to make it back again, if he ever does. All this hidden desperation and warped thinking must have deteriorated his abilities as he tried to handle it alone. Maybe because of his young age at the time of the murders, he'll be too vulnerable to make it back."

"I keep thinking that if someone had found him within a few hours maybe that would have made a difference. But he was stuck there for three days with his murdered family, too afraid to move and … who knows what could have saved him?" Dave couldn't help but wonder.

"It's hard to tell. The human mind can be so fragile and for that little child, I still find it hard to imagine what he went through. I only know Len as an adult, but he was only seven years old when this happened. I can barely remember how I felt about things at seven, but I know my parents were my rocks. If something had happened to them, I've tried to figure out what I might feel like, but I can't. It's impossible and so frustrating."

"It is, and everyone is different. Anyway, he'll finally get the help he needs and even if it's permanent, at least society will be protected and he'll be protected, too."

She nodded.

"Did you ever hear anything about those lost five years after he graduated from college?"

Sammi was cautious as she answered. "He did have some brief thoughts about it, but not enough to make any sense to me. There was one flash of him talking to someone who I thought might be a counselor of some type. Another time he thought about visiting a hospital where I think he stayed for a while. But his thoughts were quick flashes at best. It made me think that he kept trying to get help to figure himself out. Maybe it was too little, too late."

They were both quiet after that. The night-lights on the drive back to the motel seemed to have hypnotized both of them. It was a combination of exhausted emotions that were finally able to relax, fatigue and looking forward to getting back home. Sammi took a deep breath, laid her head back against the seat and seemed to mirror what was on Dave's mind. They had to pack again, get to bed early enough to be rested and be able to get up for their nine o'clock flight. But they were going home and that was a nice feeling. Home seemed far away right now, but in Sammi's mind she felt its familiarity beckoning her. Just when they pulled into the parking spot in front of their motel door, Dave's cell phone rang.

"Okay, Jim, what's up?"

Sammi thought it was strange to receive a call from Jim tonight. He knew they were coming home tomorrow. In addition, it was close to ten o'clock; she knew the call must be important.

Dave hardly said anything, but she saw an incredible look of disbelief slowly creep across on his face. He was trying to be logical about something that was a shock to him and didn't make sense at all.

Finally he put down the phone and said unsteadily, "Wait until we get inside."

They went through the door, sat down at their little table and Dave said, "Remember those two young boys who were burglarizing senior citizens, the ones who knew Roy Dawson and planned to implicate him in some way?"

"Yeah, those rich kids with influential families that were trying to bully everyone."

"Yes, that's the ones."

Sammi nodded; she remembered.

"Both of the boys have been found murdered. They were shot through the back of the head and Roy Dawson has been arrested for their murders."

CHAPTER TWELVE

Sammi's reaction said it all. "Well, so much for returning to a quiet and calming atmosphere for a while. This will be one hot issue."

"I'm not surprised Jim couldn't wait to tell me. He wanted to make sure we were coming back tomorrow. He said Sergeant Brady wants all of us working together on this one."

"Why in the world was Roy Dawson arrested? And when were they murdered? This sounds like a quick arrest."

"I'm not totally sure, I think it just happened a few days ago, but Roy was arrested this morning. Jim sounded quite uptight about everything. As far as arresting Roy, I think it had something to do with a gun, but I don't know the specifics. Guess I'll find out later tomorrow. We should be back in time for me to stop in the office later in the day."

Dave stopped talking, took a deep breath and looked over at Sammi. She smiled and said, "It's what you do, Dave. Sometimes you don't get a break between emergencies. But remember what your father told you. Concentrate on the successes and it makes everything worth it. And don't forget that you and I had a big success this past week."

Dave smiled and moved closer to her on the couch. "I don't want you to think that you're getting away with anything here. You know they're all going to want your help, too."

She laughed. "I know but you know what the difference will be?"

He looked at her surprised as he said, "What?"

"We'll all be together again working as a team. That takes the pressure off and sharing gets our brain storming working at full speed."

"Yeah, it'll be good working with Jim and Tom again, and Amilio, too. God, I miss those guys."

"We are lucky, you know. We've built up an incredible circle of friends. And we all work together so well."

"That's true; we do work best when we're together. I've got a feeling that it's going to take all of us pulling together to solve this one."

* * *

By afternoon of the next day, as soon as they got inside the door of their home, Dave started to feel anxious. He didn't say anything but Sammi knew. She purposely let him pace around for a little time and then said, "Why don't you get down to the office? That's where your mind is anyway."

He smiled, "You don't mind?"

"No, I'll get us unpacked and when you come back you can tell me what's really going on around here."

He walked over and gave her a hug and kiss before he left. "Thanks. It's what will straighten out my mind."

"I know; it's exactly what you need," she said as he left smiling.

* * *

Sammi was happy to have a little time to herself. The last few weeks had been fun and fruitful, but she was always with somebody. Dave was always with her and at other times, other people were in the vicinity needing her attention and expertise. She loved all these people, but it could be trying on her spirit.

She needed her time alone to reconnect with the universe. She pined for those moments when she could relax and allow thoughts to come to her and renew her energy. It wasn't only a special moment for her, it was a necessity and if she didn't have it, her persona changed. Maybe other people couldn't see it, but she could feel it and it was almost like a targeted pain that enveloped her until she found a way to satisfy it. Yes, she was happy to be alone and her dog Kali joined her in her gratification.

She mused around the house, walking around and staring at familiar objects as if she was seeing them for the first time. She relished the feelings of being in her environment that threw love at her from every direction. This was her home, she thought. This was where she'd made her happiness in life and she treasured it.

The phone rang. It was an advertisement for roofing needs. She let it play out. Then she remembered the mail and started sorting through the bills and junk mail until she came to the last letter. She stared at it in disbelief. Oh no, not another letter. They hadn't received one in over a year. When was this going to end? She thought it was over, but it never seemed to fade totally out of their lives, another letter from Linda Saunders. Linda had been caught in a money-laundering scheme, and had attempted to murder Dave during a sting operation. She was in jail for at least twenty-eight more years as a result. She had dated Dave a few times before he'd married Sammi and still thought she held some power over him. She was trying to get him to help her get out of jail early. She couldn't resist reading it; this time she wasn't nearly as upset as in the past.

Hi Sammi,

You can't hold onto Dave much longer. He's mine you know. He'll never be yours, not really. You're not his type of woman. He belongs to me and the sooner you realize this truth the better off you'll be. I would suggest that you leave him now – that would serve you better as far as your physical well-being is concerned. Let me tell you that I'm not going to be in jail much longer; I have plans. And when I get out the first place I'm heading is to find Dave and renew my love for him. You'd better not be around.

      Consider yourself warned.
      Linda

Sammi simply stared at the letter. She felt Linda was getting bolder the longer she remained in prison. This time she'd even signed her name to the note. The deal established was that she couldn't contact Dave, his wife, friends or anyone in their circle and she couldn't have anyone do it for her. If she did, she'd have another year tacked onto to her prison term. It had already happened once before. They all thought she had learned her lesson, but apparently not.

Sammi felt considerably more casual about the letter this time and hoped Dave would, too. Oh, he had to show it to Sergeant Brady, get it logged in, and then send it to the warden of her prison so that her sentence would be extended by another year. She was a strange girl, quite beautiful and felt she could have anyone she wanted. And she wanted Dave. Sammi knew she'd have to settle him down tonight so she was already planning a nice meal, some wine, and hopefully some time for him to relax. He'd have some enticing news to tell her regarding the latest crime, yet, she couldn't keep this letter from him. She'd done that once before and it rocked his foundation with her. They shared everything and that's what kept them solid. Suddenly she felt exhausted and was happy that she had time for a nap before Dave returned.

* * *

Dave walked eagerly into the station and managed to make his way over to his beckoning desk where his three most trusted friends met him within seconds. He smiled and greeted, Tom, Jim and Amilio.

"We're so glad you're back. It's never the same when you're not here," said Jim subtly trying to hide the fact that he was thrilled to have his friend back.

"Well, I feel the same way about you guys. I missed everyone and it's great to be back where I belong."

"We've got some crazy things going around now," Jim warned. "None of us can make much sense of the last few days."

Tom said, "And arresting Roy so fast and without warning was unbelievable; doesn't make sense to me."

Amilio couldn't help but add, "It's not that logical to me either; there's something else big time going around right now."

"What was the basis for them arresting Roy so soon?" Dave asked.

"Well," began Jim, "it seems that right after the bodies were discovered," Jim looked around for confirmation, "I mean within like ten hours, no more, there was an anonymous phone call and it said that this crime was committed by Roy Dawson and he used an extra revolver he had claimed was stolen years ago. Well, we were suspicious but we had to follow up on it and sure enough ..."

"You mean it was a pistol he used to have years ago?"

"Absolutely," said Tom. "It was registered to him when he lived and worked in Carbondale and apparently he reported it stolen, but ..."

Dave interrupted. "Who was behind pushing for such a quick arrest, surely not the mayor?"

"Oh no, not the mayor; it was a senator in Harrisburg--I forget his name," said Tom. "Now I'm not even sure how this senator got involved so fast but he put out a press release that he had gotten an anonymous call and didn't mind broadcasting it all over the media as a way to pressure the mayor to get a hold on this guy before he runs, as he put it."

"Anonymous calls seem to be getting quite popular, aren't they?" said Dave.

"And convenient," Amilio said. "This one really smells already, don't you think big brother?"

"When did these murders happen?" asked Dave.

"Three days ago and Roy was arrested right away and the TV news and the papers have been going crazy ever since."

"These are unusual circumstances, but I don't think I could buy it this fast. What did Roy have to say for himself?"

"That's another thing; he doesn't have any attorney yet. He doesn't even know anyone around here. And they only gave us a little time with him. We've talked to him twice and he denies everything. Actually," said Jim, "I thought he looked very confused, and he's sweating this one big time."

Dave asked, "They can't keep us from talking to him, can they? What did Sergeant Brady say?"

Amilio jumped on this one. "He wanted to have a meeting as soon as you got back," said Tom. "The moment after those murders, those uppity families began throwing around their positions and wealth big time. They made everything so frantic around here. And besides that, they arrested Roy really fast. Well, you can imagine why the sarge thought it would be better to wait a few days until things settled down, and by then he hoped you'd be back."

"And there's a lot of yelling and finger pointing," Jim added. "You remember that these kids were trying to implicate Roy in those thefts, so their lawyers say that's the motive; he didn't want to be found out."

Dave shook his head. "Somebody's got a plan all figured out. They seem to be covering everything from all sides, but that's okay. They always leave out something important. There's always one little clue they forget about."

"That's what I like about you, Dave," said Tom, "you always have that positive attitude, and more so since Sammi's around." He winked at Dave. "But I agree; nothing's perfect and this is only the beginning. Those family lawyers and relatives think it's cut and dried."

"They thought it was cut and dried about Lily Caulkin in Ohio, too, but that one was really bizarre and well hidden. But something always turns up." Dave paused for a minute and then asked Jim, "You've been working closely with Roy these last few weeks. What do you think about him?"

"Straight shooter. He was really trying and liked the fact that we worked as a team here. Most places he's been didn't accept him that well, but since we took him in right away I found him to be open and honest and working like we all do. I know it's kind of early to tell, but so far that's what I thought."

"And you're good with your feelings, Jim. You judge people quite accurately."

"I do kind of get a feeling about people and I thought he was going to fit in good with us."

"And now the prosecutors will be dredging up every single thing they can think of; any kind of crap that they can find will be blasted throughout the media. We'll have to get solid ourselves first and run it by the sarge because we'll have a lot of work to do," said Dave.

"The sarge won't be back until tomorrow and I don't think we have a chance of questioning Roy in the next few days. I think the sarge will have to fight for that."

"That's okay," said Dave. "We have to all get our thoughts together and I want Sammi in on the questioning."

Amilio said quickly. "That's right. She'll be able to tell us a lot."

Jim smiled, "Yes she has a way of getting to the truth pretty fast."

Dave nodded. Sammi did have her ways, he thought, and it was hard for anyone to hide any of their feelings from her.

* * *

Sammi didn't have the type of respite that she wanted. Her dream world was a little unsteady and she didn't get the usual confirmation that she was looking for. She felt her grandpa was trying to connect with her but was always a little too far away to create the bond. He had been a very important part of her younger years; he also could hear other people's thoughts. After he died, she always tried to connect with him at different times. On many occasions, she was successful.

She was undeniably struggling in her thought world trying desperately to make a connection, but to no avail. She woke up suddenly a few times but went back to sleep quickly. Yet it was a disturbed rest. Then she heard familiar voices crying out to her, but she couldn't figure out who they were. Finally, she woke up in a sweat, sat right up straight in bed and looked around expecting to see someone in her room. Her dream world and reality were beginning to blur. That's when she decided to take a shower to clear her mind. She couldn't remember much about her dream world except trying to connect with her grandpa. For some reason today, the attempt was different, and definitely more complicated. She felt it had to do with the last week that was so emotionally exhausting and let it go at that. Her shower felt wonderful and the hot water enticed her mind to try again. However, by this time she heard Dave walk in and call for her. She yelled back from the shower door.

"You look all refreshed," he said teasing.

"And I took a short nap, too. You seem to be in a better mood."

"I'm more relaxed. Jim, Tom, Amilio and I had a short meeting and got me up to speed." He told Sammi what he'd found out.

"That's not much, is it? But you'll learn more when you talk to Roy."

Dave laughed, "When 'we' talk to Roy, you mean? I need you there from the beginning. First, I need to know about this guy. None of us know him that well, although Jim seemed to feel good about him."

"Jim has good instincts and if he's been working with him for a few weeks, he must have picked up a few clues."

"But we need to know if he's involved in this crime in any way at all. That's number one, and you can tell us that. If he's totally innocent and being railroaded for some reason, then I think we've got a major problem on our hands."

Sammi agreed. "Let's assume for the moment that he's innocent. There's only one word that comes to mind-- conspiracy, but for what reason? They could be making him the fall guy for some type of cause, yet what cause?"

"I don't know; I keep wondering why they would want to set up a cop for the killing of two petty burglars; that's another thing. Someone had to think about this one carefully because they knew that killing these two particular kids would cause their families and others in their background to create a riot. Whoever did this must have known that?"

Then Dave stopped. He was confused and couldn't think straight anymore.

"We need more facts. We have to know what's going on. That's enough for me right now. Let's eat and we can talk again later."

But when later came and they were sitting together on the couch, the telephone rang. It was already past ten o'clock and that was never good.

"Hi sarge, what's up?"

"I've been working from the background lately trying to get us some time with Roy Dawson. I mean since the police arrested him we're having a hard time getting some time with him. I got a little open window for Monday afternoon. I've been told that we can see him for about an hour at that time, but we can only have three people in there. Somebody high up is really pulling strings on this one. I don't get it. Anyway, I want you, Sammi, and Jim in there. Any problem with that?"

"No, not at all. That's what I was hoping. We've got to get some basics out of the way and then we'll know what's going on and how to approach this scene. Do you have any idea why he was arrested so soon? Did the mayor insist on a quick arrest?"

"No, no, it wasn't him. I've only talked to the mayor once before the arrest and he said play it by the rules. I think the quick arrest came from the prosecutors' side and pressure from the families. They're going to make this case really difficult."

Dave said, "And they'll have all the emotions and sympathy on their sides because two young kids were murdered and they were only charged with petty theft."

"But you know, Dave, I can't figure out where all this is coming from, although I did hear someone mention the name of Berger."

That stopped Dave for a moment. "Berger? You don't mean the guy that ran for a senate seat last year in Pennsylvania. He's the only one I can think of."

"Yeah, that's the one. I'm getting hints he's involved in this in some way."

"Didn't he ever manage to get some other political office?"

"He did, but I'm not sure what. However, his name comes up often enough. He always seems to be involved in something."

"Is he the one that contacted the media because of an anonymous tip?"

"Yes, he's the one, but I don't know what his angle is."

"I wonder if Roy knows him."

"That would be interesting to find out. I've got to go. Sorry for calling you so late, but I won't be around tomorrow and I wanted to make sure that Sammi would be available on Monday."

"Sure, we'll both be there. Just let us know what time."

"Good enough and thanks Dave; I needed to know we had a plan."

* * *

Sammi didn't say a word when she heard the entire story. She had a faraway look in her eye that always worried Dave.

"Okay, what are you thinking?"

She shook her head as she realized that she had been off in space somewhere. "I was thinking that we're again involved in some type of scheme that's not what it seems to be."

"That's a good point. Nowadays it seems that everyone has a hidden plan and a secret agenda. I remember the days when crimes were evident, like a guy robbed a gas station, was caught, arrested and that was the end of that. A lot of petty crimes were like that. But I don't think these kids being murdered had anything to do with their burglaries. I just don't."

"There's got to be more to it than that," she said.

"Enough for now. I'm really beat. Glad we can sleep in tomorrow. Anything on our agenda?"

"Nope, we've got a free day, but I have one more thing to tell you."

"What's that?"

"We got another letter from Linda Saunders today."

Dave turned around stunned and totally angered. There was no doubt about it. "Damn, we haven't had a letter for quite a while now."

"I think it's been close to a year, but apparently she's not quitting yet. This time she actually signed it. She must be going nuts."

"She signed it? That's really crazy. She'll definitely get more time for this. Maybe jail has got her losing it more and more. Let me see it."

THOUGHTS CAN BE DEADLY

Dave was more upset with this letter than with some of the previous ones. She was more threatening and hinted at a plan for escape. "If she's got something going, then it's particularly stupid for her to write this letter. What the hell's the matter with her?"

"I was thinking two things. Maybe she wasn't the one who wrote it; she isn't stupid and that would have been a stupid thing to do. Someone may want us to track her again and get us off something else. On the other hand, she was such a proud woman and she might have to keep doing this to keep herself feeling in charge. Either way it's crazy."

Dave shook his head. "Well, Monday I'll get this on file with the sarge. So far, her thirty-year sentence is up to thirty-two years and I wouldn't be surprised if it keeps climbing higher. But that's enough about that. I don't plan to talk about it any more unless you want to."

"No, I've had enough of her."

"Okay, then I want to clear up a few things around here tomorrow because we're going to be busy starting Monday."

She looked at him lovingly. "This is another crime that we'll take one day at a time and have the entire group available to help."

"Yeah, I know. It's just ..."

She smiled, "It's just that you can't wait to get started. You need to relax."

"Well, let's go then. The bedroom is a great place to relax."

* * *

Sunday was almost boring to Sammi. She had time to do all the jobs that she usually found excuses to postpone. There was the laundry, cleaning the house, grocery shopping and Kali needed attention and some very serious walk time. Dave opted to walk the dog, which gave her time to be alone in her thoughts. She stood looking out the window watching Dave and Kali as they left and thought about rushing around her duties. She was anxious to get time to enjoy the beautiful day as well. Then she saw Dave returning only a few moments after they'd left. She looked to him with surprise and explanation.

"I was thinking of something," he said. "A while back when we worked together on that money-laundering case, I was quite tough on you about going anywhere alone. I know twice that you were miffed because I wouldn't let you take that walk in nature that you seem to require at times. How about we do it today?"

Sammi was immediately excited. "The housework's pretty much done and the laundry can handle itself, in fact, it should be finished by the time we get back. We've got time to get out to that great park we both like and we could take Kali."

"And we'll pick up some groceries on the way home."

"Perfect. Let me get my jeans on; ten minutes and I'm ready to go."

Dave seemed as excited as Sammi for these outdoor adventures, but Kali was the most thrilled of all.

"I'm so glad you thought of this. Housework and laundry is kind of boring, but this makes it okay."

He laughed and they packed the car and were gone within fifteen minutes.

The park was on the outskirts of town where country living began. Therefore, there were a few extra acres of roaming and running for all of them. Although populated, it was sparse enough to feel that they were the only ones out there. Sammi felt that Dave looked relaxed and calm. She liked that. He could get so uptight in his work, but he was finally learning to take problems as they came up. After all, he had three other very competent and long-term buddies whom he trusted with his life and together they could tackle anything. She knew he caught her looking at him.

"Are you staring at me?"

"Sort of. It's nice to see you relaxed when we both know there's a tough case ahead. You're taking things in stride and I like to see that."

He smiled. She knew that he was aware that she'd always worry about him.

"How's your shoulder these days? You never mention any problem."

Dave was shot twice in his left shoulder during a sting operation a few years back. It was serious, in fact, he almost died. The doctors warned him that he'd always have a weakness in that area.

"It's strange. At times, I have no weakness at all, but other times just a little. It's really under control now."

"That was only two years ago so probably as more time goes by the weakness may totally disappear."

"The important thing is that it doesn't bother me anymore."

They were sitting down taking a break on a bench that seemed to appear out of nowhere. They both stared off in the distance enjoying the time they had to be with each other and away from the stress of their jobs. Come Monday morning, it would be another story.

* * *

By the time they headed for home, the sun had disappeared and it took almost an hour for the grocery shopping. They took turns sitting in the car with Kali, as neither one liked to leave her alone for very long. Finally, they pulled into the driveway and figured that Dave could put the groceries away, and Sammi would take care of the laundry. Then they would have some time to watch TV or just unwind and let their bodies store up the memories of the wonderful day.

Dave said, "I'll get these groceries away before you finish with that laundry."

"You're on," she yelled and moved faster than she had in a long time.

Dave won. He even had to admit that it was an unfair challenge but she wouldn't relent. "No, no. You won and I accepted the challenge. So what does it mean?"

He smiled suggestively. "I'll think of something later on."

She smiled and was about to come back with an answer when the phone rang. It was about eight o'clock and that was well within non-panic time.

"Oh hi Billy. How are you and your mom doing?"

"We're fine, thank you. Mom got the charges dropped against her today. She is now a free woman, she says."

Billy was so excited that he couldn't help giggling on the phone. "I told her you had a miracle that you saved just for her. I knew you would do it, Ms. Sammi."

"I think it was your belief that helped me the most Billy. I'm so glad everything turned out okay."

"Mom wants to talk to you now."

"Hi Lily. Bet you're happy it's finally over."

"To say the least. What a strange dilemma I got involved in and I was totally clueless. Actually most people around here had no idea and without you, I don't think I'd be free. So thank you."

"I think you've thanked me enough and those home cooked meals were the icing on the cake. What's happening with Len; catch me up on that."

"He's being held in a psychiatric clinic right now. And it will take time to evaluate him. Honestly, Sammi, I'm glad that I don't have to make a decision on him; you've got to feel sorry for him."

"That's true."

"The gun did prove to be the same one that shot his little sister; did you know that or not? God, I forget what happened before and since you left."

"I think everyone assumed it was true, but I'm not sure that ballistics were back yet. So that's good news."

"And it was the same gun that shot Matthew so Joey said the evidence is irrefutable. The evidence against him is quite solid, but he has confessed, at least sort of. His mind is so messed up; it's really sad."

"Well, keep us updated on that will you? We'd both like to know what happens."

"Absolutely and Billy wants to say goodnight."

"Hi Ms. Sammi. And Mr. Larson came over for dinner again. I told you he likes my mom and my mom likes him, too. She says that he's a nice guy and smart, too."

"I couldn't blame him for liking your mom; she's a nice and special lady."

"I think so and I think you are too, and Dave. I'm glad we're all friends."

"We are, too. You keep in touch and we'll visit each other when we can, okay?"

"Oh yes. That would be nice."

"And tell Marsha we said hi, will you?"

Billy was very excited. "Oh yes, she'll be very happy about that. Goodnight."

"Goodnight, Billy."

Sammi put down the phone slowly and turned to Dave, "That special feeling even comes through over the phone. I just love Billy."

"Yeah, it's great knowing someone like him, and Lily, too for that matter."

"He lives in his own world and so does Marsha, but I think they've got it all together more than other people I know," she said.

"That's for sure. Their world is simple and somewhat pure, you know. It's nice to be associated with him."

Sammi yawned and said, "I'm getting tired."

"Me, too. And I'm ready to collect on winning that challenge."

Sammi laughed. "You know, I let you win. You know that, don't you?"

"Oh sure you did. Why would you do that?"

"Because I wanted you to collect on your challenge."

"Well, okay then. There's no problem here." And they laughed all the way to the bedroom.

CHAPTER THIRTEEN

Sammi was excited to meet Dave at the station. She was anxious to hear what was on Roy's mind so they could understand him better. She hadn't had much interaction with him, and therefore had no chance to begin to understand his thought process or his view of the world. That quick little meeting prior to his employment that had taken place in Sergeant Brady's office was all the contact she'd had with him. She felt that she needed more access, more conversation and more interaction to learn about his feelings and way of thinking.

"Hi Sammi, good to see you," said Amilio in passing.

Jim was already seated at Dave's desk, and pulled up another chair for her.

Dave said, "Okay, what we need to do is ask the right kind of questions so that Sammi can pick up the information we need."

"And what might those be?" asked Jim.

"Anything pertaining to the murders and backtracking into his prior relationship with those victims would bring up his past memories. I think that would do it, right?"

"Yeah, that's part of it," Sammi said, "but I'd also like to find out why he was moved around so much. Does he have any idea about that? Jim, you made it sound like he was happy here because we accepted him. Why didn't the other places accept him?"

"He might not know," said Jim.

"Okay, but I'd like to hear his thoughts on it. It could give us some insight into what he's all about."

Dave said, "I think if we question him like we would any other suspect that those ideas will pop up in his mind and Sammi will get what she needs. Am I right?"

"I think so," she said. "If we keep his mind thinking about the murders and the victims I think I'll be able to tell if he's playing it straight. Remember, thoughts don't lie. So where he goes in his thinking world will be the truth about him."

Dave's phone rang for some ordinary business, which gave Jim time to ask Sammi a few questions.

"So thoughts don't lie and that's how you can be sure what the truth is about him?"

"Yeah and the best part is that even though we say a few words out loud, our thoughts will take in everything we know about the subject. Might sound strange, but that's how our minds work. Think about it. Sometimes when you're asked a personal question, you will be very selective as to what you say out loud, but your mind brings up all the thoughts about the subject and then you decide what you want to share with the world."

"Yes, I see what you mean. That's an interesting world you deal in."

"And it teaches me something new all the time. To be honest, I always get a little nervous. I hope to pick up everything I can, but thoughts come and go very fast and I, too, have to be selective in what I remember because I can't remember them all. So, like today, I hope I pick the right thoughts."

Jim relaxed for a moment and smiled, "You've done excellent in the past and I'm sure if you pick up anything at all, we'll be ahead of the game. Anyway, you'll at least be able to tell us for sure if he was involved in these murders."

"That's true; that shouldn't be any problem at all."

Dave put down the phone and said, "If there's nothing else, we'd better get over there. They only gave us one hour and I want to make sure that we make the best use of it."

Sammi asked, "Where's he being held?"

"In Dalton and that's the first place he worked and was moved out of there fast after that gun episode. Apparently, that's where all of his troubles started. I don't imagine he'll have too many friends around there," said Jim.

"Why Dalton?" she asked.

"Closest to the crime scene, I guess. That's what they usually do. Probably the officers called to the scene were from that station and then they took over."

Sammi nodded and asked, "Did he get himself a lawyer yet?"

Dave and Jim looked at each other and shrugged. "He may be waiting for a little help from us on that one; probably doesn't know one."

* * *

Entering the room designated for the interview, Jim, Dave and Sammi took their seats in their usual pattern. Sammi always sat on the left side of Dave with her note pad, which he could check as time went along to verify the truthfulness of the suspect. Today was no different.

Roy Dawson walked in with drooped shoulders and a confused and dejected expression on his face. It was obvious that this entire arrest episode had rocked his world. He was nervous, sweaty, unshaven and visibly worried.

"Gees, it's good to see you guys," he said and shook Jim's hand. His eyes moved around continuously and his head nodded repeatedly as he said, "I had nothing to do with any of this. I can't believe this has happened. Somebody's got to believe me." His voice had a desperate tone.

Sammi remembered a month or so ago when Lily spoke the same way. Would this have the same type of ending? Time would tell.

Jim asked, "Did you get a lawyer yet?"

"No, I don't know who to call. God knows I need one and I haven't been with the department long enough to guarantee one."

Jim said, "But you've been with the police department around this metropolitan area long enough that you'd be entitled. Do you want me to look into it?"

"Please. That would help. Anybody you think would be good, I'll accept. God knows I'll need a good one."

Jim reminded Roy about Dave and Sammi. "I think you remember both Dave and Sammi. Sammi's going to take notes for us. Let's get started."

Jim asked the questions first. He knew Roy the best and thought that would be a comfortable way to begin.

"Do you have an alibi for that Wednesday night?"

"Not really. I worked until five thirty or six o'clock and then I stopped at that Family Restaurant on Main Street for dinner and went home."

"What time did you get home?"

"Shortly after seven; I listened to the news for a bit and sacked out early. I was exhausted. I know that's not great, but I don't have an alibi, except for the restaurant. I go there all the time and they know me, but the murders happened after eight o'clock they say and I don't have an alibi for that time."

Dave asked, "You live in an apartment, right?"

"Yes," he said.

"And you didn't see anyone, a neighbor, another tenant, anyone?"

He was thoughtful for a moment before slowly shaking his head. "No, I don't think I saw anyone."

"Well, okay," said Jim. "What's with this gun? They say it was a special that you had assigned to you years ago."

"But I lost it. Actually it was stolen right out of my locker and I reported it stolen that same day."

"It was stolen out of your police locker?" asked Dave.

"Yes it was. I went to take a shower and my locker was locked, but when I came back the lock was broken and it was gone. I still have a copy of the report. It's all in there."

Dave said, "Probably we'd be better off getting an official report. What station were you in at that time?"

"That's when I first started and I worked out of the 10th precinct in Dalton, right here and ..." he stopped instantly.

"What?" Dave asked.

"It's probably nothing."

"At this point everything might be something. Tell us what's on your mind."

"Okay, okay. At that time, I was just starting out and things had been going along real good for maybe two years. I was happy there and I felt part of the group. Then all of a sudden my gun vanishes and everything changes after that. I don't know if some of them didn't believe me or what, but the attitude of those guys really changed after that."

"How long did you stay there?"

"About two more years and it wasn't pleasant; I can tell you that. It was as if I was blackballed. I didn't do anything wrong; I mean my gun was stolen right out of my locker. But for whatever reason after that I was ignored and kept on the worst street duty you could imagine. I complained a few times because they sent me out alone in areas that previously always required two officers. I remember thinking that it was as if they wanted something to happen to me. I never understood why they did that."

"Did you have any fights or disagreements with any-body?"

"No, before that happened I got along with everybody, even socialized with a few after work. But after that everything shut down. I never could understand it."

"Did you talk to anyone about it?"

"Only my sarge when I was trying to figure out where I'd gone wrong. He didn't say much except that sometimes, things change, but I knew he wanted me out of there, too."

"So after two years where did you go?"

"That's the funny part. I knew from the gossip that they had been trying to get rid of me for a while, and they were getting increasingly irritated because there was nowhere to send me. My appraisals weren't flattering, but I hadn't done anything to warrant dismissal. Finally when an opening came up in Kingston I got shipped there as fast as they could do it."

"This does seem strange."

"And another thing," he paused, "again this might not have anything to do with anything, but ..."

"Let us decide that," said Dave.

"Okay, well, I was dating this girl, Beth, and things had been great; we were both serious and talking about making wedding plans. Then she dropped me within two weeks of the gun thing. Like I said, I always felt that something strange was in the background, but I was never able to figure it out."

"Beth who?" asked Jim.

"Beth Inglewood."

"And she lives in Kingston?"

"I'm not sure anymore; that was more than fifteen years ago. But at that time, that's where she lived."

"What reason did she give you for the breakup?"

"She didn't. She simply wasn't available anymore, wouldn't take my phone calls and once when I stopped over she wouldn't let me in. She pretended she wasn't home, but I knew she was. I heard soon after that she went away for a few months. I never saw her when she returned."

"That's strange."

"We're looking into these victims right now; maybe they were involved in other things, too."

Roy shrugged his shoulders. "I don't know. Back then, it was always petty thefts, but they were teenagers then. More like kids getting into mischief, but it was still a crime. And the fact that I was the one who caught them didn't make it any easier."

"So after Kingston you ended up in Carbondale?" asked Dave.

"Oh no, I went to Dunmore and Wilkes-Barre and then to Carbondale.

Dave puckered his lips. "That's quite a record."

"I know and try as I may, I could never get that good feeling that I was wanted. They all seemed to put up with me. I did get commended on a few crimes I solved in Wilkes-Barre and I was hoping that would make a difference, but it didn't."

Dave looked at Sammi. She seemed satisfied and they only had five more minutes left.

"Anything else you want to talk about," asked Jim.

Slowly he said, "No, I don't think so, except for the lawyer. They talked about arraigning me in the near future. So I need to be prepared."

"Okay, then, I'll look into the lawyer thing right away. I'm not sure when we'll see you again. Anyone else talk to you?"

"Yeah, some of the officers that I understand were friends of the victims' families. They tried to get me to confess, but I didn't do it. They were really miffed with me."

"How many times were you questioned without a lawyer? Did they read you your rights?"

"They said I didn't need a lawyer that they just wanted a friendly conversation, but I know the drill. The tried to trip me up in my story but I just stuck to it. It's the truth and no matter what happens, no one is going to make me say that I committed murder when I didn't."

Dave looked over at Sammi after that comment. He knew that his thoughts were telling her just what they all wanted to hear.

"I'll get you that lawyer right away," said Jim. "And those guys were out of line; we'll get them on it. You were entitled to counsel before they questioned you."

"I know that and I told them but that's when they'd say it was just a friendly conversation."

"Hopefully with a lawyer we can get to see you more often."

Just then, there was a loud knock on the door. "Time's up," said the officer roughly, and Roy was immediately led back to his cell. And the interview was shut down abruptly. Dave looked up at the large round clock glaring at him from the wall. It was exactly 3:01 PM. These officers made sure that they didn't get any more than one hour; there wouldn't be any break in this case.

* * *

They all stood beside Sammi's car for a few minutes. They didn't want to be overheard by anyone inside, but Jim, as well as Dave, needed to know immediately if Roy was telling the truth.

"He's innocent. He's not involved in these murders in any way and when he says that he's confused about everything, it's the truth."

"God," said Dave, "that means that this guy's being set up for some reason. I think this crime will be very different at the end than it seems to be at the beginning."

"Where do we start?" asked Jim. "I'm really glad that we have a good guy in Roy and when this is over we may have another good cop on our team, but where do we start?"

"I can't believe looking into the recent activities of the victims will do anything. They didn't seem to be connected with him for the last several years," said Jim. "Maybe something else happened ...."

"Well, if something happened that got him targeted for some reason, he's not aware of it. Nothing else crossed his mind that would help that I'm aware of," said Sammi.

"There's got to be something. He was targeted for a reason. The trouble is that he moved around so much there are too many people and too many instances for us to pick one."

Sammi said, "I think we should go back to when everything started going against him. You know right now that he's holding on by a thread. And he's had years of wondering why no one accepted him although he tried to play it straight, at least in his mind. It kind of messed him up mentally and I think that's why he got the reputation for being a loner. He really wanted to belong with some good police enforcement activities and was happy with the way Scranton was working with him, but his trusting ability has taken a beating over the years. Just when he saw a little hope at this station, this happens and he feels shattered again. He's very frustrated and in a precarious frame of mind."

All were quiet for a bit. They knew Sammi had assessed what was on Roy's mind and he was one person that needed someone to believe in him, something he hadn't found in years.

"We've got to go further back I think, back to when it all started," she said.

They both looked over at Sammi.

She continued, "You've got to look beyond Roy, that's for sure. Everyone around here seems to be concentrating on his guilt, maybe because of the gun. But it really was stolen like he said and that's when his troubles started."

"I wonder," said Dave in a remark that he meant to keep to himself but accidentally said aloud. They both looked over at him.

"I've got a feeling that his troubles didn't start when the gun was stolen, but before that. I think something else happened and after that, someone stole his gun and began a chain reaction of bad luck for him that has continued to this day. Look, police do get their weapons stolen, but how often are they stolen from a secured locker right in the police station? This was well planned. "

"He thinks so, too," said Sammi. "He's racked his brain over the years about that thought. But at the time it happened, he went over everything he could think of and came up blank. But it might be a good place to start."

"Right," said Dave. "I wonder what assignment he was on just before this happened. I think we have to get way back into the past and nose around a little bit."

Jim said, "And we've got the perfect person to do that."

"Amilio," they all said in unison.

Dave added, "If there's anything at all out there to be found out, he'll find it. We have to let the sarge know that we're on a mission again. We need time for this one."

"And who knows where it will lead."

"That started in Dalton right, Sammi?" asked Dave.

She nodded. "It was during his first two years and he was in Dalton at that time."

"Okay," Dave said. "I've got to run this entire case by the sarge and I'll do that first thing tomorrow. I'd like us all to be working on this first string. Jim, are you on anything else hot right now?"

He shook his head.

"Good and Amilio hasn't mentioned anything. Not sure what Tom's doing right now."

Jim said, "Oh he mentioned that he was being redirected to some political stuff for a while; not sure what it's all about."

"Well, okay. The sarge has to make the call anyway. But when it's one of our own and we know he's innocent, I'm sure he'll put a priority on this one. And I need our group working together."

* * *

Later that night Sammi still had plenty to say. She was worried about Roy and his fragile state of mind, and more so because he chose not to show it.

"He's barely holding on right now, Dave. It goes something like this. His young life was troubled; I don't think it was by him and his thoughts didn't go there enough for me to catch on to what happened, but when he thought of his early years, he was very sad. So obviously, something happened. But then he thought he found his niche in the police department. He had always been a stable person and fought hard to maintain a pleasant charisma so people would like him. That's very important to him. He was doing great until that stolen gun episode and then, for whatever reason it turned his life around and it's not been the same way since. He's lost all his confidence and belief in himself. And to what I could pick up, just a tad of it was coming back during the first few weeks in Scranton, but that's all gone now."

Dave was thoughtful. "If he was set up early on in his career for some reason, then no matter what he tried after that it didn't work. I'm thinking after a while he wouldn't know what to believe or how to act, right? That's what you're saying happened to him."

"Exactly, and I do believe this guy is strong mentally; I think he held on far past where others would have quit or given up. But he didn't. If we can get this mess straightened out, then he'll believe not only in himself again, but in you, Jim, Tom and Amilio and whoever else is standing with him. That'll go a long way to get his belief back and he definitely deserves it."

"I'm anxious to get going on this. I hope Amilio is available because I'd like to send him to Dalton immediately. With Roy held in that same station where he was harassed, I would imagine that some people are going to be happy he's in jail; he doesn't need any extra problems. And probably a lot of them will be talking again and reminiscing and that will be fertile ground for Amilio."

"I could probably pick up some stuff, too."

Dave barely answered at first. He then turned slowly to look over at Sammi and said, "Not a chance. You go back to work at the bank until we have more people to question."

"But I could be useful and I could work along with Amilio."

"We're not discussing this, Sammi. The answer is no."

She took a deep breath, and slowly let it go. He wouldn't ever let her get in on things he considered dangerous, but Amilio would be there. And if she heard something significant, it could mean a lot in solving this case fast.

She was quiet and that put Dave on alert. "You'll have plenty of other ways to help, Sammi. I won't let you do it this way."

"I think you worry too much about me."

"You're our best ally in a lot of situations and we can't take a chance."

"Okay, I give up." She knew there was no use arguing with him.

* * *

The next day Dave had a meeting with the sarge, Tom, Jim and Amilio as early as possible. He stated all the facts, as they knew them at this time and asked to have his group assigned to this case.

"I've got no problem there. If you have reason to believe that one of our own is innocent and being railroaded, that becomes high priority. I'm sure this comes under the secret ways you find out things, but I'll accept it. You're pretty sure of this?" asked the sarge.

Dave answered, "I'm very sure."

"Okay, that's good enough for me. Good time, too, because Jim and Amilio are pretty open and Tom, what's happening with you?"

"I can put some time into this, too, but I've been singled out to watch out for some politicians coming around in the next week or so. I think it's mostly normal and basic stuff so I'm not sure why they asked for me, but they did."

"Who are they?"

"Larry Laughton, he's one of our reps from the 19ᵗʰ district."

"Where's that?" asked Jim.

"Somewhere to the north of Carbondale, that's all I know right now. It seems a few of them are coming into Scranton for some meetings in a few weeks and I've been asked to ease the way and make sure their security is in place."

"That's not your usual duties," said Dave.

"I was on protection control several years back for a little while, but I was surprised, too when I was tagged for this. I don't think it'll take up too much time. I know I'll have time to help out here."

"Carbondale, isn't that the area that Roy was in just before he came here?" asked Dave.

"Yeah, I think so," said Amilio. "Wonder if that's a coincidence."

"Okay, well," said the sarge, "I've got another meeting in a few minutes, Dave, break this up any way you want, but keep me posted."

"Will do."

They ended up back at Dave's desk and thought about their plan of action.

"First things first. Amilio, we need you to get down to Dalton. That's where they're holding Roy and find out what you can about the past."

Amilio looked confused. Dave caught him up on thinking about some event that must have occurred just before they stole Roy's gun.

"And that happened when he worked in Dalton, right?"

"That's right. It seems to me if everything was so great for the first year and a half something must have happened after that. Find out especially what assignment he was on before his gun was stolen. I think we may have our first clue right there."

"Okay, amigo. I'll get right on it."

Jim said, "I've got to get an attorney lined up for him. The sarge said he's entitled."

"And I want to talk to some of those officers who found a need to question him in a 'friendly conversation' when he'd already requested a lawyer."

"Isn't that best handled by his attorney?" asked Jim.

"Oh yeah, but I want to hear their explanation about this dubious interrogation. He was blackballed for some reason and the sooner we find out the attitude of these guys in Dalton, the better."

"Maybe not all of them will be the same guys that were there way back then. How long ago was it? Maybe ten or fifteen years ago?" asked Jim.

"That's true, but we want to concentrate on the ones that were there or knew something about what happened. Fifteen years is quite a while, but things haven't been buried forever yet."

"Okay," said Jim. "You want to work together on this?"

"Later, but first Sammi and I are going to find one Beth Ingleside to see what she knew back then. Something must have scared her off."

"No doubt, and finding out might be a big part of the puzzle," said Jim.

* * *

It took a couple of days to locate Beth Inglewood who was now Beth Inglewood Canter. She presently lived in Wilkes-Barre and hadn't moved very far from the metropolitan area she'd grown up in. Getting a meeting with her proved a little difficult. She'd been married for eight years, had two children and wasn't at all thrilled at drudging up her past. Dave realized that a phone call had not been the best way to approach her. After a few more calls and her refusal to allow an interview, he had to employ other methods. Since appealing to her sense of fairness and decency didn't work, he called in Sergeant Brady's special liaison who contacted people in Wilkes-Barre that assured Beth this was a friendly interview and that she had done nothing wrong. But she was blunt about the fact that she didn't want to talk about Roy and if she had to, she wanted a lawyer with her from the beginning. It was agreed. In addition, the location for the interview was her lawyer's office. On the ride over Dave had to wonder why she was so anxious about the meeting.

"Man, I can't believe this. We only want to talk to her."

Sammi said, "I wonder if she has a jealous husband who she wants unaware of her earlier activities."

"I don't know. It seems to me more in the category of 'I don't want to get involved.' People are so afraid and many times, you can't blame them. Anyway, we should be able to pick up what we want. We'll question her about the past and her thoughts should come up, right?"

"They usually do. You really can't control your thoughts that easily, even if you try. Now Beth won't even try because she doesn't think there's any reason, but I think what she says out loud will be very telling as well. I'm curious about her story."

* * *

It turned out that the lawyer was a friend of the family so Beth felt somewhat more comfortable with someone who definitely had her best interest at heart. Mr. Ron Lawton began the conversation.

"Beth doesn't want to drudge up the past. We can't understand why this would be necessary at this time. She told me that she hasn't even seen or talked to Roy Dawson since they broke up about twelve years ago."

Ron was a very much to the point type of person, spoke with a sharp tone and manipulated his heavy body with surprising ease. His dark blond hair gave him a friendly appearance, but he could be shrewd and conniving as his roving and piercing eyes connoted. Beth, on the other hand, sat as demurely as she possibly could, but she couldn't hide the fact that she wasn't any quiet or distressed female. Her attractive appearance was compelling, while her posture and unspoken message implied she could stand her own ground with anyone. Because of her obvious strength, Dave and Sammi wondered even more why she'd been so reluctant for the interview.

Dave shot out fast to throw them both off guard. "Why did you break your engagement to Roy?"

Her mouth opened in surprise and as much as she had been warned and wanted to remain quiet, her indignation couldn't be controlled. "I don't consider that any of your business. What the hell brings you here with the audacity to ask me a personal question like that?"

Sammi didn't look up but began writing feverishly on her note pad. Dave knew that he had tripped her up from the beginning. Her thought process must really be kicking in.

Before Dave could speak again, her lawyer jumped into the fire as well. "We knew that you'd be digging into her personal past of which you have no right. That is way off base. That's Beth's private business. I'm advising her to take the 5th."

Dave finally said, "This isn't a court of law; this is an interview. You don't have to take the 5th." And he looked at that lawyer as if he had made an amateurish error, but soon realized that he was already playing games. Then he thought, *okay, I'll have to play some games of my own.*

"Roy Dawson has been arrested for the murder of two boys, Carter Olsen and Brad Nieman. To what I've heard, you used to have a very close acquaintance with him Beth. And if we have to we can subpoena you later for answers that I would assume would be more comfortable for you to answer here."

Beth and Ron sat there in shock. Beth said, "He's been arrested for murder?" For some reason her armor slipped considerably as her nervous tone of voice conveyed.

"Yes, he has and we know that he didn't do it, so we are looking wherever we can to establish his innocence."

Beth looked down at the floor. Her attitude had totally changed. "He was a nice guy; it's just that things happened."

"What kind of things?"

"My feelings changed and I didn't want to marry him, but he wasn't someone who'd commit murder. He was a very dedicated police officer. I can't believe this."

Now was the time for Dave to press harder and he did. He went for it. "To what we understand, everything was going along fine until his gun was stolen from his locker at the station. Shortly after that, you backed off from your relationship without an explanation. I feel there must have been a connection."

Beth was back on the defensive. The shock had worn off and she was combative again. "I don't know when his gun was stolen so how would I know if that had anything to do with the change in him?"

"How did he change?"

It was obvious that she wished she hadn't made that comment. Her attorney told her she didn't have to answer but she said, "Better here than in open court. And I don't doubt that you'd drag me in since it's a murder trial."

"You know we would," said Dave.

She remained quiet so Dave persisted.

"How had Roy changed?"

"He was just different," she said and clammed up.

"So you knew his gun had been stolen?"

"Yes, of course I did. He told me everything back then."

Then she panicked. She realized that she had put herself into a corner. Her lawyer shrugged his shoulders since she hadn't been listening to him anyway.

"Look, Roy was a hard worker and some were against him and they stole his gun, I guess to teach him a lesson."

"Who?"

"God, I don't know."

"What crime was he working on back then?"

"I don't remember."

"But you just said that he told you everything back then."

"That's true, but it was a long time ago."

"Were you threatened to break up with him?"

She sneered at Dave as she answered, "No," but her tone wasn't entirely convincing.

"Was your family threatened?"

She answered, "No," again, but slowly and hesitantly this time.

"Do you know why certain people were angry at Roy?"

"No," and it was clear that Beth was getting her momentum back.

Sammi had been rather quiet but kept writing throughout the interview. She signaled that she thought they had reached the end and she had collected a lot.

Dave ended by saying, "This is all for today."

Her lawyer and Beth echoed each other. "For today? You mean you may interview me again?"

"Possibly or not, I don't know at this time. This is a murder investigation and I'd think you'd want to help Roy out if you possibly could. You did leave him in a difficult way."

For some reason, Beth's armor was breaking again and she looked far away for a moment as if remembering. Then she shook her head and said no more.

Her lawyer said, "We'll fight any subpoena you send us."

"That's your right," said Dave.

Then Dave and Sammi left. They had obtained enough information for today.

* * *

As they walked to the car, Dave couldn't wait any longer. He looked over at Sammi and she nodded. "I think we've got a new direction to go."

He smiled. He was pleased. That's all he needed to know right now.

"I've really worked up an appetite. Can we eat out some place where they have wine and relax? I'll transcribe my notes as soon as we get home and then we'll discuss them."

"Sounds good to me," he said.

Watching Sammi from across the table, Dave knew that she had exhausted herself by the energy needed to concentrate for such a long time. She needed to relax and he wanted her to be at her best later. These notes could be very telling.

"She was an interesting gal," said Dave. "She tried to play the demure act at the beginning but she's a strong gal and I knew she'd speak up for herself."

"I did, too. She's too upfront acting and her lawyer had a hard time keeping her in tow. He seemed so exasperated at times. I wonder why she needed him there."

"Maybe for moral support; she's strong in one way, but did you notice how many times she checked with him before she spoke?"

"Most of the time, unless she was riled up."

"True," said Dave, "but even when he told her to make it brief or not answer, she didn't listen to him."

"Yeah, she needs to be the ruler, that's for sure."

"That lawyer did take a back seat, but I don't think that's his usual role. It's like he knew how she would act but was there more as a favor. Otherwise, I think he would have argued with her a lot more than he did."

Sammi nodded. She yawned, but they were almost finished and ready to leave.

"I think you should rest for a while when we get home. We'll have plenty of time later for discussion."

"I always do better when I get a chance to relax my mind a little, but I want to tell you up front that Beth was threatened and so was her family. There's politics all over what happened to Roy. I don't have all the specifics, but somebody thinks he saw something a while back."

"Maybe he's not aware of what he saw."

"From his thoughts I don't think he has a clue. But whatever he saw is what started him down this road where somebody I believe wanted him dead."

Dave raised an eyebrow and let out a low whistle. "That's important."

"Oh yeah. First let me get my nap to relax my mind and then we'll talk. I heard some very interesting things today."

CHAPTER FOURTEEN

Less than an hour later Sammi was excited to begin transcribing her notes. She had a lot of information for Dave and she was anxious to hear his reaction. He made coffee while she got to work. Although the interview was slightly more than an hour, Sammi seemed to have an endless amount of notes. By nine o'clock she stopped, not quite finished, but anxious to begin.

"Okay, here's what I have so far. Let me start at the beginning. She really was in love with Roy Dawson and has a soft spot for him to this day. Her mind immediately went back to 'what if,' but quickly moved on when she thought of her children. This marriage seems to be a convenience, but she wants her kids to have a stable home. Anyway, she and Roy were making plans to marry, but Roy was out on some undercover job at a bar; I tried but I couldn't make out the name of it. In fact, I'm not sure if she knew what it was. But he saw something or someone there; I think there were two people involved and they shouldn't have been there. These were political figures or friends of political figures and apparently, they still are. I got one name; it was Laughton."

That caught Dave's attention. He sat up straight in his chair and looked over at Sammi with a surprised look on his face.

"What? Who is he?" she asked.

"He's the one that Tom has just been singled out to protect when he comes to Scranton next week. He's a rep from the 19th District around Carbondale. That's all I know about him, but what's this all about?"

"Let me continue. It seems that this Laughton, or to be more exact someone from his group confronted Beth, more as a courtesy he said, and told her that it was going to be real rough around Roy in the future and that she'd be better off getting out right now. Apparently, that same night they threatened her father as well as her mother. They wanted her to break up with him immediately with no explanation given. She balked at this, but they said they wanted him out in left field wondering what was happening. If she did this, everyone would be okay."

"That's why she just dropped him that way," said Dave. "This is getting to be an intriguing plot. But what was the real reason?"

"She was told that he had seen something he shouldn't have and that he was no friend of the right side of the law."

Dave said, "I wonder what he saw. He was on stake out at a bar; what could he have seen?"

"That didn't come up and I don't think Beth even knows to this day. She has suspicions because these guys were from Laughton's office, but she didn't know anything for sure."

"We're sending Amilio out there to see what he can find out. I'll make him aware of this."

"That's one of the reasons she reacted angrily when you asked her why she broke up with Roy. She's still nervous about the situation, even after all this time."

"Probably his people are still around."

"No doubt," said Sammi, "he's still in office. And there's one more thing."

Dave turned to look at her wondering what more there could possibly be.

"Roy wasn't alone that night. There was another undercover officer with him."

"Did he get blackballed, too?"

"No, he was killed in a car accident about two days later."

"No kidding," said Dave. "That seems suspicious. Any investigation takes place?"

"That I don't know and I didn't catch his partner's name, but when this guy got killed, accident or not, that's when Beth took off for a couple of months. Apparently she was told she could come back when everything was in place."

"What does that mean?"

"Honestly, Dave, I have no idea, but it was a phrase that crossed her mind."

"I've got to let Amilio in on some of this stuff. I think he plans to head up to Carbondale sometime this week and nose around a little. He needs to be prepared with everything we've got."

Sammi only nodded; she was getting tired and it was obvious.

"Okay, enough for tonight," said Dave jokingly, "tomorrow will have its own complications."

"I'm heading for bed, you coming," she said.

"In a few minutes. I'd like to read some of your notes again."

"Don't stay up too late. You need your sleep, too."

He smiled and watched her walk to the bedroom. She was so tired and this had been a long session today. He wondered nowadays how he would ever do without her and her additional information.

* * *

At the station the next day the first item on Dave's agenda was to call a meeting with the three referees and Amilio in Sergeant Brady's office. He told them all the details that he knew and was ready for a discussion.

"I see we've got another cover up on our hands," said the sarge.

Jim said, "There's always a lot of that in politics. But Roy must have seen something serious enough to warrant possibly killing one officer and harassing another for years."

Dave said, "Sammi thinks they wanted him dead, too, but maybe two dead cops would have looked too suspicious. We need to know who this other cop was."

"That should be easy to find out," Amilio said. "A cop killed even if it was a car accident will be on file. Besides, we're forgetting that Roy would know who he was."

"That's true," said the sarge, "and since we've got him a lawyer now we should have easier access to him even though he's still being held in Carbondale."

"Still no bond?" asked Dave.

"I think there's a hearing later this week," offered Jim. "We'll see what happens."

"And I've got a lot of work to do. I'll probably get out there first thing in the morning," said Amilio.

"You need any help; do you want someone with you?"

"No, I work better on this type of stuff alone. And I have to get the name of that bar from Roy. Can I get to him today?"

"I don't think so, but let me call his lawyer," said the sarge. "I'll push it and let you know."

Amilio was thoughtful for a moment before he added, "I think I'll wait until I can get a few minutes with Roy before I go on my fishing expedition. Dave, I'd like you to come with me when I talk to him. He doesn't know me that well. But I need the name of that bar, why they were there and who that other officer was. Then I'll be ahead of the game when I go. Understand, amigo?"

They all nodded. The more background he had when he nosed around Carbondale, the better off he'd be.

Back at Dave's desk, Amilio needed more conversation. "So Sammi believes that Roy must have seen something that he shouldn't have seen on a stakeout, right?"

"That's the impression she got. But from what we've heard from him, I don't think he has a clue. He didn't even mention this stakeout at all, so I don't think he realizes there's any kind of important connection."

Amilio was thoughtful. Something wasn't making sense to him. "So he possibly saw something significant but has no clue. He was working a stakeout for some reason and went home without knowing that something important happened."

"That's what we think."

"Wow that must have made it tough on him. Then he starts getting ignored and given rotten assignments and his gun gets stolen and he has no clue why."

"That's what it seems."

"You know regardless of how this plays out, when Roy finds out the real reason for all these crappy events in his life, he's going to be relieved. It's always better to know than not to know. Me, personally, I'm damn curious what the hell he saw. Any ideas?"

"Not yet. I mean he's working a bar, anything could happen. Maybe this Laughton guy was there with some girl and he's married, or maybe he saw someone playing around big time, but obviously it didn't register with him."

"Could be anything. I can't wait to find out what bar it was and get out there and nose around a little. I'll have to spend at least one evening there to see what goes on."

"Should you have someone with you?"

"Maybe I'll take someone that night; I'll see how things play out. We've got a lot to look into."

Dave said, "As soon as we find out the name of that officer who got killed, Jim and I'll look into that. I'm curious if there was anything suspicious about the accident. Was it accepted as an accident from the beginning or what?"

"I think we're going to find a lot of things are not what they seem, big brother."

That caused Dave to laugh. Amilio always referred to him as his big brother and he had to admit he rather liked it. It came from when Amilio first came to the station and Dave taught him what he needed to know.

"You still laugh at big brother, right? But you deserve it and I like you being my big brother."

"Yeah, we're family by now you and me."

Amilio winked and slapped Dave on his back as he got up and left.

* * *

Sergeant Brady called Dave to his office about the same moment that his phone rang. It was Sammi.

"What's going on? I'm curious to know."

Dave said quickly, "We're just now trying to decide what to do. I've got to run – another meeting. I'll call you later."

"Okay, bye," she said.

Sammi realized that her mind was more on Roy Dawson than it was on her own job at the bank. She worked odd hours, as the president knew her affiliation with the police and the FBI and gave her all the space she needed. She had helped him out many times in tight spots and although he didn't know how she got her information, he was always pleased with the results.

Her private phone rang. It was the president requesting her to report to his office. She couldn't imagine what this could be about since she'd been in his staff meeting earlier in the day and he hadn't mentioned anything. She picked up her note pad, a necessary ally and immediately headed for his office. She was concerned; his voice seemed more somber than usual.

"Come in, come in," said Mr. Marconey. Although they had had a close relationship for years, she still called him Mr. Marconey and he corrected her every time.

"It's George today, Sammi," he said forcing a smile.

She sat and waited for him to continue. She sensed his agitation and although she could have read his thoughts, this was one situation where she would let the facts develop as Mr. Marconey laid them out to her.

"I'm sure you can tell I'm worried. Actually, I'm mostly suspicious about a strange request I just received and I wondered if you knew anything about it. Do you know who Thomas Rayburn is?"

She shook her head. The name meant nothing to her.

"He's one of our reps from District 19 around Carbondale."

Sammi couldn't let on, but all of her alerts were suddenly in place. That's the same area that Mr. Laughton was from – another rep from the 19th District. But more importantly, what did all this have to do with her?

"I've had a strange request and you know in the banking business anything unusual puts me in a guarded mood. So you don't know this guy?"

"No, I don't. I've never heard of him."

"What about your husband? Could Dave know him?"

"That I couldn't tell you. I could ask him."

"Tell you what. I'd really like to know that before I continue. Could you call Dave right away and ask him? Then come back here because I have a strange request to discuss with you."

Before she left the room, Sammi did read George's thoughts. At this point, she wanted to know what this was all about before she talked to Dave. And it disturbed her, too. This Thomas Rayburn wanted her to sit in on some bank business that had to do with the Carbondale area. She didn't even know him and wasn't familiar with the area. How had he heard of her? And why would he want her to sit in on any deal they were trying to complete with the bank? She had no power in helping the bank make a decision. Mr. Marconey was right; this was an unusual request that couldn't help but raise suspicions.

* * *

Sammi caught Dave just as he returned to his desk from a meeting. She repeated the request from her boss.

"You've got to be kidding, Sammi? You are, aren't you?"

"No, I'm not. Some rep from the 19th District around Carbondale has requested that I be in on some bank business meetings with Mr. Marconey. He has no idea why I was requested to be there, and wants to know if you've ever heard of him?"

Dave took a deep breath that carried over the phone. "No, I don't really know him, but guess what I just found out? Thomas Rayburn is the other rep that is involved with that Laughton fellow. Amilio was granted a quick meeting with Roy; I couldn't make it, but he told us the name of the bar that he was in and told us the name of the partner that was killed. These two reps seem to be connected in some way. What the hell do they want with you? I don't like this at all, Sammi."

"Hold off. I wouldn't be alone. Mr. Marconey and two other experts in the banking negotiations area would be there as well."

"But why do they want you? How would they have even heard of you?"

"I don't know, Dave. I've never heard of either one of them."

"This really smells bad. You have to hold off. Tell your bank president to postpone that meeting for a while. We need to find out what's going on and Amilio is heading to Carbondale tomorrow to nose around. We'll let George know when he can have that meeting. But first, I've got to make the sarge aware of this."

Sammi knew that Dave was very upset. In addition, she didn't like being the middle of anything so she had to talk plainly to her boss. Dave said she could tell him a part of the story in confidence. Due to their past work together, he knew the president of this particular bank could be trusted. And a delay would only benefit them.

"Mr. Marconey's been told they don't want this meeting until I can be there."

"Well, we may want to have a few other people added ourselves. They may want to know what's going on with Roy Dawson through you, or it could even be more sinister than that."

"But if I sat in with them I could find out what's really going on."

"I know that and it could be valuable, but not unless we have you protected. If these political figures were in on the killing of that cop and the harassment of Roy, then we have some dangerous guys dealing out protected hands here. What the hell did Roy see?"

"Okay, I'll let Mr. Marconey know where we stand and part of why."

"We may have to have a secret meeting with him before this goes any further, and you have my permission to mention that to him."

* * *

Dave had been cautious the last couple of days because Sammi was in a precarious position. He knew he couldn't tell her what to do, yet she understood the strangeness involved with this request. This had to come from the political figures that obviously had their hands in all of these affairs. In addition, people from the Laughton political office had frightened off Beth Inglewood. Okay, it was obvious that they were hiding something, but they needed to find out what. Dave was hoping both of these people would be in the meeting because Sammi could get all of the information at one time. And they definitely needed a direction to follow.

Amilio came up to his desk upon his return from Carbondale. He plopped himself down on the empty chair and stared wide-eyed at Dave daring him to guess what he'd found out.

Before either one said anything, Dave leaned back in his chair and said, "What? Am I supposed to guess?"

Amilio laughed. He liked to tease Dave with new information. "First of all, there's a complete little circle that's formed around these two political figures, amigo. I was hitting dead ends everywhere."

"So you didn't find out anything?"

"Hold on, amigo; I didn't say that. You know I have my ways."

Dave relaxed. "Yeah, you usually do."

"I didn't get the information from any place that you could guess or imagine. You see, that bar that I visited, On The Spot…"

Dave interrupted him, "On The Spot, that's the name of the bar?"

Amilio sneered, "Yep that's the name of the place. It seems that our friend Roy left out an important detail."

"What's that?" asked Dave looking intrigued.

"It's a gay bar."

"Really? He was at a stakeout in a gay bar?"

"Yep. Now he may have been there for another reason. What did he say he was there for, do you remember?"

"No, I don't."

"Well, if he saw someone who hasn't announced their preference, so to speak, this could be a huge charade to keep someone's sexual orientation quiet. For some of them, it could ruin their careers."

Dave said, "And if their career is a front for something else, this could make everything a serious offense. This certainly changes things. But who did he see?"

"You know, amigo, he was a young cop in those days and he may have seen someone or something and didn't even know who it was."

Dave nodded. "And the fact that his partner died within two days is suspicious as well."

"And the report of the accident was quite sloppy, too. Somebody's got to be hiding something."

"Now, Laughton's married, but he may have another side to his life as well. And maybe it wasn't them he saw, but he saw something, that's for sure."

Dave told Amilio about the meeting with Sammi. "And we've got to find out what it is Roy saw. I'm worried about Sammi going to that meeting. It might seem innocent enough on the surface, but why the hell did they ask her to go?

"I have a theory on that," said Amilio. "They (whoever they are) want to know what we know and they figure they'll get Sammi talking and find out at least something of what they want."

"I wish I knew it was that innocent. I want someone from our group there with her."

"I'd love to play that game, but they know me. I'm out. Who else is there?"

"Wait a minute. They wouldn't know Jeffrey Slade."

"Neither do I. Who is he?"

"We worked with him in Philadelphia on those abduction cases. He's about fifty some years old but he has this baby face and you'd think he's a lot younger. He works with Ben Collier at the FBI."

"You think they'd come in on this."

"I think they would on basic principles. They always need Sammi to help them, and besides that, if this is political and concerns a cover up on a murder, that would guarantee their involvement."

"But right now, we don't have any proof."

Dave said, "We have enough suspicions of illegal activity and this is a strange request for Sammi, so I think it'll work."

That was enough for Dave. He went immediately to check with the sarge who'd have to be the one to call Ben Collier for permission anyway. As it turned out, the process was set in motion within a few days. Jeff Slade would come in for the meeting, working as a financial bank consultant, whenever they set it up.

* * *

That night Dave arrived home before Sammi. He was glad to relax for a while and get his thoughts together. He thought she'd handle this well, especially with the additional information that Amilio had picked up. But you never knew about her, sometimes she had a mind of her own.

She walked in the door and saw him sitting, relaxing on the couch. She immediately walked over and gave him a kiss and a hug. As usual, he didn't want to let her go. She laughed.

"I'm hungry. I want to start dinner, and I know you've got something on your mind."

"Yeah," he said. "Amilio got back this afternoon and he had added another twist to this story."

Sammi turned to look at him patiently waiting.

"That stakeout bar was called 'On The Spot' and Roy left out one little detail. It's a gay bar."

He watched the wheels start to turn immediately. Sammi always had a certain stance and posture that was comfortable to her during these times. He smiled and he watched her recognize his familiarity with her thought process.

"That sure brings up a ton of possibilities, doesn't it?"

"It does and my mind has been driving me crazy with a lot of them. Amilio thinks maybe it was these politicians seen at that bar and that could have ruined their careers."

Sammi nodded. "Could be or he saw someone else connected with them. Holy cow. This could put a big problem in some of their careers. No wonder they tried to cover it up over the years.

Next Dave told her about pulling in Jeffrey Slade for that meeting.

"Ben Collier seems to think that they need FBI in on this anyway ..."

"And you'll feel a lot better, too," she said.

"Yes, I will," he answered straightforward with no apology for his feelings.

"I don't mind having Jeff around," she said. "So you talked to Ben?"

"No. Amilio and I talked to the sarge about the latest and he felt with the political twist in this story that he should call Ben and give him any hint of future trouble."

"And Ben jumped on it, right?" she said.

"With both feet. Anything political is always their first priority."

"Okay and I know that makes you happy."

"It does relieve my mind some because we don't know for sure what we're dealing with here. We still need to establish if that first cop was killed on an order or if it really was an accident. Amilio said that the information was skimpy and that the police report was changed a lot with erasures and whiteout used. It doesn't point in a good direction."

"So when do Ben and Jeff want the meeting?" Sammi asked.

"The sarge will talk to your Mr. Marconey and they'll work it out."

"That should work out good and because of the setting I shouldn't have trouble taking notes. I've got a feeling that I'm going to need them."

* * *

Amilio and Dave took time the next morning to talk and try to calm down Roy. He had a bail hearing that afternoon and he was quite nervous. He didn't yet show signs of settling down and felt quite alone in his predicament, even with the reassurance from his department.

Amilio started. "You didn't tell us that the stakeout you were on was at a gay bar?"

"Oh yeah. Why, was that important?"

Dave said, "Roy, everything is important right now. Don't leave out any details. We believe that you saw something or someone at this bar and that started all of your troubles."

Roy looked surprised. "But I don't remember seeing anyone that I knew. No one looked familiar to me."

"It seems that Larry Laughton and Thomas Rayburn representatives from the 19th District around Carbondale are involved in this. Maybe they were the two that were at this bar but you didn't know them and they might have thought that you did. Regardless they are in on this and we have to figure out their part. Do you know anything about them?"

Sadly, Roy shook his head. He was completely confused. "Actually I've never even heard of them. Let me get this straight. You're telling me that I may have seen something or someone thought I did years ago at this stakeout, and that's why I've been blackballed all these years?"

"We think there's a strong connection," said Amilio.

"And I've worked my butt off trying to figure out what I'd been doing wrong and it's possible that I hadn't done anything wrong at all? Someone was out to get me? And these same people could have scared off Beth and ruined my life because of some political game?"

"We don't know all that for sure yet," said Amilio, "but evidence is pointing in that direction."

Roy got up and punched the wall so hard that he hurt his hand. He let out a subtle groan with the pain. "They ruined my life. I've spent years trying to figure out what was wrong with me and where I went wrong. I kept getting moved around and pulling those dangerous assignments ..." he stopped pacing for a moment and turned to stare at them ... "They wanted me dead, didn't they? Holy shit, my entire life ruined because of some ... what? We still don't even know what it is."

"No, we don't," said Dave, "but we did talk to Beth and she was threatened as well as her family. This apparently isn't a little thing. But it's obvious now that someone was playing for big stakes."

Roy shook his head in disbelief. He kept thinking of all those wasted years.

"What about your partner, Jonathon Dailey."

Roy looked confused. "What about him?"

"Did he mention anything to you that night; anything at all that seemed strange or unusual to him?"

Roy thought deeply for a moment, puckered his lips and slowly shook his head. "Nothing. We both left with the idea that we got nothing that night and we'd try again."

Dave asked, "Why were you there? What were you hoping to accomplish?"

"We'd heard that some drug deals had taken place there lately. We had the pictures of a few characters we were trying to find and one was reported to be gay so we went there."

"Do you remember who that was?"

He thought for a moment. "Not off hand, but it should be in the file."

"We'll check it out," said Amilio.

Dave continued. "What about that car accident that killed your partner? Did anyone ever investigate it?"

"It was deemed an accident; I don't think anyone ever gave it a second thought. It's what I was told and I accepted it. Why? You think maybe it wasn't an accident?"

"We don't know," was all Dave would say.

Dave wrote some notes and was getting ready to end the meeting. Roy was getting increasingly agitated.

"And we still don't know who could be behind all this?"

"We're slowly getting some facts," said Dave. "And their downfall is going to be the murder of these two young boys. I think they were trying to take you out once and for all by blaming these murders on you. But I don't know why they picked these particular two kids. Any thoughts on that?"

"I used to know them; I've already told you that. And their families hated me. But I can't believe that they would have killed these kids to get back at me."

"We can't either," said Dave. "There had to be another motive. They could have dealt with you in a list of other ways. Do you know what these kids were into now?"

"No, I hadn't seen nor heard from them in years. Other than these newer burglaries, I don't have any idea what they did. I do know that their families have been on the edge of mob activities for years. That was a known fact back around Carbondale. They had money, position and a lot of power, but that was only rumors."

"But it's an interesting idea," Amilio said. "The mob has its fingers into so many more things than we could even guess. They're shrewd and clever."

The tone settled back down for a few moments. Roy was especially thoughtful, yet still obviously peeved. He finally stood up, shook his head and said, "My whole entire life has been turned upside down by whatever happened that night. I can't believe this. I really haven't had a life because of them; I mean, I lost Beth and I've had trouble making friendships at the other precincts because everyone was leery of me. I've racked my brains all these years and it probably wasn't me at all. Damn, damn, we've got to get these guys."

"We will. And we'll be at your bail hearing this afternoon," said Dave.

Roy looked surprised. "I'd appreciate that."

"We believe in you," was all Dave said in leaving, but the look on Roy's face mirrored deep gratitude.

* * *

The bail hearing was quite volatile and tempers were flying high. Dave wondered about that. After all, it was only a bail hearing. It seems that someone wanted desperately to keep Roy in jail.

Amilio whispered to Dave. "Someone is trying hard to stay in control. They have three of the highest paid prosecutors around here overseeing these proceedings. Wonder if he has a chance?"

Dave was silent, but hoped that the system would work.

Shortly into the arguments, the prosecution got very nasty and belligerent and the judge demanded an apology and took control of his courtroom again.

Then the prosecution started anew. "The victims were young innocent boys, shot through the head by this policeman's gun."

The defense popped up. "That gun was stolen years ago and the paperwork on file proves that this defendant reported the crime."

"But maybe he stole it and kept for future crimes," said the prosecution.

"There's no proof that he's ever seen the gun again."

"But he could have," said the prosecution.

"You'll need to prove that in a court of law," said the defense.

Then the hammer came down from the judge. "I'm already tired of all this bickering. This is a bail hearing, not a trial. Keep to the point. You first ..." he said as he pointed to the defense.

"Mr. Dawson has always been on the right side of the law, solving crimes and keeping the law intact. He's been a member of this metropolitan area all of his adult life working in a legal capacity and poses little chance of running. He wants to clear his name and get back to work. I think bail should be set at a minimum."

"Come one now," said the prosecution. "These are capital offenses that he's been accused of."

"Yes, accused of, not proven with very little physical proof," said the defense.

"And we will prove it in a court of law," said the prosecution in a sarcastic tone.

"And until that day, which I don't believe will ever happen, he is innocent and there's not much physical evidence unless the prosecution is holding back. No one can put him at the murder scene, no DNA, no footprints, no fingerprints ...”

Again, the judge stopped the proceedings. “Look, I thought I was dealing with two educated professionals here. But since I'm not let me again remind you that this is not the trial so I'm not listening to any opening arguments. I will take into consideration that this is a double capital offense of a horrific nature.”

At this point, the prosecution was positively glowing. They felt the judge was leaning on their side.

“On the other hand, his reputation as a police officer does not have any outstanding problems; he seems to have done a good job.”

“But he was still a street cop after fifteen years on the force. That's not any example of first-rate behavior and I beg to differ with Your Honor ...”

The judge stopped the prosecution immediately. “Since you don't apparently know when to shut up, I'll help you. I'm going to grant this defendant bail because I don't think he's a flight risk and I do believe he wants to clear his name and resume his position and especially because I can't stand you interrupting me any longer. The bail is set at $100,000.00.” He then turned to the prosecution and said, “The other thing is that you'll never know how much your interruptions caused me to flow in that direction. That's one thing you'll have to wonder about from now on.”

And down came the gavel. Roy was smiling ear to ear and conferred with his attorney immediately. Dave and Amilio said that they'd check straight away with the department and see what their panic fund held to help Roy come up with the bail money. It might take a few days but Roy would be out of jail and able to help the referees backtrack on his steps the night he was at the bar.

CHAPTER FIFTEEN

That night Sammi informed Dave that the meeting would take place early next week and it would take place at the bank.

"That's a surprise, but I like it. I thought they wanted it at an undisclosed location around Carbondale."

"I thought so, too. I think that Mr. Marconey at the request of Jeff Slade insisted that it be at our location. Jeff will attend as a new regional manager who has complete authority over loans and presides over every one. So in this case, he calls the shots."

"Great. Do you know who's coming yet?"

"I've heard both Larry Laughton and Thomas Rayburn will be there."

Dave raised an eyebrow, which prompted Sammi to explain. "They're the reps for the 19th District and this land is adjacent to their responsibilities. But I should tell you that they again wanted to be sure that I'd be there."

Dave shifted in his chair. His uneasiness was apparent. "What in the world do they have in mind? I have to think they feel they may be able to ask you pointed questions, put you on the spot and find out something."

"But I'll know what's on their minds so this should be an interesting match."

"Still I wish we knew what we were dealing with here. Amilio and Roy plan to get back to Carbondale as soon as he's out. They're going back to that bar and sniff around a little. Since this stuff is still going on, they may pick up something."

Sammi nodded and said, "But how do these young kids fit into all of this. I'm blank, how about you?"

"Most of us have come up will all kind of theories, but they're only guesses. I sure hope you pick up something at that bank meeting."

"I understand it will be a long meeting. They're bringing in lunch. They want to discuss the purchase of land that has liens and other problems attached to it. So they'll be discussing reports and scenarios positive to their side and that'll take a while."

"What does that have to do with the bank?"

"They want a rather huge loan. The bank needs to know the background, risks and everything else connected as far as infractions, possible lawsuits, legal aspects, everything and that's why Jeff is being brought in as a loan expert. I'll be working as his associate, kind of like I do with you and taking notes. I use that special shorthand so he won't be able to read it anyway, but I shouldn't miss too much."

"Will you be allowed to ask questions?"

"I'm not sure how they're working it right now. But when I talk to Jeff and Mr. Marconey that morning I plan to insist on my need for clarification in some areas. Then I can steer them where I want their thoughts to go. But I can't imagine what questions they'll ask me; although I have a strong feeling I'll be a target in some way."

"I do, too. Otherwise, why insist on you being there?"

Sammi got surprisingly quiet.

"You nervous about this?" he asked.

"No more than usual. I think its more anxious anticipation."

"You don't know what day, then?"

"Not yet, why?"

"Well, Amilio and Roy will be nosing around like I told you, and Amilio is good. He may have something we'll want you to bring up."

"I was told the middle of next week."

"It might work out – they're going out there on Monday."

That was all the conversation they could handle for the night. Dave reached over for Sammi's hand and put his head back on the couch. He felt comfortable and satisfied. They were heading in a good direction. And as long as Sammi was protected, he was satisfied; she needed to be there from their point of view also. He heard her start to breath deeply. He wanted to relax for a few minutes longer; it was a pleasing moment.

* * *

Roy left jail on Saturday afternoon in plenty of time to get his affairs straightened out and begin a logical transition to free life. He was anxious to join Amilio and head back to Carbondale, and by early Monday morning, they were on their way, but this time he was on the outside ready to discover anything to help his case. They nosed around the station asking for files and documents and although the greetings weren't friendly and seemed aloof and distant, they weren't refused any information. Amilio was mostly interested in the car accident and the lack of investigation of a hit and run of a police officer. There were erasures and white outs on almost every page of the rather extensive report and Amilio was refused access to the original report saying that it had been destroyed. He didn't believe it. He knew it was unavailable only for them.

He went back to the officer at the desk. "I can't even make out the name of the driver in this report. I need to talk to Officer Letting? Is he still around?"

"No, he retired five years ago."

"Okay, give me his address then; I'd like to talk to him."

"I think that's confidential. He's a retired police officer and wants to remain anonymous; you can understand that."

Amilio continue. "Yes, I can but I'm not going to give away his cover. I only need to talk to him about this accident."

"No can do."

"Or you won't," he replied and got a very disgusted glance in return.

As he walked away, Roy was at his side in an instant. "I guess that's that. I didn't think they'd be cooperative with us."

"Oh, I'm not finished; subpoenas do wonders if it gets to that. Let's see if we can find Officer Letting on our own. We have a wonderful computer expert by the name of Julie Mucci at the office. That girl can find anybody, anywhere, anytime. I'll get her on this one right away."

Roy seemed to perk up and they headed back to Scranton.

* * *

They stopped at Dave's desk, which was the usual proce-dure for anyone in their group. He was anxious to see what they'd found out.

"We're being shut out. Dave," said Amilio. "Whatever happened is still closed to any outsider. You should have seen that pathetic report about the hit and run of Officer Dailey. I've never seen anything like it. You would have had a fit if any of us had turned in a report like that; I'm sure you would have refused it. There wasn't even an investigation and I couldn't make out the name of the driver. There were white outs and erasures all over the pages and no one had even bothered to hide them. Sergeant Brady would probably have used it as an example of how not to write a report." He saw the surprised look on Dave's face and added, "I'm serious."

"But it proves that we're dealing with a cover up and possibly a conspiracy; who knows what else?"

"But why?" asked Roy. "We still don't have a clue."

"I think we will by the later part of this week."

Even Amilio looked stunned.

Dave told them about the meeting that Sammi was required to attend.

Amilio seemed almost smug. "Well, now we're getting somewhere." He turned to Roy to explain, "Dave's wife Sammi can find out information when everyone else fails. I still can't figure out how she does it, but she's good. So if she gets around some of these people, she'll find out something, that's for sure."

Roy turned to Dave and asked, "How does she do it?"

Dave smiled and then laughed as he said, "I'm sworn to secrecy. It's not my place to tell."

"I've been trying to figure her out for years," said Amilio. "It's not that I've completely given up, but let's just say that I'm real glad she's on our side no matter how she does it."

Roy sat back and relaxed. He felt he was part of something and it showed. Dave liked including him in this group. He knew when all this was over he'd have another good officer, and one who'd gotten his life back after having had it taken away from him for years.

Dave's phone rang. It was Sammi.

"I just found out that the meeting is set for Wednesday, and listen to this. Other than, Larry Laughton and Thomas Rayburn, they're bringing in land surveyors and one of their lawyers. The meeting is supposed to last most of the day, so I'll be pretty busy."

"That's a lot for you to handle – all day long." Dave was talking rather hesitantly.

"You're not alone at your desk, right?"

"That's right, but I'm glad it's this week. We need to move on this stuff."

"We should have enough breaks during the day to give my mind the rest it needs. I'll be okay."

"Okay, we'll talk tonight."

As he put down the phone both Roy and Amilio were satisfied the meeting was Wednesday and they knew that a

happy Sergeant Brady would be pleased that things were
finally starting to move.

* * *

That night Dave briefed Sammi on Amilio's day.
"They're still covering up stuff over there."

"I hope I'll have new input for you after our Wednesday
meeting."

"Oh and we've got Julie trying to track down that Officer
Letting. They wouldn't give us any information on him, but
he's retired now and he may be willing to let us know what
really happened back then."

"The answers are ready to come out of the woodwork,"
said Sammi. "I think the time has come and we'll finally find
out what really happened."

"Me, too. Cover ups are always the strongest at the beginning when they threaten people into silence, like they did with
Beth and her family, and usually as time goes by people are
more willing to talk."

Sammi understood.

"I want you to take it easy tomorrow and get some rest.
You've got to be at your best on Wednesday."

"I will."

"Oops, sorry. I didn't mean to put more pressure on you.
We've got a few areas we're dealing in right now, but I hope
we can come at them from all sides before they know what's
going on."

"Even though they still seem rather cautious for some
reason, they've got to have let down their guard somewhat
over the years. And we can get them at their weakest spot."

"So you feel okay about this meeting?" asked Dave.

"I do and with Jeff and Mr. Marconey there, I still wonder
why they want me. I have to think it's to get to you."

"You do have a bit of a reputation you know. It could be they've heard of you and maybe even want to see if they could coax you on their side."

Sammi's lips pursed at the idea. "I hadn't thought about that."

Dave's head tilted as he pursued the idea. "They'll follow all their angles."

"And so will we."

Sammi yawned and felt that she was ready to turn in. Dave followed her and said, "I want to make sure you get your rest."

* * *

Julie found Officer Letting within two hours. He hadn't moved very far at all; he was over in Wilkes-Barre, and Amilio and Roy got over to see him by late Monday afternoon.

An older but quite congenial William Letting let the two officers in. He acknowledged that he remembered Roy Dawson and offered them coffee.

"I retired a few months after I hit my 65th birthday. I could have stayed on longer, but I'd had enough. Things weren't always handled above board and when you're a dedicated cop, it makes it hard."

Amilio and Roy just let him relax and talk. He seemed like he had a lot to get off his mind and their questions could come later.

"Some of the superiors were on the take, but most were good guys and that put us in a bad situation. I suppose you're familiar with all that, Roy."

Roy shook his head. He didn't know.

"Well, it didn't used to be like that. When I started way back, everything was done by the book and we had a good, clean department. Later on, I'm not really sure what happened, but I know that we had some of our bosses catering to characters that I felt should have been in jail themselves. A few of us complained at times, but we were reprimanded. So we learned to keep quiet and do the best we could. That's not what being a cop is all about. We did do some good work in spite of those few, but it made it hard."

Roy asked, "Was some of this going on while I was there?"

"I know it was going on when you came, but I'm not sure exactly when it started. It really irritates me to this day because you always hear about bad cops and there aren't that many. Most of them are good and dedicated to what they do, but a few of the bad ones make all of us look bad."

"What were they doing? Did you ever find out exactly?"

"Most of it I didn't have any personal knowledge of, but I do know what happened to your buddy Jonathon Dailey was not an accident."

He leaned back in his chair and picked up his cup of coffee at that moment. As he took a sip, it was obvious that a quick thought flashed across his mind. He couldn't wait to swallow his drink and relay his thought.

"I was told to change that report you know. They sent it back to me three times because I didn't change it enough the other two times, I guess. But did you see the erasures and changes?"

"Yeah and we had to search for you. They wouldn't tell us where you lived."

"No kidding," said Bill with interest. "After all this time they're still playing games. I went to my superiors about having to change the report and I could tell they didn't like it but were in a bind. Isn't that a crock? We're the police and we had to go against crooks."

Amilio and Roy both looked confused. Bill noticed it and decided he had to let them in on what happened.

"Okay most of what I'm going to tell you I know is fact. But some of it is also guesses … pretty solid guesses from what was going on, but still a guess." He turned to Roy and asked, "You never knew why you were blackballed, did you?"

"I didn't even know I was being blackballed until about a month ago."

"No kidding," said Bill. "That's too bad. I know you were a good cop but you and Jonathon were in the wrong place at the wrong time."

Amilio asked immediately. "Do you know what happened at the On The Spot bar that night?"

He nodded. "I'm pretty sure; most of us were pretty sure. The rumors were rampant back then. Some people had proof, but no one ever came forward."

Bill took another sip of coffee and then seemed to settle in, ready to tell the story.

"I figured that was why you came here, to find out what I knew. I really thought you knew more Roy. Anyway, when you and Jonathon were at that bar, Scott Laughton came in. Do you know who he is?"

"I'd guess he's related to Larry Laughton the rep from the 19th District."

"And you'd be right. Larry fought for years to keep hidden the fact that his brother was gay. He felt it would hurt his career. Besides that, apparently he was on drugs and made a drug deal that night. I heard you were in view of him when he did it. That would mean that you could tell about his brother being gay and being a drug addict. They couldn't take a chance."

"But if I saw him, I didn't even know who he was. And Jonathon didn't mention anything either. We were there to find out about drug activity, not one or two little buys. So if this guy was around, we didn't even know."

Bill stopped Roy at this point. "You did know, whether you were aware or not. He was pretty stoned when he first entered; he tripped at your table. He spilled his drink on one of you."

Roy gasped. "I do remember some drunk spilling his drink all over Jonathon. In fact, we'd been there over an hour and decided to leave after that. That guy was Larry Laughton's brother?"

"It was."

"But so what? It still doesn't make sense."

"It would if you knew that his brother always had him tailed so that he didn't cause trouble for the family or for their careers. Now this type of information wouldn't have just done the Laughton family a lot of harm, but also the entire Rayburn clan as well. And they have tough characters in their groups."

Roy sat back in his chair completely stunned. "We didn't know anything. We even let that kid go because he wasn't alone and the guy he was with came over and got him and apologized to us. I remember now; we figured he'd take care of him and no real harm was done."

"But that guy recognized both of you as policemen from Carbondale and they couldn't take a chance that you'd remember who that boy was."

Amilio asked, "So they killed Jonathon because of that?"

"You know these characters will kill for a lot less. I never found out if the orders came from Larry or not, but this guy's task was to keep him out of the headlines with his problematic life style."

"Did you ever find out who drove the car?"

"I did and I've kept track. He's in jail right now on other crimes. I would imagine he'd be looking for a sweet deal in case you had any thoughts along those lines."

"What's his name?"

"Jordan Angler. I could never forget him. He just ran him down like a dog. We had the car, the broken headlight and all kind of evidence, but they let him go and closed the case quickly. They wouldn't even allow an investigation. It made me sick."

"We'll be following up on this and want to thank you," said Amilio. "Anything else?"

"I should be thanking the two of you. This has been heavy on my mind for years now. I'm sorry Roy that no one stepped forward to help you. They wanted you gone, probably wanted you dead as well as Jonathon."

"I do thank you now, Bill. It's a relief realizing that I wasn't screwing up but that someone had an ulterior reason for giving me all those average reviews and rotten assignments. I put in so much effort trying to do a good job, but I couldn't get recognized for anything."

"And that's why you were moved around. And with the questionable recommendations that followed you from Carbondale, you would always have a problem. Sorry for my part in it."

"I appreciate you stepping forward now."

"I know it ruined your relationship with that girl," he said. He looked over at Roy with true regret in his eyes. "But I had heard they got to her, too. Kind of changed your life, didn't it?"

"Yes, it did, totally. But I think I'll be able to go forward when we find out who killed those boys. Any ideas on that?"

"Not really. I've been out of the loop for a while, but just remember that power, politics and money is their main goal and I don't think they'd let anything stand in their way."

They left shortly after that wondering what length these families would go to save their image. If their children were causing trouble, and rumor had it that they had been in trouble for over five years, it might be very interesting to know who gave the orders.

* * *

The first thing Amilio did on Tuesday morning was make his way over to Dave's desk and sit down looking as if he'd won a prize. He knew his information would be welcomed.

After he relayed his story, he waited for Dave's comment. "Now we're getting somewhere. I was thinking that maybe Larry Laughton himself was gay or something like that, but it was his brother and he was on drugs as well. This is beginning to make sense. If anyone got a hold of that story, well, a lot would go down for him, politically as well as personally. Probably anyone connected with him would suffer as well. They must have watched him closely."

Amilio said, "I heard that they always had someone with this Scott guy to cover up and clean up after him. The kid's a mess."

"Where is he now?"

"That I don't know but we could put someone on that and keep him tailed. We may need him sometime or other."

Dave looked over searchingly. "I think we may have enough on him for now."

"Sure, he's certainly not one of the main players."

"You have something else in mind right now?" asked Dave.

"Yeah, I do. I want to get over to the prison and find out the attitude of that driver, Jonathon Angler."

"Where's he at?"

"Don't know but I'll check the computer or have Julie find him. Bill seemed to think he was in for assault and robbery, and he might be looking for a sweet deal."

"If he told us who hired him to do that hit and run on Jonathan Dailey, we'd certainly have the beginning of hard evidence."

"If we get the right answers. You think he'd admit to killing a cop?" asked Dave.

"Sure, for a plea deal. Especially if he knows the proof is out there and that it just wasn't followed through. He'd realize he had a big problem and would probably be ready to wheel and deal."

"But Sammi's going to that meeting tomorrow. She should find out something. It's still strange to me that they are so insistent that she be there. I really don't like it, but we'll have a few of our own people in this meeting."

"Can you get away with that?"

"Yes, we can. They're bringing in a few experts of their own because this land deal they want is very complicated so if we have a few extras they shouldn't question it. But I still wonder why they want Sammi in on this?"

Amilio thought for a moment and then came up with, "She's getting to be known for things. I know you're not crazy about it and neither is she, but maybe they have suspicions about her."

"I'm afraid I thought about that or they want to find out what the police are up to through her."

"That's possible, too. In fact, I think that's more likely. I mean she's married to a policeman and who better to try to lean against than her." But then, Amilio laughed.

"What? What's so funny?"

"It's just that they don't know Sammi. I think they picked the wrong person to try to pump for information."

Dave smiled. "Let's hope so. Let me know if you get there this afternoon and talk to this Angler guy. I'd like to let Sammi in on his attitude before the meeting tomorrow morning if possible."

"I'm on my way," said Amilio and walked away like a guy on a mission. And he was.

* * *

Dave's concern came through loud and clear that evening. He had trouble settling down and consistently shifted his position in his favorite brown recliner. Sammi watched him but said nothing. He had to work it out on his own.

Finally, he looked over at her and said, "How do you feel about tomorrow?"

"A little anxious on the one hand, but then I usually am in these situations. Yet all I have to do is listen to them talk and pay attention to their thoughts. It's not like I have to create anything."

Dave nodded.

"I might ask a few pointed questions if I get the chance and if I'm not picking up the thoughts I want. But Mr. Marconey is aware of me and so is Jeff, so I'm not going out in left field on my own. And they'll both cover for me should some delicate situation arise. I feel I'm on solid ground."

Dave only nodded again.

"Look, honey, I'd rather be working with you because you know what I can do and you help me by getting people thinking about what we need. In this case, I'm thinking if they wanted me there enough to request me twice, their minds will be moving pretty fast. I should be able to find their ulterior motives, but if I can't I'm sure at least I'll pick up what's really going on."

"I wish I could be there."

"I know you do, but not this time; it just wouldn't work. I really think one of those guys is going to throw some unexpected questions at me and try to find out something about the case. I really think they insisted on me being there for that objective. And personally I think they want to know the general attitude of the police department on these murders. This may be a land deal, but I'll guarantee you that part of the time will be spent talking about their son's murders. And that's when I'll get what I need."

"You're probably right. The newspapers are full of these stories so it would seem logical for someone to talk about it," said Dave.

"And I'll bet you that it isn't one of them but one of their subordinates that will bring it up to make it seem more off hand."

"Really? You think so."

"Oh sure. When the deliberations get a little touchy or possibly even going against them, one of the others will say something like, 'don't forget Mr. Laughton is under a lot of stress with his son's recent murder;' or something like that. It wouldn't surprise me at all."

Dave was quiet for a few minutes and was about to speak when the phone rang. It was Amilio. He mostly listened for the next few minutes and then made a few comments and hung up.

"Well, it seems our driver, one Jordan Angler has been ready to spill his guts for a long time. He's in for ten to twenty years for aggravated assault and robbery and from his point of view he was supposed to be protected. But everyone seems to have turned their backs on him."

"Maybe they figured if he was in jail he was out of the way."

"And they were wrong. He knows a lot of the dirt that's been swept under the rug and for a sweet deal he'll tell all."

"But doesn't a court of law take that into consideration. They might just believe that he's making things up to save his own skin."

"There's always an element of that, you're right, but if he has proof to back up his theories and if he can bring other names into the circle which he says he can, that should make everything he says more believable. Don't forget that we've got proof that he murdered that police officer by running him down with his car and he needs to cooperate now."

"I see, then it's not just his word but if others come forward, too with other stories and hopefully more proof. That makes sense."

"I really hope we can take them down this time. These are bad people."

"And they've ruined Roy's life. He's lived under a shadow and it ruined his perspective about life and trust and people and everything. They ought to pay for that, too."

"I hope they pay ... big time."

CHAPTER SIXTEEN

That Wednesday morning Sammi felt like she was doing everything in slow motion. Her mind was so sharp and alert even at home that it unnerved her some. She was always aware when she had to be and she knew how to tune into others, but today she felt a lot depended on her. She dressed slowly waiting for Dave to finish his shower and relaxed with a cup of coffee. That's when it happened.

She felt her Grandpa Logan in the area. She couldn't see him or hear him and she couldn't exactly feel his presence, but she knew he was there. And although no words were spoken, she felt a strong and welcomed relaxation cross her body and reassure her of her gift. She remembered that her grandpa, who also had the gift of hearing others' thoughts, always told her, *just do your job and the universe will do its job. Everything doesn't depend on you. Your concentration and willing attitude is all you need. Let the cosmos do the rest and you'll always get what you need.*

She needed that guarantee at this moment and that's when she knew that all the help she'd ever need would always be with her. She needn't worry at all. There were no coincidences in life and the day's happenings would follow along the course of probability. She felt relaxed, so totally relaxed that she didn't hear Dave come into the living room.

"Are you okay?"

"I'm fine. In fact, I'm real good. I'm just relaxing and getting my mind prepared for today. I'll do okay."

Dave sat down next to her on the couch.. He looked over with concern and caring.

"Whatever happens will be fine. Remember we already have something on them and they're going down. If you don't get everything we need today, we still have other ways and the chinks in the armor are giving away."

"I know," she said, "and I'll be glad to get home and transcribe my notes. Tonight ought to be an interesting session. What are you up to today?"

"I'm going back to the prison with Amilio. This Jordan Angler is supposed to have written some stuff down and is willing to start naming names. So I just might have a lot to tell you tonight as well."

Sammi got up swiftly and looked down at Dave to say, "I'm ready. I should be leaving and I'm looking forward to this."

He smiled. "Me, too. We should both find out good stuff today."

Dave walked over to Sammi gave her a kiss and a long hug. As she turned to walk out the door she said, "I love you Dave Patterson."

"Love you, too. See you tonight."

She smiled and left.

* * *

With that, she was gone. He took a few more minutes and wasted some time before he headed for the station. Kali needed to go outside and definitely wanted some food. He had a little more time than Sammi today so he sat and watched their dog gobble up her food, look for more and finally settle down satisfied. He looked around their home and thought that he'd done well with his life. For a while, things hadn't been going too well for him and he wondered if he'd ever get on the right track.

His first wife had been killed as she tried, without his knowledge, to get information for him in a murder case. He always felt the bullet was meant for someone else, but she died anyway. Although his marriage had been on the rocks it didn't lessen the pain and it took years of going from one girl to another to ease the sting he constantly felt. After working more intensely with Sammi, he realized that they had a good thing going. Taking it slowly was both their wishes, but the caring grew over time and now they'd been married for nearly two years. He realized that he'd made a good choice.

The phone rang. It was Amilio.

"What time you getting here today? I'd like to get to the prison this morning."

"I'm on my way. I'll be there in twenty minutes."

"Good enough. See you then."

They'd be going back to the prison to try to pry more information out of the hit and run driver. Actually, he didn't think it would be too hard since he was looking for a deal to reduce his sentence. And he did have a lot of information that they could use. Leave it up to Amilio to find this one and get him in a very cooperative mood. He was very good at that.

* * *

Sammi waited at her desk until Mr. Marconey called her into his office. She noticed that he seemed agitated, which surprised her. This was a meeting to insure whether a bank loan was feasible, and the decision wouldn't be made today. Why was he uptight?

"Sorry, Sammi, I didn't sleep well last night. Something about this entire thing is making me edgy."

"At least today we'll know what they want."

"But that's the problem. They've been talking about a loan to develop that land north of Carbondale. I don't know if they want condominiums, shopping malls, or whatever, but there are liens against the land so until those are satisfied there's no real reason to have a meeting. I talked to Larry about this, but he said it was just a preliminary meeting to see what the bank's position was. It seems funny to me."

"We'll know soon enough."

"Yeah and even if they hadn't insisted on you being there, I probably would have wanted you there. You pick up things and I want to know their main purpose. But why do they want you in this meeting at all?"

"I haven't figured that out."

He smiled. "Bet you'll know by the time the meeting's over."

"Hope so," was all Sammi answered.

Then Mr. Marconey's phone buzzed and his secretary said that the group had arrived for the meeting. They headed to the conference room, which was a familiar territory to Sammi.

* * *

As they walked into the room, all the men stood up. Introductions were made and Sammi took a seat on the left side of Jeff Slade. That was the position she usually took with Dave and felt comfortable with his substitute for today. She had but a few moments to get used to the atmosphere of the room as the leaders spoke a few words. The colors around Laughton and Rayburn were dark and dismal, which always connoted to her that there were secrets and ulterior motives. She did realize that today would be a difficult task with so many people's thoughts crowding in on her. But she knew how to handle a crowd; she'd done it many times before.

Mr. Marconey called the meeting to order. "Okay, gentleman, I understand that you wanted this preliminary meeting so as to get an idea how the bank feels about the possibility of a loan toward the purchase of land in the Carbondale area. Am I correct?"

"Yes, of course," said Mr. Laughton. "This is only a preliminary meeting. Depending on where our conversations go today and what you decide, we'll know if we can go ahead or not."

"You won't get an answer from me today; I'll have to take our information to my lending committee and Mr. Slade here will present it to our Board of Directors. This is quite a large loan and the decision-making process is far beyond me."

"We understand that," said Jim Andover, one of their lawyers who could also have doubled as a bodyguard. "This is preliminary remember that. We want to know where you stand depending on our presentation."

"Fair enough, but I want to know why you wanted Sammi here? She has nothing at all to do with accepting or rejecting loans."

Sammi couldn't have been happier; Mr. Marconey wasn't holding back and he did put them on the spot. Although the lawyer answered the question she was more interested in hearing the thoughts that were crossing Laughton and Rayburn's minds. And they already started to present some cautious consideration. They both knew that she had been present in other difficult negotiations that ended up being beneficial to the clients, and outwardly, that was their reason for requesting her presence. But inwardly were a very different set of ideas.

They stayed off their main topic, which was to find out what the police department thought about this deal. They didn't want any problems there. Instead, they began with the endless slides and paperwork, which was discussed in exact minute detail. It seems that these families had possession of most of the property in that area and were trying to accumulate the only parcels of land that still didn't come under their control. But it was a tremendous amount of land and would necessitate a huge loan. And their main purpose was to monopolize the area in the future.

By lunchtime, the slides and presentations were not over yet. But it seemed that Laughton and Rayburn were distracted much of the time. Sammi was concerned about certain recurring thoughts that seemed to dominate their mind. Although they kept the outward conversation centered on the land deal, many worrisome thoughts crossed everyone's mind on the opposite side of the table from Sammi. She wrote as many notes as she could because the details were sometimes sketchy and caused her confusion. She could sort them all out later.

Thomas Rayburn became pushy and aggressive at one point, which made Mr. Marconey sit back. Jeff took over and pushed back in a way foreign to his demeanor and character and with his boyish look that hid a clever and sharp mind, all were surprised that he packed such a strong personality. But then to settle down everyone Mr. Andover said, "Sorry about that, but you have to remember that Mr. Rayburn and Mr. Laughton both recently lost their sons in a horrendous murder scene and they are still distraught about it."

Both of the men apologized and Mr. Rayburn looked to Sammi as he said, "We hope the police can solve this crime." And their nosiness was one of the reasons for this meeting.

Sammi said nothing and kept a straight face, but she had received some shocking information. It was all she could do to write it down and pretend that she was the note taker for their side. It seemed to satisfy them.

However, Mr. Laughton wouldn't let it die. "It seems to me that by now the police should have found out something. I mean such young victims who didn't deserve to die should be a top priority."

Jeff looked over at Sammi who wanted him to let them continue, so he did. They both sat and let these men get everything said that they wanted and it was giving Sammi access to almost everything she needed. She found it hard to sit across from such hard-hearted men.

Finally, one of them pointed a question directly at Sammi, "Is this case progressing? Surely you should know something with your husband being one of the detectives on this case?"

Sammi paused for a moment giving them reason to wonder if she'd answer at all and then slowly said, "That's something you'd have to ask Detective Dave Patterson. I only deal with bank business."

The rebuff was not appreciated, but it was accepted. Then their lawyer said, "It was an innocent question; they wonder what's happening with their sons' murder."

"I understand and I think the police department should answer those inquiries," she said. Sammi kept a bland expression, didn't blink at all, and held eye contact with their lawyer who realized quickly enough that she could not be bullied.

She'd heard one remark cross Mr. Rayburn's mind that although she looked like a pushover, she was a strong-minded woman and they'd misread her.

Jeff said, "I think we should get back to this business deal. You've said that you still have more slides and more paperwork. It's already two o'clock. Do you think we can finish today?"

"Yes, of course. We only have about another hour. How does it sound to you this far, Mr. Marconey?" asked the lawyer.

"I've already told you that I don't make the decisions. The questions I've asked were simply for clarification so that I can present an accurate picture to my board."

"Yes, of course," said the lawyer.

They were losing points in this meeting as far as they could tell, but Sammi was getting a powerful amount of ammunition against them.

As soon as the meeting was over, they left quickly and forgot most of the pleasantries that usually accompanies the end of negotiations. They were miffed and it was obvious to all concerned.

"They didn't like the fact that our decision could take a couple of weeks," said Mr. Marconey. "God, what did they expect? They want to borrow millions and their collateral is minimal at best."

Jeff said, "They were on a fishing expedition and they didn't get very far. Although they tried to fool us with their slides and reports, they seemed more interested in the killing of their sons. And although that might be expected, if that's what was on their minds, why didn't they get a meeting with the police department? No, I think this meeting was two-fold. They want a loan, maybe later down the line, but right now they wanted some inside information about those murders."

"And they weren't too subtle about it either," said Sammi. "Where do you think they'll go from here?"

Jeff simply shook his head. "The land deal is one thing they want, but this other stuff seems heavier on their mind right now. I think they'll go fishing for information somewhere else."

Sammi had to agree with that. They were not about to give up, and at this point she was one of the few people who knew why.

* * *

Dave and Amilio met with Jordan Angler around ten o'clock that morning. Dave thought he seemed a little young for his crime sheet, but he was someone who looked younger than his years. His rap sheet said he was forty-two and Dave would have put his age closer to thirty. Sometimes you could never tell about people.

Jordan appeared eager for the meeting when he entered the interrogation room. His mouth was in gear as soon as he walked through the door.

"I've written down some stuff that I know you'll be interested in. But I want to know what's in it for me. I'm not giving out all these facts for nothing. And I've got proof so that should be worth something."

"What we'll do," said Dave slowly and methodically trying to relax Jordan "is to look over what you give us and if there's information that we can use we'll give you consideration for helping us solve the crime. What that means is we'll make our recommendation for leniency to the board and they'll make the decision."

He wrinkled his nose. He didn't like this idea at all; he wanted an answer right away.

"That's not how the system works," said Dave. "You should know that. Everything has to be checked over and verified and then if everything is true, and you helped us out, then we can help you out."

Jordan didn't like these long explanations; he was looking for yes or no answers and it was obvious. But, after he thought about it for a moment, he nodded.

"Yeah, I know that's true. I've already had a year knocked off my sentence because I cooperated on something else, so I guess I'll have to take the chance."

After that, they all sat down at the small conference table with Dave and Amilio on one side and Jordan facing them from the other side. His nervous personality still came across as he tapped his fingers on the table continuously.

"I could get killed for some of the things I've written down here ... and yes I'd be willing to testify. But I'd need some protection when I get out. They'll be some people coming after me."

"How long are you in for?" asked Amilio.

"I've still got nine years to go and even in here it'll be dangerous if I testify, but I figure I'm halfway dead anyway. My life has come to an end unless I can get something working for me."

Dave only nodded and Amilio was still reading his file.

"Can you protect me? That's what I really want to know."

"We'll have to determine that, but usually what happens is if your testimony is crucial, we'll have you testify and then moved somewhere else under another name to finish your sentence. After that, we'd have to decide later what would happen next."

Jordan stared off into space for a while and then said, "I don't really have a choice. They could come after me right here because I know they want me out of the way so that I'd no longer be considered a problem. And when I admit I ran down that cop, I'll probably get more time. But putting it all together, I might get leniency helping you get the guys behind everything and then later maybe I can start a better life. I really don't have any other choice. Someone could get me in here anyway."

Dave almost felt sorry for him. He was in a tough situation and he realized it. He wondered what his young life was like. He wondered what had gotten him to a point where he would run down a cop for money. Sammi always tried to figure out reasons behind behavior and she had him doing it, too.

"Okay, since this is my only shot, let's begin." He got out his notes and began. "First of all, I've got proof for most of this stuff and that's good because no one would believe me on most of it. Larry Laughton and Thomas Rayburn ordered the hit on that cop. Larry's brother who's gay and a drug dealer had been at a bar and caused some trouble and they thought this cop would rat on him. So I got a contract to kill him and they even suggested a hit and run."

"What type of proof do you have?"

"Two other people were with me when I took the deal and they had already asked someone else who'd turned down the job. And I've got all their names."

Dave seemed satisfied on that one.

"Admitting to killing a cop could go bad for you, but this cooperation could change a lot of things for the better," said Dave

"I know that. With everything else I've done, plus killing that cop, I know I won't get out of here anytime soon, that's for sure. But it could clear my way to get somewhere else and finish my sentence with less possibility of them getting to me. It's worth the chance to me."

"Okay," said Amilio. "Do you know anything about the murder of Carter Olsen and Brad Nieman? Those families seem to be into many things, political and otherwise. Do you know of any connection?"

A very strange look came over Jordan's face. He knew and he wasn't trying to hide it. Dave wished Sammi was here and could hear his thoughts. This guy knew something and he was debating in his mind if he should tell.

"What?" Amilio asked. "You know something about those crimes?"

"I do, but I don't have much proof. It's only rumors and stories but I know where the trail leads."

"That could go a long way to see how much time we could get off your sentence," said Amilio trying to raise the bar a little.

"I know; I know. Give me a minute."

They watched Jordan as he sat there and looked at the wall, down at the floor and back up at the ceiling. He looked down again at his notes and pursed his lips. He had a major turmoil going on inside and desperately needed to make a decision. They waited him out. He couldn't be pushed on this one.

Finally he was ready.

"I know for a fact that Olsen and Nieman were the ones who contracted to have their own sons killed. It had to do with some payback from years ago and this way all of the dangling problems could be resolved. It was done with the help and approval of Larry Laughton and Thomas Rayburn, who'd been

promised political and financial favors." After that, he stopped
and looked back and forth from Dave to Amilio trying to
figure out if they believed him or not.

Dave felt somewhat irritated with his comment at first; he
didn't believe it and felt that he was given out shocking
information to better himself. He couldn't accept such hard-
hearted tactics.

"I can tell that you don't believe me, but I know who they
talked to and these people have proof. It's recorded on one of
those phone things that can take pictures. And I know who
killed them, but they're part of the mob activity so they'll be
hard to find."

Then Jordan shut up, sat back and waited. Amilio was the
first to talk.

"Who are they?"

"You mean names; hell I don't know their names. But
both Rayburn and Laughton know them personally. They
didn't want to take any chances."

"So you're telling us that these two fathers ordered the
killings of their own sons?" Dave asked. "That's hard to
believe."

"Why? They hated those kids, and by the way, they were
their stepsons, not their real kids. Look into their backgrounds.
These kids never got along with their stepfathers and would
have been tossed out years ago if not for their mothers. They
did nothing but cause trouble. Look into their story and you'll
not only believe it, but wonder why it took them so long."

Dave noted that Jordan was quite adamant. This still
seemed far-fetched to him.

"And who has these pictures, and what good would that
do?"

"The pictures include the audio, too. One of the guys was
afraid that maybe one of them would change their minds and
wanted to have proof. The fathers don't know about the
proof."

"Holy shit," said Amilio. "If this is true, that would be real proof."

"What do you mean, if this is true? Okay, I'll tell you one more thing. You know Scott Laughton was a favorite brother although he had a lot of problems, but it seems that mostly he was kept under control. It seems that Larry Laughton and Thomas Rayburn were really pissed off about something, but I don't know what. I know it had to do with those burglaries, but also stretched back to those cops seeing his brother in that bar. Anyway, it was putting a real strain on the relationships between Nieman, Olsen and the politicians. Now the fathers of those kids had a big stake in keeping close knit with the political force around here. I heard that since the kids were always a problem for them anyway that they agreed to have them murdered and get that other cop out of the way by blaming him for the crime. This put them in real tight with the politicians."

Dave and Amilio looked at each other. They hated to believe it but this story made sense and now they were beginning to consider it. But was the proof available? They'd need to look into this for themselves.

"Okay, now," said Jordan, "you can't tell me that you don't like that information."

"No, we can't," Dave said, "but we have to find a way to check it out."

"Ask around, those stepdads never had any use for their stepsons. That's a known fact. I've told you all I can. Hell, I'm in jail, but I still have some friends who tell me what's going on. I could ask a few more questions and maybe I could get newer details, but I don't know for sure."

"We have to check the rest out for ourselves, but if this all checks out we can recommend leniency."

Jordan sat back and smiled. He was sure now that a deal was in the making.

* * *

When they walked to the parking lot, they were both silent. Amilio couldn't believe some of the stuff that he'd heard and kept shaking his head lost in thoughts that were trying desperately to make sense out of a senseless situation.

He said, "It seems hard to believe that we hit the jackpot on this one, isn't it?"

Dave said, "Yeah, but we have a lot of work to do checking all this out. If we can verify even some of this, we're going to be opening a big door that won't be closed for quite a while."

"You know," said Amilio, "I was wondering about the mothers of those two boys. They're the birth mothers and I'm sure they have no idea how their sons were killed. And if it came out in the open, I've got a feeling, amigo, that they might have plenty to tell us as well."

Dave let out a slow whistle. "That's a thought. And another thing, I can't wait to see what Sammi picked up today. Both of these guys were in that meeting at the bank."

Amilio laughed. "I'm sure she'll have plenty to say tonight. But we still need solid evidence."

"Let's get back and have a meeting with the sarge. I think he'll put out an entire unit on this one. We need this proof and we need it fast."

"Okay, amigo, but it's already past lunch time. Wouldn't it be better to wait and see what Sammi finds out?"

"I plan to mention that meeting to the sarge and I'm sure we'll all have another meeting first thing in the morning. Then we can get a plan in place. I sure hope Jordan was telling the truth, especially about those pictures and audios. That would nail them for sure."

"He probably is. You know if he lied to us he'd be in a worse spot than he is now and I could smell desperation on him," said Amilio. "I mean I think he even knows a lot more than he's saying. He's been with these people for a long time I've heard, and that's why he still hears things. His ten-year sentence is already down to nine years, but his main concern is staying alive. I really think he was telling it how it is. I wouldn't be surprised if he spiced it up a little, that's a gimme, but he needs some favors and this is his way to get them."

"Yeah you're probably right," said Dave who wished in every part of his being that Sammi could have been in this meeting. Yet he knew she was gathering a lot of information in her current situation.

* * *

Dave made it home before Sammi. That was unusual but he felt that her discussion after the meeting with Jeff Slade and Mr. Marconey would be as detailed and lengthy as the meeting itself. His own meeting with Sergeant Brady made him realize that his sarge was more excited than he had seen him in a while. He would immediately get a unit or two out in the field checking clues and names hoping for a new direction to solve some mysterious and secretive crimes. And when Dave reminded him that Sammi would probably have found out something today at her meeting, he simply nodded his head realizing that finally they were making an inroad. He immediately set up another meeting for early Thursday morning with the three referees, Amilio and Roy.

Dave had ordered a pizza hoping that Sammi would be home by the time it arrived. And she had just walked in from the garage when their front door bell rang. She looked surprised.

"I ordered a pizza," he said.

She smiled. "Great idea." Then she took a few minutes to relax and change into comfortable clothes. By the time she came out the pizza was on the table along with two glasses of wine, napkins and an inviting atmosphere.

Before she sat down, Dave came around and gave her a big hug. "Let's not discuss anything now, but wait until we eat and enjoy our wine. But I've got news, too."

She said, "So do I."

"Okay, then that's it until later."

They ate their pizza, trying to relax and stared at each other with expectancy and excitement in their body language. The pizza was especially satisfying and the wine accompanied them into the living room where they relaxed for fifteen minutes before either one of them talked.

Finally, Dave looked over and said, "You look mighty relaxed."

"And pleased. I did find out some pertinent stuff today," she said without much emotion in her voice. "Some of it wasn't very pleasant."

Dave took a deep breath and said, "Same with me. In fact, some of the interview with this Jordan person produced shocking stuff. Amilio and I both questioned him a lot about it, but he seems to be able to get some proof. So we're already looking into it."

Sammi took another sip of wine. "I've got work to do first. I have to translate my notes and that might take a while. Why don't you take a nap or something? You've been working so hard lately."

"So have you. Tell you what. I'll clean up the kitchen and probably come back here and relax until you're ready."

"Okay," she said and immediately left for her computer room.

It took a while and much emotion as she poured through her notes. She didn't take it lightly that she could hear other people's thoughts, but when she was working against evil people and criminals who wanted to rule the world in their own way, then she could handle her feelings and put them into proper context.

It was more than an hour later when she finished and found Dave already asleep on the couch. She didn't know if she should wake him or not. She stood there watching him sleep; he seemed so innocent and childlike. They could talk about this later tonight and she could use a shower to refresh her body and mind. She decided to do that first.

By the time she got out of the shower, Dave was awake. "I guess I took a little nap," he said obviously feeling a little guilty.

"It's okay," she said. "Now we're both ready; you want to go first?"

"Okay," and he went over every detail that he could remember about their meeting with Jordan. "I sure wish you'd been there. Then we would have known for sure."

"I may have picked up corroborating evidence. Larry Laughton definitely had thoughts cross his mind about his stepson's death. And he was the one who ordered the contract. In fact, he was the one who asked Thomas if he knew of anyone who could accomplish the deed. These stepfathers had their own stepchildren killed."

Dave shook his head with the confirmation.

"What bugs me is that they weren't stepfathers for just a year or a very short time. They were fathers to these kids for more than ten years. They had developed a relationship and some type of bond. My God, how could they do this?"

Sammi found this difficult to handle and her voice was quivering as she continued. "I imagine the mourning mothers don't have a clue. I wonder what will happen when they find out."

"I thought about that and hope that they might turn evidence on their loving husbands. I think the bond with their child will be stronger, don't you?"

"No doubt," she said. "Apparently the real reason that they wanted me at this meeting was because they heard I was in on the Botsford and Milliken accounts and those turned out well for the clients. So I guess they thought I'd help their cause, but they did try to get information on how the investigation was going. They said it was because their sons had just been killed and they wanted to know if the police were getting anywhere."

"So you were right?" Dave laughed.

"Yeah, I was pretty sure they'd pull something like that. However, as they were asking these questions, their thoughts were going over how they had handled the contract and whether they were still on safe ground. There's someone named Evers whom they dealt with and he was there during the negotiations for these killings."

"Wait a second," said Dave as he checked his notes. It took him more than a few minutes to get to that part. But sure enough, the name was there.

"That's one of the names that Jordan gave us. In fact, I think that's the same person who had a phone picture and audio of the meeting. It looks like this guy is checking out."

"Both of these fathers had a string of girlfriends in the last year. Maybe some of them might have a story to tell, especially if they were thrown over for someone else."

Dave agreed. "That's a good angle. Your story is checking out with ours. That's very good."

"What's next?"

"We've got an eight o'clock meeting with the sarge tomorrow morning. He's got units ready to go talk to these guys and find out what they know, and I know he plans to get us warrants so they don't have time to dispose of any evidence."

Sammi smiled for a moment, looked at Dave teasingly and then spoke. "I've saved the best for last."

"There's more?"

"Just one thing more. Mr. Laughton thought about this guy so many times there's no way I could miss this. The guy who actually shot the kids was Spike Evers. Now he was arrested on another charge just three days ago and Larry is petrified that he may try to deal his way out of his latest trouble. In fact, he was looking into something happening to him while he was awaiting trial."

"My God, Sammi. We have to get to him right away. He'll be looking for a sweet deal. In fact, this guy alone could be our main witness against the politicians and fathers, but then with all the others well, I think we're on our way. We're going to have one hell of a meeting tomorrow morning."

Sammi sighed. "At least Roy Dawson will be off the hook. He has a ways to go to heal his personality and repair the damage that was done to his self-esteem. Is he going to stay in this area when all this is over?"

"I certainly hope so. I think the referees and the others could go a long way to help him. We accept him totally and the fine job that he continuously tried to do despite the odds against him."

"I hope he does, too. He seems like a nice guy."

"He sure had to believe in his work to plod on despite what was happening."

Then they both relaxed. It didn't take fifteen minutes before Sammi fell asleep. She'd had a long fruitful day and yesterday was full of tension leading up to it. He gently tugged at her shoulder and startled her.

"It's time for bed; you're exhausted."

She didn't answer out loud but said something undecipherable through her yawns. Dave didn't think she even realized that she had automatically gotten up and headed for the bedroom. But he was tired, too, and not far behind her.

CHAPTER SEVENTEEN

The activity in the station the next morning was erratic at best. Sergeant Brady was running in at least five directions simultaneously and every time Dave tried to get his attention, he signaled a few more minutes. Dave knew that he was already moving his men out to some of the significant areas. They had several names and warrants for each one of them in case they balked about anything. It was almost a half hour later when the meeting with the sarge finally began.

"I've sent LeBron and Tyrone over to talk to the wives. We want to question them again with the thought of planting an idea in their heads that their husbands may have been involved in killing their sons. These women should know a lot of what's been going on and that could certainly help us."

"You think we should do this now," Amilio asked.

"Yes, I do. These women will know within a few days anyway. I plan to put out some new spins so that the witnesses will know they aren't alone. I think we'll get more of them to cooperate that way."

Amilio shrugged. "I can't disagree with that."

"What about the other children?" Dave asked. "Maybe they know a lot as well."

"Now I believe that will have to be down the line a bit, but I do plan to question all of them. This certainly has turned out to be a different ending than we thought it would be at the beginning."

"And what do you think about Roy? Would you keep him on after all this?"

"Hell, yes," said Sergeant Brady. "He didn't do anything wrong. He had a hell of a life because of the shadow they put on him. He deserves a break and I hope he wants to stay with us."

Dave was glad and leaned back as the phone rang.

"No kidding," was all he said. "Right … get right on it."

He stared out at his group. "We've hit pay dirt already. We were able to pick up another guy who knew of the video and audio tape of the contract transaction. Apparently he was there as well."

"That was fast, and Jordan said there were three guys there," said Amilio.

"LeBron said that when he was on the way to talk to the wives, his radio broadcasted a robbery on the way. They stopped for a moment out of curiosity and these suspects looked familiar. A call to our station confirmed that one of them was none other than Mason Denners, a close friend of Spike Evers. No surprise there. He didn't have any evidence on him, but he knew about the video and confirmed there was audio as well. My source tells me that Mason will rat on anyone to get some kind of a deal. They're on the way here with him right now. We can start questioning him right away."

"Wow," said Dave. "That was lucky."

"And if he checks out and the wives are clued in, we might have a lot of stuff real fast. I can't believe this is happening so quickly."

The sarge moved around paperwork on his desk, found what he wanted and then continued. "There are a lot of people involved in this caper. And I don't think we know all of the crimes they've committed yet. Tell you what. Dave and Jim, I want the two of you here working the phones. We need someone who can direct our people to what they should be doing. I've giving out the word that the guys out there will contact either one of you for further directions."

Dave was disappointed but didn't show it. He wanted to get out there and be where the action was. On the other hand, he'd find out by phone and radio communication what was happening.

"Where's Roy gonna be?" asked Amilio.

"On desk duty. I don't want him in on any of the action. We don't want any distractions here."

Therefore, Dave and Jim returned to their desks and waited. This was not what he wanted to do, but even Dave had to see the wisdom in this decision, but he didn't have to like it.

Immediately the phone rang and one of the field workers was already asking for some guidance. Dave knew immediately what he ought to do and moved him along. He no sooner put the phone down but it happened again. It seemed that the sarge had several units out there. It was evident he was trying to rake them all up in one day. He sat and worked the phones. Another call. It was Sammi.

"What's going on?" He briefed her.

"Not what you wanted to do, right?"

"I probably would have handled it differently, but the sergeant has his own way of doing things. So it's okay."

"As long as we get them."

"That's the plan. Look, honey, I have to go and keep this line open. Tonight, okay?"

"Bye," was all she said.

* * *

Within the next four hours, only a few people had escaped their drag net and both Larry Laughton and Thomas Rayburn were brought in for questioning. These two guys were totally stunned and walking around in their own self-created nightmare. They had no idea that anyone was on to them; they thought they were home free as they'd been in the past. In less than an hour, an entire entourage of lawyers were crowding into the station, loud, boisterous and demanding to see their clients. Dave realized that the sergeant would have a circus and a calamity on his hands for a while. But knowing Sergeant Brady, he'd get it under control quickly.

Some who walked through the door came as surprises for Dave; others were complete strangers. Many he didn't even recognize, but knew that they were probably some of lesser-known criminals closer to the bottom rung on the ladder. They were the ones out there doing the dirty work, but would pay the price as well. It always went down that way. Because of that, these guys were ready to spill their guts to get a better plea deal. And this was one of the equalizers in this nasty business.

LeBron and Tyrone were back before three o'clock. They both came over to Dave's desk, the usual resting place for tired officers.

"Okay," said Tyrone. "Those wives were shocked and totally traumatized. They had no clue and are currently in disbelief, although anger and fury did come out in the form of language not usually used by ladies." Tyrone did have to smirk a little. "We tried to present everything to them as delicately as possible, but when the idea hit them about their husbands being involved in their children's death, well, this is making everything a lot harder for them. Mrs. Rayburn already contacted a lawyer but said that she would have a lot to say later. She also said that her and Mrs. Nieman would discuss things with their lawyers first, but they were sickened and furious. I thought they would both get physically ill. It hit them that hard. I think we'll have some great allies here."

Dave nodded. "I'm sure they don't know everything about their husbands' business dealings, but they probably know enough. Either way ..." Dave paused for a moment. "This entire thing has snowballed; I've never seen anything like it. It's as if after we found the main offenders, like Laughton and Rayburn, we only had to backtrack a little and the lesser criminals involved are spilling their guts. We barely have enough officers now to get all their stories. Sergeant Brady is thrilled and the mayor is looking for a commendation for a bunch of us already."

Tyrone said, "I know what you mean. Damn, I've never before seen everything come together like this. They're coming out of the woodwork. But I'm not surprised, not really. I've seen this happen once before, but not all at the same time like this. I'll bet in a few weeks we'll have enough proof to take several of the top guys on the way to a very interesting trial."

"These guys have been a sham for a long time," said Dave.

"And brought down a lot of good people."

"That's true, and Roy Dawson was one of them. What a waste. He really is a good cop and kept trying in spite of all this."

"The worst criminals are not the obvious ones; to me, the most evil are the ones behind the scenes like these two. They do so much damage that isn't even obvious unless they get caught."

Tyrone shook his head and threw out a disgusted look.

Dave said, "Don't get bogged down on the negative side. Think of what their exposure will accomplish and remember the success we've handled."

"Good idea," he said as he got up and walked away.

Dave again thought of his father and knew he'd be proud.

* * *

That night with most of the discussions behind them was the first time in weeks that Dave could relax.

"I almost don't know what to talk about," said Dave. "We're usually so involved in these tense situations."

"I'm glad we're getting a break. I know there's a lot in front of us, but the proof is pouring in ... isn't this something?"

"Yes, it is, but it's about time. These guys have corrupted a lot of people for long enough."

"Did they ever find out who stole Roy's gun and who kept it all these years?"

"Not yet, but that should be coming out soon enough. Spike Evers got it from somebody. Still, the trail could be murky. I'm sure it leads back to those politicians who were waiting for the right time to accuse him of something big to get rid of him for good."

"Still, I'd like to know," said Sammi. She always had trouble if all the clues didn't fit in together.

"Some things we never find out. This may be one of them. At least we know that someone else had the gun. That's really all we need."

Sammi was half-satisfied, but her mind would always wonder.

"Talked to Julie and Jill today?"

Dave looked over with a devilish look and said, "Are you gals planning something sneaky again?"

She laughed. "No, not at all. This one will be totally upfront."

"This one ... this means that you are planning something."

"Absolutely. We're going to give Roy Dawson a party when the charges are dropped against him."

"No kidding," he said. "I like that idea. That should go a long way to help him realize that people understand what he went through."

"We thought so. He needs a major confidence boost put back into his psyche. I was thinking that Amilio dealt with this type of stuff somewhat, but he knew what it was all about. That was different."

"Yeah, he was playing both sides ... double agent ... and only a few of the people at the top knew he was really a good guy. Yet it was still difficult for him at times, I'm sure. All of his former friends here thought he was a mole and that got him some nasty treatment."

Sammi took a deep sigh and looked pleased.

"Okay, so what exactly are you girls planning?"

"Like I told you, as soon as the charges are dropped against Roy, we want to have a nice party for him, so that he'll know that people believe in him. He really needs that."

"I'm always suspicious when the three of you plan something together."

"You should be."

Dave laughed and left that alone. He figured this time it would be pretty much what she said with no surprises. But then, he was never sure.

* * *

It was less than two weeks later when most of the evidence was documented and lawyers were plentiful in their continued appearances with their clients, many of which couldn't make bail. The station was usually crowded.

"God, there's barely sitting room at this station most of the time now," said Amilio. "But it's a good excitement. So what's happening today?"

Dave offered, "The roundup is continuing and it's hard to believe how far and wide this group worked. We've even found out about a few other murders that took place near Philadelphia that seems to be tying in here. So let's see, the last few days brought in the wives of our favorite Nieman and Olsen, who had plenty to say about the hidden business dealings, which involved their husbands. I understand Mrs. Nieman knew about one affair her husband had a while back, but other than that, she felt they had patched up their marriage. She was in for one big shock."

"And never underestimate the fury of a woman," said Amilio.

Dave laughed. "But in this case I can't say I blame them. I know the women weren't squeaky clean either, but the shock of the far-reaching affairs of these so-called loving husbands of theirs was more than they could handle and, of course, the main shock was them realizing their husbands were involved in their children's death. They've already notified divorce attorneys."

"No kidding, already?"

"I think they want their husbands to know that they mean business. The two mothers had a meeting of their own the other day, I understand and they really want to get back at these husbands. There's no forgiveness for what they did, they said. No matter what, they did have their sons killed and I'm sure they'll tell all they know."

"You know amigo, it seems to me that these guys must have known that it was going to happen sooner or later. They couldn't keep doing what they did and think they could always cover their tracks. It just takes one forsaken lover to cause a riot."

About this time Tom walked over.

"Where have you been, amigo? I haven't seen you for the last couple of days."

"Today, I just got back from talking to that Spike Evers again. He turned over the audio and visual tape of that meeting and I personally walked that evidence over to our lab for handling. We don't want to take a chance of losing that."

"But it also seems that he's ready to testify in person, right?" asked Dave.

"Hell yes. Anything for a lighter sentence and he knows something about getting that policeman killed and getting Roy blamed for a lot of that earlier stuff. These guys play nasty games."

Just then, Sergeant Brady walked up smiling to say that another fish had been caught.

"When all this goes down we should have a much cleaner community, at least for a while."

Dave sat back and smiled. They were all proud.

"And Sammi sure brought in some nice information again. She sure can pick up information," said the sarge.

Dave looked proud. "That she can."

"I know the mayor plans to have some citations and plaques given out to us and he plans a nice celebration dinner for us. By the way, Dave, even Sammi's name was mentioned for some type of award."

Dave looked horrified. "I'd better run that by her. I'm not sure she'd want that."

"Why not? She certainly does her share in helping out around here."

"I know, but still, let me get back to you on that."

The sarge looked slightly confused, but shrugged it off.

"It's great to see us all in tight with the mayor again," said Dave. "It was barely two years ago when he had distanced himself from our entire group and that made all of our jobs harder."

"That's right. It wasn't that long ago, but in one way it seems forever."

He turned on his heel and walked away again as his name was called across the room. Other crimes were still coming in and even though they'd had phenomenal success with this one in the last few months, it had taken years of its toll on people like Roy and others caught at the beginning of this crime spree.

* * *

"I talked to Marlina today," said Sammi.

"Oh yeah, their wedding's getting close, isn't it?"

"Yes, less than a couple of months now. Does Amilio seem nervous?"

"Funny, but he said the other day that he's not anxious about marrying Marlina; he knew she was the one for him for many years now. But I guess the ceremony itself makes him nervous. I had to remind him that the marriage rite wouldn't take that long."

"What did he say about that?" she asked.

"Only that he'd be glad when it was over."

Sammi laughed. "If he can handle all of the police and double agent business he's had in his life, I guess he can handle this one wedding ceremony."

"One way or another he will; I'm sure."

Dave paused before he brought up a touchy topic. "The sarge said today that a lot of the police officers will be receiving citations and awards for their work on this case."

Sammi smiled, "And I'm sure you'll be one of them."

"That's true," he said and then added, "they want to give you an award as well."

Sammi looked shocked. "They can't do that. It wouldn't work."

Dave immediately added, "Now settle down, I told the sarge that I'd have to run it by you anyway."

Sammi took a deep breath. "I can't, Dave, for a few reasons. First, it would make me more obvious and known and I don't want that."

"People are getting to know about you anyway."

"I know, and that can't be helped. But this would broadcast it a lot more and … no, no, please, I don't want that."

"Okay, don't worry. I'll tell him. I'm sure he'll respect your wishes."

Sammi was silent for a few moments. It prompted Dave to ask, "There's more, isn't there?"

She turned her entire body in his direction as she answered, "This is a gift I've got and if I used it for personal gain … and personal recognition would be part of that, well, I'd have a price to pay. I appreciate the mayor and the sarge thinking of me, but I can't let them do it. Honestly, Dave that would frighten me in ways that I'd have trouble explaining. I think my gift might actually lessen if I let that happen."

"Yes, you've mentioned that to me before. An award never came up before, but I won't let them do it. But they do appreciate you."

Sammi sat back on the couch relaxed. "And I'm happy they do; I like the fact that they realize I do help, and that's more than enough."

Sammi was satisfied that she wouldn't be recognized and was back to her comfortable self.

"When's the party for Roy?"

"In about three weeks. It will be on a Saturday and we're having it at one of the local Roma Halls. We plan on having about three hundred people."

"Wow that should help bolster his self-confidence."

"Yeah, I know. We thought by the time we ask all of the police officers and their wives and other friends he's made over the years, we're already over two hundred people so to be on the safe side, we're getting this hall."

"Does he know about it or are we surprising him?"

"Good question. Julie and Jill thought we ought to tell him, and I agree. It'll give him time to think it over in his mind, probably get nervous about it, but also realize that he does have many friends out there who are on his side. And that's what this is all about anyway."

"That sounds good."

"Has he said anything about staying here in Scranton?"

"The way he talked the other day I think he plans on it. He hasn't said anything definite in words, but sounded like he planned to be here for a while."

"You know I think ...." The phone rang. It was Lily Caulkin.

"It's good to hear from you. How's everything with you and Billy?"

"We're fine, thanks. Hope everything is good with you and Dave. Just a minute, Billy wants to get on the extension."

"Hi Billy. You're doing well I hear."

"Hi Miss Sammi. I am doing good and I'm always happy when I'm talking to you. My mom is still dating Joey Larson and that's nice. I like him a lot."

"That sounds good Lily."

"He's a nice guy and we do have a lot in common. Didn't think so at the beginning but now I found out that we do think alike and we're so comfortable together."

Billy added. "But they're just friends, like Marsha and me, and you can love a friend."

"And how is Marsha?"

"She's fine and excited that I was going to talk to you. She said "Hi.""

"Well you tell her hi and that I miss her. I miss all of you."

"That's one of the reasons I was calling. I have a little time off in about three weeks and Billy and I'd like to come down and see you. Would that be okay?"

"Absolutely, we'd love to see you both."

"Okay, then I'll call you before we leave but I thought I'd take Friday off and come back on a Sunday. It'll be a great trip for both of us."

"And tell Mr. Dave I want to see him, too."

"I certainly will and he'll be glad to see you."

"Okay, then bye."

Dave heard the conversation and said, "I think that might be the weekend of the party, right?"

Sammi said, "Oh that's right, I forgot. We'll just invite them along. I'm sure they'll enjoy it, too."

Dave nodded and went back to reading his newspaper.

* * *

The next few weeks were busy at the station. More and more people associated with these two executives were coming forward offering testimony in an effort to help themselves. Some hadn't even been involved in any crime but didn't want their names linked to this bad publicity.

"This is sure giving us a lot of paperwork isn't it?" said Amilio.

"Not my favorite thing," replied Dave. "But it does mean that things are getting accomplished and who could have guessed that a few weeks ago?"

"Yeah, amigo, this was more like an avalanche. They started coming out of the woodwork to clear their names. And, of course, that didn't help Nieman and Olsen."

"Right. Who would have guessed that these two were involved in all these crimes? God, they had their hands in everything. And their outward persona was that they were such upstanding citizens with a lot of money and power. Many people catered to them for that reason. They sure screwed up their lives."

"So you're all ready for the party?"

"Yeah, Roy's been kind of nervous about it, I think."

About this time Roy walked up to Dave's desk asking about some paperwork that he had to finish.

"Who gets all this stuff?" he asked.

"Just give it to Sergeant Brady. He'll look it over to determine where it should go, like active files or cold or dead files. He usually likes to look them over first anyway."

Amigo said, "Are you ready for your party?"

Immediately Roy got a look of embarrassment on his face. "I guess so; ready as I'll ever be. I don't have to give a speech or anything like that, do I?"

"Oh no, no," said Dave. "It's a party. True, it's in your honor and you more than deserve it, but it's a party. Just think of it that way."

He still seemed a bit overwhelmed. "But who'll I sit with. I understand it's a sit down dinner. Those make me nervous."

Dave laughed. "A strong and very impressive cop like you gets nervous at a sit down dinner."

Roy laughed. "Well, it's different that's all."

Everyone nodded.

Amigo said, "I'm glad it's casual because I hate getting dressed up for things. And I think at first the gals were considering something more formal."

Roy looked aghast. "You're kidding right?"

"No," said Dave. "When these gals get together we never know what they're going to plan. But we thought everyone would be more comfortable with a casual party so we put in our bid," and he turned to Amilio and said, "And I can't believe we won."

"Sammi's pretty sneaky to me," said Amilio. "I'll bet she wanted a casual party from the beginning and made you think you won."

Dave laughed. "You're probably right."

And Roy added, "I don't have a date. God with everything that's happened lately I hardly know anyone anyway. Does that matter?"

"Of course not," said Dave. "You're the guest of honor, remember?"

"I don't think I can forget that."

Then Dave's phone rang and that broke up the group. Business still came first.

* * *

Roy Dawson went back to his desk and sat for a while. He really was still in shock since they told him they were giving a party in his honor. Hell, in the past years, most people didn't even want him around; now some were throwing a party for him. He shook his head. His reputation had been tarnished and in the past years, he could never figure it out. Now he knew and it did help some, but he had spent many desperate and lonely years. He finally realized that it wasn't anything he'd done wrong, but some criminals were so corrupt that they took devious paths to accomplish their evil purposes. And in doing so, they had ruined his career before it even had a chance to get started. It had also ruined the one lasting relationship of his life. He thought back.

Beth Inglewood had meant everything to him. He thought she was the most beautiful girl he'd ever seen and he liked her spicy personality. She didn't take a backseat to anyone. Things were great and they were planning their wedding, but when his gun was stolen, Beth dumped him, all of a sudden without an explanation. After two years of dating and sharing their lives completely, she dumped him without giving him any kind of reason or even seeing him again. He was devastated. He was depressed and he lost a lot of belief in himself and in the world around him. Everyone shunned him, he was given dangerous solo assignments without any explanation, ignored by previous friends, noticeably avoided and he had no clue as to why. Over and over he asked himself one question; what the hell happened?

He'd spent many hours walking around with no destination in mind. He asked a few people who simply shrugged their shoulders. But it was the other cops who wouldn't back him and in his work that could be dangerous. That's what really got to him. Your backup had your life in their hands and he couldn't trust anyone anymore. And the days turned into months and years of wondering with no answer ever coming forward. He shook his head as he now realized that it turned out to be one night at a stakeout in a bar that had changed his life forever, but he had no clue.

"Hey Roy, you ready for your party?" asked one of the officers in passing.

He waved him off shyly. He couldn't believe they were giving him a party.

"I hear you have to sit up at a table in front everybody all by yourself," joked another cop.

"You've got to be kidding," he answered horrified.

"Yeah, yeah, I'm kidding." He walked away laughing.

This is how he thought it should be, people being friendly, teasing, laughing at times, and serious and ready to back you up at other times. He had missed this over the years, but he was glad to be a part of it now. And Sergeant Brady had told him that he welcomed him on his police force, if he chose to stay. Roy planned to stay; he'd finally found a home.

* * *

Friday night dinner found Billy and Lily joining Dave and Sammi. As usual, Billy's excitement infected everyone.

"I'm so happy to see you again. I'm so happy. I counted the days until we could come, didn't I?"

Lily confirmed. "Oh yes, sometimes you counted in hours, too."

He laughed. He still had that contagious giggle and his entire body threw out warmth to everyone around.

"How's Marsha? I'll bet she misses you this weekend."

"Yes, she was sad she couldn't come, but she had another party with her mom and dad. It was her aunt's birthday and she'll have fun there, too."

Dave got more serious and asked, "Lily, it must feel good to have all this behind you. Have you seen Len again?"

"Not lately. I did see him one time, but he hardly recognized me. He seems to have retreated to his early childhood. The psychiatrist said that for a while his personality seems to have stopped around twelve years old. So he's beyond the murders, but no one knows why he's staying where he's at."

"Wow," said Sammi. "I'll bet this will take years for him to progress again and it will be slow when it does occur."

"And of course for now, there will be no trial or anything. He's not competent. It's all so sad. But I'm so torn. I know murder is wrong and he was wrong to do it, but with his mind in the precarious position it's in, it's almost hard to blame him. Do you know what I mean?"

"Absolutely," said Sammi. "I was telling Dave that I wouldn't want to be the judge or doctor who'd have to make that decision. I get totally overwhelmed when I think about it."

"He seemed like a nice man and he was nice to my mom," said Billy.

"But he was sick like I told you, remember?" said Lily.

"Yeah, I remember, you said that he was sick in his mind. That's too bad. Somebody killed his family when he was a little boy." Billy shook his head and couldn't say anymore.

Wanting to change the subject to a happier mood, Dave said, "Tomorrow night we're taking you both to a big party with us."

Billy's eyes opened wide. "A big party. Wow. Why the big party?"

Dave and Sammi took the time to explain about Roy's discouraging history, and why he deserved a big party in his honor.

"That's so nice. I think he deserves a party. And it's okay if my mom and I come, too. I'd like to celebrate at his party."

"Oh yes, you'll come as guests of Dave and I. We want you both to be there."

"This'll be so much fun. I can't wait until I tell Marsha about the big party that I went to; she'll be happy for me."

Later, the evening went on with talk centering on reminiscing about the last few months and looking forward to the party on Saturday night. Lily was still celebrating her new lease on life.

* * *

Walking into the Roma Hall was a delight. The room was decorated properly befitting a police officer's party and a large picture of Roy Dawson hung in front. The tables were decorated in blue and white and there was no main table per a request by Roy himself. About fifty people had already arrived although Dave and Sammi made sure to get there early. By 7:30 PM, more than two hundred people were there to applaud and blow whistles as Roy arrived.

He was shocked and couldn't help a few tears escape from his eyes. One man walked up to him immediately and he was in awe of the fact that Officer William Letting was coming forward to shake his hand. As he put out his hand, William grabbed him and gave him a hug.

"You've been a strong guy all of these years, working it alone and hanging in there. I'm real proud of you. I wish I had done more, but..." Roy stopped him. He couldn't speak anymore; he was overcome with emotion.

"I understand," said Roy. "You were in a spot, too; a lot of the guys were. I'm just happy that I found out why I was poison all those years. Now it makes sense."

"A lot of guys would have given up, but you didn't. I hope we can be friends."

"Absolutely. I heard how you helped me out and I want to thank you."

"It's the least I could do."

As he walked around the room, he was shocked to see a few other officers he had known years ago and acknowledged them and finally had a chance to hear a few welcoming words from them. He understood. Many were in a tight spot themselves. But everything was opening up now.

Later just before dinner was served, Sergeant Brady got up to say a few words.

"Don't worry, Roy, we promised that you wouldn't have to give a speech, and you won't. I gave him my word and I'll stick to it, but I have a few things to say. Without going into a lot of details that are best left unsaid, I want to commend a very strong and loyal police officer who never gave up when he had to stand alone against many who didn't believe in him. Our courage proves the strongest when we can stand unaided because it shows what we're really made of. Roy Dawson has always been a reliable and dedicated police officer in spite of the unbelievable odds against him. We're all proud of you and if we're really lucky, you'll decide to stay with us in Scranton."

There was thunderous applause that lasted for more than a few minutes. It did much to awaken a delightful and uncomplicated feeling deep inside of Roy. He felt that he belonged somewhere and it felt good.

After dinner, which found Billy in a contemplative mood, he suddenly spoke up. "I know who he is. I remember him now." Then he turned to his mother, Sammi and Dave as he asked, "Would you come with me? I'd like to talk to Mr. Roy."

Sammi knew the thoughts on Billy's mind, but the others had to wait to find out about a special happening. Billy was afraid that Mr. Roy wouldn't remember him, but felt that he had to make the effort.

Sammi introduced everyone to Roy, and Billy waited. Then he couldn't wait any longer and said, "Mr. Roy, do you remember me? It's Billy, Billy G. Simpson?" and he smiled and rocked on his feet as he waited.

Suddenly Roy got up slowly from his chair and pointed to Billy as he said, "Yes, I remember now. You were the one on the sidewalk trying to get home from school."

Billy shook his head up and down as he said, "Can I tell them the story?"

"Of course," said Roy, "But I'm happy to see you looking so well."

"Thanks. Mr. Roy," said Billy as he turned to the others "was there when I needed him. I was walking home from school one day and I was alone after I got off the bus. These three boys came up to me and started to hit me and make fun of me. They were real mean and nasty. But Mr. Roy came along, and you weren't dressed like a police officer, but he made those boys stop and told them that I would have special protection from then on so they'd better leave me alone. They ran away and never bothered me again. He was my hero for the day. But I didn't know your name."

"Well, you know it now, it's Roy Dawson."

"Can I give you a hug?"

"Absolutely," laughed Roy and he was caught in Billy's world as quickly and completely as everyone else.

The party did a lot for everyone and mended many fences so that Roy Dawson could finally start healing. His entire body had been in limbo for so long, but now he was ready to go forward and he had many supporters with him, ready to rally around.

* * *

At home, Dave and Sammi were tired but delighted.

"Did you know that Billy knew Roy?"

"No, not until a few minutes before, when he finally recognized him. Then his mind was ablaze with excitement and gratitude. Isn't it nice that Roy always had a good heart? You know, he'd be a good catch for someone. I hope a nice gal comes along and completes his life."

"You do, do you? Anyone in mind?"

"No, I wish I did, but we'll have to let the universe handle that one."

Dave laughed. "Oh yeah, back to the universe."

Sammi laughed as well. "It's always a part of our lives."

Sammi felt that the universe would take care of Roy Dawson. He'd paid his dues and hung in there through tough times. She felt he had a good life ahead of him.